HOW WE END

LM JUNIPER

How We End

ISBN 13: 978-91-527-3825-2

Cover Art by LM Juniper
Editing by Kimberly Dawn
Sensitivity Read by Ashia Monet

Content Information

Violence
Gore
Addiction
Mass death, including the young and vulnerable
Suicidal thoughts (no one dies)
Transphobia (mentioned, not explicit)
Dead naming (once)
Child Abuse (mentioned, not graphic)

♥

Please take care of yourself while reading!

To Graeme
For whom the sun sets.

♥

Playlist

- *Santa Monica Dream* – Angus & Julia Stone
- *S.O.B* – Nathaniel Ratecliff & The Night Sweats
- *In Hell I'll Be In Good Company* – The Dead South
- *And So It Begins* – Klergy
- *Pieces* – Sum 41
- *Run With Me (Kara)* – Philip Sheppard
- *Brother Run Fast* – KALEO
- *Survivor* – 2WEI
- *Dust & Light* – Twelve Titans Music
- *Farewell to Earth* – Audiomachine
- *Funeral March* – 2WEI
- *The Devil Inside* – Daniel Murphy, Anthony Sanudo, Eric Serna
- *Take You Down* – Illenium
- *Ain't No Mountain High Enough* – Marvin Gaye, Tammi Terrell
- *Godmanchester Chinese Bridge* – The Howl & The Hum
- *When Was That* – Angus & Julia Stone
- *Desert Rose* – Faouzia
- *God's Gonna Cut You Down* – Johnny Cash
- *Mountain* – Faouzia

- *Through the Valley* – Shawn James
- *Tessa* – Steve Jablonsky
- *Without You* – Ursine Vulpine & Annaca
- *Goodbye* – Ramsey
- *Future Days* – Pearl Jam

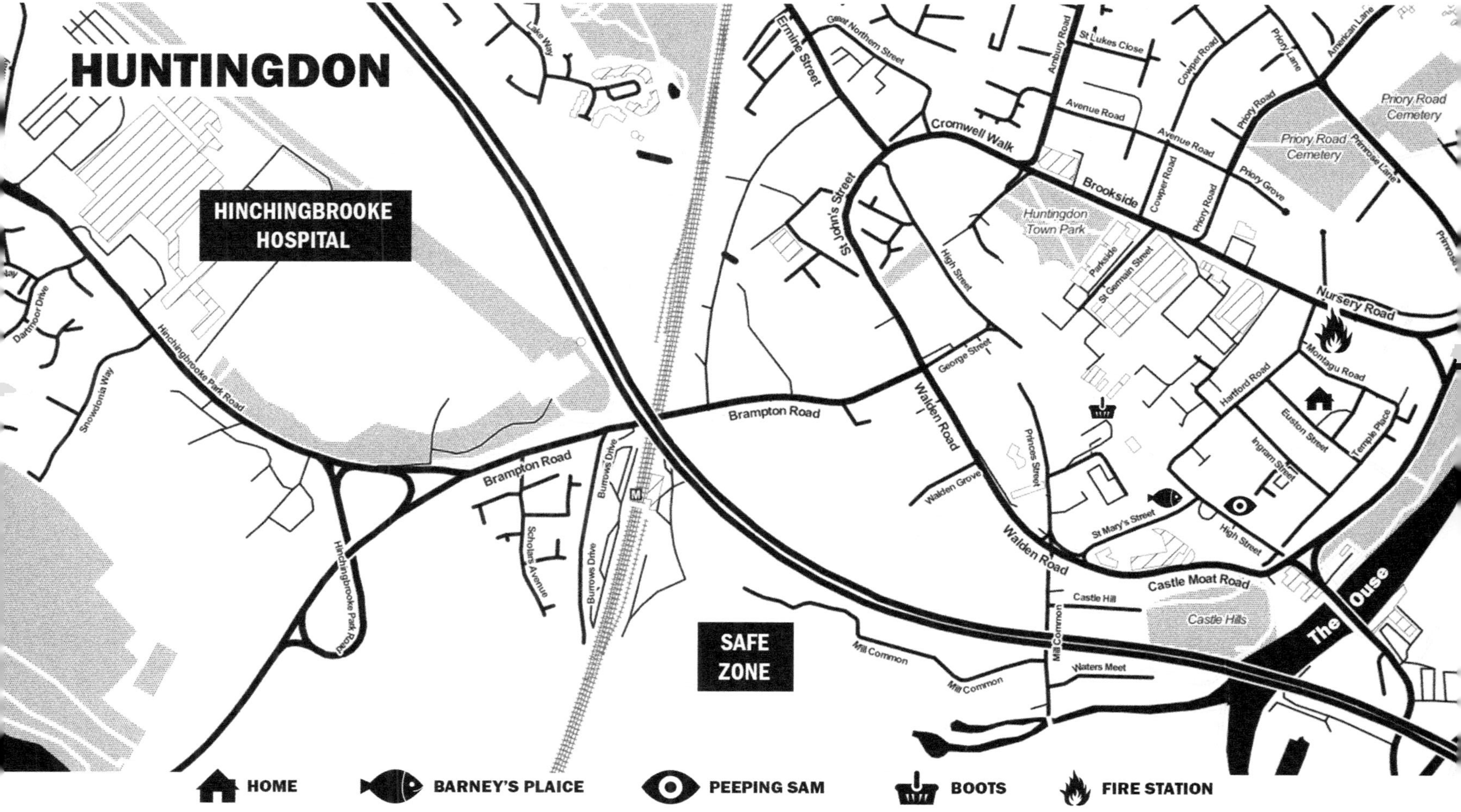
HUNTINGDON
HINCHINGBROOKE HOSPITAL
SAFE ZONE
The Ouse
Hinchingbrooke Park Road
Brampton Road
Walden Road
St John's Street
High Street
Cromwell Walk
Brookside
Nursery Road
Castle Moat Road
Ermine Street
Great Northern Street
St Lukes Close
Ambury Road
Avenue Road
Cowper Road
Priory Road
Priory Lane
Priory Grove
American Lane
Primrose Lane
Priory Road Cemetery
Huntingdon Town Park
Parkside
St Germain Street
George Street
Princes Street
St Mary's Street
Montagu Road
Hartford Road
Euston Street
Ingram Street
Temple Place
Walden Grove
Castle Hill
Castle Hills
Mill Common
Waters Meet
Burrows Drive
Scholars Avenue
Lake Way
Snowdonia Way
Dartmoor Drive
HOME
BARNEY'S PLAICE
PEEPING SAM
BOOTS
FIRE STATION

1
JAKE

THE BEST STORIES ALWAYS start with failure. At least that's what my dad always told me. I think my life would make a great story then, even though it isn't filled with magical wonders. My life is more like this train ride—filled with a lot of stops and a lot of people coming and going.

I laugh to myself and shake my head. The guy opposite me glares at me, and I realise working in the tube has me way too comfortable with my own company.

The train gives a sharp jolt, and a girl dressed for Friday success—a short dress and nine-inch heels—stumbles into the man beside her. A layer of sweat coats the man's red face, and the way he tucks his chin and grimaces at the girl brings to mind a pudgy toad. He curls his lips in disapproval, but, in the tradition of perfectly British manners, he says nothing.

"Sorry," she apologises in a silky-smooth voice, but the man-toad has turned his back, effectively ignoring her.

If it's one thing we Londoners dislike more than tourists, it's people in our personal space, breaking the sacred rule of "my dance space, your dance space."

I turn my attention back to the girl. With her golden-brown skin, a copper glow at her cheeks, and curly black hair that gives Aphrodite a run for her money, she is undeniably beautiful. She's perfectly matched her thin black dress and leather jacket that hangs open in the front with a chunky silver necklace. For a guy who knows nothing about fashion, I think she looks nice.

The train lurches once more, shaking the commuters in the carriage. Predictably, the girl stumbles again on her high heels, loses her grip of the metal rail, and crashes into the man beside her.

He wears an expensive-looking suit and has an unhealthy amount of wax in his slicked-back dirty-blond hair. His brows draw together, reddening cheeks puffing out as if he got punched in the stomach.

"Jesus!" he snaps and shoves her off him.

Charming. The girl lets out a scoff somewhere between disbelief and indignancy. I can't help but feel bad for her. She's likely meeting up with friends for a fun night out and before her night has even begun, two men have glared or otherwise acted aggressively towards her.

Everyday life for a woman, one of my best friends has informed me on multiple occasions. As if I couldn't possibly know.

We're in between Waterloo and Westminster stations, where there's one more piece of track which causes the train to jerk. I know every inch of this line. Driving the same line eight hours a day for six years has that effect. I should probably warn her, or she might get herself into a brawl before she reaches the bar.

I pull out one of my earbuds and lean to tap her shoulder. Maybe it's because she expects someone else to have a go at her, verbal or nonverbal, but she turns with her brows knit together.

With my stretched earlobes and tattoos covering my arms and neck, I know I don't look like the most approachable guy, but at least I've got a good smile. Looking friendly takes away the edge. I smile and her initial anger softens slightly.

"Why don't we swap places?" I motion to my spot beside the train door. It's at the end, by the window, and a padded bumper for your butt makes it easy to keep your balance. Especially if you're wearing heels.

What remains of her irritation melts from her face and she gives what I think is a grateful nod. I catch a waft of sweet-smelling perfume when she brushes past me. "These shoes." She leans back against the window with a sigh.

"Not the best for venturing out on a shaky train?" I ask.

"Really not." She rolls her eyes when the train pulls to a slow stop in the tunnel.

The commuters don't notice, but since I know this route, I know there's no reason for us to stop here. I peer out the window to figure out where we are. Call it an occupational hazard, but it's so ingrained after six years working as a tube driver that it's second nature. Wires of all sizes run horizontal along the wall outside, lifting and dipping into hooks that hold them in place.

I tilt my head for a better view and frown when I spot the white sign to our left. We're stopped between two stations. It's too late to be train queues; there aren't enough trains on the line this late.

I've heard people had gathered at Trafalgar, and that the gathering was fast becoming a riot. This could be the cause of our delay.

I pull my phone from my pocket to check my messages even though the tube is the most hated notspot in London. Blame the reptile part of my brain.

The phone lights purple with a message, and I swipe my thumb across the glass screen. One missed call from Megan, seventeen minutes ago, and an unread message. *Meet you at The Cross at nine. Love you.* It's the 'love you'

you use instead of "bye," "talk to you later," or "whatever, I can't be arsed right now." The 'love you' that you don't mean in the same way anymore, but you procrastinate rather than deal with it.

She must have rung before I returned underground after having an after-work pint with Andrew. I have forty-five minutes to make it on time. Providing we move soon, I can still make it.

"Why are we stopped?" Nine-inch girl is the first one to twig, and her face scrunches my way. I guess offering her my space means we're now on speaking terms.

"I don't know," I say.

"Haven't we been stopped for some time now?"

I look at my watch. One minute and thirty-four seconds, but who's counting?

The girl lets out a frustrated sigh. "I can't be late. Not tonight." The last word is a whine.

A sardonic chuckle sounds beside us, and we both turn in that direction. It's Prince Charming, his face arranged in a patronising expression. "Yes, because I'm sure your shots and drunk girlfriends can't possibly wait," he says in an upper class, posh voice. His attitude is obviously payback for the earlier collision.

I frown at him and notice a tall Black man wearing a fedora a few seats away. He gives Prince Charming a sidelong look that reminds me of a copper. Neutral but calculating, as if he's assessing the situation. I don't blame him. It's the tube on a Friday night, after all. Anything could happen. Thankfully, the girl has the good grace to ignore Prince Charming, and the potential conflict dies out.

The train hums as people squirm impatiently. Somehow the carriage feels more crowded than it did before. What is taking so long?

"Ladies and gentlemen," a voice crackles from the speakers above, as if it heard my question and answered. Everyone's heads lift like people waiting for the rapture. "A Passenger Emergency Alarm has been operated on the train in front of us at Westminster station. There will be a brief delay while we investigate this."

"Oh," I say out loud. It's not so much surprise, more of a *well that must suck for the driver* sort of empathy. A few heavy sighs and grunts meet the train operator's message, but at least now the commuters are more annoyed than apprehensive. Annoyed is better than scared. Annoyed people moan but resign themselves to their fate; scared people, on the other hand... they do stupid shit.

"This better not take forever," nine-inch heels says and sweeps her thick curls from one side of her head to the other with her arm.

I grin. There it is, the London commuter spirit.

"Oh, you think this is funny?" she asks with an eyebrow quirked in my direction.

I'm about to answer when Mr. Toad coughs loud enough to rattle his chest and bump into my side. The collar on his white shirt is grey from the sweat that coats his thick neck, and the hair at his hairline curls into small, wet tendrils. His face red as his lips open and close with wheezy breaths, like an old-time bellows. That can't be good.

I finished my shift two hours ago, but some habits die hard. I lean forward to catch his eye. "Sir?" He watches me through piglike eyes, one of which twitches. It's only now that I notice how it sits at an odd angle. "Are you alright?"

He grunts as if to tell me to bugger off. Maybe his glaring should bother me, but I've seen too much during work. What bothers me is the thought of being stuck on a train in a tunnel with a man who isn't well. And this one might be close to a heart attack. He gives a harking cough, his windpipe hissing. His eyes bulge and veins protrude from his temples with the spasms of his chest. People step away, not bothering to mask the revulsion on their faces. I take a step backwards, although I hope I'm masking my disgust a little better.

A woman in a purple coat and an eye-searing pink blouse asks the man if he really is alright and if he would like some water.

"I'm fine!" he snaps. A line of red trickles from his nose and splatters to his white shirt. He jerks his head as if to keep his shirt from getting stained, but all it serves to do is throw droplets of blood in an arc around the carriage.

A girl yelps as a few drops splatter against her handbag, and her chavvy boyfriend cusses at the man. Don't get me wrong, throwing your nosebleed around is pretty minging, but I'm pretty sure he didn't do it on purpose.

"Alright, mate, calm down." Clearly my brain hasn't clocked off, and I grab tissues from my bag and pass one to the girl with the leather bag. Then I turn to Mr. Toad, who's grabbing at his nose with a pair of chubby fingers. "Here, take these."

He snatches them, instantly stuffing sheets of tissue against his nostrils, and I try not to grimace when his fingers brush against mine. I hope whatever that guy has, it's not contagious. A closed train car, spattering blood, and packed people would make for a nice end-of-the-world scenario.

Pulling my alcogel from my bag, I glimpse my watch. I'm going to be late, and Megan is going to be pissed. As usual. In fact, that end-of-the-world scenario might be preferable to her wrath. I snort to myself. I should be so lucky.

2
LIV

PRISON. TWO THINGS HAPPENED when someone went to prison. First, they took what little things the new inmate brought with them, and then guards strip-searched the inmate in a sort of degrading initiation rite. Warden Callister had taken extra delight in the strip search on Liv's first day of prison. *You better figure things out quickly. People like you don't last very long in here,* Warden Callister's voice rang in Liv's head where she sat.

She poked the glass resting on the counter in front of her. Things could go badly in prison. After the frisking with Warden Callister, the other inmates had given her two broken ribs, a split lip, and a nice cut across her eyebrow. To welcome her to the block.

Callister hadn't been wrong. People like Liv didn't last long in prison. Some days, she'd wished they would just end it. That way she wouldn't have to.

It had been both a relief and a curse when she was released early. She'd survived prison; she was still alive. And yet, she wasn't sure if that was a good or bad thing.

A sudden shattering startled her from her thoughts, and she glanced up at a young-looking bartender. "Sorry"—he held up a broken glass bottle—"butter fingers tonight."

She was holding his gaze, eyes narrowed, when a blonde woman with a serious expression on the large monitor next to the bartender caught Liv's attention.

"Rioters have taken to Trafalgar Square to show their discontent, and we estimate a whopping sixty thousand people to have gathered at one of Britain's most well-known landmarks." The news reporter's forehead creased, and she leaned forward, one finger pressed to her ear. "We are getting reports of unrest at the square amongst the rioters, various sources citing fighting with minor to severe injuries..."

"Good old Britannia, gathering to protest and ends up fighting." The bartender shook his head and turned down the volume of the TV that hung behind him. "Makes you wonder though. What they're really fighting for."

Liv let her gaze slide back to the bartender, Lou, according to his name tag. Was he trying to make conversation? She had specifically come to the bar to avoid conversation or hearing the news. The same news that had been circulating for over a week.

Lou watched her as he wiped down the bar, waiting for her answer. Annoying.

"Beats me," she said with a glare and sipped her drink, hoping to kill the conversation before it started. The smoky rich whiskey burned its way down her throat, and she closed her eyes while the warm buzz wrapped her in its comforting embrace.

She revelled in the sense of calm that settled in her chest. All the things that annoyed her seemed to wash away with the liquor, and she couldn't remember what had annoyed her anymore. Whatever it was, it had been enough to go to a bar and get drunk. *See! Alcohol did solve everything.*

"Pffft." She toasted her own thoughts and took another sip. She was going to savour this fifth drink.

"Rough night?" Lou asked as if they'd known each other for years, not less than five minutes. Although "know" was a bit on the generous side.

"Lou"—she straightened herself on the barstool—"a wise woman once said, 'the less you annoy strangers, the bigger the chance of not getting slugged.'"

A smile crossed Lou's face, flashing white teeth through the dark stubble. "I haven't heard that saying before, but I can see how she might be right."

"You are officially not as dumb as you look."

He laughed. "Why, you're a proper charmer."

"And you just became my least favourite person in this bar."

Lou glanced around them. "There's only you and me here..."

"Exactly."

"And who's your favourite? You?"

It was her turn to laugh. "This fucker." She raised her glass.

"That how good you are at relationships?" Lou winked and slid a dried wineglass into its place on the rack above him. It was a joke—anyone would know that—but his words pushed all the right buttons.

"And what are you, a fucking shrink?" That should send him packing, leaving her alone.

"Actually," he said in amusement, and she groaned inwardly. Why was he still talking to her? "I am. And a very good one at that." He tapped the tip jar with his finger, drawing a scoff from her.

"Only because obviously you heavily medicate your patients." Liv held up her glass in the air that was still—amazingly enough—half-full of whiskey.

"Medicine *and* therapy." Lou grinned. "And to think you only pay one third of market prices."

Liv narrowed her eyes in a way she hoped conveyed how utterly unimpressed she felt. She wanted to be left alone, but this bloke was annoyingly persistent. Why? What did he want from her? People always wanted something.

"Heh." Lou dropped his head with an embarrassed chuckle. "Guess that one missed its mark by a smidge."

"A smidge?" Now *that* was funny. She laughed and made a whooshing noise arching her hand above her head.

"Alright." He laughed. "Well, it was worth a try."

She studied him for a while. It seemed like everyone around her wanted to try. Try to fix her. Try to help her, rescue her. Even this mildly handsome stranger with his long face and body of someone who took care of himself but still liked his pizza. He wasn't a bad catch. His pickup lines were terrible, and he obviously had no sense of when people were better left alone, but there was still something likable about him.

She downed the last of her drink before she leaned over the bartop and pulled Lou closer by his shirt. "Well, *A* for effort."

"Pretty sure they spell that with an *E*." He grinned back at her.

She rolled her eyes. As long as he kept his mouth shut, he was a catch, she corrected herself. To keep him from saying anything else stupid, she silenced him with her lips. He tasted of mint gum. Unlike herself, who most likely tasted like an expensive Irish whiskey.

She released his shirt and pulled away from him before she could decide to indulge in a night of meaningless and most likely average sex. Though the distraction was welcomed, the morning after was not.

She slid off the barstool in the most graceful manner she could muster while drunk as a skunk. She flashed him a coy smile, spun on her heel, then headed for the door.

"For real?" His voice reached her ears and she turned to see his blue eyes sparkle with half amusement, half disappointment. "You going to leave me like this?"

"You're cute, love, but you're also a *bartender*. I get clams just looking at you."

Lou guffawed and shook his head. "Can I at least walk you home? I get off in like five. You know, with the rioters and all." He hooked his thumb in the direction of Trafalgar Square.

"Darling." Liv quirked a dark eyebrow at him. Perhaps chivalry wasn't dead, though she wasn't one to care for it. "I've been walking myself home for twenty-six years. I think I can handle it." She fired off one last smile and walked out the door.

The cool late-night air hit her straight in the face when she stepped out from the pub, almost, but not quite, sobering her up as she strolled along the crowded sidewalk. A typical packed Friday night. She grunted. Every weekend was the same: tourists and Londoners alike poured into the central city like the faithful on a pilgrimage.

Rounding the corner, her head spun and she slowed her pace, throwing a quick glance at her watch. Eight p.m. If she took the long way around to her car, she might sober up enough to drive back to her favourite parking spot: a secluded construction site where her pickup truck almost never looked out of place. The nightly police patrols rarely bothered her when she crashed there.

Liv pulled the collar of her green utility jacket closer while she passed dark shop windows as drunk and merry people stumbled past her. She let her eyes wander the different displays of all the things she'd never be able to afford.

She stopped to look at something ghostlike fluttering at the bottom of the windows. A pale, tired version of herself with hollowed eyes and dark messy hair.

"Ugh," she let out a moan, her gaze still scrutinising the woman. "What the fuck happened to you?" *What hadn't happened?* That would probably be easier to answer, but the woman—the ghost—didn't reply. She only looked back like a hopeless, powerless thing.

"Bet you don't even know, do you?" Liv said before catching herself talking to her own reflection. *Well, if that ain't a sign you're drunk, I don't know what is.*

Her slurred mind wasn't wrong. She wasn't buzzed; she was intoxicated. As always. It was her favourite state after all, once she got off her eight-hour shift at the shelter. She huffed. The gig at the shelter was a crappy job, with crappy pay, kindly bestowed upon her by some do-gooder judge. But at least it got her out on parole. At least it got her out of prison. Alive.

She rubbed her face. Alive. Was that really what she wanted? What did that even mean anymore when all she could feel was a numbing emptiness?

Liv let her gaze trail the length of the stranger's face, studying the nose she inherited from an Indian mother, though Liv's skin was a lighter shade of brown. She blamed her father for that. She blamed her father for a lot of things. *Must be nice to blame all your misfortunes on someone else.* The woman sneered back at her.

"Whatever," Liv muttered and did what she did best with people she disliked. She turned her back and walked away.

She walked for another fifteen minutes, turning onto side streets and back streets to take the longest possible way around. Still, when she finally came to a stop by her pickup, she felt no more sober than when she'd started her walk. In fact, she felt drunker.

It took her longer to unlock the door than she'd be proud to admit, and she let out a sigh of relief when it finally opened. Slapping at the light switch, she let out a triumphant sound when her fingers accidentally turned the interior light on. Little victories in life!

She climbed into the pickup, slamming the door hard behind her before stretching out on the long bench seat with a drunk sigh. She'd left the light on. From where she lay, she thought she heard screaming as she pulled the blanket over her head to keep out the cold. It was probably the thousands of people rioting not far from her current sleeping place. Or not. She was too tired to care. A little rioting wasn't the end of the world.

London and her smog would still stand in the morning when she woke.

3

JAKE

"I BEAT YOUR KINGS with my three of a kind." Fareena, the girl with nine-inch heels, throws her cards to the floor with a triumphant flick of her hand.

I shake my head and give her my handful of purple Skittles. This is the third time in a row I've lost my bet. I could be a sore loser and ask if she's hiding cards somewhere, but I find it hard to imagine where she'd hide them. Her black leather jacket lays underneath her on the floor, and her tight black dress is sleeveless. Dismissing the idea, I grab the pile of cards and shuffle them.

It's been nearly an hour since the driver informed us we'd be hanging around for a while, and, although people are annoyed, most just seem tired and want to go home. It took us thirty minutes before we realised this wasn't going to be over anytime soon. I resigned myself to my fate, sat down, and pulled the deck of playing cards from my survival kit. The kit any sensible Londoner would keep in their bag, though I know I'm likely one of the few who walks around with a stash of snacks, water, a roll of toilet paper, and emergency entertainment. You never know when you'll get stuck in the middle of a breakdown and spend hours sitting around waiting.

Five flapjacks, two apples, three pork pies, three sausage rolls, two bags of crisps, and another two bags of Skittles make out the emergency diet in my survival kit. All the important parts of a varied diet—sweet and savoury.

I was enjoying one of my sausage rolls, playing solitaire, and listening to Julia Stone sing about Santa Monica dreams when something in the corner of my eye caught my attention—nine-inch girl scrutinising me with pursed plump lips and light-brown, almost amber, eyes.

I held up the cards and raised an eyebrow.

"I thought you'd never ask." She'd fired off a sweet smile and shuffled closer on the floor.

Now we play poker on a dingy train floor with sweets as our precious chips.

"So," Fareena says and eyes my diminishing pile of Skittles. "This how you planned on spending your Friday night?"

"Being a loser?"

"Yeah," she agrees with a grin.

"Let me see." I deal us new cards and set the rest on the floor. If I didn't know better, I'd say we were at a proper fashionable casino. "I'm late for a meeting with my fiancée who's supposed to be dumping me tonight... so yeah. I guess tonight's the night, huh?"

"Oh." She looks a little taken aback. "I didn't mean to..."

If this was a conversation with someone I'd have to see again tomorrow, I wouldn't have said it, but after tonight, I'll never see Fareena again. Why not be daring and tell the truth for once? The three pints with Andrew might also be a factor. I change the subject. "So, what is it you can't be late for tonight?"

She heaves a sigh. "I had my first real gig booked tonight."

"Oh, wow."

"I've been practising for a month, all the songs, the lyrics... and now"—she sighs forlornly—"my boyfriend and all our friends are going to sit there and wonder where the hell I am."

"I'm sure you'll make it." I try to sound more convinced than I feel.

"Nice try. I'm supposed to be in Islington in fifteen minutes, and I only have an hour slot."

I suck air through my teeth. Even if we get this wrapped up in ten minutes or so, she'll have a hard time making it before halftime. "Ah, I'm sorry. Guess we're two losers here tonight..."

"Oh gee, thanks." She purses her lips, her eyes thinning. "I'm so glad I got to join your little club."

"There's a club?" A girl in her mid-twenties drops to the floor beside me. Jet-black hair drapes the sides of her face, and her blood-red lips are a stark contrast to her pale, almost white skin. "Mind if I join?"

Fareena eyes her with a somewhat guarded expression. "You good at poker?"

"Staking out the competition?" The girl raises an eyebrow. "I can hold my own."

"Oh, great." Fareena sighs in relief. "What's your stake?"

"Well, I haven't got any sweets, but I have this." She slips a bottle of Bacardi from her shoulder bag and wiggles it in the air.

I chuckle. "Alright, now we're talking."

"Yes, you can stay." Fareena nods in approval.

"Right, well, got any other takers while we're at it?" I look around the car, only to be met by glaring looks of disinterest. Except for the guy in the tawny fedora.

"What y'all playing over there?" he asks in a thick Southern American accent. "Is that Texas Hold'Em?"

"Yeah," I say. Fareena gives a smug *and-he's-losing-big-time* grin.

"Alright," he says in amusement. "I'll play."

"Cool, we'll take all Jake's Skittles," Fareena says.

The man and his female companion sit down next to us.

"Okay, well, I think it's time for some introductions. I'm Jules," the girl with the Bacardi says. She gives a small wave of her hand. And then in true 'first day at school' fashion, everyone introduces themselves.

The guy with the fedora is Roy. He wears a grey jacket and maroon scarf with such style it makes me more than a little jealous. The woman, Angela, is his wife. Angela is almost as tall as her husband, with cropped charcoal-black hair, and her kind eyes and smile remind me a little of my mother. She tells us they were on their way to Heathrow to fly home to Louisiana. Instead of stressing about whether they'll make their flight, a game of poker seemed like the best kind of distraction.

"So who gets to drink?" Roy points at the bottle of liquor on the dirty floor. "Losers or winner?"

"Winner." Fareena clicks her tongue and winks.

"How about losers drink?" he asks and something glints in his eyes. Maybe inviting him wasn't such a good idea.

Jules frowns. "But then everyone will want to lose."

"Trust me, y'all are going to beg me not to have to drink." Roy smirks and Angela rolls her eyes at him before mouthing 'show off' to the rest of us.

"Alright." I hand the shuffled cards to Fareena, who's the dealer this round. "Let's do this."

It's a bit of Bacardi. How bad can it be?

4

JAKE

I LICK MY LIPS, my cheeks hot from the buzz that's working its way towards a drunken state. My vision blurs and my head spins. Next to me, Jules tries to focus on her cards, though Angela downs another sip of rum and shrugs it off like a seasoned sailor.

Fareena, on the other hand, wears her poker face, eyes narrowed at her cards, not even breaking a sweat. She and Roy have taken turns at winning while the rest of us are slowly but surely getting pickled.

Jules flaps her cards in front of her face with a grimace. "Is it me or is it boiling in here?"

"It's just your drunk arse," Fareena says.

This draws a throaty chortle from Angela, who quickly covers her mouth and, in doing so, shows us all her cards. A few commuters glare at our raucous laughter, but I don't care. They had the chance to join the fun. And surprising as it may be, I'm actually having fun with the strangers I just met. Of course, the alcohol could have something to do it. Or maybe I genuinely like these people.

I've learnt that Jules can burp the national anthem. Fareena has a weakness for sloths. Angela wishes she could do the splits, and, according to Angela, Roy wants to be a magician.

Jules grabs the bottle and takes a sip as Fareena swats at her hand. "Oi! Stop drinking the chips!"

I reach for the deck of cards when the speakers in the car crackle with static. The few of us who speak fall silent, and the rest unplug their earbuds when they notice our attention turned towards the round speakers.

"If there is a member of Underground staff on this train, please make yourself known to the train operator."

My first instinct is to groan. I've just finished a seven-day stint of shifts. The last thing I want to do is clock in extra hours, but then I realise that if the train operator is asking for help, things might be worse than he let on. The thought sobers me up enough to put my cards facedown on the floor.

"Sorry." My fellow card players watch in surprise as I get to my feet and make my way to the intercom. I stare at the aluminium button. I could say nothing.

No one would ever know. But if I were operating the train right now, I'd be fucking pissed if I needed help. I sigh and press the button. "Operator 936024 reporting for duty."

There's a long silence, and I squirm as the passengers eye me. Now that they know I work for the underground, I'm more than likely going to be bombarded with questions. It's how people are. If you work for one part of public transport, people assume you know everything about *all* public transport.

"Operator 936024," the train driver's voice cuts through the silence in the car, "glad to have you on board. Which car are you currently in?"

My eyes dart towards the far end of the car where a five-number combination is printed in black. "I'm in 96118, the seventh car."

"Great. Inspector Sands is on his way, so everything should be fine, but please make your way to the driver's cab..." There's a brief pause. "...for further instructions."

The speaker holes gape up at me like hungry little mouths from the wall panel. Inspector Sands? It's the code we most commonly use when fire alarms have been triggered or for other safety-related issues. I look around my carriage and peer into the adjoining one. No smoke, and the commuters look as bored and displeased as the people in this one. I frown. The safety of this train is somehow compromised, so everything can't be fine. And, if it is, why did I need to identify myself?

"Operator?" the driver asks through the speaker. Now that I know what to look for, it sounds tense and on edge.

"Yes, copy that, operator out," I reply, an uneasy feeling settling in my stomach. What is he not telling us?

"Excuse me." The girl with the handbag looks up from where she sits. "How long will this take?" *Here we go again*. Other passengers murmur and nod as if none heard the same message I did.

"I don't know," I say with a scowl. I move towards the card game and my bag.

"Uh," an annoyingly pompous voice sounds behind my back. "Are you going to return to acting like a child? Didn't you hear him?"

Prince Charming holds on to the ceiling bar and glares at me. The surrounding commuters look my way as well, a small buzz growing as they mutter amongst themselves. I knew I shouldn't have made myself known. Instead of being grateful that I'm stepping up, people jump at the chance to vent their frustrations at the nearest, most convenient target. Me.

"I heard him fine. Like he said, I'll be making my way to the cabin for further information."

"Oh, that's great!" Prince Charming throws his hands in the air in disbelief. A chunk of his hair flops from its wax confinement. "I guess you get paid for being useless."

I understand most commuters think I get paid to press a button and be insulted all day long, but it's poncey wankers like this that really get to me. They think their cotton shirts, silk ties, and four-hundred-pound suits mean they're better than anyone. I'm used to the staring when people see the ink that rises to my chin and my black earplugs. They have certain ideas about people like me. Right now, I feel like living up to their expectations. I take a deep breath when Angela comes to where I stand, hands on her hips like policemen you see on TV.

"Is there a problem here?" she asks in a stern but calm voice. Huh. I was wrong. *She* is the copper.

Prince Charming's glare falters, but he quickly regains himself. "This man shouldn't be mucking about when all of us are stuck and wanting to go home."

Angela turns to look at me. I think she might actually agree with Prince Charming and the other annoyed commuters who nod, but then her brows knit and she tilts her head at Prince Charming. "Does this man look like he's still on the clock to you?" She motions towards where I stand in my causal pub night clothes.

"Well, no, but..." Prince Charming purses his lips in annoyance.

"Okay, well." Angela cocks her head, and her mouth thins. "Then why don't we let him get on with it and be thankful he's willing to help?"

The look on Prince Charming's face makes me want to smirk, but Angela has just defused the situation, so a cocky attitude would help no one. "Thanks," I say in a low voice as we both turn to the others.

"You're welcome." She smiles and gives me a gentle pat on the shoulder. "Now get us the hell out of here."

"Sure." I chuckle and reach for my bag on the floor, but before I can reach it, Jules grabs it and pushes to her feet.

"Are you an undercover operator as well?"

"Wait, *you* drive the tube?" I look at her dubiously.

"Mm-hmm." She nods, but thanks to all the alcohol, her poker face is about as good as a five-year-old's. I cock an eyebrow at her. "Fine." She leans in close and lowers her voice. "But I always really, really wanted to see the inside of the driver's cabin."

For a few ridiculous seconds, I consider letting her follow me into the cab, but then I remember the train operator's serious voice and Inspector Sands. "How about, after this, I'll give you a personal tour of the cab? When we're not stuck with, you know..." I jut my chin in Prince Charming's direction.

She grins, eyes sparkling. "You asking me out on a date?"

I laugh. "I should go."

She watches me intently, head canted before she nods. "See you around, Jakey."

I hope so. It's all I have time to think before the train gives a weary sigh and the gentle thrumming of its engine dies out, thrusting the entire train into darkness.

5

JAKE

I *HATE* THE DARK. Yes, I know how that sounds. If I spend too long in the dark, my mind conjures up all the horrible things that might crawl out from spaces I didn't even know exist. Maybe all the Asian horror movies I've seen contributed to my vivid imagination.

Panic rakes its nails along my spine, my skin rippling under its icy touch. I need light and I need it ***now***, before my inner five-year-old takes over. I shove my hand into my pocket and my fingers graze the metal casing of my phone.

I turn on the flashlight and shine it across the crowd. Almost instantly, small dots of light flare to life as more people have the same bright idea as me. I snort at the unintentional pun.

My beam finds Fareena and the others. Jules gives a little wave, but it doesn't escape me that she and Fareena hold hands. Both seem a little shaken.

"Hey!" Prince Charming shouts, startling me. I turn to face him. "What the fuck are you doing?"

Because, clearly, I am King of Electricity.

"Sir," I use the politest get-the-fuck-out-of-my-face voice I can muster while intentionally shining my light in his eyes. "Please try to remain calm."

"Calm?" he splutters. "The electricity is out, and we haven't moved in over an ***hour***." The man with the nosebleed coughs, drawing Prince Charming's attention away from me. He looks at the man with distaste. "And we've got someone bleeding over half the fucking train."

Mr. Toad squints as some commuters shine their lights in his face.

"This man needs medical attention." A woman in her mid-forties steps forward, her brows one hard line. "What are you going to do about him? He can't be bleeding all over the train."

I would like to believe they care about the man. But the truth is commuters are selfish knobs. They're only using this excuse to get the train moving faster. They care that his blood might stain their shoes, not about his health. It's people like this that make every bad situation worse because all they care about is themselves. If it would work, they'd wave their annual gold bonus card at me and demand we "resume traffic at once."

"Like I said earlier, I'm not on duty. I know as much as you." I impress myself with how calm I sound.

She puts her hands on her hips. "You could call emergency services to get to the man."

I don't mention that the underground has its own response unit. "Ma'am, I can't make a call any more than anyone else here. I have to hear what further instructions the operator has for me."

I leave out the fact that, without electricity, I can't contact the other driver. Worst case, I'll walk through the train to talk to him. But that's a worst-case scenario—hopefully, this is a glitch, and we'll have electricity back in no time. There's a reason I've never heard of a blackout in London: our grid is hooked up to France's grid. If ours goes down, we piggyback off theirs.

"So, when you've talked to your little friend, will you know when the train will leave?"

I blink at him. Do I look like I've got a fortune teller up my arse or something? "I *don't* know."

"Fucking ridiculous," Prince Charming scolds.

There's nothing more I can do to calm anyone. I shrug and push past him towards the cab door.

Hoisting my keys from my bag, I ignore the people in the car and push the thin door to the cabin open. My phone vibrates in my hands. At first, I think it's my reminder I'm due my shot. It takes me a good few seconds before I realise that my phone, unlike anyone else's, is ringing.

6

LIV

SHE DREAMT OF A young boy that had her eyes. He spoke to her through a large window, his mouth moving with silent words. She shook her head, trying to let him know she couldn't hear him, but his face grew angrier and angrier. He slammed his palms against the window.

"Toby?" she tried to call out to him.

His mouth gaped until it cracked the corners of his lips, splitting open to reveal a ghoulish grey, dry tongue. Flies skittered across the velvety grey mass that covered his palate and landed in the small spots of black rot dotted throughout. His head twitched uncontrollably until it banged against her window. Faster and faster. One. Two. Three. The last bang so loud it jolted her awake.

"Toby!" Liv called out, still half-asleep.

"Miss?" A stern voice cut through her confusion. "Miss, you need to wake up."

Liv pushed herself up from the seat. Her head spun as she let her eyes adjust to the dark. How long had she been asleep? It didn't feel like very long. She dropped her head into her hands when another bang on her window sent her bolting upright.

"Hey!" The voice cut through the fog. "*Wake up*!"

She blinked at the two people outside her car. Not even police officers were that eager to wake her. A woman in a vaguely familiar blue uniform stared through the window, her eyes wide and afflicted.

"Please, you need to open up," the woman pleaded. *Open up?*

"The military!" a young man with short mousy-brown hair and a similar uniform shouted. "They're shooting people, please let us in!" He pointed in the opposite direction.

Who was shooting...? What? Liv clasped her head between her hands, her mind reeling.

"Hurry, goddamn it!" the man hissed in a thick cockney accent.

"Shut up!" Liv snapped. "Let me think!" She was still far too drunk to have someone talk this loudly at this time of night. She glared at them. They wanted her to let them into her car? Two strangers, just like that? "Why should I let you in?"

"Because they're *shooting* at us," the man who looked to be in his late twenties said.

"Well, shit, how do I know you didn't rob a bank?" Giving their frazzled appearance another look, she pursed her lips. "Or something worse."

"Love," the woman who looked to be in her early fifties said in a calm, soothing voice, "something's not right with the rioters. They've shown signs of extreme aggression. Some have even attacked people."

"By biting," the man said, his face a mixture of horror and disbelief.

The rioters? The sixty *thousand* rioters on the news last night. Attacking and biting people? Sure, they'd been breaking windows and cars, but skin and bones? The thought sobered her up faster than a walk around the block ever could.

Liv strained her ears and heard a popping sound echo in the distance. Should she trust this woman? Probably not, but for all the liars and dishonest people she'd met in her life, this woman didn't seem to be one of them.

"I'm Frances Bradigan. I work at St. Thomas Hospital with Andy. It's only around the corner." Beads of sweat clung to Frances's face. Everything about her, from her clothes to her hair, gave her a harried appearance. Andy didn't look much better. His uniform was torn at the shoulder and something dark stained the side of his top.

"I'm a nurse," Frances said and pointed at the badge clipped to the chest pocket next to the familiar nurse's watch.

Distant clattering pierced the late September night and was followed by shouting. The two ducked as if on cue.

"Please let us in," Frances said, shaking wildly from what Liv could only assume was stress or adrenaline. Maybe both.

"And where exactly do you need to go?" she asked. She might—*might*—be willing to give them a lift somewhere near.

"Anywhere out of the city," Frances said with a smile, one that mothers would give their kids to reassure them everything was going to be alright. Liv let out a frustrated scoff. She'd always been a sucker for mother figures. She didn't normally trust people she'd just met. Or anyone, really. But Frances seemed genuine. Truth be told, if it were her mum, she'd sure as shit hope someone wouldn't leave her stranded in a city gone haywire.

"Fine," she muttered. "But one of you suckers is buying me a coffee when we get out of here."

"Thank you," Frances and Andy said in unified relief as they climbed into the truck.

"We really need to get out of here," Andy said. His eyes darted from side to side as he wiped sweat from his brows.

Liv nodded and fired up the engine. It spluttered and coughed, then gave a loud groan before dying. "Oh, come on!" Her frustrated moan ended in a whine. This was *not* the time for her trusty old—with an emphasis on old—truck to give up. "Please, please..." The engine roared to life along with a unanimous "Yes!" from the three of them.

"Can't go that way." Andy pointed at the main road that crossed the street ahead. "Military and rioters clashing. They don't even care. They just shoot. *Anyone*."

Liv followed his pointing finger. That was Westminster Bridge Road. How could the military be shooting there? What about all the civilians *and* rioters? *They just shoot. Anyone.* Andy's voice rang in her head. But surely they couldn't shoot people for inciting civil unrest? This was the UK. Or if they could... then what had made something like that a reality in London? She shook her head. These two, Frances and Andy, they weren't lying. And the smoke... whatever was burning was *really* burning.

"Okay, I think I know a way," she said and grabbed the wheel, taking a deep breath she hoped would sober her up. Turning the pickup around, she steered them away from the main road until they came to an end on Chicheley Street. She took a right turn, about to congratulate herself for her quick thinking, when a roadblock of police and military vehicles stopped them in their tracks.

"Oh, bugger," Frances said through clenched teeth.

"What do we do now?" Liv gripped the wheel tightly.

Andy's eyes fixed on the heavily armed soldiers. "We hope they think before they shoot."

7

JAKE

DAD, THE SCREEN READS. Dad? I frown. My dad and I haven't spoken in five years, not since— Another sharp vibration rips me from my stupor, and I swipe at the flashing green icon on the screen.

"Hello?"

"Soo-Yun?" he says in Korean.

"Don't call me that."

"I'm sorry," he apologises quickly. Something must be terribly wrong if my dad is apologising. "I must talk to you. Two weeks ago, there was an explosion in a lab."

"Okay..." I'm unsure where he's going with this, but I have more important things to deal with than a news update. "That's not good, but I'm kind of busy, Dad. I can't talk—"

"Jake," my dad cuts me off. "The explosion was up in Yorkshire, but you won't hear about it. They're putting a lid on it."

"Why?" I ask, curious to hear what he has to say. Why put a lid on an explosion?

"The explosion was in one of our bases."

"Oh, shit..."

"Language, Jake."

"Sorry."

If my father was an ordinary military guy, I wouldn't feel so stunned. My dad, however, is *not* an ordinary military guy. He's the head of the military's biochemical engineers unit. Meaning the British Prime Minister is the one who gets to press the red button, but my dad is the one who created that button to begin with.

The thought of one of my dad's bases being taken out makes my blood curdle. There's a reason military research facilities and labs are built to withstand explosions, earthquakes, and even terror attacks. The amount of hazardous stuff in those labs is—according to Dad—incomprehensible to the average person. If any of that were to get out, we'd be in for one hell of a shitstorm.

"Why are they covering it up?"

"Well, the lab in Danby technically doesn't exist. Imagine having to explain that to the press." He whispers the last part.

"Yeah," I say and for a minute I remember what it was like talking to Dad every day.

Dad was the stereotypical stone-faced, stern military father. The one who expected the best from his children. If I ever left the house with my bed unmade, I could be damn sure my weekly allowance would get suspended.

I want to say I don't miss him. I want to say I don't care, but he's my dad. Whether or not he agrees with my life choices, I can't ignore that fact. Knowing he's been in London a lot lately for work without trying to reach out to me, well, in less eloquent words, it sucks.

"Listen," he interrupts my thoughts. "I want you to get your mother and brother and bring them to Aldershot. I would go, but they're flying me out to Catterick. I've spoken to your mother, and she'll go get Tim, so go straight to our house and get them out."

"But Yorkshire is miles away from Huntingdon," I say. "Is it really necessary?"

"The entire facility got destroyed." His voice tightens at those words.

"Okay, but—"

"Don't talk back, just obey me!" He barks in Korean, then switches back to English. "Go get your mother and brother *now*; that's an order!" He talks as if I'm one of his military minions, but there's something in his voice when he quietly whispers, "Please," that catches me off guard.

It's a quiver, barely there, but I hear it and my initial annoyance subsides. My dad isn't angry. The grim-looking military man who had perfected the death stare is scared. Of what I don't know, and that sends shivers up my spine.

8

LIV

CARS LINED THE STREET in front of a roadblock where a large group of police and soldiers had gathered. A tripod floodlight loomed over the police and military vehicles parked lengthwise across the street to create the improvised blockade. The lamps shone bright, a stark contrast to the dark September night, and it took Liv's eyes a good few seconds to adjust.

A man dressed in camouflage stood in the middle, surrounded by a crowd of military. His hands moved, ordering officers and soldiers in different directions before pointing to the cars.

Liv slowed. "What the hell is going on?"

"More soldiers," Frances said, her jaw tight, "I don't like the look of this."

"We should get out of here." Andy shifted his weight nervously.

"But how?" Liv squinted against the bright light to search for any usable side streets. Thinking she'd spotted one, she cursed under her breath as two soldiers placed themselves in the way. They wore masks and held rifles firmly in their hands.

She shook her head with an annoyed sigh. She should have driven to her regular spot. If she hadn't gotten drunk, she could have done that. And be long gone by now, not stuck in this mess. Whatever the hell this mess was. But, no, instead she was stuck wishing she'd done things differently. Once again, regretting the choices of her past. *Story of my fucking life.*

She turned on the truck's radio. They couldn't have set up a big-arse roadblock right outside Central London without it being all over the news.

"...police and military oversee these roadblocks together because the police don't have enough forces," the radio presenter said in a soft but clear voice. "Others claim the military is in place, as the Prime Minister will declare martial law if the riots don't end. What do you think of this, Susan?"

"Well, as you pointed out earlier, Robert, we don't have a lot of information on what is currently happening in London regarding the riots," the woman replied in a posh, crisp voice that reminded Liv of the barrister who'd worked her case.

"What set it off initially?" Robert cut in quickly.

"Well, from what has been reported, the riots were sparked by the multiple deaths that they feel resulted from people not receiving help when turning to the NHS. Which is a direct result of understaffed hospitals leading to overworked personnel. And not enough time for new patients."

Understaffed hospitals, underpaid and overworked staff. Since when was that anything new? Liv frowned at the radio.

"Ah, yes," the male presenter said in a pompous, posh voice, "the LYM-1 virus. A new strain of the influenza thought to attack the lungs and lymph nodes in particular."

"Yes, minor virus outbreaks happen every year. Although it is fairly unusual for influenza season during the summer."

"And this one certainly seems much more aggressive."

"Certainly. For whatever reason, the riots are bordering on extreme at this very moment. Now, I don't think the Prime Minister will impose martial law tonight. Though they have indeed grown beyond expectations. It is a very serious issue that both civilians and law enforcement face. If we look at the riots of 2011, they lasted approximately five days. We're only on our third day."

"So, you think this will blow over?"

A pause followed the presenter's voice, lasting so long Liv checked to be sure the radio was still on.

"Well, the riots will indeed die out, but we're missing something here." The woman—Susan—paused dramatically, and Liv could imagine how she locked eyes with every person in the studio for maximum effect. "The talk of martial law is there to disguise the *real* question. If we were dealing with regular rioters, why has the government issued an order of roadblocks? When the largest part of the riots is still in the city? An estimated number of nearly seventy thousand by now. Instead of herding them *out* of the city, separating them from each other, they're being rounded up together and kept inside. Why?"

9

JAKE

I'VE NEVER SEEN OR heard my dad scared. I've seen him angry, drunk, happy, even sad. And judgmental, of course. But never scared. If Dad's scared, then I should be terrified.

"Okay," I say and glance out the train window into the darkness. "I'll go, but I need to find a way to get out of here. I'm stuck at work."

"What do you mean?" I can hear the frown in his voice. "I thought you were staying home from work this week?"

"Who said that?" Why would he think I was staying home from work?

"Well, I thought with the riots you'd stay home from work."

"No... I just finished work"—I scowl as if he can see—"and we're trapped underground."

"What do you mean, trapped?" He sounds more perplexed than anything else.

"The train at Westminster station hasn't moved in nearly two hours. The entire network isn't moving, and we just lost electricity. Everything is completely dead."

"*Shit*!" My dad, who's never had to pay a penny to the swear jar, curses. It's a weak one, but still more than I've heard until this point in my life. "Jake, you need to get out! You need to—"

A loud bang whips through the tunnel and shakes the train beneath my feet. I jump, my pulse slamming wildly. I can't see anything and shining my torch out the window only results in a blinding reflection off the glass. I raise the phone to ask Dad what he meant to say, but when I press my ear against the phone, it's silent. Dead silent.

I'm trying to make sense of the panic in my dad's voice when a low hum catches my attention. The small lamp next to the familiar black receiver blinks with urgency. The driver has activated the train's battery mode.

"Driver 936024," I breathe down the receiver.

"What's your name, driver?" the voice asks in its distinct London accent.

"Jake."

"Nice to meet you, Jake. I'm Gary. Listen, control radioed. Things are really bad in the city."

"How bad?" I ask, although I already know the answer. Even if I hadn't talked to Dad. There's no way Jane Remington at control would let the tube network go down for this long if things weren't bad. During normal cases, Remington would have gotten the trains running again, no matter the cost. Drag the sick person off the train, stick a newspaper on top of the vomit, leave the coat hanging out. Go, go, go. It's all about seconds down here.

"Remington said the military has ordered Dead Man's Barrier."

Dead Man's Barrier, or, as the suits call it, the "Catastrophe Barriers." Not sure which is more dramatic. In an event of flooding, the gates come down, slowing the flow until Westminster or Waterloo, or both, have been evacuated. Urban legend has it that during a catastrophe, if a train got trapped between the two gates, London Underground would sacrifice that train if it meant saving Westminster or Waterloo from flooding.

The thought sends a shiver up my spine, but then I remember that we're not flooded. "But there's no flooding."

"Not to stop flooding, mate," Gary says in a gruff voice. "The rioters are off their rockers, biting and attacking people around them. All over the city, and the military want them contained."

Contained? That's the word important people use in movies before ordering an assassination or taking drastic measures to stop something truly awful from happening. Either way, it always ends in casualties.

"But we're still in here!" I hiss down the receiver so that no one nearby will hear. There's another long silence before Gary speaks again.

"We're the train, Jake." We're the train?

"But it makes no sense," I say, my voice at normal volume. The gates only slow the flooding; to keep them from giving way under the water pressure, they've been fitted with large holes at the top. "Closing the gates won't stop the rioters from getting out. Unless..."

I look into the pitch-black tunnel, and it hits me like a bucket of cold water. *You need to get out!* My dad's terrified voice rings in my ears. *He knew!*

"They're flooding the tunnels," I say.

When Gary doesn't answer, I know I'm right. *Fuck! Fuck, fuck, fuck!* My heart slams with adrenaline as my brain desperately tries to think of a solution.

"Deactivate your cabin." I fumble with the train keys in my hands that shake from the stress pumping through my veins. "I can drive this train back to Waterloo."

We've only used the intercom, and during battery mode the train can travel three minutes before shutting down. Three minutes is all I need.

"No, you can't." Gary sounds terse, as if he wears a scowl.

"We haven't used much battery. I can get us there."

"No, you *can't*," Gary says, his voice tight.

"Listen," I say, but he interrupts me.

"They're already down." It's barely a whisper, but it makes me wish he'd yelled instead. My brain can comprehend angry, yelling people, but people so scared that they don't have a voice...

Gary clears his throat from the other line. "We don't have much time."

"How much?"

"Twenty at most."

Twenty? It's not much, but if we work together, we can get everyone off the train and use the emergency exits to return to street level. "That gives us time to—"

"I've got an emergency exit right here. I'm taking it." His voice is firm and decisive now.

"Okay, you take the first half of the train, I take the second."

"No..." he says slowly. "I'm taking it *now*."

"What?" I splutter, dumbfounded.

"You should get out of here as well. You've got quite the walk ahead of you to the next exit." I hear him move about in his cabin, gathering his things for the trip.

"Mate, what about the passengers?"

"I'm sorry, kid," he says. The receiver drops with a clunk as he scrambles out of the cab. I stand there with the receiver to my ear for few seconds. Maybe he'll come back and tell me this is just an elaborate joke.

I hang up and clasp my head between my hands. *What the fuck am I supposed to do?* Yes, commuters are a pain in my arse, but I can't leave them to die. I release my head and exhale. I need to get as many as possible out of here, and quick.

The exit Gary used is closer, but there's a flaw with his plan. That emergency exit leads straight to the corner of Richmond Terrace and Whitehall, barely a heartbeat away from Trafalgar Square. If things are bad enough for the military to step in, ground zero is the last place you want to be. The second exit leads to the far side of the river. It'll take longer, but it should lead us to safety.

I glance at my wristwatch. If Gary's right, I have fifteen minutes to reach the exit. That includes evacuating people and travel time. Nausea washes over me as I realise there's not enough time to get everyone out.

10

LIV

"HEY." A SUDDEN KNOCK on the truck's window startled Liv into a jolt.

"Jesus fuck!" The amount of people knocking on her bloody window was reaching its limit. Fast.

A soldier with bushy eyebrows and a scraggly beard peered back at her from the other side of the window. "Miss, are you coming from Central London?"

She frowned. What stupid kind of question was that? She sure as hell wasn't coming from *out*side the barricade. "Yes."

"Okay, well, I need you and your..." His voice trailed off with his glance at Frances and Andy. "Do you guys know each other?" The way his eyes narrowed made her nervous, and the slide of his finger to rest on the trigger of his rifle only added to her unease.

"No, I pick up strangers from the street every day." She scowled at him. Liv hated being scared, and she hated when other people made her feel scared. It made her feel weak and small, and that pissed her off. Not a great combination where confrontations were concerned.

Her words seemed to resonate with him. He gave a small nod and straightened when his eyes landed on Andy's dirty shirt. "Sir?" His voice turned sharp. "Is that blood on your shirt?"

Liv's insides grew cold. Blood on a shirt was always a bad thing. In front of a roadblock full of police officers and soldiers... *really* bad.

"No." Andy shook his head. "I work at the hospi—"

"Sir!" The soldier moved so fast Liv hardly had time to register it before the barrel of his rifle pointed straight at them. "Get out of the vehicle!"

"What are you doing?" Frances shouted, her voice skirting the edges of hysteria.

"Get out of the vehicle! Sir, I'm giving you one more warning. Get out of the vehicle or I will shoot!"

The others heard the soldier's shouts, and dozens of them swarmed her car, their rifles ready to fire.

"We've got an infected!" the first soldier shouted to the approaching soldiers.

Time slowed. Frances's screaming ricocheted through Liv's head, and Andy's desperate pleas not to shoot him echoed along with the stampede of footsteps. She should probably throw her hands in the air. That's what a normal person would do, but Liv was anything but normal. As in past moments of terror, anger swirled to life. She hadn't survived all the bollocks growing up to end up a bloody smear on some shitty street in the middle of London. So what if she lived in her car, worked for crap pay, and had a criminal record? Hell would freeze over before someone else decided when *her* life was over. One day, but today was not that day. Over her dead body.

The sharp sound of glass breaking cut through her thoughts as one soldier used the rifle butt to break the window next to Andy.

"Did you just break my window?" She glared at the soldier, ignoring the rifle in his hand. Just because he was the one with a gun didn't mean he could go around breaking shit. Especially not her shit. The truck might be a pile of junk on wheels, but it was *her* pile of junk. Her home. "You bellend!"

The soldier ignored her, threw the door open, and locked his arm around Andy's neck before he dragged him out kicking and screaming.

"What the fuck!" She turned to open the door, but the bushy-browed soldier moved closer, the barrel of his rifle glaring back at her. If she tried to open it, it would no doubt hit the rifle and she'd have a gaping hole in her head. Despite that, she grabbed the door in defiance as more soldiers neared.

"Miss, he's infected. Stay in your car!" the soldier shouted at her.

"Infected with *what*? How do you even know he's infected?" She pointed at where Andy stood in the midst of soldiers, hands on the back of his head, his chest moving in rapid, short gasps. "Hey!" she shouted again when he didn't answer.

"Shut up and stay in your car or I'll—"

"Fucking shoot me?" The people in nearby cars watched the spectacle from the safety of their metallic hulls, but none tried to defuse the situation or help. *Fucking humans! Scum of the Earth*. She grabbed the door handle and kicked it open just as the deafening boom of an explosion shook the ground and rattled her eardrums. Liv curled into a ball on her seat, instinctively wrapping her arms around her head.

Silence shrouded the street as soldiers and civilians alike slowly rose to their feet. Black smoke billowed into the sky. Liv dropped her arms to stare in shock at the clouds. Was that an explosion in the centre of London? She couldn't tell from where the smoke came. Sirens wailed from somewhere behind them. The hospital? Westminster?

"Infected! Breaching the left perimeter!" an alarmed voice cried out.

"They're coming from the hospital!" another voice shouted. An ear-shattering staccato of bangs followed, and the armed forces withdrew, rushing towards the side street Liv had considered earlier.

Her heart slammed wildly in her chest, and her body shook with barely controlled panic when she saw Andy slumped on his side. *Bollocks!* She grabbed the bottle of water that lay discarded on her floor and rushed to the young man. Blood pooled from a wound on his side, creating a puddle in which he lay.

Bullets and screams blended into a racket so loud Liv could barely hear her own thoughts as she lifted Andy's shirt. The gunshot wound—a small hole dug through the pale skin and flesh. She wrestled off the thick sweater she wore and pressed it hard against the wound.

The screams and footsteps of people fleeing the scene around them thudded across on the asphalt all around her. She inhaled and steeled her focus on Andy.

Frances landed with a heavy thud on the ground opposite her. "Oh my God," the older woman whispered with a shaky breath.

Liv ignored her and jabbed two fingers against Andy's pulse point. A thready, fast, and weak pulse. Clammy skin and the point of entry much too close to the abdominal area. She made mental notes, her trained eyes assessing the situation.

"Andy?" His breaths came in rapid, shallow gasps, and his head lolled to the side. "Andy, look at me."

She thought she could see him try, but his eyes remained closed. In normal cases she would have dialled nine-nine-nine by now, but nine-nine-nine was part of the group that had shot at them. And who were currently busy shooting at rioters. She had to get Andy back in the car and out of this place. Now seemed a better time than ever. "Hey, Andy, you goofing on Elvis?"

A weak smile tugged at the corner of his mouth before a moan escaped his lips.

"Listen to me, Andy, I need to have a look at your back, okay?" she asked him, but he merely whimpered in reply. "Come on, Andy, I need you to stay with me."

She was all business now. Treating a gunshot wound on the street without proper equipment was bad enough, but with all the shooting and shouting around them, she needed Andy to cooperate. She squeezed his shoulder gently when he still hadn't answered and was rewarded with a barely audible, "Okay."

"I need you to help me turn him over," she said to Frances.

"Understood." Something flickered across Frances's face. Surprise? Curiosity? But then the nurse lowered her head as she gently pushed Andy to his side. The faintest sigh slipped past his lips and Liv peered across the pinkish skin of his waist. A gold-coloured bullet lay on the ground. At least that saved them the hassle of removing the bullet. She let her gaze sweep the area around the two holes, prodding the surrounding flesh with gentle fingers. She could find no direct sign of anything else being damaged, although without an X-ray, she couldn't know for sure. Bullets had a nasty tendency to wreak havoc inside the body, pulverising bones and liquifying muscles.

"Unscrew the bottle and give it to me." Liv pointed at the small water bottle with her free hand. The nurse gave her a resolute nod, uncapped the bottle, and handed it to her. "Andy, this might sting."

She poured the water onto the entry wound. Andy hissed as the liquid mixed and mingled with the blood until she could peer inside. Thankfully, no intestines were visible. Blood bubbled up through the wound as quick as the water had washed it away, and she pressed the sweater against the wound. "Stay here and hold this in place. Keep talking to him."

"Hurry." Frances's voice shook slightly as Liv pushed to her feet.

She hadn't paid attention to her surroundings, but standing up was like stepping into a war zone. People in the cars around them screamed. Some threw their doors open and ran past her, terror contorting their faces. A man dragged a crying young girl with him as he sprinted away from the roadblock towards the river behind them. The constant blast of rifles and guns ricocheted between the buildings as thick clouds of smoke rolled across the street. Her ears rang from the loud bangs, each one sharp and painful.

She ran towards her car, arms held protectively around her head. Fat lot of good that would do if someone shot her in the back.

She slid to a stop by her truck and ripped open the back cover of her pickup, her gaze darting from side to side until she saw the toolbox filled with a bit of everything. Heaving herself onto the back of her truck, she grabbed it and flung it open.

The small package lay like the purest of diamonds among a pile of useless rubbish, and she snatched it up before racing back to Frances. She ripped the black vacuum patch open with her teeth and the green bandage dropped into her open hand.

She'd meant to get rid of everything from the life she had before this. She didn't need the reminders. But after they finished wrapping Andy up and dragged him into the back of her truck, she thanked her messy self for keeping it around.

11

JAKE

I TAKE A DEEP breath, hold it for a few seconds, then exhale again. Once my ritual is over, I step outside.

The carriage explodes with upset voices the moment I appear. Frantic, frightened voices.

"What's happening?"

"We need answers!"

"Are we being attacked?"

They blend into a cacophony. I don't know how to deal with this situation, which is quickly escalating into something that might explode. I don't blame them. With recent events, people fear this could be another terror attack. But the worst thing that could happen is for people to panic more than they already are. It's up to me to keep that from happening. The air feels raw, so raw it almost vibrates around my hands as I raise them into the air, palms facing out.

"Listen," I say as calmly as my nerves allow. As in all other situations like this one, they continue peppering me with questions. "You need to let me talk."

They only raise their voices. Obviously, reason isn't going to work.

"Quiet!" I finally bellow, and the entire carriage falls silent with the expressions of scolded schoolchildren. I observe them for a short moment, weighing my words.

Work once sent me to a customer service workshop, where they taught us how to communicate with customers and avoid conflict. To foster a conversation where the customer would listen, understand, and remain calm. The words "can't," "don't know," "I'm afraid not," and "no" were not to be used.

Which, in actual life situations, leaves me with a handful of "yes, I understand" phrases. Oh, and we should always smile when talking to customers. If I say, "Yes, we are trapped underground and will be flooded by the military shortly," and smile, I think someone might actually try to gouge my eyes out with their Oyster card.

I settle for something less aggravating. "They have instructed me to evacuate this train. Rioters from Trafalgar currently occupy Westminster, and the situation won't be resolved for another few hours." I pause, wondering if anyone's going to question this sort-of-a-lie-but-not-exactly-a-lie talk, but they don't. I follow it up with the magic words, "It'll get you home faster."

Most of the commuters shine their phones around the carriage to find their things, preparing to leave, but some remain seated, looking confused or dismayed.

A middle-aged white man with glasses and a shaved head raises his voice. "Exactly how are we being evacuated?"

I put on my friendliest smile because this next part might be a bone of contention. "A short walk through the tunnels to the nearest exit."

"Through the tunnels?" a young girl pipes up, an apprehensive look on her face.

"It's perfectly safe," I reassure her.

"Are you serious?" the man asks me, his forehead drawn into a deep frown.

I press my lips together and try not to scowl at him. I *do not* have time for this. "It's the only way out."

"Walking through the tunnels? Have you seen how dark it is out there, mate?" The man points with a large meaty finger towards the window, and when I simply stare back at him, he drops his arm to his side with a dramatic flick of his head. "So, to get home, instead of riding the train like we pay for, we're going to have to walk in a dark tunnel like some animals?"

"This is so typical of the underground. Chaos, *chaos* as always," another commuter says.

"You know what? I have an entire train to evacuate. If you want to stay, then *stay*. If not, get yourself ready to leave."

"I'm going to file a complaint," the man snaps, and I almost laugh at him. Almost.

"I don't even give a shit. Now if you'll excuse me." I look away from him. "Anyone who wants to be evacuated stand in a line over there." I point to the far side of the carriage. Much to my relief, almost all the passengers line up. It doesn't escape me that Mr. 'I will file a report' is also lining up. I brush past them and walk to where Roy and the others stand in the line.

"Hey." I give them a tired sigh, and Roy gives me a small fist bump on my shoulder.

"Being all fierce." Jules grins at me, and Fareena nods.

"Thanks." I chuckle, then turn towards Angela. "Can I ask you a favour?"

"Sure," she says and looks at me with curiosity. "What can I do to help?"

"I need someone to take charge in the front. You seem like the right person for the job." I pull a pad and pen from my bag. If I didn't know better, I'd say she looks a bit chuffed where she stands.

"I do, don't I?" She winks at me and dips her head with a sly smile.

“Look what you did.” Roy rolls his eyes at me. I laugh, both from relief at a pair of friendly faces and a small bit of panic.

“Listen carefully, okay?” I put my pen on the paper and write down the instructions. “Use the walkway on the left-hand side of the tunnel. Follow it until you see a large electricity box with a white sign on it. It should read something like Waterloo 1:5. There should be an exit right after. Take it then follow the stairs all the way up.” I pluck the key chain from my pocket and hand it to Angela. “These keys will get you through the doors.”

“And what about you?” Angela frowns.

“I’ll try to evacuate the rest of the train before...” I fall silent. What do I say? If I tell them what’s at stake, they’ll most likely panic and set off into the tunnels, but I need to warn them. “Don’t stop for anything, okay?”

“Jake?” Jules takes a step forward, her square features serious and sober. “What’s wrong?”

“Everything,” I whisper in a low voice. “Get out of here. Now.”

I walk away before they can protest, and I’m glad to hear Angela move to the front, instructing the other commuters on what to do. I move for the door connecting the next carriage with ours and allow myself another glance at the time. Twelve minutes to go. If this is how long every carriage will take, the next one might be the only one I have time for. That leaves five carriages full of passengers. Five carriages of passengers left to die.

I swallow, my throat as dry as sandpaper. If the military really floods the tunnels, their blood will be on my hands. But what can I do? There’s no time. My hands shake. This is real. This is *happening*. Right now. Even with all our drills, I never thought it possible.

I push the thoughts aside and put the key in the lock. Something slams against the glass door. Despite myself, I scream and recoil from the sight.

A woman stares back at me, her long, pale hair glowing white in the light of my torch. Something moves behind her in the dark, but I can’t see more than her ghostlike face. Her lips are drawn back into a twisted grimace, and blood trickles down her nose. She bangs her hands against the window.

I take another step back when I notice the strange, tilted angle of her eyes. An ice-cold sensation snakes up my back, and I spin to where Mr. Toad sits and shine my light at him. His left eye has turned so far to one side, his pupil is no longer visible. His veiny hands twitch in an irregular pattern. The more I stare at him, the faster my heart starts beating. Behind me, a guttural, unnatural noise rips from the woman’s lips, and she claws at the window like a frenzied animal.

I trip backwards into Fareena, who grabs me by the arm just as the first crack appears in the window.

"Run!"

12
LIV

OF ALL THE SHITSHOWS Liv had found herself in, this one took the biscuit. Grabbing the wheel with her hands, she let out a laugh that sounded a lot more hysterical than she had intended.

Her eyes snapped to the soldiers. They were shooting at the oncoming rioters. Or... *infected?* That was what they'd called Andy when they'd seen his stained shirt. They'd said the same about this group of rioters. *Infected by what?*

Whatever it was, bullets didn't stop them. The infected poured from the side street, the sounds from the screaming people and firing guns drawing their attention. Like beacons in the dark.

Bullets dug into their bodies, but the infected kept moving, their mouths mimicking the open, roaring mouths of the soldiers as they fired their weapons.

How was that possible? One bullet had shot Andy, and he was hanging on by a thread. These people, whatever they were, shouldn't be able to keep going, but they did.

A chill darted up Liv's spine as the infected rioters stormed across the street, encompassing the soldiers like a swarm of bees. Their speed, and the way their bodies charged forward with abandon, reminded her of the horses at the racetracks.

Nothing could stop them. Just like the horses at the track, they raced forward, lips drawn back and nostrils flaring, until they reached the soldiers. The hands and mouths of the infected ripped at any part they could reach. They buried their teeth into the soldiers' flesh like hungry children digging into food, blood showering across their faces, but instead of lurching backwards in disgust like any normal person would, it only seemed to spur their hunger.

Nausea washed over her. The infected were *eating* people. It was like a bizarre alternate universe. None of it made any sense.

The shooting stopped as the last of the soldiers was pulled from his feet and into the swarm of the feeding rioters.

Another group—thirty or so—rounded the corner with torn clothes and bloody faces. They stopped to sniff the air like wild animals, then raced towards the screaming people still inside their cars.

A middle-aged woman in a nice-looking suit dragged herself along the street. Her shoulder hung at a grotesquely unnatural angle, the white of her collar drenched in blood. Her milky grey eyes flickered wildly from side to side.

She pulled to a stop at the car in front of Liv's truck and pressed her cheek against the window as if eavesdropping. A shrill shriek erupted from within the car. The infected woman's face pressed harder against the glass while more infected swarmed the vehicle. Hands and faces rammed the windows as they tried to reach the screaming people.

A spiderweb of cracks crawled across the thick glass of the rocking car, and for an instant they almost looked like normal rioters. A scream cut through the mindless snarling of the infected, and Liv saw the small, round face wet with tears as it screamed in sheer terror. There were children in the car.

"Oh my God," she whispered in horror. She moved in an attempt to do something, *anything*. It was ridiculously foolish, she knew, and when Frances's hand gently grabbed her shoulder, she knew what the nurse would say. Yet she refused to look at her.

"We can't help them." The nurse's voice was eerily calm and soft. "There's too many of them. There's nothing we can do."

The first window broke underneath the weight of the snarling bodies. Liv thought she heard it shatter, but between the sounds of the infected and the people screaming, it was difficult to hear anything.

"We can't just do nothing!" She shook off Frances's hand and reached for the door handle, but more infected closed in. They smothered both the car and the screams, leaving her mind to imagine the rest.

It was almost worse, and her throat closed tight.

"We *have* to leave," Frances said and paused before continuing, "while they're too busy to pay us any attention."

Liv's head throbbed as she tried to comprehend what the nurse was saying. How could she be so cold? How could she consider leaving them to this fate? She turned to say as much, but where she'd expected to find Frances's flinty stare, she found two damp eyes watching her in despair. Not the eyes of someone who didn't care, but of someone who knew there was nothing to be done.

She took in the full depth of the anguished determination written across the nurse's features. "Okay..." Liv took a deep breath. There was no time for emotions. Not if they wanted to survive. She shook her head—she needed to snap out of it.

"Maybe we can find a way out further up the Thames," Frances said.

She reached for the keys when a sudden high-pitched, piercing noise sounded above their heads.

Five dark objects sped across the sky towards the city behind them, a tail of greyish smoke trailing each one.

"What is that?" she asked, her eyes following the objects until they disappeared behind buildings.

"They look like-" A sharp bang shot through the air, a cloud of orange and yellow billowing from the ground and soaring towards the sky.

One by one, the tall buildings crumbled like sandcastles in the tide.

13

JAKE

THE TUNNELS HAVE BEEN thrown into an impenetrable darkness, but somehow we scramble along without pushing each other over. I'd advised using the walkway, but we run along the tracks, the bloodcurdling, shrill shrieks chasing after us in the dark. I don't know how Fareena is running in her nine-inch heels, but she moves like a sprinter. Steady and fast, only stumbling a few times when the tunnel shook from four thunderous bangs that sent us all staggering before we hunched down in the spoil between the tracks.

A few commuters reacted too slowly and stumbled or fell over, injuring themselves. A young man twisted his ankle, and another man banged his forehead. Blood stains his shirt, but luckily one bloke is a doctor, and he crouches beside the man who sits in the macadam, patching him together with a makeshift bandage using bits of fabrics from scarfs and someone's leftover top.

I've walked up to Angela, who's been taking the lead, when the distinct sound of trickling water reaches my ear. I use my phone to illuminate the tracks ahead. It takes a few seconds before I see the transparent liquid rolling across the tracks, black as oil, mirroring the cave walls around us. It splashes against the tracks and walls, flowing our way.

I glance down at my watch. Our fifteen minutes were up four minutes ago.

"Guys," I yell, urging them to listen to me, "guys, we really need to go." To my surprise, everyone listens. When the first water reaches our feet, we burst into motion.

Half the time when something goes wrong in the tube, Londoners instantly think the underground purposefully does it to cause them extra hassle. It's the human need to put blame somewhere, but even Londoners know that leaking water in an underground tunnel isn't a plot to piss them off.

Maybe it's because I'm the only one who knows the way out, or maybe they've finally realised I know a little more than them. Whatever the reason, they follow me without argument or question. Our feet slap against the wet ground that's quickly filling up with water. Thirty seconds of running, and the water has already reached our ankles. Where's that bloody electricity box?

A loud splashing, followed by a yelp, echoes through the tunnel as one commuter falls over, tripping the ones behind them. I spin on my heel, shining my light, and feel relief when it's neither Angela, Fareena, or Jules. I know it's not Roy because he's taken my spot at the back to make sure no one gets left behind.

It surprises me, the sense of relief. I've only known them for a few hours, after all.

Prince Charming climbs to his feet, the woman in the eye-searing pink blouse helping him up. They're both soaked, water dripping down their faces, wet hair clinging like slugs to their skin. If this had been twenty minutes earlier, I would have laughed, but there's nothing funny about our situation. Instead, I wait to make sure the others who also fell climb to their feet, then I continue our race towards the exit.

It shouldn't be much further, but perhaps my memory is playing tricks on me. Driving through these tunnels isn't the same as walking or running. By the time my eyes finally land on the dirty metal box, brown from too many years spent in the tube, the water reaches my knees.

We wade the last twenty metres, legs struggling against the current until we reach the door, where Angela hands me my keys. The water rises faster now, covering the bottom of the door. It opens with a loud moan, and we spill into the stairwell with the water.

"Up, keep going up, all the way!" I say. People pile up the stairs, exhausted, wet, and scared, moving painstakingly slow as their hands clasp the railing for support.

"Jake?" Jules runs to me, her long, peacock-blue dress stuck to her legs. She still holds Fareena's hand, as if they're anchored to each other, helping the other one to keep going. The way she says my name leaves the unspoken question hanging in the air: what's happening?

"I'll explain when we get out of here. Now get a move on." I nod towards the stairs, and Roy puts a hand on Fareena's shoulder, motioning for them to keep moving. I slam the door and race to follow the line of dark heads that climb the stairs. These stairs will lead us up one floor, then take us out on the other side of the Thames through the maintenance tunnel underneath the County Hall. Once in that tunnel, it's only one last push until we'll see the exit at Queen's Walk.

The stairwell is grey concrete, and our phones cast eerie shadows along the walls. Dust and spiderwebs enhance the dank smell. The last set of stairs leads to a white door that's grey and dirtied from years of maintenance activity.

A hard push opens the door into the maintenance tunnel. Like everything else so far, lack of power leaves the corridor cloaked in complete darkness.

This time I take the lead; I know the corridor is long and turns steep farther ahead.

"Are you going to tell us what's going on?" I hear Jules' voice as she and Fareena step up next to me, apparently having elbowed their way past the other people.

She walks briskly at my side. The light from her phone illuminates the concrete floor, but enough light bleeds into the darkness above to cast soft shadows on her square face and defined jawline. She glances at me, eyes sharp and inquisitive. I was going to tell them when we got out, but I guess now is as good a time as any.

"Where's Roy and Angela?" I ask and Fareena motions to where the couple walks. Angela lifts her eyes from the ground, and I wave for them to come over.

"You got any news?" Roy asks when they catch up to us.

"Not exactly, but before everything went down, I got a call," I say, watching their faces. "From my dad."

"How did you manage that?" A tiny frown crosses Jules' face.

"I'm not sure." I don't know how my dad got through. No one else had reception. "My dad's work might have had something to do with it. He's this military guy." I say *military guy* as if that explains everything. It doesn't, but I'm not sure how else to explain it.

"What did you say your father does?" Angela asks.

"I didn't," I say. "He works as a biochemical engineer for the military. I know my dad, if he says something is wrong..."

"Then we better listen the hell up," Roy says.

"My thoughts exactly."

"So, what do we do?" Angela asks, a wrinkle forming between her eyes.

"Dad told me to get my mum and little brother. Something about taking them to a military base."

"A military base?" An irritatingly familiar voice sounds from my left side as Prince Charming comes into view. "And when were you going to tell the rest of us this little tidbit of information?"

"I don't see how my private conversation is anyone else's business." I scowl at him.

"Well, you're telling this lot." He wears a smug face as he motions towards the others.

I sigh. "Listen, Mister...?"

"Coleman, Noah Coleman."

"Mister Coleman, first, it's private business. Second, I don't think it's beneficial worrying everyone just because my dad asked for my mother and brother to stay with him at the base." I put forward my argument like a politician at a debate. Hopefully, he'll buy it and leave it alone. Though by the way he flattens his lips into a thin line, I'm not sure he will.

"So, you don't know what's happening?"

This time, I don't even have to sugarcoat my answer. "No, I don't know what's going on out there."

"You'll find out soon enough," Fareena says to Noah.

She points at the orange glow that dances at the top of the rise, and I quicken my steps. The closer we get to the entrance, the harder it is to see. Our eyes have grown accustomed to the dark and the orange light, which I assume is streetlights, are sharp and blinding. I squint when the smell of smoke reaches my nose.

"What's that?" Jules asks.

The smoke smells strange. Sniffing it, I slow down. The sound of car alarms and sirens makes its way into the tunnel, and foreboding constricts my chest.

"That noise sure doesn't sound good," Roy says.

As we draw closer to the entrance, I sense the others slowing down behind me, uncertain of what's going on outside. The sirens and car alarms were loud enough to find their way down the long tunnel, but it's only by the entrance that I hear the screams and shouting, followed by popping sounds that resemble gunfire. Or what I think is gunfire, based on every shooter game and action movie I've seen.

I barely have time to glimpse the shattered glass doors, thousands of shards littering the floor, before the smell of rotten, burnt flesh reaches my nose. I bend forward as I gag.

Others heave behind me. Even Noah, who stands at my back, can't keep his face straight. He looks pale, his face seemingly trying to crawl back into itself as he swallows thickly, fighting the urge to throw up.

Roy, stoic as ever, only looks as if he tasted something slightly unpleasant, but other than that, the man hosts an unfazed expression. It takes me a moment and several deep breaths before I can stand upright again, and I cover my mouth and nose before stepping into the blinding light.

Jules gasps, grabbing my arm, and I stare at the sight before us.

London is burning.

14
LIV

"OH GOD," FRANCES GASPED, eyes glued to the city behind them. Fire swallowed it whole, black smoke rising towards the sky.

Liv watched in horror, her ears still ringing from the blasts. Air forces had dropped bombs on London. She wasn't an expert, but she was pretty sure that if enemy aircraft entered their airspace, the military would be on it. So far, the only military she'd seen had been shooting at them, not the enemy.

They're being rounded up together and kept inside. Why? The radio presenter's voice prickled at the back of her mind. It wasn't the enemy who had kept them from leaving. Did that mean those airplanes were their own?

"This can't be real." Frances shook her head, then straightened to peer down the street behind them.

"What is it?"

"Reinforcements."

Of course! Turning in her seat, Liv saw the large, sand-coloured vehicle thundering towards them.

"Shit!" They'd left Andy in the back of her pickup and covered him as much as they could, but anyone with good enough eyesight would see the injured man if they drove past. The last thing they needed was for someone else to think Andy was infected. She threw a quick glance at Andy. Beads of sweat coated his pale skin like tiny diamonds.

Maybe if the reinforcements focused on the attacking rioters, they'd ignore Liv and her new friends? Perhaps it was even too dark for them to notice Andy.

She watched the heavily armoured truck as it sped towards them. Grating covered the entire truck, giving its already massive bulk an imposing appearance. She'd started the engine in case the reinforcements spotted Andy and they needed to make a quick escape. As it drew closer, Liv realised trying to outdrive it would be futile. Theirs was a military vehicle, hers a junk pile that was a spark plug away from being sent to the scrapyard. Like a snail trying to outrun a greyhound.

She held her breath as the truck pulled up next to hers. *Maybe I can talk my way out of this.* She sighed and reached for the window handle. Might as well try to bullshit them. Maybe if she appeared cooperative, they'd forget to check the back of her truck.

A gust of wind rattled the pickup as the military truck thundered past. She blinked in surprise. Then, as if the cars blocking the road were little more than cardboard, the truck crashed into them, sending them spinning to the sides.

That was their way out.

15

JAKE

THE OTHER SIDE OF the Thames, which once hosted Big Ben, Westminster Abbey, Downing Street, and all the other places that made this city beautiful, lies in ruins.

The London Eye, once the world's tallest Ferris wheel, has fallen on its side. Half of it and its pods are caught in the Thames. The dark water mirrors the buildings around the river, and just like the city, the Thames resembles a blazing inferno.

I stare in disbelief. A smoking, gnarled skeleton is all that remains of Big Ben. Westminster Bridge, which has connected the city centre to south of London for nearly two hundred years, sports a gaping hole in the middle. Concrete slabs hang off rebars, and burning cars line the intact sides of the bridge.

Bodies litter the bridge and the walkway in front of us. Most are charred by the fire, and some appear mauled by an animal. Their chests and throats shredded and flayed open, limbs ripped and discarded on the ground. What the hell did that?

Screaming and shouting travels across the river. Or is it coming from behind us? I can't tell, but it sounds too far away to be close by.

"Good God," Roy says next to me. He lifts his fedora from his clean-shaven head and rests it on his chest, his face set and serious as he wraps his arm around his wife. We all stand for a good few minutes, shell-shocked into silence underneath a sky of auburn flames.

Sobbing draws my attention from the devastation in front of us. Fareena covers her mouth with trembling hands. Tears roll down her cheeks, and I remember our conversation from earlier. Fareena's boyfriend and all their friends were waiting for her somewhere in there.

I feel a lump in my throat. Like Megan was waiting for me. I look at the complete and utter destruction of the city I love. *Had* been waiting for me. The Cross lays at the very heart of the city, the same one that rages with fires, gnarled and blackened metal bending under the carnage. And she's in there. Somewhere.

I clench my jaw and shake my head. Maybe she got out. She can't be gone. I only just texted with her. I think up a thousand ways she could be alive, but then my eyes land on the destruction again, and it hits me like a punch in the gut. Nothing could have survived that.

The world shifts beneath my feet. Fear and grief roll through me. If I don't stop myself, the ground will open and swallow me whole. I can't think of this. Not now. Instead, I walk over to Fareena, doing what I do best; I push my emotions aside to deal with them later.

"Hey." I touch Fareena's shoulder as she hides her face in her hands.

I get it, do I ever. When we went down into the tube this evening, save for some rioting, the world was fine, and now... the whole world is on fire, flakes of ashes falling on us like snow.

Behind us, someone mumbles, "Oh my God" repeatedly, like a mantra or a prayer. More begin to sob. And once again, I struggle against my emotions to stay in control. Our previous nightmare in the tube feels like nothing compared to this.

"I'm sorry, Fareena," I mumble. I wish there was some way I could comfort her and say we'd find him. Even if I didn't know better, the heaps of dead bodies littering the ground aren't a good sign, and the blown bridge makes getting there impossible. Unless we use the tunnels. But there's no guarantee they haven't been affected by the destruction aboveground.

"They were all there because of me," she cries.

I hate it when people cry because I don't know what to say. At least that's what I think is the reason, but Megan thinks it's because I fear other people's vulnerability.

Having met and interacted with my dad, she always blamed my upbringing for my inability to handle both my own and others' emotions.

My dad never talked about his feelings, and he would rarely show them. Unless, of course, he was angry. Then you'd know for sure. But the deeper emotions, the ones that connect you to other people, were always off-limits. To Dad, showing your emotions was a sign of weakness. One of the many reasons Megan never liked him.

My throat and chest constrain with emotions, and for too many heartbeats, it feels like I can't breathe. I always knew I'd lose Megan. But not like this. Not forever. I blink at the sudden dampness in my eyes, trying not to think of her, of us. The way we used to be. The way she always smelled faintly of wildflowers and how her body fit right in my arms. How she would shiver underneath me and whisper my name. When everything was perfect. Before we fell apart. Maybe she was right. Maybe I never trusted her enough to let her in.

I sigh and scrub my face with my hands. There's nothing I can do about it now, so I return my focus to Fareena. As per usual, I have no idea what to say, but I doubt there's anything that would make her feel better.

"Oh, hon." Angela puts her arm around Fareena's shaking shoulders, and Jules strokes her arm. I'm grateful someone else takes care of the comforting bit. "This is awful," Angela continues, her eyes damp. "Just awful."

"What the hell happened here?" Roy finally says, his hat returned to his head.

I shake my head. "I don't know, I—" My shoulders slump as my throat tightens. How far did this destruction reach? I grab my phone and swipe the screen with my thumb. There's reception, but when I press the dial button, I get a busy tone.

The others are doing the same. Finally, I drop my phone into my pocket. I've tried Megan, Mum, and Dad, but every time my screen reads: user busy.

"Anyone get through?" I ask, and the others shake their heads.

"I even tried calling nine-nine-nine," a square-shouldered young woman adds, "and I can't get through."

"What do we do now?" a woman asks from behind us.

Everyone's eyes turn my way. I want to sigh and tell them I'm not in charge, never was nor wanted to be. I just happened to know the way out. I've done my part and they're on their own. I have my own shit to deal with. I need to get to my mother and brother, and I don't have time to help everyone else.

I bite my cheek. I made my choice back in that tunnel. There's no going back. I guess we're in this together.

16

JAKE

"I DON'T KNOW WHAT to do," I say.

"What do you mean you don't know?" Noah raises his voice and pushes his way past a few people. "What do you *mean* you don't know?"

"Look," I say, but Noah's angry voice drowns out my own.

"You said you'd evacuate us. You said you'd help! You *fix* this!" Noah's face reddens with every breath and every step brings him closer to me, his fists balled so tightly his knuckles pale. I'm not sure why he thinks I have the power to fix any of this, and for a fraction of a second I feel like laughing, but I clamp down on whatever shock-fuelled reaction I'm about to have. Just like me, he must be trying to work his frantic mind around this insane situation.

"Jake," Jules hisses next to me, "Jake, let's get out of his way."

I should do as she says, but I'm tired and confused, like everyone else. And I'm sick of this knob trying to push me around. As if I can fix a burning fucking city! Instead of moving, I cross my arms over my chest and stare at him.

"You incompetent son of a bitch!" Saliva flies from Noah's mouth as he spits out the words, then his tall frame lunges towards me. I welcome him with open arms. Like meeting a long-lost friend. A long-lost friend I hate.

"Hey!" Angela snaps, her voice surprisingly sharp.

"Stop it!" Jules raises her voice to stop the two of us fighting. I've already got Noah's collar twisted between my fists and I use all my strength to twist him around and away from me. He spins, giving me momentum to shove him to the ground, but he's got his own hands wrapped in the front of my shirt, and I follow him down as he falls.

Growing up, I was always the smallest. I didn't have much strength to fight back with, and as my anger and frustration seep into my muscles, I fight the only way I know how: dirty. Pushing my knuckles hard against his collarbone, I grind them roughly against the sensitive bone. He groans in pain. I push him to the ground and jerk my left arm free from his grasp. The loud whack of my fist connecting with something fleshy and bony reaches my ears.

Noah's cry echoes as he rolls over, clutching his nose. Blood spurts from between his fingers. I release his shirt in shock. *Shit...* I punched him. I sit back and stare at him. I actually hit him and now he's got a nosebleed and I've got a sore hand. Grimacing, I open and close my fingers. Fighting isn't what we need right now. We need to work together and be levelheaded.

"Hey, hey, hey," Angela says calmly and pulls me to my feet. "Settle down, settle down." Her voice is kind, but her eyes are hard. Telling me she won't take any more of our childish fighting.

"He-he broke my nose!" Noah splutters from the ground.

The doctor that came with us kneels by his side, carefully removing Noah's hands to look at the nose.

"Sir," the doctor says calmly, "it's not broken; you'll be fine. Let's just stop that bleeding." It wasn't a smile, but I swear I can see the corner of the doctor's eyes wrinkle as he looks back at me and Angela.

"Gentlemen." Angela takes a step forward and holds her hand out in the air, palm downward. "I understand we are all under a lot of pressure and scared, but we cannot be fighting among ourselves." She nods towards the scene across the water, then the debris and rubble further down the walkway. "Take a good look around." Her voice is solemn and serious.

I take in the destroyed city around me once more. My gaze trails the bridge. Only a few sad-looking columns remain in the middle. The rest have plummeted into the Thames, separating us from the inner city. Jules stares at the city, her eyes damp with tears. Fareena stands next to her, just as shaken.

"How could this have happened?" Jules whispers. Her voice trembles.

"I don't think anyone knows, honey." Angela gives her arm a soft squeeze.

"Hey." Jules puts her hand on my arm. "Are you okay?"

"Yeah, thanks, I'm fine." I rub my cheek. I wasn't the only one who got a punch in.

"Well," Roy's voice reaches my ear. "We can't access the most central part of London. I suspect no one wanted to in the first place."

Angela shoots a careful glance at Fareena sniffling next to her, but I suspect that even though Fareena's boyfriend was in the city, she isn't foolish enough to insist on looking for him. At least not now.

"I guess whoever wants to can go to the nearest station and ask for help," Roy says and motions towards the city behind us.

"The nearest tube is Waterloo, but I think Westminster is..." I remember the rushing waters in the tunnels as we fled across the tracks. "I think Westminster is gone." The words and the memories of our escape linger in the air, and silence settles for a minute.

"I'm going to the nearest station," the doctor finally says, taking a step forward. "If there are people there, they might need a doctor." Some of the commuters exchange looks before walking to stand next to the doctor. I'd want to stick around a doctor as well, but I have to get to my parents. I don't have a choice but to keep on moving.

"What about the rest of us?" someone says. My eyes glide to where Jules crouches next to a woman. The woman wears a scarf the same colour as her hair, and she slumps back against the stony wall of the building behind us.

A burly man with a weathered face and a bald head steps forward, and I return my attention to the group in front of me.

"We're going to make our way home," he says in a gruff voice. "We all live in the same area, so we'll be safe if we stick together. I think that's the best for everyone. Group up with people who live near you and go home."

Roy's grimace says he thinks it's a bad idea, but the burly man and his group seem to have made up their minds, and with one last look at us, they turn and walk away. A few of the remaining people discuss among themselves, then set off towards their homes, some in pairs, some in a bigger group.

"Listen." I turn to the doctor. "If you get to the station and things go bad, you might have to hunker down for a while."

He gives me a dubious look, but then the reflection of the burning city dances against his eyes, and he nods.

"If that would happen, and help doesn't arrive, you'll be needing water." I scratch my beard. "And possibly the loos."

"Surely the tube has some sort of water?"

"Yes, which is why I'm giving you these." I unclasp a set of keys from my key chain. "Many rooms in there have water; these keys will let you in to the loos and lunchroom."

"And you're giving them to me? Just like that?" he asks, looking slightly sceptical.

I shrug. "Seen the city? I think work has bigger issues than getting on my back for losing my keys."

"Yeah." He chuckles weakly. "Well, thanks, mate. I'm sure we'll be fine. When they come to get us, I'll make sure they find the keys you 'dropped.'"

"Be careful." I give him a small nod and then watch the group make their way down the walkway towards The Eye to take a sharp right turn towards Waterloo.

I watch them until they disappear around the corner, then I turn and look around at the remaining few. Jules, the woman in a scarf, Fareena, Roy, Angela, and... I frown in surprise. Noah?

17

JAKE

I HAVEN'T ALWAYS BEEN the nicest person in this world. Sometimes, especially if you ask Megan, I can be a bit of a dick. She says I can be very selfish. That I can come off cold and be too blunt. Apparently, I also have a "glare" that makes me look as if I want to punch people. Which might not be entirely untrue, but anyone who had my job for a day or two would want to punch people on a daily basis, too. She also says I'm very judgy, and yes, that one is also true. Maybe I'm a terrible person at times, but do I really deserve to be stranded in a destroyed city with the biggest dick of them all?

Noah's nose is starting to swell. Maybe because of my punch or the two gigantic balls of tissue he's got stuffed up both his nostrils. He looks miserable, and I find myself feeling a *little* bad about punching him. I shouldn't have. It was very cathartic, but I still shouldn't have.

"We were talking on our way here," Roy says, nudging me from my thoughts, "and we were thinking of trying to catch a bus or a cab to get to Heathrow."

I turn to look at him and I have to keep from laughing.

"Obviously that plan has been blown all the way to hell," Angela says with a tinge of sarcasm bordering on amusement in her voice.

"Even if the destruction has only affected Central London, the airports will be shut down," Jules says.

"We need to find someone who can tell us what's going on," Angela fills in. "I mean, we've got to get home."

"I guess we could go to the nearest police station," I say.

There's a loud snort behind me, and we all look at Noah. His eyes go round when he notices us, as if he hadn't meant for anyone to hear him, but he quickly regains his composure.

"Got something on your mind?" I say with a frown.

"Look around you, mate," he scoffs. "You see any police? Any military?"

I hate to admit it, but he's right. Despite sirens and blaring car alarms, there are no police, no military, no one around. The staccato popping sounds we heard earlier had stopped by the time we left the maintenance tunnel, and we haven't heard anything since.

"Exactly," he says smugly to my silence. "Where are they, if they're not here? Military brat like you should know what that means."

Once again, he's not wrong. I do know what that means. It either means they've got more serious things to deal with. Or... I stare at the burning city across the river. Or they've been forced to retreat. The military forced to retreat? That certainly doesn't bode well...

My dad's words ring in my ear, and I realise why he'd sounded so scared. He knew. Not just about the train, but about everything. Who would do something like this? Surely, a few riots couldn't cause it.

The US? Russia? Terrorists? I know England has been the target of terror attacks lately, and just like the commuters back at Westminster, fear bubbles up inside. What if this is a terror attack? What if this isn't only to incite fear, but to really take us out? Throw England into chaos.

"Claire?" Jules turns towards the pale woman sitting on the ground. Claire holds her head between her hands and pinches her eyes together with a small sob. Jules kneels next to her and puts a hand on her shoulder.

"My head won't stop hurting," Claire says weakly.

"Drink this," Jules says, holding out a bottle of water.

"I'm too tired," Claire sobs. "I just want to go home."

"Okay, hon, we will get you home soon." Jules drops the bottle into her lap and looks back at us with a worried expression.

Maybe it's the shock combined with being ill, but I think that if we don't get Claire home soon, she might crack.

"We need to find help. There has to be *someone* out there," Roy says.

"I wish I'd known earlier, before that doctor left," Jules says quietly as she stands back up. "He could have looked at her."

"There's a hospital across the road," Fareena says, her voice thick from having cried. Clearing her throat, she points to the steps behind us that lead to the big street.

"And you think because it's a hospital it'll still be standing?" Noah scoffs.

"No." Fareena glowers at him. "But maybe there are people there who survived this..." She waves her hand around in the air. "Whatever this is."

"I think she's right," Roy says. "There must be others like us. Who survived."

"Why don't we split up? Some stay here, some go there to check it out," I say.

"What, are you stupid?" Jules slaps my arm.

"Uh..." I look at her suspiciously. Is this one of those arguments? The ones Megan and I used to have where I always lost.

"Have you never watched a single scary movie in your whole life?" She glares daggers at me. "Don't you know splitting up is the number one fast lane to death?"

"I..." I scratch the nape of my neck. She has a point, but this isn't a movie. We can't do things the way we'd like to do things in a movie. We have to be logical and sensible.

"We *don't* split up," she insists, "unless we all want to die."

"Sugar," Angela says in her calm voice softened by her light Southern accent, "someone needs to stay with Claire. If there aren't any survivors at the hospital, then whoever leaves comes back here."

Jules looks at Angela. "But..."

"But at least Claire won't have to exert herself when she's feeling this bad, and what if it's dangerous over there?"

"Why don't you, Angela, and Fareena stay with Claire?" Roy suggests. "The rest of us can quickly run over there and check things out."

"Whoa!" Noah raises his hands in the air in protest. Of course he would. "Why do I have to go? I could just as well stay here with them."

"Because, son," Roy drawls and locks eyes with Noah, "I don't trust you for a second not to leave my wife in a pickle. Or Miss Jules, Fareena, or Claire, for that matter. Should you feel the instinct to save yourself."

"All right, honey. You know I'm perfectly capable of taking care of myself." Angela waves her hands dismissively at her protective husband, and I grin. Roy is a big guy, and I mean big as in all muscles and bulk, and he probably towers my five feet eight by at least four inches. Big as he may be, though, I can see that no one's running this household but Angela.

Roy narrows his eyes, his thumbs hooked on his belt. "I would let you stay," he says, but then nods in Fareena's direction, "but have you seen her shoes?"

"I will take your eyes out if you make me run in these again." She holds her shoe up, heel pointed outwards, and I swear Noah's face slackens briefly.

"Actually," Jules' voice lilts as she digs around in her bag. Not more Bacardi, I hope. Or maybe, now that I think about it, we could all need some to calm our nerves. Her face breaks into a smile when she finds what she's looking for, and she holds out a pair of black ballerina shoes.

"Oi," Fareena growls and snatches them from Jules. "You had these all along and let me traverse those tunnels in those heels?"

Jules fires off an innocent smile that I'm sure has gotten her out of trouble more times than she'd ever admit.

"See, Fareena will come with you boys, and we'll be fine here with Noah." Angela pats Roy's arm lovingly.

"One hair," Roy warns Noah, moving his two fingers from his own eyes towards Noah's.

Ever since we got stranded at Westminster, Noah's sole priority has been himself. So, I can't exactly blame Roy for not trusting him, but I'm relieved that I don't have to rely on Noah to watch my back.

"Whatever." Noah scowls at Roy. He doesn't protest or try to argue with the defamation of his character, though. Not even Noah is stupid enough to pick a fight with Roy.

"It's barely a nip across the street," Fareena says.

The way Jules narrows her eyes at Noah means she won't let anything happen to Angela if she can prevent it.

I look at her determined face and dark hair that looks as if she woke up and rolled straight out of bed. But it's her eyes that give me pause. I haven't noticed them until now. It's not the startling blue colour that surprises me; it's the fire that burns within.

18
JAKE

SMOKE DRIFTS DOWN THE street as we zigzag between two rows of cars packed impossibly tight. Burnt bodies scatter the ground around us and some have been seared into the seats of their cars. The smoke is so thick it could almost be mistaken for fog, but the pungent stench of burnt flesh and blood gives it away.

We round a double-decker that lays tossed to its side, flames licking its hull like hungry wolves, and I glance at the dark figures inside. Roy's hand gently nudges me to keep moving, and we duck through the smoke, hiding our faces in the crook of our elbows as we pass a van that lies upside down on the coarse asphalt. Its entire front is decimated, and the windows must have exploded with the impact. Remnants of glass cover the surrounding ground, and a large puddle of dark liquid stains the asphalt.

My stomach twists. I look away, but not before my eye catches the sticker on the rear window. Two parents, two children, and a dog. I hope none of those children were in that car. That they were somewhere safe, far away from the city.

"Over there!" Fareena points through the smoke across a big grass-filled square ahead.

A multi-storey building rises towards the sky. A chunk of the right wing has been torn off. Hospital furniture and rubble spills from it like a bleeding wound.

"The entrance." Roy nods to our left where a set of railings cleverly diverts the visitors off the road, towards the main entrance of the hospital.

I pick up speed and jog along the sidewalk, Fareena and Roy following closely. Turning a sharp right, we follow the metal railing towards the entrance. I'm surprised to see the bottom part of the hospital fairly undamaged. Reflective film covers the panoramic windows near the entrance and our reflections grow larger the closer we draw to the entrance.

"Look!" Fareena juts her chin towards the glass entrance. "There are others in there."

"Thank God." Roy breathes a sigh of relief. I can't blame him. For a moment, I'd feared the worst.

The windows reflect the city behind us, and I have to squint to see beyond the reflection. Dark shadows move around, but I can't make out how many there are or even who they are. What if most of them are patients who need as much help as we do?

"That ambulance," Fareena says with a quizzical expression on her face.

I take my eyes off the windows and let my gaze slide to where the yellow vehicle stands parked right in front of the main entrance, blocking it off.

"Balls," I mutter. I was hoping entry would be easier.

"Why on earth is it keeping us from getting in?" Roy asks.

We're almost by the entrance when something catches my attention. Someone's banging on the window.

"Do you guys see that?" I ask. I'm not sure they heard me because I get no response, so I take a step closer. *What is that?* I press my face against the glass.

The room is full of people. They move in an odd, erratic manner, and their bodies twitch, causing their heads to shake eerily. I recognise the odd twitching. I've seen it before, on Mr. Toad and that woman on the train.

I try to see if any of the people's eyes are acting as strange, but they're too far away. A large sign on the wall catches my attention. Infected Patient Drop-Off, the sign reads. Infected patients? What the shit? What kind of infection? I search the opulent foyer for more clues and spot a yellow sign on one of the doors. "Quarantined Waiting Room, infected patients and authorised personnel only."

I read it twice in case I read it wrong. Anything that begins with the word quarantine is bad, and with the state of the world outside, we don't need things to get any worse.

"Guys," I say slowly, "there's some sort of infection here."

"Infection?" Roy asks behind my back.

My breath fogs up the window. I wipe it away and spot a small figure on the floor—a teenage girl.

She's crouched on top of something, picking at it with her fingers. *What the hell?* It appears to be a cushion from the hospital furniture. Her thin fingers rip at the stuffing. Red stuffing? Red, gooey stuffing.

My brain tries to comprehend what it's seeing when a face slams against the window inches away. I scream and jump back into Roy, my heart racing.

"Son?" Roy steadies me, and Fareena stares with a startled expression.

"I saw something.". A cold sensation spreads through my chest and head, as a loud banging begins where I just face-planted at the window.

Roy takes a step forward. "Someone needs help."

"No, don't!" I reach to grab him, but he's already peering into the hospital lounge. A crack forms on the window, the patter of multiple hands and heads banging against the glass wall reverberating through it.

I want to run. I want to grab Roy and Fareena and get the hell out of here. Whatever is in there *can't* be real. It must be my imagination. Spent too much time playing those fucking video games, I tell myself, but I can't forget the image of a teenage girl feeding on another human being and the large letters spelling "Infection."

The cracks expand. Soon the white face will be out. Here. With me.

"The ambulance." I breathe so low it's almost a whisper.

"What?" Fareena says next to me, but she's not moving closer to the windows like Roy.

"The ambulance," I say, louder this time. "It's not there to keep us out." Panic races up my spine, rippling my skin in its wake, and the hair on my neck stands on end.

"It's to keep them in." Fareena blanches with realisation.

A bloodied arm crashes through the thick window.

"Jesus!" Roy cries out.

The fingers are brown with dirt and filthy around the nails. The broken glass has shredded the hand and arm into fleshy ribbons, but it continues to claw at Roy. He backs to where we stand.

More arms and hands push through the small hole, tearing at it in an effort to escape. Dark blood washes down the glass. I want to stop looking. My brain screams at us to run, but we're frozen. Then a loud thudding shakes the whole wall as people in hospital gowns throw themselves at the window.

The small hole takes four hits, then it shatters, allowing a stream of kicking and flailing bodies to wash onto the ground. My brain finally kick-starts my body into motion. I grab Fareena and Roy by the arm and spin us around.

"Go!" I shout. "Run!" It takes them a few seconds before they break into a mad dash. I can barely hear my own footsteps through my heavy breathing and pounding head, and Roy—who until this point hasn't dropped a single swear word—curses with every step.

Fareena doesn't make a sound, but I see the fear in her eyes. We round the overturned van, and this time I don't stop to hope for a happy ending. This time I just keep my legs moving. I'm not entirely sure what's fuelling me more—my stamina or my fear.

19

LIV

THE TRUCK SWERVED FROM between the cars, the wheels screeching in protest as Liv yanked the handbrake and turned the steering wheel hard. Her stomach flipped with the sudden surge when the truck spun, buildings blurring all around them. Releasing the handbrake, she pulled them out of the sharp turn then she slammed the accelerator and steered them down the empty street.

"You alright?" she asked, her eyes still on the road. If they were lucky, this would lead them away from the infected rioters and to the suburbs.

"Wig is still in place, so I believe so." If she wasn't busy driving like a car thief, Liv would have turned to the nurse, but she thought she could detect the faintest of smiles in the voice.

"That makes two of us." She smiled despite everything, then shook her head. "What a mess."

Frances nodded. "What do we do with Andy? We can't go back to St. Thomas."

Liv kept her eyes on the empty road. The military had done a good job of keeping cars from reaching this part of the city. "What really happened at St. Thomas? Why exactly can't we go there?"

"I don't know," Frances said, but Liv could hear the slight hesitation in the nurse's voice.

"No." She shook her head. "No more lies. Tell me."

"I don't know. I wasn't one of the nurses working in the quarantine. The only thing I know is that the hospital set one up. A new kind of virus."

"A *quarantine*?" Liv's brows pulled together. Last time a quarantine was set up in England was during the Ebola outbreak. Could it be something like that?

"I was finishing my shift when it all started." Frances's voice was low as she spoke. "I heard the most horrendous screaming, when Andy came running from the main area. Then it all went so fast. He blocked the doors and told me to run."

Not saying anything, Liv turned the corner of Ravensdon Street while she waited for the nurse to continue.

"Then we ran into the military. They were just... *slaughtering* people. Shooting at anything that moved. Inside the hospital." Frances let out a shuddering breath. "We left through a back corridor. Just ran, leaving everyone behind. And then we found you."

Liv heaved a sigh. What had happened to make the military execute people in a hospital? Was it St. Thomas only, or was it more widespread than that?

"Is there a possibility Lambeth Hospital is still working? Maybe this was just something..." She fell silent, uncertain of what to say. Something what? A one-time thing? That's why they dropped bombs on London? A one-time thing wouldn't explain the infected rioters.

"Yes," Frances said, interrupting her thoughts, "perhaps Lambeth isn't affected by... by the..."

"Infected," Liv finished the sentence, glad she wasn't the only one who had hard time wrapping her head around everything.

"Yes, that."

"Then we go there," Liv said with determination. Hopefully Lambeth and everywhere else was still like it had been earlier that day: normal. Only regular life where people woke up, went to work, bitched about work, went home, bitched about life, went to bed, only to do it all over again the next day.

"What's your name?" She saw Frances look at her from the corner of her eye. In all the commotion, there hadn't been time for introductions. The plan had been to drop them off before any of that was necessary. Now, it seemed rude not to let the person she might die with know her name.

"Liv."

"Well, Liv," Frances said, her clever eyes noticing everything, "I've seen a lot of people try to play the good Samaritan when someone's injured. Most people do pretty well with a cut or two."

Manoeuvring the pickup between two cars pushed to the side, Liv frowned, not liking where the nurse was going with this new story.

"You know what normal people don't do very well?"

Speeding up, she ignored the question.

"Efficiently examine and patch up gunshot wounds. With an Israeli bandage no less," Frances answered the question for her, and Liv gave Frances points for recognising the military issued first-aid device. "But you..." There was a pause as the nurse let her words sink in. "You knew exactly what you were doing."

Liv didn't reply but kept her eyes firmly on the street in front of her. It was dark, and thick smoke rolled between the only vehicles they passed, making it hard to see.

"It was like watching an A&E doctor work."

Her skin prickled with unease. A doctor. Someone who saved lives. That was the last thing she was. She was the David Copperfield of alcohol and a convict. But a doctor? She snorted. No, that was not her. Not anymore.

"I don't know what you're talking about," she said with a glare at Frances who just smiled in return. *Oh God...* Liv thought tiredly to herself. Frances wouldn't let this one go. "Listen, I don't—" She slammed the brakes hard.

The military truck lay toppled over, engulfed in flames that illuminated the dark night. Flames licked the sandy-coloured body. Bright fire darted up and down along the vehicle before skittering across the road to the other cars.

Another goddamn roadblock.

20

JAKE

JULES NUDGES CLAIRE WITH her elbow as the three of us scramble down the steps.

"We need to go!" I shout, taking the stairs three at a time. I almost stumble as I come to a stop.

"What do you mean?" Jules stares at me.

"Just trust me, there's not a lot of time to explain. There are..." I have to stop and breathe.

"Things," Roy says, taking charge, "things that shouldn't be possible."

"Things?" Angela asks.

"Humans," Roy breathes, struggling for air as he leans with his hands onto his knees. "*Infected* humans. There was a quarantine and everything. Something ain't right with them; they've lost their minds! Eating people and throwing themselves against the window." Roy gesticulates wildly. His accent has thickened, his voice a pitch higher than usual, in what could be mistaken for marvel. Like a man who just found God.

"They attacked?" Jules echoes. "Were they rioters?"

I shake my head. "No, I saw... I saw a girl." I swallow as if that might keep the horror from my face. "She was eating another patient."

"Are you high?" Noah grimaces at us. I can't really blame him. I would have asked the same thing.

"Listen to me," Roy barks and straightens. "This is all wrong. It can't be true, but I saw it. I *saw* it."

Maybe it's how Roy holds himself when he talks. Or perhaps because Roy seems like the unshakable type who doesn't walk around making stories up about monsters. Whatever it is, Noah's eyes widen, and he jerks his head in a stiff nod.

"Now listen," Roy says, sounding calmer, "it ain't safe here and we need to move. Fast. We have to find somewhere safe if we want to survive."

"But what about Claire?" Jules looks down at the woman leaning against the wall. "I don't think she can walk very far, much less run."

"Then leave her," Noah snarls impatiently. "Didn't you hear? We have to go. *Now*."

"No!" Jules exclaims.

"She can't run!" Noah snaps, and his greasy hair falls in his face.

"So, we just leave her?"

It's annoying how much sense Noah has made so far. We have to run, and God forgive me, but Claire will only slow us down. That doesn't mean we can leave the woman here. Alone and defenceless against those things from the hospital who chase us.

"No," I say firmly, "we *won't*."

"Do you want to die?" Noah throws his arms out wide.

"No, but I also don't want to leave someone else to." I wrap my arm around Claire, then grab her hand and gently help her to her feet. Ill or not, I won't leave this woman on her own.

"Funny," Noah's lips twist sourly, "because I'm pretty sure you left quite some people behind on the train. Didn't seem to have a problem with it then."

Now I'm glad I punched him, and I wish I could do it again, but I fix him with a hard stare. "She's coming with us. If you don't like it, you can leave."

"Here, let me help," Roy says, holding out his hand to Claire who takes it.

"You boys sure know how to make a girl feel special," she jokes between us. Though I suspect that's her way to say thank you.

"Where do we go?" Fareena asks. "We can't go to the hospital."

"I say we go to the nearest tube station," Noah says.

"No." I shake my head. "That lady on the train, and the man with the nosebleed. They were acting like the infected. If Waterloo also has infected, I don't want to be stuck there."

Noah narrows his eyes and folds his arms across his chest. "Then where to?"

"Listen, I live in Brixton. If we run, we can make it in under an hour. It's longer, but fewer people and less chance of infected," I say, trying to ease the tension. We can hate each other once we're safe, but right now we're wasting time. "If we go now, we can cross the street we came from and run along the riverside."

"Sounds like a good plan to me. Let's move." Roy nods towards the stairs. "And let's be real quick about it."

There's no more time for talking, and, once we see the others set into motion, we sprint towards the stairs, lifting Clair between us as if she weighs no more than a leaf.

I turn to make sure no cars are speeding our way when the broken bridge catches my attention. No cars will come speeding down that road anytime soon. It's a surreal realisation. Half of London has been blown up, and infected people who looked more dead than alive were eating other people.

21

JAKE

WE SCAMPER ACROSS THE road and down the steps to the walkway. Once there, we break into a jog, Claire dangling like a rag doll between us. I'm glad I don't have to carry her on my own. I may go to the gym a few times a week, but this isn't something I've ever trained for: panic-spurred running with an extra hundred and forty pounds in my arms.

"Wait!" Angela gulps for air behind us when a shrill shriek cuts through the air. We both spin around.

Noah bolts down the steps, his hair springing wildly from his head as he pelts towards us.

"Where's Fareena and Jules?" I ask when neither of the girls follows him down the steps.

"I don't know," Noah pants, arrogant features wrinkled in annoyance.

"You ran past them?" This time, even the levelheaded Angela sounds cross.

"Jesus," I mutter. So busy saving himself, he didn't care to look out for the rest of the group.

"What, are we holding hands?" he snaps.

"No, Noah, but decent human beings look after each other," Angela scolds him.

"I didn't mean to..." Noah holds his hands out to his sides, fingers splayed. "They're grown-ups; they can take care of themselves."

"Hold her," I say to Roy who looks as if he wants to shove his fist down Noah's throat.

"Son," he growls. His voice rumbles with the simple word.

Fareena dashes down the steps, her hand gripping Jules' arm as she pulls the shell-shocked girl along with her.

"Go, go, *go*!" she yells as a dozen ghoul-like faces appear behind her. They moan and growl, and one man's head appears split in half. And yet he moves. How, I don't know.

Unlike the ones at the hospital, these don't shuffle or move like someone who woke up the day after a wild party. These move with a speed that matches our own.

"Oh, shit!" Roy hoists Claire further up on his shoulder. "Time to haul ass, people!"

We break into a sprint, bolting down the walkway. Behind us, loud moans and cries mingle into a morbid symphony.

Scratching noises and pattering come from the wall to our left.

They're like ants, climbing each other onto the wall that separates us from the hospital. Guts, blood, and shit-coloured muck smudge the white wall, and a repulsive smell of rotten fish and shit assaults my nose.

One by one, infected dressed in white gowns hurl themselves from the thick wall onto the paved walkway. They land face-first, bones crunching against the ground on impact, but instead of pain stunning them, they get back up and warble as if nothing had happened.

A construction worker in bright-orange trousers and a t-shirt ripped to shreds stands. His arms are torn to shreds, skin curling around the rips in his flesh.

"How much farther?" Roy looks at me. "If they keep coming, we need to get off this street."

"It's not far!" I force myself to say through my quick intake of breaths.

I know this bit well. Megan and I used to walk this walkway during the early morning hours, back when we'd dance the night away and miss the last tube home. Now, instead of stumbling along drunk and merry, I race down the street, the pungent smell and guttural moans propelling me forward.

One of the infected lands feet away, flailing and flopping like a fish on dry land. It's a woman with half her face ripped off. Fire has burnt her hair to rolled-up black stumps.

Roy reacts as fast as lightning and spins us away from her. I try to keep up with him as he navigates us between and over dead bodies. It's like an obstacle course, only much deadlier.

Noah races past, not caring if we keep up with him or not. The only thing he cares about is getting out of here alive. He's so busy looking ahead that he misses one of the infected who gets to its feet.

It lunges at him, mouth gaping and arms held out like a long-lost lover, but Noah moves effortlessly, like a dancer, sidestepping the infected. It crashes into the stone railing with a frustrated shriek.

Noah stares at it for a split second, then, without hesitation, he grabs hold of the infected's tattered shirt and hurls it on top of the short stone wall at the river's edge. The infected hisses and snarls futilely in Noah's tight grasp. With one hard push, Noah shoves it across the small wall, where it falls face-first into the river.

Holy shit! Holy motherfucking shit! He just killed someone!

"Fuuuck..." Something clamps down on my arm and my whisper turns to a surprised yell. A man has his jaws around my arm, his teeth digging into the leather of my jacket.

"Jesus!" Roy shouts and kicks at the infected man.

I shake my arm as hard as I can without dropping Claire, but the man hangs on like a rabid dog. He digs his teeth deeper and I scream as searing hot pain shoots through my arm. No matter how I try, I can't get him to release those jaws.

All I see is the crimson blood that seeps from his eyes, blackish veins webbing across his face as his mouth froths around my arm. The eyes bulge and roll. I can't pull my arm away. I can't move an inch.

Panic claws at my frenzied mind. The harder I pull, the harder he bites and pain pulses through my arm. Then, without warning, the man digs his heels in and yanks like a dog playing with his favourite bone.

I topple to the ground, releasing Claire, and the man lands squarely on my chest. He thrashes and claws. My arm, firmly caught between his teeth, is the only thing that keeps him from reaching my face with his filth-covered nails. I throw my head from side to side, continuously dodging him.

I let out another yell. A mixture of fear and frustration. My arms shake from the pressure of holding the crazed man away from my face. My right arm throbs from the teeth trying to grind their way through the leather jacket. I can't last much longer.

I've used every last bit of my strength, every ounce of adrenaline, but they're about to run out. I can feel it. These are the horrifying seconds before death, the millisecond before you realise that your time is up and there is nothing, absolutely fuck all you can do about it.

"No!" I shout in anger as my arms weaken. This is it. This is where I die. On a shitty tourist walk in London.

Something flashes in the corner of my eye, and I turn my head as Fareena's black ballerina shoe lands inches from my nose. An eerie cracking sound is followed by a sludge of hot, wet, sticky goo that washes over my chest and the side of my neck. I instinctively shut my eyes and mouth as the infected man's body collapses on top of me. I kick and push at the body in panic, and when it finally rolls off, I drop back to my elbows and pant with exertion.

"Stop slacking," Fareena says and pulls me to standing. She's joking, but I feel her hands shaking in mine, matching my own jacked-up heart rate.

My gaze drops to the lifeless body by my feet. A black umbrella pierces the side of his neck, a silvery metal tip gleaming from the exit wound.

"You alright?" I look at Fareena. Dark blood and brown fluid stain the skirt of her dress.

"I had to..."

I give Fareena's hands a gentle squeeze. "I know. Thank you." It's all I have time to say before more infected begin to pour down the wall behind us like a deadly wave of snapping mouths.

I yank at the umbrella, but it's wedged stuck. Another tug at it only jostles the body. Grimacing, I step down hard on the head and it crunches against the asphalt as I yank the umbrella out. "Let's go."

We catch up with the rest of our group, and I take Claire from Angela.

"Over there!" Fareena points towards where the walkway splits open into a side street. It will lead us from where we're trapped between two stone walls and a horde of infected people.

"We made it!" Noah pants in relief, completely disregarding the fact that all we've done is run a few hundred metres down the street. A walk that usually takes five minutes.

And there's a long way to go before we're home.

22

JAKE

I think it's universally known that saying, "we did it" before we've actually done "it," is the surest way to jinx just about anything. I want to strangle Noah when the street that would give us more space to manoeuvre is packed with cars. Cars that contain dead drivers. At least I *think* they're dead.

At the far end of the path leading off the walkway, infected feed on the remains of people. The infected are too busy to notice us, and we turn quickly and quietly, motioning for the others to follow.

It's the last day of September, and the weather is cool. Despite that, I wipe sweat from my face as we speed through the night. Claire does her best to paddle with her feet in an effort to help, but it only makes it worse, and I strain under her weight.

"Oh!" Fareena suddenly calls out. "In here!"

"Where are you going?" Noah grunts after her but follows nonetheless.

"Boris bikes!" Fareena explains as we draw closer to the bicycle station. "Give me your credit card." She holds her hand out as she runs.

"Why are you looking at me?" Noah snaps.

"Just. Give. Me." She doesn't stop, but still manages to give him a glare that no one in their right mind would dare defy. That and the infected hot on our heels don't give him a lot of choice.

He stops and fumbles with his wallet and cards before giving it to her. She flashes a grin. "That wasn't so bad, was it?"

"I don't know, guess I'll find out," Noah replies in what I now realise is his standard sour voice.

Fareena runs up to the docking station, card held in front of her like a runner's baton. "Ugh. Screen's dead." She frowns and circles the docking station predatorily until she's behind it. "It's still got juice in it though." Her face lights up, and she drops to her knees.

Unlike near Westminster, this part seems to have electricity. Every now and then, I spot lit windows with dark figures peering out at the chaos outside. Fareena makes a rustling noise from behind the square post, and I throw a quick glance across my shoulders. We've lost the infected for now, but the groans and gurgles from somewhere close means it won't be long before they find us again. And every little sound we make alerts them to our presence.

Roy and I walk around to watch her work, while I do my best to not think about the infected people that roam the city. However, their cries grow louder and louder, and it's an impossible task. *Come on...*

The plate that covers the wires inside the docking station clatters noisily to the ground and I grimace, hoping we were the only ones near enough to hear it.

"Bollocks," Jules whispers with a nod at the street behind us.

Five or more infected move towards the noise. I remember the girl from the hospital and the infected all along the walkway. My stomach twists at the memory, fear racing up my spine.

"Fareena." I try to keep the urgency in my voice under control, but I doubt I'm doing a good job of it, as she starts muttering.

The infected sniff the air, their heads tilting side to side as if listening for something. *Listening for prey,* I correct myself.

"Fareena..." Roy's voice is tight with apprehension.

The infected snap their heads our way and break into a fast limp. Their bodies hunch forward and their mouths open and close while they hiss, as if they can taste our smell.

"What are we doing?" I say through clenched teeth as we back up behind the long row of bikes locked in place.

The infected aren't as fast as normal people, but they're still too fast for my liking.

A series of loud, echoing clicks moves down the row of bikes, as if guiding the infected towards us. Fareena flies to her feet with a triumphant, "Yes!"

She sprints towards a bike and pulls it from the stand. In seconds, she's seated and pedalling. She shouts over her shoulder, "Come on, what are you waiting for?" Her voice, although low, still taunts the infected coming towards us, and they growl in what resembles hunger.

We bolt for the bikes and rip them from the stand. Jules and Noah swing their legs across the saddle and speed after Fareena.

"Claire, I need you to hold on to me, okay?"

She nods weakly. "Yes, of course."

"Roy, put her on the handlebars."

He helps Claire perch on my handlebars. She wraps her arms around my neck and leans into me.

She gives a heavy sigh. "Ready."

"Not so bad, huh?" I joke. I'm rewarded by a small chuckle and a low mumble I can't make out.

"You going to be alright like that?" Roy asks as he pulls a bike for Angela before grabbing one for himself.

"Yeah." I kick down on the pedals. I used to ride around with Megan on my handlebars, her skirt and hair flapping wildly in the wind as she re-enacted some scene from *Titanic* with her arms spread wide. It makes me remember the way Megan used to make me feel. How we'd bike like this everywhere around London. I got this.

It's a race the rest of the way as we speed through narrow backstreets and forgotten alleyways, avoiding all the larger, more crowded streets.

Wooden garden walls and lines of thick fir trees shield us from the street alongside us, and if it weren't for the noises of the infected, I could pretend the world hasn't gone to absolute shit. But the grotesque hacking and grating screeches spoil my illusion. The screaming from behind us doesn't help, either. Whether or not I can see them, infected roam the streets only feet away.

We've passed people fleeing into buildings or trying to drive through the congested streets, only to find themselves overwhelmed by a group of infected. It's surreal and nightmarish. My heart hammers so hard it makes my body tremble.

The thin alleyway opens onto a bigger street, and we slow down, listening for sounds of infected nearby. Aside from a few abandoned cars, the street is empty. No infected. At least not near us.

I jut my chin to our right, signalling where to go. I don't like being out on a street this big. With all the brick houses packed together behind lush, growing hedges and garden trees, it's difficult to see anything lurking.

I'm not sure how much time has passed when we pull beside a brick church. Roy stops, waving his hand at us, and I slow down.

Five infected feed on something. Or rather, *someone*, I shudder as I correct myself. They bury their faces in the body before throwing their heads up like someone breaking the surface for a gasp of air. Rolling to a stop behind me, my ragtag group stares, disbelief and horror mixing in their expressions.

"What now?" Jules says so quietly it's barely audible.

"I'm not sure." I turn back to them. "Do you think we could out-bike them?"

Roy shakes his head. "Those sons of bitches are fast. First lot might get through, but they'll be on the rest of us in no time."

"Unless..." Angela whispers.

"Unless?" Roy turns to his wife, and the look they exchange gives me an uneasy feeling. Like two teenagers executing a well-planned but somewhat reckless scheme.

"Well, what if we distracted them with something?" Angela holds my eyes with hers, and I realise what they're thinking.

"You want us to be bait?"

"I'm sorry, what?" Jules shifts on her saddle.

"Well," Angela says slowly, "if someone leads them away, the rest of us could cross into the next alley."

Jules' dark eyes bore into me. It's an insane idea, but what's the alternative? I'm painfully aware we have nothing to defend ourselves with. Not a single stick. We can't fight them, and we most likely can't out-bike them.

A gazillion questions have time to present themselves to me, but Jules' eyes burn with the million-dollar question.

Who will be the bait?

23
LIV

"FUCKING SHIT-WANK." TURNING OFF the main street and onto Lorn Road, Liv cursed under her breath. It was their third roadblock in less than ten minutes. Whoever was in charge of roadblocks was clearly an overenthusiastic prick.

"I must say," Frances said, "you're quite the artist when it comes to swearing."

Liv huffed. Oh, she was an artist alright, with swearing, drinking, and fucking up. "I'll admit." She steered them down the street, where at the end—fittingly to the conversation—an old church stood. "I don't think I've ever heard it put in such a... *positive* light before."

"You know, I grew up in a big Irish Catholic family where swear words were exchanged as freely as Bible passages. And I don't think I've ever heard such colourful swearing."

The corners of Liv's mouth curled in a smile. *Crap...* People didn't make her smile, and if they did, it often meant they'd managed to—despite her best efforts—break through her well-guarded walls. There were few people she liked. Mostly she accepted people's existence, but "like" wasn't a word she used often. Maybe it was Frances's eyes, warm and kind, that reminded Liv of her mother, but something about Frances felt familiar, almost... safe. She pushed the thought aside quickly. Nothing in life was safe. Nothing was certain. A fact that became more apparent as they crept down the street past fenced-in brick houses and abandoned cars.

They'd made their way through numerous side streets and alleyways, but so far, the only living thing they'd seen was the infected. If living was a word you could use to describe them. Other than that, the only signs of life were the broken shop windows and items littering the ground from the looting. Because who wouldn't prioritise a new flat screen when the city was being blown to hell? Anyone who wanted to survive, that's who.

A loud clang came from her left, and she snapped her head towards the sound. A streetlight illuminated where two wheelie bins had crashed into the railings between the pavement and the street. In the dark alley behind the bins, figures loomed.

A crowd of infected. Hungry and speeding towards the car whose engine rumbled in the quiet street. They were moving, but the bins blocked the opening to the alleyway and slowed them down.

A memory from the first roadblock flashed through her mind. The ear-shattering staccato from guns fired, the screams of terror, the smell of blood permeating the air. And the faces of the infected. Contorted with blind rage and hunger.

She turned to the nurse. "Look in the glove box; there's a bottle of whiskey there."

Frances shot her a look, but opened the glove box nonetheless, pulling the square glass bottle from its confinement. The black label with a vintage-looking font smiled back at her, inviting her to take a sip, and for a fraction of a heartbeat, she considered asking Frances to put it back.

"You wouldn't happen to have a spare sock, would you?" she asked, taking the bottle from the nurse.

"I have the ones I'm wearing?" Frances offered, and Liv gave an affirmative nod. Any socks would do, as long as it wasn't hers. She didn't own enough to set them on fire.

"While I stuff it in the bottle, find me a lighter, will you?" Liv nodded towards the door compartment.

"Who *are* you?" Frances asked incredulously, mouth slightly ajar. "Okay, when we find somewhere safe, you're definitely telling me your story," Frances muttered, sparking the lighter.

Taking a swig from the bottle, Liv gave Frances a lopsided grin, then rammed the sock into its rounded neck.

Flames erupted along the makeshift wick, and, with a final silent goodbye, Liv launched her whiskey out the window.

Farewell, old friend.

24

JAKE

"I'LL GO." JULES ROLLS up the long skirt of her dress and ties it in a knot above her knees. I was never big on wearing skirts, but even I know it would get in the way.

Everyone seems uneasy at her words. I would offer to go. I know this place like the back of my hand, but I have Claire.

"I don't know..." Uncertainty bleeds into Fareena's face. "How are you going to find us again? What if you don't?"

A small smile touches the corners of Jules' mouth. "Don't worry, I know this area. I work nearby. If worse comes to worst, I'll go there and look for help."

"Do you know Streatham Hill?"

She nods. "Have a few clients I check up on there."

"That's where I live. Go to one-oh-five, and into Amesbury, then past the bank until you see an orange and white house. That's mine. There's only one."

"Okay." She nods, square jaw set and eyes firm, then sets her foot on the pedal. "See you around, Jakey."

I swallow. It doesn't feel right. Everything about this is wrong. Using someone as bait.

Jules has just got on her saddle to take off when shattering glass breaks through the moans of the infected. It's followed by a high-pitched whistle. Wheels spinning on asphalt?

The infected on the ground scramble to their feet. Their heads swivel as they listen for what made the sound, their arms thrown back in a predatory stance. Like rugby players ready to launch themselves at the ball. Before they can move, a red pickup truck swerves in a smooth turn and hits them full force with its side.

An unpleasant crunching sounds from underneath the heavy truck as it rams into the bodies. The wheels screech against the asphalt, no doubt alerting every single infected within a mile's radius.

We stare at the red pickup as a girl leans through the driver's window. "Quick!" she shouts and a mess of dark-brown hair tangles down her face. "Get in the back!"

I gawk for a few seconds as if she's an apparition. She looks like she just got spat out from a tumble dryer. Clothes wrinkled and bedraggled, but she talks like she spent most of her time in fancy restaurants in Notting Hill.

"Get. In!" The girl gives the door two hard slaps, waking us from our stupor.

"Let's go, people!" Roy barks, and bikes clatters to the ground as we run to the pickup.

Roy and Noah grab Claire from my bike and help her into the truck as I run up to the driver. "Where are you going?"

She glares at me for a split second, stormy hazel eyes narrowed below a deep frown. "The hospital," she finally says.

"That's a bad idea." I shake my head. "We just barely managed to escape from one."

"We *have* to get to a hospital. I have an injured man with me."

Jules shoves me to the side and fires off a friendly smile. "I'm Jules. And you?"

Either this woman doesn't enjoy talking, or maybe she's got her mind set about where to go. Whichever it is, she levels Jules with a flinty stare, but when Jules' smile doesn't falter she grumbles a short, "Liv."

"I understand that you don't know us, but the last hospital we saw had been overrun." Jules motions at the bodies on the road. "Judging by the state of the city, I can't see any other hospitals being better off."

Liv turns and looks at an older-looking woman next to her. The woman shrugs and gives an uncertain shake of her head.

"You'd be putting your friend's life at a greater risk if you take him to a hospital. The infected, they're *everywhere*," Jules says. Though her voice has taken on a softer tone, her face is grim and hard.

"Listen." I lean to catch Liv's eyes. "I live nearby and, if it helps, I have a pretty decent first aid kit you can use."

"Yes, because plaster and some antiseptic wipes are exactly what I need." She snorts, her scowl deepening.

"Err... it's a little more extensive than your regular first aid kit."

She heaves a sigh and shakes her head. "Fine, just get in the damn truck before you get us all killed."

25

LIV

USING THE THIN ALLEYWAYS and backstreets, they slowly made their way through the city until they reached Cricklade Avenue, where two old bangers blocked their path.

Jules and her group leapt off the back of the truck and scrambled towards the cars, spending a few painstakingly long heartbeats having a discussion between themselves. They motioned at the grey Honda every now and then, until finally the guy with greasy hair stomped to one of the cars and gave it a hard shove.

"No, no, no!" Two Black women, one with short hair and the younger one with curly hair, waved their arms in protest.

The car rocked. Liv watched in horror as its orange hazards started blinking. Then, in objection to the hard push, the car's alarm broke into a howling wail.

The group scattered and sprinted back to the car, infected appearing at every street corner. Their feet beat the ground in time with her racing pulse before the group clambered into the truck's bed. Once in, she threw the truck in gear, sending it into a lurching start. She was too close to the cars. She needed more momentum if her truck, held together by sheer stubbornness and a pinch of luck, would be able to bust through them.

"Hold on." Eyes glued to the rearview mirror, she reversed as far as she dared, considering the swarm of crazed infected racing towards them.

"You're going the wrong way!" Greasy shouted from the back. *No shit, Sherlock.*

She pulled to a hard stop, then rammed the gear stick into first. The engine sputtered and died. *No!*

"Go! Fucking go!" Greasy slammed the side of her truck as if doing so would make it start faster.

Adrenaline made her hands shake. Her fingers fumbled at the keys, her arms and legs feeling as if they were made from lead. The engine gave a pitiful sputter before dying again.

Fuck! She punched the steering wheel as the sounds of the infected came closer.

A soft hand squeezed hers. "You've got this. Just take a deep breath and focus. Ignore everything else."

Holding her breath, she pushed the clutch and turned the keys again. The engine rumbled to life.

A loud thud and a shrill scream cut through the air. Her gaze darted to her rearview mirror. Ghoulishly green hands, stained with brown and red, tangled themselves into Jules' black hair. Arms snaked around her chest, pulling her off the back of the truck. The tall Black man and hipster guy pulled at her legs in a futile attempt to help her. They held on desperately, but her kicking only sent the two of them stumbling.

The greasy-haired man who'd caused all of this grabbed at one of the black plastic bags and jerked it up. *No, no! Not all my—*

The bag sailed through the air—her clothes, underwear, and jeans trailing behind it—before planting itself in the face of one of the infected. It stopped the infected for mere seconds, but it returned to slap its grimy fingers at the screaming girl.

Should she take off and hope they had a good grip on her? Or should she reverse, buying Jules more time? As if to answer her question, one of the infected closed her mouth around the soft, fleshy part of Jules' neck. Her eyes widened in pain or horror or maybe both. Blood spurted down Jules' pale neck, stirring the rest of the infected into a frenzy. Liv floored the pedal, forcing the two men to let go, leaving Jules drowned by a swarm of hungry infected.

"Hey!" The hipster slammed the roof of her truck. "Stop!"

She didn't stop. But she also didn't blame him for not understanding, for not giving up.

"Stop the fucking car!" he bellowed again. He slammed the roof until the Black man who had tried to help him grabbed him by the shoulder, gently but firmly. They slid down to the floor, shoulders slouching, heads hanging between their knees.

No one moved or spoke until she pulled to a stop at the address she'd been given, where they piled out from the back of her truck, and the Asian guy walked up to her.

He scratched the side of his full beard, his dark eyes observing her intently. She sucked in a breath, preparing for him to rip into her.

"Hey," he said in a low voice, "I'm sorry I shouted..." He smiled wanly, running a hand through the thick hair at the top of his undercut.

"Oh," she said, uncertain of what else to say. She'd expected, and therefore prepared for, an argument.

"I know there wasn't anything we could have done. I just..."

"Wanted to do something," she said, studying him.

He was taller than her, and his grey top and tattooed neck were covered in a dark-red sludge. She wrinkled her nose. Sludge that was rather iffy smelling. Like something dead.

"Yeah..." He chuckled. "Had a run-in with..." His voice trailed off. He wasn't a born and bred Londoner. She could tell by the way his voice curled around the syllables without cutting out necessary letters when he talked. He seemed nice. Maybe this bloke, these people, weren't like the rest of the Londoners, selfish and self-absorbed. She hoped they were. But she knew better than to believe that. Right now, though, they could provide what she needed. That would have to do. For now.

26
LIV

"MEGAN?" HIPSTER GUY CALLED out as he opened the front door. They stumbled into the dark hallway. "Megan!" He threw his keys onto a small hallway table and rounded the corner into the open plan living room. His head swivelled as he swept through the lower floor, his jaw tight, brows furrowed with what Liv assumed was worry.

"Shit," she heard him mutter as he brushed past. "Shit!"

Megan was either a girlfriend or... a red digit on an old-looking box flashed up at her from a table next to the door. An answering machine? What kind of loser still owned an answering machine? She watched the hipster pace back and forth. On second thought, maybe it made sense this hippie owned an ancient telephone device.

"Oi, mate," she called out to him and pointed at the thing. "You got a message here."

"An answering machine?" The Black guy with a thick American accent sounded highly amused.

It had a large rectangular silver button, one of those that screams 'push me!' and so, with a shrug, she did.

"Jake," a woman's voice said with an odd mixture of panic and trying to sound absolutely normal. "You're not here, and I don't know what's going on. Something is really wrong with these people. I'm going to Cait's. I can't wait for you anymore. I hope you get this, I lo—" A scream cut her sentence short, then the call cut out.

Jake's shoulders slumped, and he shook his head as he breathed out another desperate, "Shit."

"I'm sure she's fine," was all Liv could think to say to this stranger. She cringed at her own words. 'Fine' usually meant, *I hope she's alright, but you know, I just don't know*. But what the hell could she say? Megan was most likely dead, but no one would say that. Liv shook her head. She may be socially inept, but she wasn't a complete idiot.

"Yeah, maybe." Jake nodded, unconvinced.

"Are you... okay?" she asked. It seemed like the appropriate thing to ask, although how could he be alright? How could any of them be? They'd just seen a person get dragged off her truck and chewed to pieces. And that probably wasn't the only grisly, fucked-up thing any of them had encountered this evening.

He sighed and shook his head. Not so much to say no as to shake off her question. "We have to prepare to leave."

"Leave?"

"I'm heading up towards Cambridge. Anyone who wants to can come along. You could stay," he paused, "but I don't think this city is safe anymore. Either way, we need to pack some supplies."

He turned his back to her and stalked through the white-walled living room into the narrow hallway.

"Guys." He turned to the group who stood huddled in his entranceway. "There are rooms upstairs. Claire and the injured guy can have one each. The rest of us can share."

"I will help you with the sick woman," Frances said to the tall Black guy and the woman Liv thought could be his wife. "I'm a nurse. I can take a look at her when we get upstairs."

Jake nodded, then looked at Liv. "The others will help your friend, but I'll show you the first aid kit."

The man with greasy hair muttered something. She ignored him and trailed after Jake. The sooner she got to look through this special first aid kit of his, the sooner she could do something about Andy's wounds.

"So, Liv, was it?"

"Yeah."

"Cool. I'm Jake."

"Yes. I gathered that from the message..."

As they made their way down the dark hallway, she noted framed photos lining its wall. Photos of exquisite landscapes and places Liv could only dream of ever visiting.

In one photo, a girl with long ginger hair and faint freckles scattered across her face laughed into the camera. Her laugh looked *incredible*, red lips spread wide in a perfect *Pretty Woman* smile, and her eyes were startling green. Her body, Liv noticed, was covered in tattoos. They snaked their way up across her arms and shoulders, then dived across her collarbones.

Jake, the hipster, stood next to her in a loose-fitting vest. Its open side revealed dark tattoos on his ribs and arms, all the way up and around his shoulders, down across his chest, then up towards his neck. The two of them, Jake and the girl who Liv guessed was Megan, resembled that cool hipster couple who shared a popular Instagram account where they posted pictures of themselves and their homemade sourdough bread.

She studied the photo closer, her eyes dissecting every minor detail. The way Jake seemed to look at something over on Megan's right side, and how Megan clutched the front of his vest with one of her hands as she laughed into the camera. They seemed happy, although Jake seemed expert at avoiding the camera with his eyes.

"Uh, Liv?" Jake stepped out from the kitchen and gave her a quizzical look.

"Hmm?" She hadn't realised she'd was full-on staring at the photo.

"Are you coming?"

"Yes, of course." She nodded and walked over to where Jake stood by a bookcase.

"If you look on the second shelf, you might find what you need."

"You mean your 'extensive first aid kit.'" Liv pulled a face at him.

"Yeah, I might have downplayed that part a bit." Jake grinned and swung the bookcase open, revealing a hidden cupboard.

27
LIV

"You have a look through that. I'm going to grab some extra bags," Jake said before walking away, leaving her alone with the hidden cupboard.

What the fuck? Liv stared at the small storeroom. Small was perhaps too generous a word. It was barely deep enough for two people to stand next to each other and just about wide enough for one person to fit between the rows of shelves that snaked from one side of the cupboard to the other.

It was still bigger than the space she had in her car. She quirked her eyebrow at the cupboard. Definitely a lot cosier than her car, too.

She let her eyes follow the rows from one side to the other, taking in the surreal sight. Rows upon rows of neatly stacked cans and jars filled the bottom shelves. Bottles of water, boxes full of different-sized bags, and large jars with wheat and flour filled the next set of shelves.

The top shelves hosted a curious assembly of toothpaste, hygiene products, and... standing on her tiptoes, she peered closer at a row of enormous jars containing what could've been large chunks of dried meat. They were the only jars labelled with stylish parchment-coloured labels. "Karma" the labels read in tall spindly letters. What the *hell* was this Karma jar for?

A low growl came from behind, and she groaned inwardly. *You just had to ask, didn't you?* Another growl, this one even deeper, like the low menacing rumble before lightning hits, sent shivers up her spine. She closed her eyes and instinctively raised her hands in the air. If it hadn't been for the infected outside, she wouldn't have been so paranoid, but seeing a woman have her face chewed off had Liv on the jumpy side. She bit her lip and steadied her breath as the growl grew deeper and angrier. It was just a dog, she told herself. Plus, experience had taught Liv one thing, and that was the smaller the dog, the bigger the growl.

Turning around, Liv put on the friendliest face she could muster, the same one she pasted onto her face whenever she met with her probation officer. *Just like greeting Mr. Douche-kinson*. She stopped mid-turn and stared at the beast. It was not a small dog.

The thing baring its teeth in disapproval was made of pure muscle and bulk, its hackles raised and alert, and the ears on its wide, gigantic head drawn back. Fiery-orange fur covered the bulk, and muscles rippled with every hiss of its breath. Its nostrils flared, wrinkles and big folds of hanging skin shaking with each snarl. Sharp white teeth gleamed, the fangs looking particularly nasty.

"Karma!" Jake breathed in relief as he came jogging down the stairs.

"I found your dog..." She tried to sound a lot less unnerved than she felt.

"Good girl," he praised the dog, scratching behind her ears, "but this is a friend. Stand down, girl."

A *friend*? She'd known the guy for all of two seconds and he called her a friend. *Typical spoiled have-it-all people.* Karma dropped her stance, her whole posture relaxing and the face, which had been little more than gum and teeth, now revealed eerily human eyes.

"I'm sorry if she scared you." Jake patted the big dog's side.

"What *is* that?" Liv finally breathed and dropped her hands to her sides.

"This," Jake chuckled, "is Karma, my Dogue."

Liv frowned. "Dog? That's a fucking horse."

Laughter bubbled from his throat. "I meant Dogue as in Dogue de Bordeaux."

Now that Karma wasn't trying to rip her head off, Liv thought she almost seemed apologetic. Large friendly amber eyes and an underbite that Liv had been too scared to notice before gave Karma a crooked, but amiable smile.

Jake scratched the dog behind her ears and regarded Karma the way parents did their children. "Who's a good puppy?"

Karma wagged her tail, the motion causing her to shimmy forward on her butt as she generously kissed Jake.

"You're my big girl, yes, you are." Jake grabbed one ear in each hand and ruffled them, sending Karma wiggling even closer.

Liv grinned. This Jake dude was a bit of a knob, but the two of them were pretty entertaining. Then she remembered the psycho-kidnapper cupboard behind her.

"So," she said slowly, "before I actually commit to being your..." She crossed her arms. "...*friend*. Why the fuck do you have a creepy hidden killer room?" She hooked her thumb across her shoulder. "Were you planning on kidnapping someone and keeping them locked up in here?"

Jake laughed and stood up. "No, nothing quite that dramatic." He walked around her and stepped into the cupboard, Karma following him close behind. "Me and Megan, we had this just in case..."

"In case *what*?" Liv asked, the ends of her brow raised in disbelief. By the looks of it, Jake and his girlfriend had expected some sort of event that meant they needed to sit on a year's worth of food in a cupboard. A *hidden* cupboard.

"Oh, you know," Jake said and flashed her a row of charmingly imperfect teeth, "the zombie apocalypse."

Liv stared at him and guffawed. It was a joke, right? It had to be a joke, but despite his smile, nothing about it made his comment feel like a joke, and she bit down on her laughter.

"Come... again?" She could see the tips of Jake's ears grow red with embarrassment.

"The end of the world," he said, but before Liv could say something, Jake raised a hand in the air. "Have you read the *Until the End of the World* books?"

Liv shook her head and folded her arms across her chest as she waited for his explanation.

"We started listening to the first book a few summers ago. They became our favourite books, and we decided to not be one of those schmucks caught with their butts hanging out of their pants when the zombie apocalypse happened," Jake explained.

"Are you..." Liv squinted at him. "...taking the piss?"

"I'm afraid I'm not. It started for fun really, but you know with the threat of severe climate changes, the import and export treaties going to shit with Brexit, not to mention the dreaded EMP... it seemed like the smart thing to do."

"An EMP?" Liv looked at him dubiously. "That would take out all the electricity in London? I don't think I've ever even experienced a blackout."

"In England," he corrected her, "but, yeah, I know, it's virtually impossible for our grid to go down."

"So, you guys seriously prepared for the end of the world?" Liv wasn't sure if she was impressed or slightly concerned.

Jake chuckled, a grin growing on his face. "It started as something we did together. Out in the back garden."

Liv looked at the tiny green patch he called a garden. A rug of fake green grass covered the concrete ground, and wood boxes lifted a small but lush garden towards the sun. Large terracotta pots lined the white walls, full of greenery, and she wondered what might be growing in them.

"We got an allotment over at Rosedale where we used to plant things together; every spring we'd go. Every damn spring, planting things, then harvesting it in the summer and fall. Do you know how cold it is to dig dirt in early spring?" Jake gave her a rueful look.

She sure as hell knew how cold it was to sleep in a car in early spring, but that was about it. "Can't say I do."

"Really fucking cold."

Liv looked at the growing garden again. That, plus an allotment, must produce quite a lot of vegetables. "What did you do with it all?"

"Canned a lot of it"—he motioned towards the cans that lined the shelves—"or gave it to Brixton's Soup Kitchen."

"Huh." She watched him, both intrigued and sceptical. This bearded hipster grew vegetables and simply gave them away? It was weird, but the way Jake explained it made it seem a lot less cuckoo and a bit more like something nice he and his girlfriend did together. Jake wore a distant expression on his face. Almost as if for a few precious seconds he was back at that allotment, and not in a house in Brixton that may or may not be surrounded by infected.

"Anyway..." He motioned towards the floor.

Three bags rested on the floor. One a forest-green bag with a skull pin, the other military green with a pink, white, and blue patch sewed on to it, and the third marked BOB.

Jake pulled a book from the skull pin bag. "This one is her favourite," he said and handed Liv the book.

She turned it in her hand and eyed the large white font on the cover. *Until the End of the World.*

The book had been read so many times the blue cover had grown deep wrinkles and creases on its back. Air had snuck in between every other page and made the book look double its original size, reminding Liv of a well-read Bible. Curious, she opened the cover, revealing a handwritten note.

"Happy Birthday, Space Cadet. Love, Sarah Lyons Fleming."

Liv grinned. What a sappy bitch this Jake was. She kind of liked it. "You know," she said and looked up at him, "despite it being cheesy as fuck... this is kind of nice."

"Yeah, well, that was before I—" Jake caught himself as if he'd spoken without thinking. "We just stopped."

"Stopped?" she asked when she'd finished reading the summary on the back of the book. It did sound interesting.

"Stopped recognising each other, I guess."

"Oh..." Liv said and handed him the book.

"It's even better as an audiobook," Jake said and tucked the book into the top pocket of the khaki military bag. Then carefully, almost as if it might break, he pushed the skull pin bag to the side before grabbing one of the other bags and holding it out towards Liv. "Here, take this one."

She blinked at the military-green bag tagged BOB. He was offering her the bag? Just like that? Or did he want something in return? People always wanted something in return. That or they started to expect things from her. Things she wouldn't be able to live up to. But maybe this group was different? She shook her head. Even if this group was different, she wasn't.

And she deserved neither Jake's bag nor his trust.

Liv shook her head. She didn't accept things from anyone, least of all strangers she'd just met. Even if that stranger happened to actually be a pretty decent person. Besides, if she were Bob, she might not be so happy if Jake gave her bag away. "I couldn't."

"Don't worry." Jake smiled, "There's nothing in there that I can't replace with stuff from in here." Jake motioned around the cupboard. "Preppers, remember?"

"Won't Bob be upset you're giving his bag away though?"

Jake's face split with the laughter that bubbled up from his throat, his shoulders shaking with amusement. She glared at him, folding her arms over her chest as he pinched the bridge of his nose with his fingers.

"Ahem." He cleared his throat, trying and failing to clamp down on his laughter. "That's B-O-B, Bug Out Bag."

"Well, fuck you," Liv sniped at Jake, who was so graciously laughing at her. Wiping *tears* from his face. She scowled.

"I'm sorry," he apologised, though she could still hear the amusement in his voice. "Before prepping, I didn't know what it was either." He smiled at her and, much to her irritation, she found she couldn't be all that angry. He was, after all, offering her something that would most certainly help her stay alive should she choose to tag along.

"Please." Jake looked at her sincerely. "I would feel much better if I knew you had it. Since you seem to know your way around medical stuff."

"Just so you know," she said as she accepted the bag, "this still doesn't mean I don't think you're batshit crazy. And I *will* be sleeping with one eye open."

"Sure," Jake replied, his eyes glittering with amusement.

"Also, I have to ask. Why the bookcase?"

"What?" Brown eyes sparkled. "You never wanted a hidden room behind a bookcase as a kid?"

That was a fair point. She nodded.

Throwing a quick glance at his watch, Jake started to fill an empty bag he'd been holding in his hand. Cans, toothpaste, various bottles of what looked like aspirin, and some other sort of pills got shoved into the bag. Turning around, he reached for another box, then fished out lanterns and flashlights. "Just in case."

"I thought you said a blackout was virtually impossible."

"It is," he said and tossed them into the bag. "We're hooked up to France's grid, so even if ours goes down, it'll instantly piggyback off it. But these might come in handy anyway."

When he reached the large box filled with plastic vacuum-packed packages, he hesitated briefly and glanced at what she assumed was Megan's bag. Then he nodded and scooped as many as he could fit into his bag. Before he was done, he pulled out a small bag that looked similar to a cooler bag. He handled it carefully, as if its contents was worth its weight in gold.

Unlike the other supplies, Jake placed this at the top, gently securing it into place between the other supplies. She watched him grab a vest with a bag, a water bottle, and a few pockets hooked onto it. She frowned. It didn't look like it would fit him.

He filled the pockets with a small bandage package, more medicine, the kibble and dried meat. Oh! The vest wasn't meant for one of them. It was Karma's. Once done with Karma's vest, he rummaged around the second shelf until he found the box he was looking for.

"What is it you need?" He looked up at her.

"Surgical suture."

His forehead wrinkled in confusion.

"Needle and thread, for stitching." She clarified, a little amused to see him flounder for a bit. "Gauze and antiseptic wash."

"What happened to him?"

"Got shot."

Jake's brows knitted together. "I thought *that* only happened over in the US. Or maybe Sweden. I hear it's the gun capital of Europe."

"Apparently not."

"Is he going to be alright?"

Andy had been shot in the abdomen. Bullet had passed right through, but that was no guarantee of anything, and according to protocol, all injuries to the abdomen needed a laparotomy. Andy most likely needed surgery. There could be internal bleeding, or remaining bullet fragments, or a ruptured bowel. There were any number of complications that she couldn't foresee without the proper instruments.

She rubbed her face in frustration. "I don't know."

"Well... shit," Jake said before returning to dig around with his one hand. He reminded Liv of a gorilla the way he hunched over the box, his eyes fixed on the contents.

"Maybe I should take the whole box? I'll bring it back, I promise."

"Yeah, sure." He pushed the box into her arms. Giving her a friendly smile, he hooked the bag across his shoulder, Karma's vest still in his hand. "This and your bag should be enough for all of us until we get to my parents' place."

"They've got a hidden cupboard as well?" Liv raised her eyebrows.

"No." He laughed. "But the closest military facility isn't far from there. We make it there, we'll be safe."

Military facility. She followed Jake through the hallway. Her morning had started off with her running *from* the military, and now she was trying to make her way towards a military facility.

This day had definitely taken an unexpected turn, and the next day? She clenched her teeth. She didn't even want to think about the next day. For now, surviving this day was all that mattered. Whatever any of their lives had been like before, whoever they had been, had changed irrevocably. And just like in prison, the only thing they could do was adapt and survive.

28
JAKE

"As I speak to the nation, London has once again become the victim of a terror attack. In the late hours of this Friday evening, terrorists set off multiple bombs in Central London, causing mass destruction. This was a strategic bombing that tried—but ultimately failed—to take out the government." The blonde woman looks into the camera as she speaks, her face gaunt, lines of tension around her eyes and mouth tightening with each word.

The Prime Minister almost always speaks to the nation from outside her home, but instead of the familiar brick walls and black metal fence that line the houses on Downing Street, grey walls and an ambient blue light surround the Prime Minister.

Noah, *claiming* to be more exhausted than everyone else, decided to watch TV while those of us who weren't looking after Claire prepared food. The Prime Minister's voice had caught everyone's attention and now we all stand in the living room, watching intently as she speaks.

"As of now, we can confirm these were chemical bombs set off in the city, which cost the lives of many innocent civilians and officials. The fire department, police, military forces, and countless men and women who helped and aided the people of London. Today we lost many brave souls." The Prime Minister lowers her gaze, as if to give the people who lost their lives the respect they deserve, before she looks up again.

"I urge all of you, the people of Greater London, and the rest of our nation, to have faith in and aid the authorities and officials by staying indoors. At this point, we are uncertain of how many may have been affected by the fallout from these chemical explosives. Until we are certain and have established that no other cities may be targeted in the days to come, we ask that you stay in your houses.

"If you or a family member experience any side effects of potential residue or witness something out of the ordinary and require aid, we have set up an emergency number. The symptoms observed so far are high fever, pain in one's arms and legs, and extreme aggression. Please call this number if you or your family show any symptoms." She takes a deep breath before continuing, and I throw a quick glance at the others to gauge their reactions.

Residue? I'm no genius scientist like my dad, but I'm fairly fucking sure that residue doesn't cause the symptoms we've seen today. I drag my attention back to the TV where an o-eight hundred number rolls along the bottom of the screen.

"This is an attack not only on our capital, but on our nation. But hear this." The Prime Minister's eyes, which have been sympathetic and as genuine as a politician's eyes can be, turn dark and serious. "We will not bow; we will not negotiate with terrorists or falter in the wake of their destruction. We, the British people, will rise again. We will show them that we cannot—will not—be broken. Our nation will prevail."

There's a long pause, but the Prime Minister doesn't take her eyes away; she simply looks into the camera, chin held high as if to say, "I will be steadfast, and I will not bow."

I'm surprised to see it's actually working, as my chest buzzes with a renewed sense of determination. But then the throbbing of my arm where a man tried to chew it off returns, and I survey the others. Liv's blood-stained shirt, Roy's goo-splattered trousers, and everyone's dirty faces. Everyone except Jules. My chest pains at the memory of Jules being dragged off the back of the truck, her frightened, desperate screams. I close my eyes and try to push it out of my head. When that doesn't help, I turn to the TV and focus on the Prime Minister's words. I've heard some cock and bull in my life, but this definitely takes the biscuit.

A terror attack did this? In what world was it believable that residue caused people to feed on each other?

"Residue?" Fareena's jaw hangs open, her face pulling a grimace. "Why aren't they even talking about the infection we saw? Or the crazy people chasing us?"

"And remember how we didn't see any military or police?" I point out.

"What's interesting is that they didn't show us any footage of the city," Angela says. "Why wouldn't they show us any footage?"

"Because it wasn't a terror attack," Liv speaks up from where she leans against the doorframe. "We saw the military, and they were shooting at us. They *shot* one of us, and he's upstairs dying from his wounds."

Frances, the older Irish nurse who introduced herself once everyone got settled in, nods solemnly. "The officials we met were certainly British military and police, and they had fences and vehicles blocking off entire areas."

"There's no way this has got nothing to do with the infected we saw," I say, slashing my hand through the air.

"You saw them *eat* people." Liv's eyes are flinty and hard. "Infected? They're fucking zombies."

Fareena lets out a laugh, but it dies out when she sees Liv's face. "Oh." She clears her throat. "I thought you were joking. I mean, zombies aren't real, they're—"

Noah gets to his feet and throws the remote onto the sofa. "Zombie and conspiracy theories? Can't you hear how fucking stupid you sound? Stop making things worse than they already are. I just wanted to watch some fucking TV, but this bollocks is all they're showing." He swears and stomps from the room.

No one goes after him. I might dislike the guy, but I can't say I'm not feeling his frustration. Parts of me want to believe everything the Prime Minister said, but another part of me wants to shake my TV, make it show something besides the pre-recorded message.

"That's an excellent point." Angela follows Noah with her gaze. "If this was a normal attack, why aren't we seeing any news reports about it? Why can't we access the internet or get a phone call through? Maybe the network is overloaded, but at some point we should have gotten at least one call through."

"I told you," Liv says with annoyance.

"I know, sugar." Angela squeezes Liv's forearm lightly, then turns to us as if we're students in a classroom. "The roadblocks, the fences, the shooting by your own Army. They *all* point to the same conclusion."

We nod. The government is lying to us. Whatever this is, it's much worse than they say.

29

JAKE

"THEY COULD BE TELLING the truth," Noah says where we stand around my small kitchen table.

"Like hell they are." Liv crosses her arms.

A map from Megan's and my prepper lair lays on the table, and I scratch the bridge of my nose as I search for the best route to my parents' place.

The others remain quiet, most likely lost in their own thoughts of what to do or where to go. Fareena chews her lips, her red and swollen eyes locked with the floor, and Noah stares out the window, his shoulders curled forward, his hands shoved deep into his pockets.

Roy and Angela talk in low murmurs, and Frances picks at the corner of the map. I don't expect many of them will want to follow me. If it weren't for my mum and Tim, I'd stay hunkered down here. I have everything I need to survive—food, gear, shelter, and medicines. But I can't leave Mum and Tim on their own.

I try to focus, ignoring the pain in my arm that's been growing more and more intense over the past few hours. My forearm has swollen like a balloon, and even though the bite didn't go through the leather, it sports an uncanny purple colour. It looks like a massive whale hangs from my elbow.

I turn my focus away from the whale, back to the red circle on the map. Our house. If I leave for Huntington, it would mean leaving Megan behind. Is that really something I can do? Regardless of how things are between us, I would never want her to get caught up in all of this. To have to fight to survive on her own through a zombie apocalypse.

Zombie-fucking-apocalypse. I scrub my face with my hand. Yeah, we used to joke about the zompoc, but it was a *joke*. Everyone knows zombies *don't* exist. Or? I look past Noah and out the window, remembering the so-called infected feeding on people. I guess a more accurate statement would be: everyone thought they *knew* zombies didn't exist.

I let out a heavy breath. I don't want to leave Megan, but I can't leave Mum and Tim either, and I can't be in two places at the same time, so I have to choose.

Mum and Tim have Dad flying in; maybe I should stay here. For Megan. I snort and shake my head, my eyes still locked on our house. Megan would kill me if she knew I thought of her like this, like some damsel in distress who might need saving by a man. I know she can handle herself, and I know she isn't stupid. If she is still alive, she will make her way here. Like me, she knows that everything she needs to survive is in this house.

I'm going to Cait's. I can't wait for you anymore.

My thoughts drift back to the message and all its double meanings. I shake my head. Those were problems for another time. I bite the inside of my cheek. If she'd gone to Cait's, she would have been caught in the destruction of Central London. Either way, there is no way I can find Megan, and if she's not here by tomorrow morning, I'll know she's not coming back. At least not in time. I clear my throat in an unsuccessful attempt to clear my thoughts and take a sip from my tea.

"I'll go with," Fareena says. "I've got family in Leeds, so I'll go with you to Huntingdon and make my way home from there."

"Ange and I were thinking of trying to make our way to the airport," Roy says slowly as he leans onto the knuckles of his hand.

"Maybe Stansted is still running," I offer. "If things are only affecting Central and Greater London, there's a chance."

"Perhaps, although I think with the way things are out there, that's hoping for too much," Angela says. "From experience, I think we all better stick together."

"Your dad's the military, isn't he?" Noah has stopped staring out the window, his blue eyes observing me with a penetrating stare.

"I guess," I say and shrug.

"Then I agree with Angela. I think anyone who wants to survive this should stick with us until we get to Jake's parents'. Then his dad can get us into a safe military facility."

It shouldn't surprise me that the only reason Noah would consider staying is because I'm the ticket to a safe place. Survival at all costs, isn't that what they say? I'd probably do the same thing if I were in his shoes. Although I'd be less obvious about it.

"I think I will go with you, if you don't mind," Frances says. "My sister lives in Dublin. Maybe... well, the farther north I get, the better."

Frances is an older woman in her mid-fifties with a slightly angular, happy face. Grey and white streak through her brown hair and a pair of oval glasses frame her face.

I smile because Frances, with her warm smile and soft Irish accent, is hard not to like. "Of course, I don't mind."

"What do we do about Claire and the shot guy?" Noah asks.

Right. There's that. Claire was sick, there was no doubt about that, but what kind of sick is she? With the flu or with the infection? We could bring her, but could it be a threat to our own safety? Getting her from Westminster to my house was hard. Travelling with her to Cambridge will be even more difficult.

I look around the table to see if anyone else is thinking the same thing. Judging by their faces, they are.

"We can ask Claire if she's able, and, if Andy can make the trip, we'll bring him too," I say and ignore the way Noah sucks in a breath and holds it as he looks away. I know he's all about surviving, and though Claire and Andy are definitely not the ones you want on your team, if survival is the game, we can't just leave them. Noah was right about one thing: I've already left an entire train full of people to die. I can't—I won't—leave more people behind.

My gaze slides to Liv, who's got her arms folded over her chest. She doesn't say anything.

"Alright," I say, once I realise she's not going to chime in, "at least that gives us an idea of how many we might be." I place my finger at the red circle on the map. "This is where we are." I drag it from the circle, across London, all the way up and beyond Cambridge until the tip of my finger lands at Huntingdon. "This is where we need to get to."

They lean in across the table and peer closer at where my finger points.

"That's one hell of a way to go." Roy leans away from the table.

"Yeah." I sigh. "Better yet, how do we get there?"

"From what we saw, we can't go through Central London." Fareena circles the central area of London with her finger. "That's a pretty big area we can't get through."

"I guess there are always tunnels we could use, but do we *want* to go through Ground Zero?" I say.

"Ah, hell no." Roy shakes his head.

"So, we go around," I say. "Surely there must be somewhere we can cross the Thames and head north."

"We could go out towards Greenwich and see if we can cross anywhere there." Frances suggests with a nod towards the map.

"Okay." It's not a bad plan. "But how do we get there?"

"We can still drive the pickup," Roy says.

"Don't count on it," Noah snorts.

"Yeah, there's no guarantee roads won't be crammed," Fareena agrees. "London traffic is a nightmare, with or without a terror attack. One car stops on the M11 and it completely blocks the rest of the route up. It's a *nightmare*."

"Now you double that car by hundreds," Noah says, and I can almost imagine the shitshow it would be trying to drive through this mess.

"What about bikes?" Biking all the way up to Huntingdon is probably one of my worst nightmares, but it sure as hell beats walking up there. Or, as it would most likely end up being, running.

"We left the bikes by the church," Angela points out.

"Maybe one of your neighbours has bikes we could borrow?" Roy says. Borrow bikes? From neighbours? I laugh. Where's this guy from? We're in London; we don't talk to our neighbours, let alone ask to borrow their bikes.

"I have two and I'm sure we can borrow bikes from the neighbours who've already left."

Roy chortles. "Oh. You mean *borrow*. Don't let my wife hear that."

"I'm right here, hon." Angela pats him on the shoulder and side-eyes him.

I laugh. "If they're not here, they're not going to miss them."

"I'm not leaving my truck," Liv interjects, her voice leaving no room for discussion. I guess she's coming with.

Thinking back to the truck, I remember seeing black plastic bags packed to the rim. And there was the bag of clothes Noah chucked at the infected in a frantic attempt to get them off Jules. There's definitely more to this truck business than meets the eye.

"What about taking it as far as we possibly can?" I ask. Liv scowls but gives a reluctant nod after a while, then leaves the room again. Well, that's one problem solved. I scratch my beard. The truck could be useful if we find streets clear enough to drive. I think about how we had to navigate every single small street we could find to get here, and the cars blocking the roads.

A sudden gasp sounds from my side and all of us look over at Fareena, who looks as if she just won the jackpot.

"What?" I ask.

"Boats," she whispers, her hands held out to her sides, fingers splayed, her amber eyes wide and round in excitement.

"I'm sorry, what?" I know what I heard; I'm just not sure what she wants to say.

"My aunt, she lived on a boat," Fareena grabs my arm and I'm surprised she's not pulling at it in excitement. "She used to tell me that the best thing about living on a boat was that she could live anywhere, *go* anywhere."

"Oh my God," I hear myself whisper as the brilliance of her idea takes root.

"If we find a boat, we could travel the canals up to Cambridge," Fareena explains to the others.

I grin. "The Great Ouse. If we can get onto the Great Ouse, we can go all the way to my parents' front door."

"So, all we need now is a boat," Noah says and looks at Fareena who—much to our disappointment—shakes her head.

"She passed away a few years back."

"Surely there must be other boats," Angela says, her forehead wrinkling in thought.

"That we could *borrow*, you mean?" I joke.

"Actually, there are boats all over London." Fareena plants her finger on the wide light-blue line that curls its way through London. "Londoners have been complaining about too many boats mooring in the city. I bet we can find one that no one's using. There has to be at least *one*."

"The boats nearest the city will have taken a hit during the attack," I say. It's ridiculous to call it an attack when we all know there's more to it than that, but for now, I guess it's the only thing we know to call it. I point a little further to the east on the map. "Maybe over in Kingston, things won't be so bad."

"So, the plan is"—Roy folds his arms across his chest—"we borrow bikes, sling 'em onto the pickup, make our way east, and then borrow a boat."

Everyone watches him in silence, as though waiting for his approval. Maybe it's because of his no-nonsense attitude or the thick Southern accent, but whatever it is, it seems I'm not the only one to look to Roy for some reassurance. Roy, in turn, looks at Angela.

Her eyes narrow in thought, lips curling. "I've heard worse plans," she says after a while.

"It sure as hell beats staying close to a city of infected humans running rampant. Now there's only one more thing." Roy drops his hands onto his hips and looks at us with a serious expression. "Guns."

I can practically see everyone's reaction before they even think about having it. The non-American members of our group look at Roy as if he just asked for the Crown jewels.

"Yeah, we don't really do that here," I say.

"I *know* you don't walk around with guns," Roy scolds me, "but there has to be some lying around."

"Yeah, alright, mate." Noah gives a snort of derision. "This ain't the US. Unless you go to some pretty dodgy places, you're not going to find any guns just 'lying around.'"

"Then what?" Roy scratches the side of his face. "Let's be realistic here; we ain't going to survive for long out there without weapons."

"Alright there, Louisiana." I slap him on the shoulder. "I said we don't really have any guns; I never said I didn't have any weapons." I grab one of my bags and empty it onto the kitchen table.

Slingshots, knives, two crossbows, a small camping axe, and a nail gun tumble onto the table.

"I also have a fire axe and a cricket bat," I say and nod at the bat that rests in one corner of the kitchen. It's not much, but it's something, and by the others' looks, I think they're slightly impressed. Or worried. It could go either way.

"A nail gun?" Fareena looks at me. "I thought that was a movie thing."

I grin. Megan and I had gone back and forth between getting it when we made our pallet furniture or saving the money and doing the hammering ourselves. Our laziness won out and we'd spent half a fortune on it. If we'd known London would get overrun by infected, we probably wouldn't have felt so bad about it.

"Holy shit," Liv gasps as she walks in from the living room and takes a swig from a glass bottle. *Is that my thirty-year-old Comber?*

"Is that my whiskey?" I stare at the rare bottle of whiskey in her hand.

"Yes," she says with an uninterested look on her face before her mouth forms a silent 'oh.' "Do you want some?"

"That's a limited edition from my collection," I say stiffly as I watch my well-kept, precious whiskey being downed by some barbarian.

"Well, are you going to leave it there? Because at this rate you'll just have a lot of stupidly expensive whiskey go to waste."

"Ugh." I drop my face into my hands as Angela breaks into a soft laughter. *Who is this woman?* I know she has a point, but goddamn it, couldn't she at least have waited until after dinner?

A see-through bottleneck dances below my nose as Liv waves it in front of my mouth. I snatch it from her. What the hell, this place is going to shit, anyway. Might as well enjoy parts of it. Taking a big gulp, I shake my head at Liv. She fires off a coy smile. I hand the bottle to Angela, who takes a sip and passes it along until everyone has had a nip. Like an Irishman's holy communion.

Maybe it's the whiskey, maybe it's the absurdity of the situation, but just like before, Angela's laugh spreads like a wildfire and soon we're laughing so hard tears run from my eyes.

"Well, I guess that's settled." Roy wipes his eyes when we finally stop laughing. Everyone nods. Before today, these were people I didn't know at all. But despite our differences, we've decided to stick together.

Now all we need to do is survive.

30

JAKE

DARKNESS HAS SWALLOWED THE world whole. At least that's how it feels now that all of London is without power.

The Prime Minister announced that they had misjudged the damage done to the infrastructure of London, and that many more than they could have expected had become very ill as a side effect of the residue. With more than seventy-five percent of hospitals on lockdown due to the contagious residue, all resources needed to be rerouted to essential facilities.

We've been without electricity since midnight. I want to think people would worry about how to stay warm or keep their refrigerators cool, maybe even charge their phones. But despite the expensive whiskey warming my insides, calming my nerves, I know some people will think about how this could be to their advantage. Opportunists that, instead of rising to the occasion, will rise to the idea of power over others.

Of all the things out there, the infected or an invisible illness spread by residue, the opportunists—my fellow humans—are the ones I really fear. I gaze through the window and imagine someone waiting for us to fall asleep so they can kill us. *For fuck's sake, Jake.*

The darkness presses closer and leaves nothing but my thoughts to distract me. And they're doing a shit job of it. I see Jules' face moments before she's dragged off the truck, and I hear her scream. It plays over and over in my head no matter what I do.

Roy's face was as ashen as mine felt when we sunk to the floor, shocked and defeated. We had her in our hands. What if we'd tried a little harder? I let out a sigh. All these mind traps keep me walking in circles.

Someone stirring catches my attention. Liv sits in the armchair we got from Megan's aunt Edith. It's covered in a deep-red velvety fabric with an embroidered pattern. Megan insists it's flowers, but I swear they look more like vaginas than any flower I ever saw.

I used to call it the Twat Chair, much to Megan's horror and amusement. She'd laugh and then shush herself and me as if poor aunt Edith would take great offence.

Ugly as it may be, it's extremely comfortable. I shift my weight from my left butt cheek to the right before my entire butt falls asleep. Aunt Edith's chair definitely beats the rug on the floor.

Karma sleeps next to me, her loud snores rumbling through the otherwise silent house. I rest my hand on her warm, furry neck, and she looks up at me with tired eyes. She doesn't even lift her head, merely rolls her eyes to the side. Once she's decided I haven't got any food to offer her, she closes her eyes again.

A soft thud sounds as Liv stands and walks across the living room. I watch her move towards me, jaw set, dark hair twisting and turning across her shoulders.

She slides down onto the rug beside me but remains silent, so I watch the sleeping people at the other end of the room. Noah lays sprawled across the camping bed we set up, and Fareena is curled like a shrimp on the sofa. I should probably have asked Fareena how she was doing, but that would no doubt lead to a discussion about Andy, which would lead to crying, which would lead to me squirming awkwardly before thinking up a poor excuse to leave. I like Fareena, I do, but I don't know her well enough to let all my guards down. I don't think I'll ever know anyone enough to do that.

"This..." Liv's quiet voice reaches my ears, and I can smell the alcohol on her breath, "has been one fucked-up day."

"Tell me about it." Parts of it feel like a dream, while others feel frighteningly real. *It is real*, I remind myself.

"How can this be happening?" Her voice is so soft and subtle I'm not entirely sure she meant to say it aloud. That, and the fact I haven't got a good guess, makes me lift my shoulders and drop them again.

We remain silent, Liv's fingers tapping another of my ridiculously expensive whiskey bottles, but I can see her watching me out of the corner of my eye.

"So, what is she like?" she finally says.

"Who?" I ask, not quite following Liv's trail of thoughts. With the amount of alcohol she's consumed, I'm not even sure she does.

"Megan," she says pointedly. "I saw your picture in the hallway. She's pretty fucking hot."

"Oh," I say. I hadn't quite expected that one. "She's, uh... Megan?"

"Well, obviously," Liv hisses, "but besides that?"

"Why do you want to know?" I ask a little more defensively than I meant to.

"Why don't you want to tell me?"

"Err... Because it's private."

She heaves a heavy sigh and hugs herself. "Fine."

Nice, Jake, I tell myself as an awkward silence settles between us. *Girl tries to make conversation, and you shoot her down because you'd have to talk about your feelings.* Yep, that's me, good old Jake. Making things awkward since 1997.

“She’s a Scorpio,” I say and grab the bottle from Liv, “and that should really tell you all you need to know about her, but, if it doesn’t...” I take a deep breath and dig around my pocket for my pack of cigarettes. Fishing it out, I stand up. I need a fag. “She’s intense. It’s all or nothing, heaven and hell.”

“She sounds...” Liv holds up her hand and I grab it, helping her to her feet.

“Crazy?” I laugh softly as we tiptoe through the kitchen and out to my small backyard. “She is. And when you’re with her, it makes you crazy too. In a good way. And sometimes bad.”

She snatches a cigarette from my pack. “Oi, shitbag, you’ve had these fags all along and not shared?”

I light my cigarette. “My whiskey isn’t enough?”

She huffs in response and lights her own. “So, what happened?”

I snort inwardly and take a drag from my cigarette. *What didn’t happen?*

“You know what I always wanted to do?” Liv interrupts me. I’m glad she does because talking about Megan opens a can of worms I’ve been doing my best to keep sealed for a very long time.

All the late-night fights, the shouting and slamming of doors. Megan was like a criminal with a loaded gun, her words leaving wounds that at times still felt raw and new. It was always the same fight. It would start out about something else, but always come back to that one particular thing.

“No?” I reply to Liv’s question that I can barely remember what it was.

“There’s a restaurant, Cork & Bottle, at Leicester Square. Super expensive, but their food—especially the ham and cheese pie—is to die for,” Liv says. There’s a dreamy edge to her voice that’s cut short as she scowls. “Do you know how I know this?”

I shake my head, not sure where she’s going with this.

“I read it. Fucking read it. On TripAdvisor.” She waves her hands in the air. “On a fucking website.”

“It could have been on the app; that would have been even worse.” I grin at the slightly odd conversation.

She pulls a face at me. “I always wanted to go there and try out their pie. The best thing on their menu, but I kept pushing it off. I’d say, ‘next week, next week.’ And then what happened?”

I suck on my lip. “Uh...”

“And then someone went and blew the whole bloody city to shit.” She huffs, a puff of smoke shooting from her lips as she does. “I thought...”

“You’d have more time?” I give a soft chuckle. “Me too.” If I’d gotten a penny for everything I’d do later, I’d be a millionaire by now. Now, I’m not so sure I’ll ever get to do any of those things. I was going to write a book, open a small café on one of London's smaller streets. I was going to go back to school and finish my degree, and I was going to visit my family more often.

My family. Mum and Tim. In a day, I'll be seeing them. That's more than some of the people in this house. I feel a pang of guilt for the pity party I'm throwing myself. At least I got to go home. Megan wasn't here, but at least I know I went home and checked. And I have Karma. Some of these people might never have that luxury.

It hadn't occurred to me until now that Angela and Roy have family in the US they can't contact, and that the others might have family or friends they can't reach. I look at where Liv stands next to me under a sea of stars. It's the first time I've seen them from the backyard of my house. And all it took was an apocalypse.

"Liv?"

"Yeah?"

"Do you have someone? Someone you'd want to see?"

"Pfft," she snorts, "No."

"No one at all?" I stump out the last of my cig on the concrete stairs and open the door.

"Wow, Jake. Thanks for rubbing it in," she whispers as we tiptoe back into the living room.

Slick, mate. Very slick. I berate myself until I see her amused expression. "Shut up."

She hands me back my bottle of whiskey. My empty bottle of whiskey. Damn, this girl can really hold her liquor.

"Right, Hipster. That was my nightcap."

"Thanks," I say and hold up the bottle as if toasting her. "Good night." I drop back to the floor.

She curls up in the twat chair and ignores me. I shrug and lie back on the floor, using Karma's butt as my pillow. Just I as close my eyes, I hear a quiet whisper.

"Good night, Hipster. Don't let the zombies bite."

31

LIV

SHE SLEPT RESTLESSLY, DRIFTING in and out of sleep and dreaming of ghoulish, haggard faces with jaws full of dull brown teeth that chased her down narrow corridors. The further she got, the darker and narrower the corridors got until finally the ghouls caught up with her, their teeth shredding her neck and hands.

She jolted awake with a gasp, instinctively fighting off the hand on her shoulder.

"Oh, hey," a girl with soft features and warm eyes said. "Bad dreams?"

Liv blinked in confusion. She couldn't remember inviting a girl to stay in her car.

"Yeah," the girl scoffed softly, "I had a hard time remembering where I was as well."

She allowed her brain a few seconds to recognise her surroundings. The small room was lit by a lantern and candles, allowing her to see the worn wooden flooring covered by an antique rug and various mismatched furniture. The hipster bloke's house.

"Ah, bollocks." She sagged on the chair, memories from the day before coming back to her. She'd thought it'd been another one of her alcohol-fuelled, messed-up dreams, but it seemed dreams imitated life.

"Right?" Fareena, the girl with the amazing curly hair, said with a sad smile. She stood and walked towards the small kitchen with its yellow walls and cluttered surfaces.

"What time is it?" Liv asked, scrubbing sleep from her eyes.

"Three in the morning."

"Ugh." She let out a groan, feeling like a train had hit her. Twice.

Fareena, on the other hand, looked as if she'd just stepped from a juice commercial—fresh, wide awake, and ready to tackle the day. She had tied her hair into a large bun, though the most stubborn curls still found a way to spring loose from their confinement. Her light-brown eyes studied Liv from behind the rounded rim of the mug pressed to her lips. Good God, how could anyone wake up and look that gorgeous? Liv grimaced when she imagined what she must look like in comparison. One of those infected, no doubt.

"I hear you. Don't think anyone got a good night's sleep," Fareena said, making polite small talk. "If that's what you can call three hours of sleep." She wrinkled her nose.

"Please tell me that's coffee." Liv felt her knees crunch as she pushed up from the comfortable chair.

"Oh." Fareena chuckled softly and tilted her head. "Yes. Thank God for gas stoves, eh? Angela made it when she couldn't sleep. Speaking of which, I can't believe you fell asleep like that."

Ugh. Liv rubbed her face. Her conversational skills were bad at best. Her conversational skills before her mandatory intake of caffeine were nothing short of a train wreck. "I've had worse. Now, can you *please*... Give. Me. Coffee. Before I deck someone." The last words came out as a snarl. *Well, at least I said please.*

"Ah, another morning person." Pouring coffee into a mug, a flash of amusement touched Fareena's face.

"Is three really morning though? Or is it just stupid o'clock?"

Fareena laughed. "The rest of the grouch squad is out there." She motioned with a nod towards the backyard.

Taking the mug, Liv stepped out into the crisp early morning, her breath fogging up the air.

Jake and Angela sat in silence on a wooden bench, both staring off into space as they sipped from their mugs. Now this was the sort of morning conversation Liv appreciated. Angela wore a big winter jacket and a scarf in green and red colours, making her look like she was about to go on a hunt. Jake wore a black coat with a grey hoodie pulled up over his head, bits of spiky hair sticking out from it.

He pushed his thick-rimmed glasses up and gave a curt nod. She gave what she hoped was a somewhat friendly nod and sat next to Angela.

Taking a sip from the hot coffee, she let out a low moan of pleasure at the rich flavour and closed her eyes in bliss. Of all the things she couldn't live without, coffee was definitely one of them.

Something tapped her hand and she looked up to see a cigarette being offered. She grabbed the green lighter and lit it, then took a deep drag. Okay, maybe cigarettes had to be squeezed into the "cannot live without" category as well. And a good scotch.

By the time she had finished both her coffee and the cigarette, Angela and Jake had started making small talk about what remained to do before they left.

She scratched her head, effectively messing up the stylish bird's nest she had managed to conjure at the back of her head while sleeping. "I thought we weren't leaving until late morning?"

"We were," Jake said, his voice low with a pleasant ruggedness to it, "but Ange couldn't sleep and now we will all suffer."

Laughing softly, Angela took a deep breath. "I... I remembered the Sierra Leone Ebola epidemic and how that situation progressed."

The Ebola epidemic in 2014. The outbreak happened around the same time Doctor Anwar accepted Liv to train with him. He'd spent their first week talking about Sierra Leone. He wasn't the only one though. The whole medical community had been buzzing with horrified fascination. "What about it? It's not Ebola, if that's what you're worried about."

Angela tsked in dismay and gave Liv's knee a playful slap. "I know that. But by the time the government declared a state of emergency, the death toll had risen to nearly a hundred cases."

A hundred cases. It had been a staggering amount back then, and it hadn't only been the deaths, but the number of confirmed infections that had everyone worried. The virus had seemed unstoppable, all attempts to stop it futile.

Judging by the number of infected they'd seen in the city, they were way past a hundred cases. "Are you saying we're in a state of emergency?"

Nodding slowly, Angela narrowed her eyes in thought. "They put up roadblocks all around the city centre, but I'm a police officer. I've seen my fair share of barricades. That was not a simple roadblock."

"A quarantine?" She could feel the ends of her brows draw together in disbelief. *A quarantine!* Of course it was! Now that she had the answer right in front of her, it made perfect sense. It would explain why the military shot at them—to keep them from leaving the quarantine. *No one in, no one out.* That's what Doctor Anwar had said about the lockdown Sierra Leone announced.

"Bastards..." she whispered.

"But as we all know, the Sierra Leone lockdown failed," Jake said before taking another drag of his cigarette.

Angela nodded. "And apparently, so did this one. And since it failed, they might try to quarantine a larger area..."

"We might get stuck inside the quarantine," Liv said slowly, "even though we're not actually sick."

"That's pretty much what Angela figured as well. So, we thought we'd better hustle before it's too late."

"Hustle?" She jutted out her chin. "Who under the age of fifty even says that anymore?"

Jake let out a snakelike sound and scratched his head. The grey hood slipped off to reveal thick black hair that matched her own bird's nest, making him look ruggedly handsome despite being up when everyone else was still asleep.

"Guess I'm not down with what the kids say nowadays."

Liv snorted. He couldn't be that much older than her. In fact, despite his beard, his baby face made him look much younger.

"Liv?" Fareena poked her head out the kitchen door, her forehead creased. "Frances wants you to check on Andy. He's been throwing up."

Throwing up? Liv doubted Frances would need her help with something as mundane as vomiting. She went over Andy's injury in her head. Blunt abdominal trauma. They already knew Andy's chances for survival were slim to none, so if Frances needed her help with vomiting... she already knew what the nurse was going to say. Blood. Andy must be vomiting blood. *Shit.* Liv had hoped things today would prove better, but vomiting blood? In Andy's condition, it was without a doubt the result of internal bleeding. *So fucking stupid.* She cursed herself. She should know better than to hope for miracles. There was a reason they almost always sent patients with blunt abdominal trauma to surgery.

"Thanks," she murmured to Jake as she stood up and made her way back into the house.

"She's upstairs," Fareena said, her face tight with worry as she walked past. "Is everything okay?"

Liv tried to keep her face expressionless. "I can't really..."

The sound of a door slamming shut sounded somewhere above them, and they both lifted their heads towards the ceiling.

Footsteps thudded loudly, then a loud *whack* cut through the house, followed by Roy's exasperated voice. "Jesus Christ!"

The two of them moved to the bottom of the stairs.

"Roy? What's going on?" Fareena asked apprehensively.

"Claire attacked Frances and tried to bite me!" The tall man lifted the side of his shirt where a chunk of the collar had been torn off.

Frances stood behind him holding a blue bucket in her hand. She looked rattled, but unharmed.

"Bite?" Liv's brows knit together. "Like the infected?"

A loud *thunk* shook the wall as someone threw themself against the bedroom door. Its hinges creaked loudly in protest. A throaty moan came from the other side of the wood, low and trembling until it grew in strength to a rabid snarl, then another displeased cracking whipped through the air as Claire's body slammed the door.

"Claire," Roy said slowly, like a person trying to calm a rabid dog, "you need to calm down so we can help you." He was rewarded with another coughing hiss. Or it could have been a cackle.

Fareena grabbed Liv's arm as Claire slammed the door again, and the sudden *thunk* made them all jump.

"Help... me..." came the frail voice from behind the door. "Please..."

"What's going on?" Jake's forehead puckered as he and Angela entered from the kitchen.

"Claire tried to bite Roy," Fareena whispered.

"What?" Angela's eyes widened. "Are you alright?"

"Yes, yes." Another *whack* cracked from the door. "Guys... I don't think this door will hold up much longer."

A retching from one of the other rooms sent Frances into motion, blue bucket held firmly in her hands. Claire's shoving at the door accompanied Frances's quick footsteps.

Vomiting and people going crazy, like a regular Friday night at A&E.

"Roy." Liv leaned over to catch his gaze. "What did she look like?"

"I don't know." He lifted his shoulders and shook his head. "I mean, she looked a little... pale."

"Pale?" That was the best he could do? She shook her head. This guy had to give her something more than that. "Anything else?"

"Well, she was trying to bite me," Roy drawled.

Well, yes, there was that. "I thought you guys said she had the *flu*. The flu doesn't exactly have you trying to chew away at other people."

"I mean, we don't know, that's what she said," Fareena said slowly.

"She's football tackling that door like she's trying to get a fucking home run," Liv snorted.

"Touchdown," Jake said, and she turned to look at him. "It's called a 'touc hdown.'" A smile tugged at the corners of his mouth as he lifted his shoulders and dropped them again.

"Same shit, different name." She wiggled her fingers dismissively at him. "What it means is we need to skedaddle the fuck out of here."

As if to cement her point, the sickening crunch of wood reached their ears.

"I don't think she's wrong," Roy said, his eyes darting towards the door.

"Alright, everybody." Jake nodded. "Let's get our shit together!"

Fareena's grip on her arm disappeared as she and Angela bounced into motion, their footsteps pattering in an eerie cohesive symphony with Claire's banging on the door.

"I need to check on Andy quickly." She took a step up the stairs when Jake's hand caught her arm. She spun and glared at him.

"You need to get your bag and put it in the car. Roy and I will grab Andy."

"I'll put my damn bag in the car *after* I've checked on him," she hissed through her teeth.

"Listen," Jake insisted, "we need to go. Now. Will Andy be able to go?"

She stared at him, swallowing hard. If she said no, then what? Would they leave him behind? If she said yes, would they try to bring him along? Causing him more pain than if left at the house?

"I brought Claire here. I didn't know she's infected." He threw a quick glance up at the walkway above them. "I risked everyone's lives to help someone. So, I get wanting to save your friend."

She shook her head. "It's most likely internal bleeding. He needs surgery. I don't have the right instruments. I don't... I don't know."

Movement sounded from the walkway above as Frances stepped out from Andy's room, eyes downcast as she shook her head. "I don't think he'll be able to move."

"Damn." Roy sighed and ran a hand over his shaved head.

Thunk.

"Roy, love, let's get away from that door." Frances held out her hand in a nurse-like manner, as though helping a patient.

"We can't bring him if that isn't what's best for him," Jake said. His voice was firm, full of reason, but his eyes were soft and sympathetic.

"What about the number?" Roy asked, the stairs creaking underneath his weight as he and Frances made their way down.

"You mean the number to the same people who lied on national TV?" Liv fixed him with a penetrating stare.

"If you were the government and had a zombie outbreak on your hands," Roy began, completely unfazed by her stare, "would you tell everyone and risk panic? Or would you try to get everyone to stay indoors and call for help where needed?"

Goddamn it, he had a point. "Okay, fine," she said with a sigh.

There was a sickening crack as the door finally gave way to Crazy Claire's weight.

They froze on the spot, Liv's eyes darting to find something she could use to protect herself, but unless she used one of the other people in the stairs as a weapon—or fodder, rather—there was little she could use to protect herself.

She'd seen a documentary about a man who lived with wolves. He'd said that if one ever came face-to-face with a real-life wild wolf, one should stand still until the wolf decided that there was no threat and moved on.

Holding her breath, she tried to not think about how the wolf man had been torn to pieces and eaten only months after the documentary was filmed.

Claire darted from the door, hunched and growling, a strong putrid smell following in her wake. Her hair hung in long wet tendrils from her head, sticking to her greying, wrinkled face. She stopped at the top of the stairs.

"Shit," Roy hissed.

Claire spun on her heel. Her head twitched erratically, mouth opening and closing. Her white eyes fell on their small group. Her lips pulled back in a snarl, revealing corpse grey gum and yellowing teeth. She sniffed the air like a dog that'd caught a scent.

Claire's head swung from one side to the other, to the bedroom where Andy lay, then back to them. Back to Andy and back to them. Almost as if she were sizing them up. *What the hell?*

Roy shifted, and the boards creaked underneath him. Claire lurched forward, a grating, high-pitched screech erupting from her lips. They all stumbled backwards, instinct taking them away from the monster. But instead of following, Claire gave one last hacking snarl and then scrambled into Andy's room.

Liv opened her lips to scream, but she was pulled backwards, a big hand wrapping itself over her mouth. All that came out was a muffled, "Hmph."

"Shh," Jake whispered in her ear.

She heard teeth ripping at flesh and sinew, and she clawed at Jake to release her. Something dropped to the floor with a wet splosh, and she shuddered to think which part of Andy it might have been.

"We need to go." His voice thrummed with tension as he pulled her out of the house and onto the street. The others piled out after them, rushing towards the car. "It's too late now; we can't do anything for either of them."

Noah carried two of the backpacks Jake had prepared, and Fareena threw the third onto the back of the truck before heaving herself after it.

Liv jerked in frustration, but Jake held her firm until Roy had slammed the door. Karma stood in front of it like a big, menacing bear, waiting to pounce at anything that emerged.

"If I let you go, will you get in your truck?"

She gave one hard nod and jerked free as he released her, then shoved him hard. For good measure.

"Karma!" Jake's voice came out firm, but Liv thought she could detect a tinge of panic in it. "Get in car, *now*."

She opened the door, and the big dog moved from the front door to her car in seconds. Karma's enormous bulk blurred as the dog skidded into the seat next to hers.

She followed right after, throwing herself a lot less gracefully into her seat, then turned on the ignition and floored it.

This time she didn't look back. Andy was gone. What good would looking back do? She never had before, so why start now?

They got as far as Wimbledon, which was a lot farther than most of them had expected. If she'd been wondering where all the people were yesterday, the answer was right in front of her as they'd turned onto Wimbledon Hill.

Cars were stopped in every direction. On the street, on the pavement, in the right direction, in the wrong direction. Everyone desperately trying to get somewhere. Drivers honked and put their heads out their windows to shout, as if by some miracle that would get the entire line to shift.

Unlike most people in their cars, they had gotten out the bikes, as well as an impressive cart that now held their bags and Karma as they pedalled like bats out of hell.

Sweat poured down Liv's back, her calves burning from exertion, and she fixed her gaze on Noah's back.

"You alright?" Fareena asked from where she sat on the rear rack of her bike.

Liv grunted a reply.

"Let me know when you want to swap and let me have all the fun," Fareena teased.

Biking at insanity miles an hour with someone sitting on the rear rack was not Liv's idea of fun, and she snarled through her breathing. Fareena had already done all the 'fun' work. And, sure, Liv could let her get back to it, but she'd rather not have the person keeping them from getting caught by infected be so tired that a pensioner with a Zimmer frame could outrun them. So she kept her gaze firm on Noah's back.

Houses and streets blurred past in a multicoloured frenzy as people who'd just woken up rushed the streets, either stocking up their houses or preparing to leave. Apparently, they weren't the only ones who thought the government was hiding something. Hopefully, all these people didn't have the same great idea about the boats as they had. Fighting and running from the infected was one thing, but fighting humans would be a whole other ball game.

Turning a sharp right, they rolled past two-storey brick houses until Fareena gave a cry of excitement. "There!"

The ripples on the river mirrored the sky above them. Green foliage and trees separated the water from the T junction ahead, but a small opening in between the trees gaped back at them. Without hesitation, and with barely a look around, Noah flew through it, Frances jiggling like a rag doll on the rear rack.

The rest of them followed just as recklessly. Liv's heart slammed, adrenaline and excitement rushing through her, but then she saw Jake's face, his eyes downcast, a wrinkle of hopelessness between his brows.

She followed his gaze. Her heart lurched before it dropped to the pit of her stomach.

The docks were empty. Not a single boat was in sight. And to top it all off, a crescendo of moans and guttural groans rose from somewhere behind them.

They'd come all this way, thinking they'd be able to find a boat. Not once had they stopped to think they wouldn't find one. For some reason, their idea seemed original, as if someone else with half a brain wouldn't have thought of it as well. Her jaw tightened with annoyance that once again—in less than twenty-four hours—she'd relied on something so ludicrous as hope to solve her problems.

"Well, isn't this fucktastic?" Maybe it was shitty karma from another life, or just this arsehole universe constantly dropping obstacles in front of her. But she'd hoped, for once, it could cut her some fucking slack. Liv glared at the empty riverside.

"No." Jake gave an adamant shake of his head. "There has to be more."

"Over there!" Angela pointed from the rear rack of Roy's bike.

In the distance, on the other bank, where the river bent and turned, Liv saw vague shapes in the water. Boats. Lots of boats!

Karma gave an excited bark that rumbled through the air. Liv dropped on the saddle, kicking down furiously on the pedals. Not only because she wanted to get to the boats, but also because Karma's excitement had alerted the shambling infected of their presence. However, they weren't shambling—they were *running* after Liv and the others. Weren't zombies supposed to be slow and flail around with their arms going, "Braaaaiiins?"

They zoomed down the gravelled path, putting some distance between themselves and the infected, although their rotten, decayed aroma followed closely, and their groans seemed to stick in her ears.

A stone bridge with an arched underside crossed the river ahead. They'd never pedal that up slope fast enough. Without exchanging a word, she and Fareena leapt from the bike and jogged to the bridge's peak before jumping on to coast down.

"In there!" Fareena called as they drew closer to a pine-coloured floating house. "I can't hot-wire these things. We need the keys."

"I'm sorry, hot-wire?" This girl certainly had some hidden talents. Fareena fired off an innocent smile as everyone pulled to a stop and got off their bikes.

A loud bang shot through the air as Noah, Roy, and Jake flung themselves against the door. It gave way with a crack, and the three men landed on the floor with a hard thud, followed by one or two *oomphs*.

Stepping over them, Fareena moved towards a cheap white desk that stood by the windows with a view of the river and boats. A wooden cabinet hung on the wall next to it. Fareena flipped it open, her eyes narrowing.

She let out an exasperated, "Oh." Three keys, but at least double the number of boats mooring at the dock.

"Grab all of them." Jake brushed himself off. "We'll split up and try all the boats."

Liv glanced over her shoulder at the bridge. Dark shadows moved along it, fast and determined like marathon runners. "We don't have much time."

"Then we better haul ass." Roy adjusted his fedora and caught the set of keys that flew his way.

Fareena moved past him, dropped one of the keys in Jake's hand, then grinned at Liv. "Girl team, let's find this boat." She jiggled the keys in the air.

A metal keyring hung from the keys, large golden letters tracing a name. Gloria. She frowned. The name looked somewhat familiar, as if she'd just seen it somewhere. Her eyes darted back and forth until it landed on an indigo-blue narrowboat, whose white curly letters spelled out *Gloria*.

"Holy shit." She laughed. "Holy motherfucking shit, it's right there!"

"Yes!" Fareena pumped her fist in the air and raced past her. "We totally won."

Liv let out a snort and feigned an American accent as she said, "Yes, girl," then raced after her.

"Get the ropes!" Fareena hauled herself on board using the stern's railing and jammed the key into the ignition.

Angela and Roy bent above one set of the ropes, tugging hard, and Liv pelted to where the second rope held the boat in its place. She pulled. It didn't budge.

Sweat rolled down her back and her heart pounded like a jackhammer as she tugged. The moans and groans from the infected increased in strength. Their scuffling feet on the gravel announced they would arrive any second.

Someone knelt beside her. A stench of rotten fish and days' old vomit reached her nose.

Not someone. *Something.*

32

JAKE

THE INFECTED ROUND THE corner, coming at us at a speed that still shocks me. They're so fast. Too fast.

Angela, Roy, and Liv throw themselves at the ropes and tug with frantic motions. We've biked thirty minutes at breakneck speed with bags full of supplies. My legs feel like jelly, and my chest burns.

"Get off her!" Noah yells behind my back. It's followed by Karma's sharp bark. I pivot, ready to spring to her protection.

Noah pulls at an old man with wispy white hair who's got his hands wrapped in Frances's thick hair. She screams and tries to elbow him away from her, but his fingers are threaded through.

He growls, blood-soaked teeth snapping.

Noah tugs at him, the motion twisting the infected man's fingers deeper into Frances's hair. Her screams spur him on, and his snarls turn to frenzied howls.

Karma sinks her teeth into his calf and I suck in my breath. She's never bitten anyone. Dogs who bite people are put down, and I can't lose—

"Fucking do something!" Noah's howl snaps me out of my absurd tailspin. It's not a person, and Karma knows that as well as I do.

This man will chew Frances's face off. He won't let go. Unless his arms come flying off. *Come flying off...*

My gaze drops to the axe in my hand. *Shit.* There isn't another way, but I really don't fancy cutting a man's arms off. I don't even like cutting through sinewy steak.

Fuck!

Noah stares at me, his eyes tight with frustration. "Come on!" he roars.

Frances screams again, her voice vibrating with pain and fear, and I spring into motion. Closing the distance, I swing the axe above my head. A jolt travels up the handle when the blade hits flesh and bones.

My stomach turns as thick, dark blood sprays from the severed arm. The man doesn't react. It's as if he can't feel a thing, too hell-bent on digging his teeth into Frances.

I swing the axe again at his other arm that is still tugging at Frances' hair. Without the momentum from running, the axe slices through the sticky, soft flesh, then buries itself in bone. *Fuck!*

Frances grasps at her hair, tears streaming down her face.

I yank the axe free and swing once more. It breaks through the last bit with a crack that makes my skin crawl.

Frances stumbles forwards, tugging at the hands in her hair. Noah and the old man tumble to the ground, stumps flailing. Noah gives a hard push, jamming his knee between him and the infected man on top of him. His arms shake from the effort.

I can't risk grabbing the man by the arms. He's still got a mouthful of teeth to bite me with.

Karma yanks at the man's leg while Noah pushes with his knee. Rounding Noah, I help Karma pull the man off when something blurs in my peripheral vision.

A young woman with torn jeans and a bright-red scarf wrapped around her neck lunges at Noah. The back of her head is torn to shreds, the hanging skin and hair flapping as she rips and claws at Noah with frenzied, guttural snarls. Blood seeps from her eyes and nose, trickling down on a screaming Noah.

I need to help, but I can't release the old man. These infected don't stop. Not until they're dead. I shudder. It's Noah or them. Us or them.

Karma jerks and pulls, growls rumbling as she helps me pull the man away. He snarls in protest. I round him, his stumps flailing in the air as he tries to grab me. I can use my axe without the risk of hitting Noah instead. But I have to do it now. I *have* to do it.

I raise my arms and avoid looking at the bloodshot eyes that leak dark fluids, then push the thought of who he might have been before the infection aside.

When I bring the blade down on his throat, the ringing in my ears deafens me to any squelching sound. I force myself to lift the axe again. And again. Until his body goes limp, and my shirt is warm and sticky with his blood.

My chest rises and falls with the horror of what I've done, but I spin away and race back to Noah.

I don't have time to be horrified. I have to help Noah. The woman snapping and clawing at him isn't alive. She can't be. Not with that gaping hole in her head. I grab the red scarf with both hands and wrap it around her neck in quick motions. One, two, three times. Then I pull as hard as I can. Until my arms shake. Until I feel something snap, and she drops lifelessly to the ground by my feet.

I stare at the dead woman, my ears ringing. I killed her. I killed the old man. I had no choice, but I killed them. I stumble backwards and drop the scarf like it's burning hot coal.

Her pale white wrist lolls to the side. A golden chain curls around it, rounded gold letters dangling from it. Mum. Nausea washes over me, and I gasp for air, my shallow panting making me light-headed.

"Liv!" Frances gasps and I drag my gaze to where Frances darts past me.

A muscled young guy, with red bite marks puncturing his white sweater, reaches for Liv.

Her fingers wrap around his throat while his beefy arms slap at her. The corners of his mouth bubble with reddish-brown froth. Teeth marks blaze on his cheekbones and chin.

Despite being much smaller than him, she manages to keep him at an arm's length.

Noah scrambles to his feet. We set off to help her, but Frances swings her cricket bat like a pro player. It connects with Buff Dude's face, throwing him to the side.

Liv wastes no time and tugs at the rope again. I drop to my knees to help, our fingers shaking with adrenaline as Buff Dude rises to his feet.

With a mighty crack, Frances lands another hit straight in his face. He stumbles backwards. A primal roar erupts from her lips, and another cracking smack echoes through the air.

We pull and push with frantic desperation until the rope finally slips from the mooring ring.

"Go, go, go!" I grab Liv by the elbow and drag us to our knees.

Another group of infected swarms towards us. Frances swivels, and I point at the boat. She dashes the short distance, and Noah and I grab her hands to launch her across the short gap between the boat and dock.

Liv follows, then Karma pushes past Noah and leaps onto the boat, claws scratching against the deck.

Noah looks at me as though waiting for instructions.

"Push her out, then get on," I say.

He nods, and we push for all we're worth, then we scramble onto the boat.

Roy and Angela grab us by the shoulders. It's the only thing that keeps me from falling arse over tit.

We made it. I didn't think we would. I thought we were done for and the relief that we're alive has me shaking.

"You're okay, you're okay," Roy's voice soothes me as I try to catch my breath. "You're okay, kiddo."

I'm okay. Alive. I killed two people. I took their lives, felt their life force bleed out of them. But we're alive.

"I killed them..."

"You had to." Angela clasps my face with her hands, her warm brown eyes anchoring me to something real. It's only then I realise I'm crying.

33
LIV

JAKE STOOD BENT OVER, hands on his knees, head dropped. His back and shoulders bounced as he struggled for air. Noah flopped down on the wooden seating, not looking much better.

"Well." Roy wiped his forehead. "That didn't exactly go as planned."

"You think?" Liv could practically hear the glare in Angela's voice.

Liv had been too busy trying to keep the infected jock off her to see what happened. But she'd heard it all.

Infected prowled along the edge of the dock. A handful of lifeless bodies lay on the ground behind them.

Jake hadn't done all of that. She studied the large stains on his hoodie and joggers. Brown gunk mixed with blood covered him, some of it on his face as well. Maybe not all of it, but most of it.

Angela murmured something to him, rubbing his back, and he nodded in a stiff motion. Like he wasn't really listening. She turned to Noah, who leaned forwards onto his elbows. Bright-red blood soaked the blue silk shirt he wore.

She frowned. That looked an awful lot like fresh, uninfected human blood. Was he bit?

"Are you alright?" she asked.

"I'm fine," he said in a clipped tone.

If she were the regular pleasant type of person, she might have believed him. But she was not. Humans weren't trustworthy. Not selfish ones like Noah. She had a feeling that if he could gain something from it, he would sooner turn into an infected before admitting he was bit.

"Are you sure? Because..." She poked his shoulder. "You got something on you."

He slapped her hand away, his entire face wrinkled in annoyance. "I said I'm fine!"

She crossed her arms. "I understand that you're in shock right now, so I'll let this slide. But touch me again and I'll break your fingers."

His gaze flickered.

"Now I'm asking you because you've got enough fresh blood on you to not be alright."

His eyes grew into moons. "You think *I'm* infected?" He pointed a shaking finger at himself. As though it was the most shocking thing in the world that someone would hide the fact that they'd got bitten by... she glanced at the dock. Bitten by zombies. God, she hated that word.

"I don't know. Which is *why* I'm asking."

The others had stopped talking, all eyes on them and Noah's bloodied shoulder.

Frances cleared her throat. "I think what Liv is trying to say, dear, is that you're in shock."

Liv held back a snort. That was not what she'd been trying to say. That's what a doctor would say. And she was *not* a doctor. Doctors saved people's lives.

"Let's have a look at you, love."

"Fine." Noah glowered up at her but let Frances pull his shirt aside. No bite marks.

"I *told* you so."

The others glanced awkwardly at her.

"So I was wrong." She shrugged. "But aren't you glad we know I was?"

Judging by the look on the others' faces, they were. Frances gave her a berating look. "Of course we are, but would it have hurt you to handle things a little nicer?"

She shrugged again. They'd known each other for all of two minutes. What made Frances think there was anything nice about her? If she knew—if the rest of them knew—what she'd done, they wouldn't think of her as nice. They would see a monster. And they would be right.

She looked away from Frances and back at the shore they were leaving behind. Slowly, and—she cringed—loudly. Fareena had forgotten to mention one not so tiny, vital part: how fucking loud a narrowboat was.

The sounds attracted more infected to the dock. A man with a hollow eye socket and torn lips howled. For a brief moment, it looked as if he were going to launch himself after the boat, but then his body jerked backwards, and he let out another gargled scream.

She looked on in horrified fascination as he fought an internal battle of instinct versus logic, but in the end, survival instinct won out.

A tiny figure moved behind the man. A young boy. His glazed eyes pushed to the sides. His lips twisted around bared teeth.

His stripy blue sweater was covered in dark stains and the side of his head looked wet and sticky.

She wanted to look away, but she couldn't, as if looking away would somehow make it worse. What could make this worse? This crazy situation in which children turned to monsters. Attacked by God knows who, perhaps their own parents.

Egged on by the moans from other infected, the boy made a start towards the edge of the dock and stumbled on a dark lump that lay discarded on the ground.

He fell forward, and for a split moment, she wanted to run to him. To make sure he was alright. But then she saw the gaping hole in the side of his head. He wasn't a little boy anymore. Not the way he had been.

She shuddered. If the boy had been there only moments earlier, would they have had to kill him too?

She dragged her eyes away from the boy to the dark lump. Their bags.

"Shit... We lost two bags."

Jake's head whipped up, his big eyes even rounder. "What?"

She pointed towards the yellow and black bag. Jake's shoulders tightened at the sight of them. "That was most of the food we brought."

"Well, I know there are a lot of shops along the canals." Fareena gave the tiller a gentle nudge. "We can stock up there."

Jake dragged a hand through his hair. If he kept that up, that man was going to be prematurely bald. "Yeah, that could work."

"Perhaps there's food inside. Hopefully, they were Irish. Might find some beans under the bed."

"What?" Liv looked at Frances.

"Or spuds." It drew a breathy chuckle from Jake.

Liv blinked in confusion. Potatoes or beans. Under the bed. "You're even crazier than I thought."

"Aww, 'tis alright, love. I still got some stocked up for later." Frances smiled saintly and tapped the side of her head, then motioned towards the door. "But let's see what we find inside."

Noah was the first to duck inside. Angela gave Jake's arm one final rub before following after Roy and Frances.

"Hey, Hipster." Liv held out the one bag they hadn't lost, nodding towards the door. "Want to check out the boat we've knocked off?"

He let out a groan, pinching the nose of his bridge.

"Relax," she drawled, "it's not really theft if you have the key."

"That we stole."

"Borrowed."

"Fine. Borrowed."

She fired off a smile. “You learn fast, Hipster.” And with that, she followed the others down the small steps into the boat.

Painted wood panelling covered the inside, and the nice white colour lent an air of spaciousness. A modest kitchen opened to a small seating area where a black heater stove stood next to two windows. Outside, the water glided past, autumn-orange leaves floating on its surface.

A small pamphlet lay on the oak kitchen counter. “Look, they even gave us a boating for dummies.” She waved the small pamphlet at Jake.

Colour had crept back into his face, and a small smile tugged at his lips.

“Well, as knocked-off stuff goes, this one is pretty sweet,” he admitted. “Let’s hope it’ll get us all the way home.”

34
JAKE

It's two in the morning when Angela wakes us for our shift at the tiller. Fareena rolls out of bed and sits on the edge for a good minute, but then she's up and about as if well rested after a good night's sleep. With barely four hours of sleep, I feel like a hungover wreck.

"Tea for you and first-class powdered coffee for Fareena." Angela—bless her—points at a kettle and two mugs.

"You're awesome," I mumble. I'm rewarded with a tired smile and a quick hug before I shamble into the small kitchen. "Hear anything on the radio?"

Angela shakes her head. "Nothing new. All the stations say the same, no new information coming out of London."

We'd gotten halfway to Windsor when I'd remembered the windup radio stuffed in my bag. It's a cheap plastic thing, but it tunes in all the reliable radio stations. We'd gathered around it when the news anchor's voice cut through the chilly morning air. London was under quarantine.

The news reported that millions of people had been caught in the attack and even more were locked inside the quarantine zone. Fences covered with black fabric shield off large parts of London, keeping both the public and the reporters from seeing inside the Cordon Sanitaire. That's the fancy term being used by the authorities. Although it's already been dubbed The Wrap and The Outbreak Zone by the people.

I shiver at the memory. Too close. If we'd waited just a few more hours, we wouldn't have been able to leave. I try to shrug off the unease as I drag my tired arse around the kitchen to find my clothes. Karma cracks one eye open as if to say *nope, not leaving this bed* before going back to sleep.

"Traitor," I whisper before giving Angela an apologetic smile. "Sorry, guess it's a package deal."

"Oh, it's fine. Our daughter has three French bulldogs we babysit sometimes. *All* of them sleep in the bed..."

I pause where I stand. I didn't know she had a daughter. She folds her trousers before placing them carefully on the chair beside the bed. With her outward calm, it's difficult to imagine she might be worrying about her daughter, but now I sense a certain weariness to her movements. Maybe I should ask if she's alright, but now isn't the time or the place. And maybe it's none of my business. I settle for slipping into a pair of light-grey joggers, then I pull on my grey hoodie and black coat.

I'll admit it's not the most efficient clothing, unless one's goal is to look like a bum, and it doesn't provide much warmth. Despite having planned for something like this, the plan to leave in an orderly, calm fashion flew out the window the moment Claire smashed that door. As a result, we share two beanies and four pairs of gloves between seven people.

Beanies and gloves aside, we need to do something about clothes. Fareena, Angela, and Liv borrowed some of Megan's. Noah is taller than me, but he's also leaner, and while he fits into my clothes, my jeans are short enough that his ankles stick out. He could use new clothes as could Frances and Roy. I'm lucky; even though my grey joggers, clean and dried after today's mayhem, are all that I managed to bring, I still have clothes in my old room at Mum and Dad's.

I grab the mug, then kneel by the stove to add more wood. Angela and Roy have been out in the cold for four hours. They've earned a little toastiness.

"Sleep well," I say quietly to Angela so as not to wake the sleeping people in the bow.

"You be careful out there." Worry flashes across her face. It's the parent kind of worry, the kind my mum and dad occasionally wore.

"We will, I promise. Now go to sleep." I don't have to tell her twice—she's already crawling into bed when I step into the crisp October night.

Fareena leans against the railing next to the tiller with a tired-looking Roy, who still manages a friendly smile.

"Well." He holds out a beanie. "Looks like I'm about to finally get myself some sleep."

"Cabin's all toasty for you." I put the beanie in my pocket for now.

"Exactly what I like to hear," he says in his deep voice, "now y'all be safe." He gives one last nod, then disappears inside.

"Morning," I say and take a sip of my tea. I'm not usually this nice when I'm newly awake. I like my peace and quiet in the mornings, but this doesn't count as morning, and we're stuck out here for four hours. We're stuck on this tiny boat for a week, if not more. It's better to make it as pleasant as possible.

Fareena yawns out a "Good morning," her face scrunching with sleep. So not always an early bird. She takes the mug I offer, studying me as I sip my tea.

"Let me guess, PG tea?" She leans back against the railing, the tiller held firmly in her hand.

"Hell no." I grimace at the thought of what tourists call English Breakfast tea. "I don't even know how people drink that dishwater."

"Dishwater?" She feigns shock, puts a hand across her chest, and juts her chin as if deeply insulted.

I laugh quietly. "Seriously though, who thought that was a good idea?"

"It's an acquired taste, something you peasants wouldn't understand."

"Sure." I raise my eyebrows in mock agreement. "You know what I think happened? I bet someone brought some tea back from colonising China and it all went stale, and some knobhead aristocrat went and sold it as this exotic tea thing. And now every single Brit drinks horrible tea every morning and thinks that they made it."

She shakes her head. The universal *I'm not listening to you* shake.

"It's one thing to insult the crown." She sips her coffee with a serious expression. "But to insult our tea..."

I laugh and hold up my hands in surrender. "Oh, your highness, I meant no offence."

"I shall forgive your ignorance. This once." She gives me a playful nudge before we fall silent.

I drink the rest of my tea and watch the river behind her. I wonder if she's thinking of Andy. How long has it been since she realised her fiancé was most likely dead? A little over twenty-four hours.

I always thought the world without lights would be scarily dark, but without all the streetlamps and light pollution, the moon shines like a spotlight above us. The surface of the river reflects its light and the starry sky, although the night is pitch-black and impenetrable beyond the moonlight's reach.

We crawl through the canal, past fields, streets, and the occasional houses, with the engine chugging through the still night. I watch the water's skin ripple and curl as we slice through, listen to it splashing softly to the sides. Between running and avoiding crazed infected, I've been able to avoid talking with Fareena, leaving the *how are you doing* talk to others, but now it's just the two of us.

I scowl into the dark. It's not like I have to talk about *my* feelings. All I have to do is get over myself and be a decent human being. I take a quiet, deep breath. "How you holding up?"

"You mean besides the zombie outbreak and the destruction of the capital?" Her exasperated laugh turns into a sob. She clamps her mouth shut and shakes her head, but the tears she fights keep on falling, leaving liquid trails down her cheeks.

I shouldn't have asked. If I'd kept my stupid mouth shut, maybe she wouldn't be thinking about her dead fiancé and crying her eyes out. I suck. And I don't even have a cup of tea to offer the girl. I mean, I do, but I don't think she wants my leftovers.

I bite the inside of my lip and look away. *Not at all awkward, Jake.* My mind needs to shut up and stop being an arsehole.

Fareena turns her head so I can't see her crying, but her shoulders shake, and I try to imagine what I'd do if she were Megan. When Megan cries, I don't feel awkward; I feel heartbroken, helpless, and I want to wrap her in my arms to keep her safe from hurt.

An odd sort of ache fills my chest. I surprise both myself and Fareena when I pull her into my arms and hold her close, the same way I'd hold Megan.

Megan called it the burrito. She thought it was the perfect kind of hug because it made her feel safe. A memory of when things were better between us flitters through my mind. I know I shouldn't be thinking of Megan. Thinking about her hurts, and I'm not good at hurting, but it's as if the heart or the brain—one of those fuckers—is prone to arseholishness, and it messes with my head at inopportune times.

Fareena presses her face to my chest. I'm glad she isn't as tall as Megan, because then her face would be buried at my neck. It would remind me too much of her. Of how her lips would trail up my neck as she shivered on top of me and the way she'd look at me sometimes. Before everything changed. Before *I* changed. I close my eyes. Thinking of Megan only awakens all kinds of locked away, crazy emotions. And this is not the time for crazy. The infected handle that part well enough on their own.

I don't know what to say, but then again, sometimes words aren't needed. I stay as I am, and—responsibly enough—keep a watchful eye on the canal so we don't veer into the bank.

When her shoulders stop shaking, I let her go and lean back to look at her. "Better?"

"Ish." She smiles and pulls a napkin from a pocket. "I mean... what the fuck is happening? And then Andy and all my friends, and even Jules. They..." She pauses briefly. "They just took her. And I'm worried about my family, and I..."

"I know," I say and draw a breath. "I'm really sorry."

She swipes at her cheeks and blows her nose into a piece of tissue. She brushes at a wet patch on my coat. "Sorry for getting you all messy."

"A few tears never hurt anyone."

"Actually"—she smiles sheepishly—"crying has a tendency to involve snot. Especially ugly crying."

I shrug. "Well, we're sharing a bed already, so I guess we're at that stage in our relationship."

She bursts into sparkling laughter, only this time it doesn't end with crying. And, yes, I will totally take credit for that.

"How are *you* holding up?" she asks.

"What do you mean?"

"I'm not the only one who's lost people," she says. "I know you told me you were breaking up, but not like this."

I dig my teeth into my lip and scratch the nape of my neck. "No, this isn't quite how I pictured it..."

She doesn't say anything, only waits for me to elaborate. Parts of me want to, parts of me don't. I don't know Fareena. I don't know what I feel comfortable telling her.

"I mean, we've been broken for so long"—I brush the back of my hand against my beard—"but we just kept going."

"Why?"

I shake my head. Damned if I knew. "We've been together for seven years—"

"Seven?" Fareena gasps, her eyes growing moonlike as if I've grown a second head, "how do you even do that? Three years, that's my longest."

"You don't even want to know how long my parents have been together then."

She waves her hand dismissively at me. "No, that's different. Parents *have* to stick together. Because they're still part of the *no divorce* generation."

"Yeah, well, I don't even know if our seven years really count. Four of them have been sort of... a struggle."

"Do you still love her?"

The question takes me by surprise, and I inhale slowly as I ponder the question. We still say *I love you*, but it's more out of habit than real love. Obviously, it doesn't mean the same thing it used to mean. It no longer means we can't get enough of the other's company, that their presence is the one thing that makes us feel whole.

I picture Megan's face, picture us how we used to be, how we used to laugh together, take on the world as if—together—we were invincible. I love that Megan. That Megan still gets my heart racing wildly, but that Megan also loved me. Unconditionally. Well, I grimace, that's what I used to believe. Now I know that there isn't such thing as *unconditionally*.

"I don't know," I admit. I've been telling myself for so long that I'm over Megan, and I am, but I don't know if I've worked through what that actually means. Right now, the only thing I feel is pain, but that is something I can't tell someone I barely know.

"Hmm." Fareena averts her eyes and gazes out across the length of the boat.

I watch her, how the moonlight shadows half her face, as her almond-shaped eyes rest on the river ahead of us. I like Fareena. I don't know her, but what little I know I like. A lot. She's genuine, and I get the feeling that I can trust her. Maybe it's her kindness or her disarming personality. Or the fact that she can hot-wire almost anything, but having someone like Fareena on my side is a good thing. Maybe, this one time, I should risk trusting someone new.

"She's sleeping with my best friend."

Her head snaps towards me. "Oh, Jake..."

"Yeah." I give her a lopsided smile. "We've been broken for a long time. I knew we'd have to address it sooner or later. But... I guess it's hard to digest the fact that she's happier with someone else. And now, she's most likely gone." I release a frustrated breath. "I'm a little fucked up about it."

"What she did, for whatever reason, it wasn't right. You deserve better." Her brows draw together to emphasise the last word.

I can't help but smile; she sounds so convinced it's true. "In fairness, I'm not perfect," I say, because God knows that's true.

"Err... you got us out of Westminster, let us crash your entire plan to get to your parents, *and* you're sharing all your supplies. That makes you pretty perfect in my book."

"I'm not going to be able to convince you otherwise, am I?"

She shakes her head.

"You're taking my side?" I narrow my eyes at her in suspicion. "Just like that?"

"*Just like that*?" she repeats. "Don't you understand? You confided in me, and I've plastered my tears and snot all over your chest. We are truly comrades in arms now."

"And you saved my life."

"That too."

"Does this mean we're Best Bitches Forever or something now?"

"For*ever*." She leans back with a satisfied smile on her face. "Now, bestie, fetch us a cuppa, would you?"

We spend the rest of our shift exchanging stories. Fareena reveals the basics of picking a lock. Her older brother Affie suffers from the inability to not lose his keys. Instead of backup keys, he taught Fareena and her two younger brothers how to hot-wire and break into his car.

And was this the only car she ever broke into? I ask, drawing that laughter from her that makes her already incredible eyes bright. It doesn't escape me that we change the subject to me and that she never actually answers the question.

I list the most painful places to get tattooed on. Unsurprisingly, she cringes when I point at the thin skin on my throat, right above my Adam's apple.

I'd worried the night would drag and that I'd have trouble staying awake, but by now we've passed so many locks, I've stopped counting. As it is, jumping in and out of the boat to manoeuvre the locks keeps us both warm and awake. The ten cups of tea might also have helped.

I lean against the railing with a yawn and slip my hand into my coat pocket. I dig out my pack of cigarettes as dawn breaks through the darkness, maroon and orange bleeding into the sky as the sun starts to climb the horizon.

I slip out the cigarette that isn't turned upside down. Four more in this one, then I need to crack open the box of ten packs. After that, if this thing doesn't blow over, and I can't get more cigarettes... I grimace. Well, my life is pretty much over. Not to be dramatic or anything.

"I knew I could smell fags." The lilt in Liv's voice sounds from the door.

I scowl. "Oh, she's back." My cigarette bobs up and down on my lip as I speak.

"That is no way to speak to the person who is currently holding your breakfast hostage."

The mention of breakfast gets my stomach rumbling. Liv cradles two bowls of what looks like oatmeal from a few of the field rations that made it onto the boat. Until we've got some more food, we rationed whatever we managed to bring. Never thought I'd say it, but I'm dying for some oatmeal right now. Unless I'm completely absorbed by something, hunger is one of the things I don't deal well with, so right now, any food will do.

"Trade you breakfast for a fag." I wiggle a cigarette in the air.

"Deal." Her head gives a little bob. She holds out the bowl, but before I can grab it, she yanks it away. "Not allergic to peanut butter, are you?"

"Not really." I frown, hand still out.

"Good." She hands me a bowl and snatches the cigarette. "You'd make a good prison daddy, Jake."

"Err... thanks?" I shove a spoonful into my mouth, careful not to get oatmeal stuck in my beard. "How did you sleep?"

Liv snorts. "Well, if it wasn't the endless noise I had to put up with, I would have slept perfectly fine."

"Engine that bad?" I grimace. Back here by the tiller, the chugging noise isn't so bad, but where Liv and Frances sleep, it might be worse.

"Engine? I'm talking about Frat Boy who snores like someone's demented grandma."

Ah, yes, Noah. Who insisted on sleeping in the only single bed because he's "not comfortable sharing a bed with someone he doesn't know."

"That better not be me you're talking about," Frances says as she and Angela climb to where we're sitting.

"Wouldn't dream of it." Liv's features soften ever so slightly. "You're not demented."

"Cheeky bugger." Frances gives her a gentle slap and sits down next to Fareena.

"Why are you guys already up?" Fareena asks with a yawn.

"Well..." Angela rubs sleep from her eyes as Roy ducks out from the small door. "Liv wanted cigarettes, but the rest of us wanted to keep you company."

I chew my oatmeal, my chest warm with the feeling of companionship, and marvel at the taste of my breakfast. Usually, oatmeal is a big lump of glue-like goo. This is smooth, slightly salty, with a velvety texture. Surprisingly good for field rations used by the military. "This tastes better than I expected."

"It's not very common in your cuisine, is it?"

Despite my best efforts, I look at Noah with one of my say-what-now expressions. Not because I don't want to take this fight, but because I know he's trying to connect. This is what people always do. They try to compliment you by inadvertently exotifying you. I know I'm different. I know I look and act different. What I don't know is why people feel the need to always point that out to me.

"I don't think peanut butter is that uncommon here in Britain, but you should know that as well," I say casually and wait for the inevitable protest.

"No, but I mean, like, *your* cuisine. Where you're from," he clarifies.

"I know." I put the spoon down and look at him with a tired expression. "I'm from Huntingdon."

"Well, yeah, I know that," he starts in a defiant, almost annoyed voice, "but I mean—"

"Oh, for goodness' sake, Noah." Frances rolls her eyes. "It's like you've never seen an Asian man in your life. Now shut up and eat your oatmeal."

He glares at her with the anger of a thousand fiery suns. "I was only trying to make conversation."

"I know, love, but next time try the weather." She pats his hand gently.

"Well, you have this handsome fella to thank for the oatmeal." Angela changes the subject, leaning into her husband, who wraps his arm around her. Roy?

Roy lifts a shoulder and drops it with a self-conscious pull at his lips.

Angela gives him a gentle nudge with her elbow. "He's acting modest, which doesn't suit him."

"Why would anyone be modest about cooking oatmeal?" Liv asks.

"Because once everyone finds out you can cook, you're the one stuck in the kitchen," he replies, clearly speaking from experience.

"Just how well can you cook?" Fareena asks before taking another bite of her oatmeal.

"Well enough to own the best seafood restaurant in all of Louisiana," Angela replies when Roy doesn't answer, instantly prompting the others to pepper him with questions.

I frown into my oatmeal as I realise I don't know much about the others, not even the basics like what they do for a living. I know Frances is a nurse, Angela is a copper, Fareena works in a clothes store, and now I know that Roy is a restaurant owner. That leaves Liv and Noah.

Noah, with his slicked-back hair, can't be anything but a broker or banker. Definitely something that rhymes with banker, at least.

Liv. She sits at the far end, away from the rest of us. She seems to purposely distance herself. I watch her with thinly veiled curiosity. She looks weary, with dark circles around her eyes and lines I hadn't noticed before. Her hair hangs limp as she slouches to stare somewhere beyond the canal, and her fingers tremble ever so slightly. She brings to mind the homeless junkies I see on my trains. The restless skittishness as they wait for their next fix, the eyes that constantly scan their surroundings while avoiding any and all contact with other humans.

She notices me watching, and her fingers curl into a fist. I blink at the sudden, antagonistic reaction. "You okay?" I ask.

"Fine." She stuffs her fisted hand between her arm and ribs, pretending to warm it.

"Okay, cool." I shrug. Six years as a tube driver has given me the ability to read people, and I know she's hiding something. But there's no point in pressuring her. If there's one thing I understand, it's privacy. We might have fled London together, but that doesn't mean we know each other yet. Until then, I think we're allowed our own secrets.

I thumb my leg absentmindedly. The canal is wide here, and lines of bushes and trees race along its sides. Beyond the trees, hills of brown and green dip at the horizon, with a greying sky looming above. It's October, and England doesn't disappoint with its crisp autumn mornings.

We're somewhere between Reading and Oxford, though we can't pinpoint where. I once dated a guy in Oxford. I used to complain about the three-hour train journey it took from home to Dominic's, but this boat is even slower. We're starting our second day and we haven't even reached Oxford yet. Once we do, we still have four days left to go.

Four days is a lot of time for things to go haywire, but I'm hoping Dad gets to Mum and Tim before me. Most of all, I hope the military has quarantined the infection. But I've read too many books, played too many games, and watched too many films to put my faith in that.

I pull the collar of my coat closer. No point in stressing out about things I can't control—as if that logic has ever kept me from fretting about things. I clear my throat to chase away my worries and take a drag from a new cigarette. For a moment, I think that maybe this is a habit I need to kick. I snort to myself. If this infection doesn't die out, I might have to quit, unless we stock up on some much-needed supplies soon. Maybe the next lock will have a shop.

I pull out my phone and swipe until I get to Google Maps, hoping it would help me locate some shops near the canal. The blue GPS pin still hovers over my house. I tap it, and it doesn't move. I hold my phone up in the air as if that might help my poor reception.

"How's that working out for you, mate?" Liv looks at me in amusement.

"Taking a selfie." I drop my arm into my lap. "Am I the only one who can't get my phone to connect to anything?"

"Haven't been able to get anything on either of our phones." Roy shakes his head.

Fareena, because of her previous experiences on the canal, is the unspoken boss of this ship. And she's the one currently sitting with the canal maps in her hands. If anyone would be able to find a nearby shop, it would be her.

"Hey, bezzie mate," I say, and she looks over with a grin, "do we know when we'll find some shops?"

"We don't know, but *I* do."

I snort. "Only because you've probably memorised the entire route, nerd."

"Okay, hold my tiller," she orders Noah, who gives her a sour frown.

"Why?"

"Because I'm going to kick some ninja boy arse."

"I don't even know karate!" I protest, hands held up in the air, which draws laughter from the others. Noah might not be aware of it, but a grin works its way onto his face before he resumes glaring into space.

"Sure, you don't," Fareena says dismissively. She sits down beside me and unfolds the map on her lap, then points at the blue winding line. "This is where we are. About eight miles up is the closest shop."

"Eight miles?" I ask. "Surely there must be something closer?"

"Of course, there is, but if you know of any shop that opens before eight, I'm open to suggestions."

Ah, yes. There was that.

“It’s only eight miles. What’s the worst that could happen?” Noah says from the tiller, drawing groans from the rest of us. Normally? Not much. Now? Let’s hope we don’t find out.

35
LIV

ONE MISTAKE. THAT'S HOW it always started, whether it was hers or someone else's. Infected people were running around the streets in London, eating other people. The government was trying to blame it on terrorists, but Liv could sniff a liar from miles away. And the Prime Minister was lying through her teeth. Someone important had screwed up somewhere along the line. Whether it was the military, the government, or the bloody PM herself, someone else's mistake had landed Liv on a boat full of strangers. Whether this was a good or bad thing, she was yet to find out.

She glanced at Roy and Noah, who stood by the railing. Being stuck with a bunch of strangers was, without a doubt, a downside. On the other hand, she was far away from London. Whatever was happening there—the military, the quarantine—she'd seen scenarios like that before. In case studies, in catastrophe simulations, and on the news.

The morning had started on a good note. She'd woken up fairly well rested; someone had fed her, and Jake had given her the mandatory morning fag. And even if life dictated that all good things must come to an end, she wasn't planning on letting her head demons get to her just yet. Not until she had something to battle it with.

She fidgeted, her leg bouncing up and down. Breakfast and nicotine could only get her so far before the crawling underneath her skin began, shortly followed by the shaking and sweating. Normally she could counter the shakes and cold sweats by popping a few Xanax or Valium, but she only had one blister pack left. One. After that, she was out. Of both alcohol and her medicine. Or as her therapist had called it: her comforter.

She'd laughed when her two-hundred-quid-per-hour therapist had told her that drugs and alcohol, in cases like hers, were often used to keep people at a distance. She could pull better proverbs out of her arse and she didn't have a degree in psychology. At least the session had been part of her so-called rehabilitation and therefore paid by the crown.

She grimaced at the first sensation of an odd tingle, her skin prickling as if ants were crawling all over her. Clenching and unclenching her fist briefly suffocated the increasing intensity of the ants.

She blinked, trying to focus on something other than the unpleasant sensation that crept through her muscles.

Roy's voice drifted towards her, and she shifted her gaze towards him and Noah. The two men were talking by the tiller, Roy pointing at the canal, then back at his hand that moved the tiller. Noah followed Roy's movements, and he almost looked interested. But then when Roy looked up at him, he averted his eyes and crossed his arms.

Roy didn't seem to notice, or if he did, it certainly didn't bother him as he kept instructing Noah on what to look out for when steering the boat.

She watched them for a while, then turned her attention elsewhere. It was only so long you could watch people before it went from curious watching to creepy staring.

A creaking noise caught her attention. Karma's wide head pushed the door open before she climbed out of the cabin. Liv stared at her, still not entirely convinced Karma wasn't a small horse.

Karma stood sniffing the air, then turned her big, sad eyes towards Liv. Another sniff. A heavy sigh, then the big dog walked over and plonked her butt down right in front of Liv.

She frowned at the dog who sat there staring at her, looking forlorn. "What?" she finally asked. Karma replied by moving her weight from one hip to the other, her enormous paws tapping the floor.

"No." Liv slashed with her hand through the air. "I'm not doing that."

Karma let out a half growl, half whine, stretching her neck as she lifted her head towards Liv. She shook her head, drawing a frustrated snort from Karma.

"I am *not* doing this whole 'who's a good girl' thing." Liv narrowed her eyes at the dog, whose tail instantly started to wag at the words. It started at the tip that reminded Liv of a paintbrush. A small wag, then despite Liv shaking her head, it spread along the entire tail until it beat happily against the wooden flooring.

"You." She finally succumbed and scratched the big ears, much to Karma's delight. "Are such a brat."

"Oh, boy." Sitting down next to them, Roy wiped his bald head with his hand. "You're in for it now."

"Don't I know it?" She sighed at the squishy-faced beast sitting by her feet.

They fell quiet for a while, she gently pulling at Karma's ears, Roy staring out across the canal somewhere.

She watched him for a bit. From what she'd seen so far, Roy always looked so together. Like he had all his ducks in a row. Like someone reliable.

Reliable. Now that was a word she didn't much like. All the reliable men she'd ever met turned out to be anything but. Doctor Pratt, the chief surgeon who had a wife and three children and an acquired taste in expensive women. The coppers who looked away for the right price, who protected their own over the people. The politicians, the weed of the galaxy. They all seemed so reliable, so trustworthy, offering empty promises and complacency.

She considered the man sitting next to her. His entire presence radiated a sense of dependability, and he didn't seem to fit in with the other men she'd met. Not only because of the way he acted towards the people around him, but because of the way Angela was around him–strong, confident, and happy. How Angela would glance at him for reassurance or even to just sneak a peek of him.

Liv grimaced. Maybe her good people radar was just broken.

"You'd think they'd let us get a call through." Roy's voice interrupted her thoughts.

"You know, you can barely get a call through on New Year's Eve. This is probably ten times worse than that, with all the people trying to ring family," she pointed out. "And don't forget, we're in the middle of nowhere now. Reception here is shit on a good day."

He gave a slow nod. "Maybe once we get closer to a bigger city we can get a call through."

Who was he so desperately trying to get through to? "Miss your restaurant that much?" she joked.

"Miss my kid that much," he said in a voice that was softer than usual.

"Oh." She averted her eyes, gluing them to the riverbank. If she looked at Roy, something in his face would remind her too much of herself. Another silence settled between them. She wrung her hands together, pressed in the softer spot between thumb and index finger to add sensation. Taking focus away from other thoughts.

"She, uh, was starting her new job this week, so we wanted to celebrate with dinner on Friday." Worry tinged his words, and she remembered a time when worried parents would look to her for comfort. What was it Doctor Tennant had said? Always ensure your patients that all efforts were made to bring the situation under control.

"I'm sure they'll have it fixed by then."

He chuckled. "You are an even worse liar than my kid, but thank you for trying to help an old man feel better."

She bit into the stupid grin that tugged at her lips at the simple compliment. These people were too nice, and parts of her wanted to believe in it, but she couldn't afford to trust them, to make another mistake. Not again. Not when her life might depend on it, and right now that was the only thing she had left to lose.

36

JAKE

"WHAT IS THAT?" IT'S noon by the time we reach Wallingford and Fareena points at the white web that coats the trees and bushes along the canal, which look like gigantic cocoons. They remind me of all the oversized spiders I've killed in World of Warcraft. I shudder. I really hate spiders. Please don't let those be cocoons full of giant spiders.

Liv leans out the side of the boat and squints at the web. She's brushed her hair back into a ponytail and yet somehow—inexplicable to me—it still looks as messy as a bird's nest. She, Roy, and Noah took the watch while Fareena and I got some much-needed sleep.

Frances woke us up when BBC aired news footage for the first time since the attack on London. The telly on the boat was small, but showed us all we needed to see. When the reporter started by saying that The Wall around the centre of London now reaches nearly ten feet, I thought he must have got that wrong. But then the camera panned over to the wall and the entire boat drew in a sharp breath.

Large shipping containers stacked on top of each other dwarfed the military in front of it, making them look like miniature tin soldiers. A shot from above the Cordon showed large gaps in the wall where instead of containers, high-rising barbed wire fences have been erected.

When asked about the containers, viewers are told that our fellow EU countries have loaned us as many as possible to help with the Cordon.

"Would you say the other countries are doing it to help or to protect themselves?"

There's a long moment of silence, the spokesman staring awkwardly at the black microphone muffler as if it might launch itself at him at any given moment.

"I assure you, our fellow European countries simply want to assist with the Cordon Sanitaire." For everyone's safety, the spokesman explains, then expertly changes the subject. But in a voice that is too calm and too polished.

More than a few million are still stuck in the quarantine zone, and I wonder if those fences will keep a few hundred thousand frustrated people at bay.

But then I see the military helicopters circling the air above the Cordon, and the troops stationed on top of the containers. The military has already shot at civilians. By the looks of it, they won't hesitate to do it again. Infected or not.

"There have been reports of infected attacking people by biting them. How safe are the rest of England and UK from this infection?"

There was no way to avoid the question now that it's been asked. "It is true that patients infected by the residue show signs of extreme aggression, and unfortunately some have been physically violent towards others." Most of what he said was true, but he left out the part where the infected feed on the noninfected people.

The public is still advised to stay indoors, and the immediate areas around London have been evacuated as a precaution. Other larger cities like Manchester, Birmingham, and Leeds have implemented a lockdown: residents are not to go to work or school for the next week. They're doing everything they can to prevent the spread of the virus whose infection rate has increased in the past twenty-four hours. The sick are being transported to a safe facility outside the Cordon Sanitaire. But to where, the spokesman won't answer. We'd been discussing all of this until Fareena spotted the creepy webbing.

"Is that spiderweb?" Noah asks from the tiller. "If that is spiderweb someone else will have to go instead of me."

"Oh, don't be daft," Frances says in an amused voice. "They're more scared of you."

"Also, they're not even spiderwebs, genius." The annoyance in Liv's voice is obvious. "They're larvae."

Noah glowers. It seems the two of them have a rivalry going, and I think it might have something to do with that bag full of clothes Noah chucked at the infected.

"That's not making me feel any better, Liv." Fareena shoots Liv a dirty look.

"You know in some countries they say it's protein," Liv says flatly, but I swear I can see her bite down on a smile as Fareena pulls a disgusted face and slaps her.

I study the eerie webbing and have to fight the urge to slap the sudden crawling feeling on my neck. I'm still slightly freaked out, but I'd rather dodge slow larvae than fast spiders. Or infected humans, for that matter, but so far, we've spotted no signs of infection.

A tinny trill cuts through our chatter, and we look around in confusion. It sounds again, then Roy flies to his feet, shoving his hand into his pocket.

"Baby girl?" his voice quivers as he presses his phone to his ear. We watch him for a few dumbfound seconds before the rest of us quickly pull out our own mobiles and start dialling.

It rings three times before I hear the familiar click as someone picks up the phone.

"Jake?" my mum's voice whispers down the phone in disbelief.

"Mum?" I almost laugh from sheer shock and relief when I hear her voice. It feels like a lifetime ago since I last heard it.

She lets out a noisy breath. Her voice trembles. "You got out. I thought..."

"Mum, I'm alright, but what's happening? Did Dad tell you? The infected were attacking each other, and the military were shooting at civilians." I've switched to Korean now, and it feels like my words tumble out of me. I'm surprised she can even hear half of them.

"Your dad didn't tell me, but they flew him out to Catterick. Jake, I don't like this one bit. He told me to prepare."

"For what? Mum, do you have enough food and water to last until I can get to you?" The prepper in me kicks in. I don't have time to worry if I want to help my mother prepare.

"Jake..." she says in the same voice that would ask if birds fly.

"Alright, okay. You and Tim should stay indoors until I get there. But prepare a bag with the essentials, enough for seventy-two hours, in case you need you leave. Keep it near you at all times, okay? The PM isn't telling the truth."

"If she was telling the truth, your father wouldn't be at Catterick," Mum mutters.

"No, Mum, listen, they're not just infected, they're eating people."

There's a long silence before Mum speaks again. "The Lysurus... Your..." Static crackles through the line. "...in London... months... your work..."

"What? Mum? You're breaking up. Hello?" I look at my phone. The call dropped, and I redial her number, praying I can still get through.

"Jake?"

"Yes, our call got cut. Listen, Mum, stay hunkered down, don't go out. They say it's in Manchester now. If we got out, how many more did?"

"I will. I'm going to go pick up your brother from school." Her voice is tight with tension.

"Okay, promise me you'll go straight back home, Mum. No dillydallying."

She laughs. That's what she used to tell me when I first started walking home from school on my own. "No dillydallying," she promises. "I love you."

"I love you too. See you soon."

"See you soon, darling. Be careful."

"I will," I say, then we hang up and I look up from my phone.

Fareena grins, and her head bobs as she speaks to someone on the phone and wipes her eyes. The others are on their phones as well, but whereas Angela and Roy tell their daughter they're alright, and Frances speaks in soft whispers to her sister, Noah thumbs rapidly at his screen.

Noah's face is all hard angles, giving him an attractive, masculine edge as his jaw clenches, brows dropping low, eyes scanning up and down his screen.

He looks up, eyes locking with mine. Now I don't know whether to quickly look away as if I haven't been staring, which only makes it more obvious I was, in fact, staring.

I settle for smoothing it over with a question. "You get a billion notifications as well?" I thought he would give me one final hard stare, but he moves towards me.

"Look at this."

I'm not sure whether I should be appalled or impressed at his Twitter feed. Someone's started the hashtags #ItsAWrap and #LondonFastFood, because why wouldn't you?

The feed updates with new tweets every second. Tweets from family members that haven't heard from their loved ones within the Cordon. Others tweet theories of what's going on or why we aren't hearing from within The Wrap. Jokes about wraps and fast food fill the timeline.

"They think it's a joke." Noah's brows pinch together. "How can they think it's a joke?"

"People are arseholes, that's why." Liv squeezes in between us and peers down at the screen.

"Wait, stop." A few tweets stand out, but one in particular has caught my attention. 'It's not a joke. It's real. #FromWithinTheCordon.' A video sits at the bottom of the tweet, and I press it.

It's a video dated October 1. The video is dark and blurry with a large building lit up in the background. Loud and shrill voices ring out while dark shapes push past the camera. It's unclear what they're fleeing from until something at the far back claws and rips its way through the screaming people. One infected, followed by hundreds more, throw themselves at the crowd, dragging the fleeing people to the ground. The video catches the first few seconds when the infected digs its teeth into a screaming man's shoulder, then the video starts shaking wildly as the filmmaker runs.

"What the fuck?" Liv whispers and presses the replay button. It plays again, and the next time we update, the view count has gone from fifty-two views to three thousand and counting.

"Check the replies," I say.

Eighty-nine replies. Some doubt the video is real. I would have as well, but I was there. We all were, and we know the video isn't fake.

"Look at that one." Noah points at a tweet.

@SylWindrunner *If this is real, the video has made it outside the Cordon. What else did?*

@ThreeNugsTall *No. Who else did?*

37
LIV

WALLINGFORD WAS A SMALL village with thin roads that barely fit one car, yet somehow was still considered a two-lane road. Brick terrace houses with white walls and large gardens lined the street they walked on. It was like something out of a TV show or as if someone had dropped her down in the middle of a secret childhood dream.

Apple trees with red apples, perfectly mowed lawns, families who strolled along the uneven pavement holding hands with their curious but well-behaved children. It was almost as if London wasn't being swarmed by infected and quarantined. If she didn't know any better, she could almost forget the chaos and mayhem they'd left behind.

It left a bitter taste in her mouth.

They passed a hatter, a pub, a wool shop, and a pizza place, where the smell of newly baked pizza made her stomach rumble. She glanced at Jake, whose steps slowed ever so slightly, his head turning towards the restaurant's windows before he continued walking.

"Vegan Giardiniera," she said, loud enough for Jake to hear it.

He turned his head. Something often seemed to sparkle in his eyes, and she couldn't tell if it was amusement or curiosity. Maybe even both. "Calamari."

"Pizza dough balls," Frances said, encouraging Liv's appetite.

"Their Caesar salad with anchovies." She pulled a disgusted face at Jake and even Angela looked a little doubtful which, considering her husband owned a seafood restaurant, said quite a lot.

"Anchovies on salad, what even is that? The chavs' idea of luxury?" Noah said, his voice sardonic.

Jake tutted. "And there I was almost contemplating getting us all pizza, but apparently it's not good enough for Noah."

"You lost me a pizza." She glared daggers at Noah. She could murder a nice pizza right about now. Or perhaps after a glass of whiskey. Sharp pain coursed through her veins, and she swallowed to keep the nausea at bay. Yes, whiskey first, food after. Priorities and all that.

"Noah," Frances said in a berating tone, "I wouldn't have minded a pizza." She continued in disappointment. To Liv's surprise, Noah had the good grace to look a little ashamed.

"Well, I thought it was funny..."

Frances turned away from him. "Now I know we're bit pressed for time, but I've got to stop at Costa."

They had left Fareena and Roy to guard the boat by the boat club's mooring spot, which technically was breaking the "upper class's boating laws." But they wanted to get to safety sooner rather than later, which had them up against the clock, and they'd all agreed to break the rules one more time.

Frowning, Liv followed the older woman as the street opened to a quaint-looking marketplace with flower beds and brick paving. There, squeezed between Lloyds Bank and Barclays, like some poor sod caught between two enemies, was Costa. "Why Costa?"

"If I'm not going senile, I remember owing someone a cup of coffee for getting me out of the city."

Liv let out a laugh. She'd forgotten all about that, but Frances remembered. Not that she had planned on cashing in on that coffee. With running away from human-eating people and all. But it still made her feel like someone cared for her. It was stupid, of course it was, and she should know better than to allow herself that feeling.

"Actually, that's perfect. While you do that, I'm going to pop into the pharmacy." Jake hooked a thumb at the white building they just passed.

"Would you like anything from Costa, love?" Whenever Frances spoke, she reminded Liv of what she had imagined a loving mother must sound like. It was what she thought she remembered her own mother's voice had been like.

"No, I'm good. Thanks." He gave a small wave with his hand before he strode off towards the pharmacy.

Liv followed him with her gaze. He looked like a proper bum. Grey joggers, a black coat, and a beanie to keep his thick hair in place. In London, no one would bat an eye, but she'd lived and worked in a small town. Jake looking like he did, tattoos and all, might not get the warmest of welcomes. She'd already seen how some villagers had eyed him when they passed them on the street. Jake, however, seemed oblivious to it.

"Hey." She put her hand on Frances's arm. "We'll meet you outside Waitrose in ten?" *I'm helping him because if he gets stuck arguing, then this will all just take longer*. That was the only reason she was willing to waste time and effort going with him.

"Alright, dear. Black or with milk?"

"Just black, please." She smiled and set off after Jake.

"What are you doing?" he asked, suspicion in his voice.

"You look like an absolute bum."

"And just how is your presence supposed to help with that?"

"You really woke up this morning and chose violence, huh?" She gave him a playful dirty look, drawing a chuckle from him before continuing. "Unlike you, I had a shower this morning."

He stopped in his tracks. "I only didn't because I'm working out later."

Working out? Where? They were on a narrowboat, and it was called narrow for a reason. "So, what's this working out deal, anyway?" She watched him out of the corner of her eye as he started to walk again.

"I like to keep in shape."

"Are you one of those who *has* to work out without a shirt on?"

A soft laugh slipped across his lips. "Sometimes."

"Can I watch?" It was a joke. Mostly. Jake guffawed. *Well, this is different.* Making people laugh wasn't what many would call her strong suit.

"How about you join me?" Jake's voice interrupted her thoughts.

"Uh... no." She pushed the marine-blue door open. "I don't work out at the best of times, let alone without a shirt."

"That's not what I meant." A blush climbed to his cheeks as they stepped into the pharmacy.

"Sure, you didn't."

The pharmacy was small, and she let her gaze wander around the mint-green walls as Jake made his way towards the blue letters that spelled out 'prescription.' They were so big even her dead grandma would be able to read them.

"Hello," he said politely once he reached the counter. She grinned and shook her head. He was such a Boy Scout.

"Hello!" The young girl, whose nametag read Chloe, smiled sweetly. "How can I help you today?"

"Can I pick up a prescription for Jake Hyun, please?"

"What is the prescription?" The girl, with her—obviously dyed—red hair, was all bubbles and sunshine. Liv already hated her. No one could be that nice for real.

"Sustanon, but is there any possibility that I could get an extra lot? I'm visiting family and won't be going home for a bit. You might have seen what's going on in London?"

Chloe's eyes widen in a mixture of excitement and apprehension. "Oh, yeah, it's crazy what's going on there. Lucky timing you were visiting family now."

"Yeah." He chuckled softly. "My house is on the inside of The Wrap, so I can't get my meds."

Chloe gave him a soft-eyed look, though a small wrinkle creased her forehead. "Unfortunately, we can't do that, though. I'm sorry. You could contact your doctor. They might arrange extra prescriptions due to your circumstances."

"Okay, yeah, I've had to do that before," he said, a flash of disappointment touching his face.

"What's wrong?" Liv asked as Chloe left to fetch his prescription.

He let out a long breath. "I lost all the medicine I brought. Back at the marina. Three months' worth of medicine down the drain."

She studied him carefully. This could be the excuse she'd been looking for. She chewed her thumb. As far as other human beings went, Jake wasn't half bad. She watched the small crease between his brows grow deeper as he tapped the counter with his debit card. *Click. Click. Click-click-click.*

"Okay. Stop, stop." She put her hand on top of his. She had to help him, if for no other reason than to stop the irritating tapping. He looked at her in surprise, and she quickly withdrew her hand. "What's your dosage?"

"Why?" He narrowed his eyes at her. *Ah, a fellow sceptic.*

"Tell me or I won't help you."

"Right now, one ml every two weeks. Wait, what are you doing?" he said, sounding alarmed when she reached for the phone hidden behind the counter and dialled the number.

"Hello," a familiar voice answered.

"Hello, David."

"Olivia?" To say he sounded baffled could possibly be the understatement of the century, but for all the things Liv could blame him for, that wasn't one of them. She did tell him to get bent last time they spoke.

"You know I hate it when you call me that," she said, channelling her inner Chloe. She was met by silence, and she sighed. "Oh, don't sound so happy to hear from me."

"I am. Of course, I am," he amended quickly. Just like old times. "I didn't expect to hear from you. You weren't exactly happy when last we spoke."

Still talks like a poncey twat. "Yes, well, I need a favour."

"A favour?" Amusement filtered into his upper-class accent.

"For a friend." She grinned into the receiver.

"I don't hear from you for—what—six months and when I do, you're asking for a favour." He paused. "For a *friend*."

"Yes." She knew where he was trying to go with this. "No, I'm not shagging him." Somewhere behind her, Jake coughed.

"Alright, I guess that's in his favour," he said, the amusement gone from his voice.

"Right, well, if you hadn't gotten engaged six months after our divorce, that might actually offend me."

"Yes, well, if you hadn't been otherwise," he paused purposefully, "occupied, I might not have."

What was the reply to that? She could tell him she hated him. It would be true. But it would help no one, least of all her. And however much she hated him, there was one person she loathed more, and it wasn't David. "I need a prescription."

"A prescription? For what?"

"I need three months' worth of Sustanon prescribed to Jake..." She turned to look at Jake.

"Hyun."

"Hung?" She cocked her head at him, her mind going to inappropriate places.

"No, *H-y-u-n.*"

"Oh. That would be Hyun."

"And would you like some chips with that, ma'am?" David said, his voice dripping with sarcasm. Although she could still hear his fingers tapping on the keyboard.

"Actually, I'm having pizza later." She put on a fake jovial tone. She might need David's help right now, but she'd be damned before letting him know the emotions coursing through her.

"Of course you are," he replied dryly.

"And make that pronto. We're at the pharmacy right now." She looked up at the perky pharmacist who stood, arms folded, lips pursed, looking decidedly unimpressed. "Oh! And while you're at it, throw in some Diazepam with that."

"Diazepam?" *And who would that be for?* She could hear the unspoken question in his voice.

"So how is Lisa? Not chewing someone's face off, I hope."

"Christ, Olivia!" he said in disgust, forgetting his question. "She's fine. We're *both* fine."

"Right. Well, thanks for helping." In an odd way, she meant it, even if she made it sound more sarcastic than even he deserved.

"Wait!" His voice stopped her before she could hang up. "You didn't have to go. I never wanted you to go."

She laughed, and she could imagine the indignant expression growing on his face. Of all the empty words he'd ever had spouted at her, those might be the winner. She could have stayed? In the guestroom of her old house with her ex-husband and his newfound love. Sure, if she had no self-respect whatsoever. And if being near him wasn't too much. Too complicated, reminding her of what she'd been and done. Of what she'd lost.

"Bye, David." She hung up before his voice made her remember things that were best locked away.

"Are you quite done?" The pharmacist glared her down.

"Yes. Thank you." She fired off a smile that was ignored by the pharmacist. "You should have a few new prescriptions for this guy." She patted Jake on the chest, drawing a bemused look from him.

"Thank you, Liv," he said in a pleasant low voice. His brown eyes were almost black as he studied her. "You didn't have to do that."

She felt like he could see right through her. Past the rough exterior and into a place where no one was allowed. She'd noticed it before, on the boat earlier that morning. It was the kind of look that could tear down walls.

"Yes, well." She turned away from him. "You owe me pizza."

38

JAKE

Liv pours whiskey into her coffee as we make our way down a particularly dull aisle at the grocery store. It's the aisle no one really goes to, unless they forgot Aunt Dorothy's birthday, and are in dire need of an overpriced, cheap-looking birthday card. At least that's Liv's explanation for its existence.

She sips her coffee and closes her eyes with a sigh. Whether from the alcohol or the coffee, she looks a lot more relaxed.

"You know, I don't think that's what Frances had in mind when she bought you the coffee."

"Of course she did. Irish coffee."

"I don't know," I say sceptically. "I think you might just be a pirate."

At that she simply spins around mid-walk, *arrs* like a pirate, and wiggles the mug in the air, then continues her saunter and disappears around the corner.

I shake my head and grin as I follow into the next set of aisles.

"We should get cereals." She slips her finger along a shelf as she makes her way through the aisle. "And yoghurt. Everyone likes yoghurt. If not, I'll eat it for them."

I have the completely rational fear of finding slugs in my yoghurt or anything that comes out of a carton. Cait used to joke about it being a wonder that I can function as a normal human being with all my "eccentricities."

"The expiry date on those things isn't optimal." It's a sound excuse. Liv shoots me a glare before returning to peer into the shelves.

She's wearing Megan's lumber jacket and the bird's nest in her hair almost looks like part of the ensemble as she inspects the shelves. They're stocked with colourful packages of blue, red, orange, and whatnot. A stark contrast to the bland white walls and lime-green labels.

She pulls to a stop, peers into the shelf, then digs around with her free hand. "Gotcha," she snarls victoriously, then a blue package sails towards the trolley and lands with the loud rustle of plastic wrapping.

"Jaffa cakes?" I pick up the package. I'm not sure what Liv thinks we're doing, but I've had to put back a handful of "useful" things she's added to our groceries. A latte wisp for her Irish coffees, a pan which she planned to use as a zombie smacker, and dummies to shut up Noah's whining. It was very tempting to keep them, but I'm also considering a change in shopping partner. Sending the others to get clothes from the secondhand store next door might not have been my smartest move.

"For when everyone's grumpy because of all that inspiring food..." She lifts her chin and purses her lips at the cans that make up the majority of our shop.

"Somehow, I think food that lasts takes priority over old lady snacks."

She gasps and narrows her eyes. "What did you call me?" She snatches at the package, but I've had years of practice with Megan and easily pull it out of arm's reach.

"Nice try." I chuckle, but it catches in my throat when she pushes me backwards against the shelves and reaches for the cakes. To her credit, she gets a good grip on my wrist, then pulls herself closer to the package—and me.

She's almost as tall as me and when I tiptoe out of her way, her face is level with mine. Her clothes smell like Megan, and she's pressed so close I can't protect myself from the onslaught of emotions.

It seems like only yesterday since Megan and I were like this, when she was this close. It hits like a freight train. Megan's gone. I lost her. And yet all my senses tell me she's right here with me. Her scent, the warmth of her body against mine, and the red and black of her favourite jacket.

We used to muck around like this and every time she'd win because I adored her smile when she did. I let her have the package as I gently cup her face with my hands, revelling in the soft skin I know so well. This is usually the part where she turns away, pushes me away, leaving me aching for her. This time, she doesn't.

I swallow against the burning sensation in my throat as hazel eyes blink in surprise. Dark-brown—not red—hair tangles around my fingers. I don't know which hurts the most—that she's gone, or that if she were here, she'd push me away.

"Liv?" My brain is fuzzy, like I just woke up from a weird dream. Liv's eyes dart side to side, and I can't tell whether her expression is bewildered or if she's about to punch me. "I'm sorry, I don't know what... you smell like her and..."

"Oh, there you are, we been loo—" Frances stops abruptly, and I drop my hands to my sides as we quickly withdraw a safe distance from each other. Frances tilts her head ever so slightly, giving us a once-over.

An awkward silence settles between the three of us as Liv guzzles her coffee. Frances's lips twitch in an amused smile. "Right, well, why have hormones if you're not going to use them?"

I open my mouth to protest. "That's not what I was doing."

"Mm-hmm." She takes the Jaffa cakes from Liv's hand and drops them in the trolley. "Let's get on with it, then."

"Right." I clear my throat and watch her stride past only to catch Liv sign to me from where she stands, pointing at the Jaffa cakes, then me, then herself.

You–me, nil–one.

39

LIV

She should have punched Jake. Or kissed him. Maybe even both. She let out a frustrated grunt. The upside of alcohol was that it settled the crawling in her skin and the whispering voices from her past. It gave her stomach that warm, fuzzy feeling that made everything and everyone so much more tolerable. On the flip side, it also turned her libido into an unreliable, middle-aged man with a midlife crisis connected to his crotch.

At least Frances had impeccable timing and, Liv noted, looked curiously different in her new clothes. Gone was the starch nurse's uniform, replaced by a blue shirt, jeans, and leather boots. So this was Frances when she wasn't being Nurse Bradigan.

"I see you clean up well," she said, leading them into the next set of aisles. "For an old lady," she amended at the amused look on Frances's face.

"Oi!"

"You look great. I'd take you on a date, but I fear you might break my heart." Jake put a hand on his chest and fired off a wickedly charming smile.

"Piss off, you!" Frances chuckled, the corners of her eyes crinkling as she swatted his hand from his broken heart.

"You're such a knob." Liv rolled her eyes just as a sharp voice carried down the aisle, catching their attention.

"This is not the brand I usually buy." An older, frail-looking woman shook a tin can at a shop assistant.

"I'm sorry, we only have the brands that are on the shelves," the shop assistant, a young boy no more than sixteen, replied. He gave an uncertain wave of his hand towards the shelves, following it with one of those youthful, polite smiles. The unsure smiles that were followed by an awkward squirming that only young people displayed. With his ginger hair styled with too much gel, he reminded her an awful lot of a boy called Ed.

"I have come here for fourteen years and bought the same bloody soup, and now you're telling me this rubbish is all you have?" She wore an old lady pink smock dress with an eye-dizzying floral pattern. Her wrinkled, veiny hand clutched the can so hard the knuckles turned bright white. "I don't know *what* this country is becoming."

The assistant, Liv noticed, had the great misfortune to wear a grey vest on top of a stripy shirt with a pin badge the size of a fist. She could read the text all the way from where they stood watching the pair. *Ask me anything*. Poor sod.

Old people were the worst. They had this well-earned fuck off and die attitude about pretty much everything. Stealing? It's not stealing when you worked hard your entire life, raised five children with some bloke you could barely stand, and then got left to survive on pittance.

They had earned that jar of pickled eggs stashed somewhere in their Zimmer frame. They didn't need to pay; they had sacrificed enough. Standing in line? Filter what they say? Sod that, they had sacrificed *enough*. This was the privilege of age.

"Someone's in a bit of a strop," Frances said in a low voice.

"Old people are the worst though," Liv replied. If she had to list three things that she avoided at all costs, old people would definitely be on that list.

"Ruthless." Frances dropped a can of peas into the trolley.

Liv wrinkled her nose. "Poor Ed."

"How do you know his name is Ed?" Frances's forehead wrinkled.

"He looks like an Ed."

Frances shook her head. "Whatever that looks like, numpty."

"Madame, we have many other quality pea soups. I can help you find one you like."

"Are you simple? Don't speak English?" the old lady asked, overpronouncing every word, the white of her dentures showing. "I said I wanted the *same* brand I've always bought."

Liv frowned. This one was nasty even by mean old people standard.

"Yes, but—" Ed said in an attempt to placate her.

"Listen, you snivelling brat," the old lady snarled, "I've had a headache for days, and I want some fucking soup." Metal flashed, then a startled yelp followed a loud thwack as tin connected with the young man's eyebrow.

"Whoa!" Jake pushed into motion, arms held out in front of him as he moved to stand between the two. Although Liv was fairly certain he was trying to protect Ed more than the old lady who stood wielding her can like a pair of nunchakus.

"You're crazy!" Blood trickled down the side of Ed's face as he dropped his hands to his sides, balling them into fists. But instead of taking a step forward towards the can-wielding lady, Jake's body stopped him.

"Alright, calm down." Jake's gaze dropped towards the nametag on Ed's chest. "Jonah."

Jonah? She stared at the boy. That was not a Jonah. Clearly, his parents failed this whole name giving process, not that hers had been much better at it.

"Yeah," the lady's voice came out in a hiss, a nasty grin spreading on her lips. "Stay calm, *Jonah*."

Way to bring up the creep-o-meter, lady.

"Please, put the can dow—" Jake's words caught in his throat at the sight of the old woman. "Your eyes..."

"What the fuck?" Ed whispered.

A rattling cough silenced them both. Liv wasn't sure Jake was aware of it, but he grabbed Ed by the shoulders and steered him towards where Liv and Frances stood. She frowned. What was it about the woman's eyes that made Jake back away like a man facing a bear, hoping his movements wouldn't cause it to attack?

"What?" the old lady asked, watching Jake and Ed. "I just wanted some soup." Her eyes rolled back and forth like she was trying to keep them straight but something kept pulling at them. *Exactly like Claire*. Intraocular pressure?

"Some soup? You *hit* me in the face!" Ed howled, holding up his hand to show her the blood.

"Alright, come on, chicken." Frances put her hand on Ed's arm and gave it a gentle squeeze. "Let's get you patched up."

He turned to look at her, eyes wide, his anger slowly draining. "Yeah, okay." He gave a weak nod and allowed Frances to guide him away from the old lady.

Liv studied the old lady closer, looking for anything out of the ordinary, something she could attribute to the infection. Headaches and severe pressure on the eyes. And the flu. Claire had displayed flu-like symptoms like coughing, muscle aches, and a high fever. Could Claire have caught the influenza before getting infected? Maybe the influenza and the infection were separate from each other.

Or maybe... she felt a chill run through her. Maybe the influenza and the new infection were the same thing.

"What is the likelihood of influenza and infection being two different diseases?" she asked Jake.

"I'm no genius like my dad, but it's too much of a coincidence."

She nodded. Jake was thinking the same thing. The new influenza, the infection. They were connected somehow. And despite what the government might claim, they didn't have things under control.

This was Wallingford, a small village out in bumfuck nowhere, and yet this eighty-something-year-old lady was showing similar symptoms as Claire.

Her train of thought was broken by the can clattering to the floor. Smock Lady lifted her hand to her nose and wiped crimson blood from it with surprise.

"We should go." Jake nudged Liv by the shoulder.

"What about her? If she's infected, we have to warn people."

"We'll tell the cashier at checkout and call that government number. Come on." He nodded towards the end of the aisle. "We should get a move on. We don't want to be here once the cavalry rolls in, not if it's anything like London."

40

JAKE

"WAIT, SO WHAT, THIS bloke didn't notice her eyes at all?" Fareena asks in disbelief.

Frances clicks her tongue and shakes her head. "He thought she was just cross-eyed, bless him."

"What did the manager say?" Angela says.

"I don't know; he seemed like he didn't believe me but said he'd look into it."

We made our way back from Waitrose and now we sit around the small dining table, waiting for the pizzas baking in the oven. I promised Liv pizza, and I'm a man of my word.

I look through the door to the tiller where Liv stands. It may not be fancy Pizza Express, but I'm pretty sure she won't say no to hot cheese and peperoni while stuck in the cold to keep watch.

"And you're sure she was infected?" Roy looks at us solemnly.

I'd asked Liv the same question on our way back. To make sure I wasn't being paranoid after London. But she'd said the same thing. The coughing, nosebleed, and weird eyes couldn't all be a coincidence. "Liv says she's certain. With the eyes and everything else, I think she's right."

"Well... shit." Roy scratches the back of his head.

"Did you see anyone else who could've been infected?" Fareena's eyes dart between our faces.

"Well, it's bloody difficult not seeing infected everywhere when the symptoms are sneezing and coughing," Frances says and sets down the mug she's been sipping tea from.

"I'm glad we're getting the hell out of here." Roy slaps the table with his palm, then gets up to check the pizza.

I grin. He might say he doesn't want to be stuck cooking, but it hasn't escaped me that every time a meal is being prepped, Roy's the one to do it. And not because no one else will do it, but he hovers. Behind you. And he's a big guy; he casts a very large shadow. In every sense of the word.

"But if it's in the big cities and now a small town like Wallingford..." For the first time since we got stuck in the tunnel together, Angela's positive mask falters. Her eyes dart towards Roy. She wants to go home. Maybe even more so after having spoken to their daughter.

Roy moves from the oven to his wife and starts humming a song. His voice is deep like a rumble, and he squeezes in next to Angela, who smiles and leans into him.

At first, I think it must be an inside joke or something only they'd know, but then slowly I recognise the song and I laugh as Roy sings the chorus to "Ain't No Mountain High Enough." It's a higher pitch than he can sing and halfway through the song he forgets the words. But it doesn't matter. Not to Angela. And it's pretty clear to the rest of us why.

Nothing in this world will stop Roy from bringing them home and, for now, she believes him. For now, it's the only promise she needs. I hope he can keep his promise, but as I get up from my seat, unease creeps up my back.

If this infection keeps spreading, if we're on the verge of an epidemic, the airports will shut down to prevent further spread. They're already trying to quarantine cities. If the quarantines don't work, the rest of England will be next.

41

LIV

THE EVENING WAS QUIET, the others busying themselves preparing dinner. She usually enjoyed the quietness, but lately the only time she was left with her own thoughts was during the nights when everyone was either asleep or on watch. She'd handled it like she had in prison. Simply blacking out memories, names, and faces. Like redacting a document in case it fell into the wrong hands.

Her eyes wandered the dusky evening landscape past tall oak trees, buckthorn bushes, and open fields with yellowing tall grass. The green water mirrored the lifeless sky above them, impenetrable clouds giving the appearance of being stuck inside a snow globe. It was the kind of sky that best described England's weather in October: cold, bleak, and depressing.

She lifted her gaze and spotted a small bridge arched above the canal, the multiple shades of its grey stones reminding her of the small flower bed David had insisted on building in the garden of their new home.

It had been late October when they'd first gone to see it. If she thought about that day long enough, she could almost smell the wooden floors.

The walls were white, and the tall windows opened into a well-kept garden. A glossy white panel skirted the lower part of the walls, adding—what David called—a fresh and modern look to it. More like sterile.

She let her fingers slide along the panelling as she walked around the room. Not a single speck of dust. She wanted to scoff, but the owners were in the hallway behind them, so she settled for a simple frown. Who the hell kept their flat this clean? She barely had time to change nappies, let alone keep their place tidy.

"It's perfect, isn't it?" His footsteps echoed oddly against the tigerwood floorboards that matched the colour of his leather shoes. "I know *you* think it's perfect at least," he murmured. Not to her, but to a small boy with David's dark eyes and her pout when he got in a sulk.

"Fine." She smiled and shook her head, then turned to look at them. Slowly. Savouring the moment for some other time.

Liv sucked in her breath sharply, ripping herself out of the memory. Some places weren't meant to be visited again. Not ever.

She closed her eyes, pinching the bridge of her nose. She shouldn't have called him. She knew this would happen. A shiver ran through her, and she shoved her hands into her pockets. Her fingers brushed against the small package. Her pills, the black marker pen to redact her memories with.

Pulling it from her pocket, she squeezed one, two, three pills into her palm. She could worry about running out later. She raised her hand towards her mouth, then grabbed the bottle from the other pocket. Throwing her head backwards, she guzzled as much as she could, then closed her eyes and counted the seconds until numbness settled in.

"Holy hell, you drink *a lot*." Fareena heaved herself up on the deck.

"Thank you." She could see a frown working its way across Fareena's face.

"That wasn't a compliment..."

Liv ignored her as a lovely calm buzzed through her limbs, settling like a warm glow behind her eyes. It made her feel so good. Made her forget.

Fareena shuffled beside her, and when Liv bothered to look, she saw Fareena sat on the railing, legs dangling. Fareena didn't say anything else, only stared—perhaps in contemplation—across the canal.

They both stayed silent for a long time, simply focusing on keeping watch.

"I remember going on the boat with my aunt, but I don't remember it being this beautiful," Fareena broke the silence, hands clutching the railing for support. The clouds from earlier had dispersed, or maybe it was the pills doing their job. Either way, the evening sun painted the side of Fareena's face golden, giving the illusion of a warm summer's night as they glided through still waters.

They'd passed a few moored boats earlier, but other than those few boats, the canal was quiet and calm. Travelling on the narrowboat was like stepping into a magical fantasy world. The pace was completely different on the canal. Not only because they weren't allowed to go faster than four miles per hour. There was something peaceful about being surrounded by fat geese and curious ducks calmly going about their business. Even Liv had to admit that.

"It's nice."

"Oh, it is more than nice." Fareena let go of the railing and reached for the plate on a stool between them. Two cakes remained. Liv was pretty sure Fareena had managed to eat most of them by herself.

"It is awesome because—Jaffa cakes." Fareena popped an entire cake into her mouth. She looked like a chipmunk as she closed her eyes and chewed it. "Jake got us cake," she said around the spongy cake and orange jam in her mouth. "But not only that, he also brought *pizza*. He's kind of perfect."

"So, your standard is set to a pizza delivery boy?" Liv took another sip from her coffee.

"When it's possibly the end of the world? Um, yes."

"You realise *I* was the one who picked up the Jaffa and helped him with his prescriptions? Therefore, I'm the one who made it happen."

Fareena quirked a fashionably bushy eyebrow in Liv's direction.

"So really, I should be your standard." Now that was a sad thought. A standard even lower than that of a pizza delivery boy.

"Maybe if you combed your hair once in a while..."

"It's called naturally chic." She shrugged and peered at the rest of their group through the door's small window.

She'd been left to her own devices while they prepped dinner. Not that she was complaining. A small narrowboat with six other people didn't allow for many opportunities to be alone. Though her solitude had been short-lived now that Fareena had come to keep her company. Company. Of all the things she didn't need more of...

Karma lay sleeping by her feet. The dog didn't count because she didn't try to make pointless conversation. Karma didn't pry or ask questions. And that was how Liv liked it. Questions led to answers, and answers always led to people thinking they knew her. Or inevitably—if she didn't answer—led to them trying to figure her out. With Karma there were no awkward silences, and she really wasn't comfortable with uncomfortable silences.

"So, what do you think Noah's deal is?" Fareena mused with a jut of her chin towards the window where Noah stood, eyes focused on something in front of him.

"I don't know, I think he's just an arsehole in five different directions." It drew bright laughter from Fareena, who leaned backwards and eyed her.

"I like you. I think we're going to be good friends, you and I."

Liv snorted. Friendships were never what one expected them to be. They were always a letdown. Loyalty and honesty in friendships was like finding the Scottish unicorn. "Friendships are a fickle thing."

"Maybe you've just had the wrong friends."

"It's nothing personal." She looked away from Fareena's soft expression. Trusting people left you vulnerable to deception. The fewer you trusted, the less likely you were to be betrayed. "I don't have friends because I don't need them."

Liv stiffened, thrown when Fareena wrapped her arms around her in a long, hard hug.

"Everybody needs a friend," Fareena said. Then, releasing her grip, she smiled and ducked back inside the boat.

Liv glared in annoyance after the girl who'd dared to steam wheel into her personal sphere. And it wasn't only Fareena. It was everyone on this godforsaken boat. They kept coming at her with friendly gestures and kindness. It made her feel like she was part of something. Only, she didn't know how to do that. She never had, and she never would. It was simple. One couldn't sow in poisoned soil. Nothing grew there. It would only wither and die or grow into something ugly. Still, there it was, the tiniest feeling threatening to grow into something unless she squashed it before it grew too big.

42

LIV

When Jake had described his arm as a 'big fat whale,' she thought he'd exaggerated just a tad.

She stared at the monstrosity that was his lower arm. It was dark purple, almost black, and swollen to the point of bursting.

"Jesus." She prodded the yellowing around the bruise, which drew a hiss from Jake. No wonder he had trouble carrying some of the groceries back.

She'd first noticed something when he ducked through the door and dropped the cricket bat. The funny thing about having an enormous swollen bruise on one's forearm was that bending over caused a considerable amount of blood to rush towards the arms, resulting in a throbbing that must have felt as if it was going to split his skin apart. Judging by his loud grunt and sudden jerk upwards, she'd known he was hiding something.

She prodded it again, which drew an annoyed yelp from him. "Do you have to keep poking at it?"

"Yes, I need to know the extent of the damage." She twisted his forearm back and forth. There were no visible bite marks, and his skin was unbroken but swollen. "He bit you, you said?"

Jake nodded. "Like a rabid dog. He wouldn't let go."

"Human bites are extremely dangerous. There's so much shit in our mouths that the bite can cause some serious infections. You're lucky he didn't break your skin."

"Felt like he was going to break my entire arm." He snorted, but she was too busy thinking about what she'd just said to reply. Infections caused by bites. She blinked, feeling her forehead crease with thought.

"Jake, that woman, Claire. Do you know if she was bit?"

"Err..." He scratched the back of his head. "I don't know. Jules said she had the flu."

"Hmm." Maybe she was being paranoid. She let go of his wrist and pointed at the swollen bit. "Care to explain why you didn't tell anyone about this?"

"I thought it would go down."

Her irritation flared to life. "Well, it won't if you don't treat it properly. Did you put ice on it?" She couldn't remember seeing him with ice at his house. Unsurprisingly, Jake shook his head. "You're an idiot. Even a child knows you ice an injury like that."

"Wow, you really have a way with people." A dark scowl pulled at his mouth as he carefully rolled down the sleeve of his hoodie. It was the first time she'd seen him look anything resembling angry, and though it shouldn't bother her, for some reason it did.

"I only meant that..." She paused. If the infected had attacked them on their way back from town and his arm didn't work properly, he could have been hurt. The same went for the others.

She kept the frown from her face. The thought bothered her. Why the hell was she even worrying about them in the first place? And why was it Jake's responsibility to keep the others safe? Shame and guilt reared their ugly heads and she turned away.

It was his responsibility because she didn't trust Noah or herself. She had since long perfected the ability to drink and take her pills with no one noticing, but that didn't mean her mind worked as it should. There was a reason she couldn't look down at her feet too long, or even dream about running in a straight line, when she was on her medication.

Medication. A voice in her head snorted. *Mixing alcohol with drugs isn't being on medication. It's being an alcoholic junkie.*

"Hey." Jake frowned, his eyes cast downwards. "Your hands. They're shaking."

She quickly shoved them in her pockets. They shouldn't be shaking already, not after such a short time without... what she needed. "I'm just cold."

"Here." His expression softened as he held his hands in the air in front of her, palms facing each other.

She hesitated. But then a smile tugged at his lips and she sighed, holding up her own hands between his. She'd expected his hands to be warm. Why else would he offer them? But sweet baby Jesus, they were like hot furnaces, almost melting her hands between them.

"Holy shit."

"Yeah." He grinned. "It's my superpower."

"My hands are also cold. Are you going to affectionately warm mine as well?" Noah's voice drawled from behind Jake's back.

Turning his head, Jake quirked an eyebrow. "My hands are all full up."

"I bet they are."

"You can have my armpits though," Jake offered and was rewarded by a disgusted noise from Noah. "Some people are so ungrateful." Jake shrugged as Noah went back to reading his book.

"Aren't you supposed to be main watch?" Liv asked, though she already knew the answer. Noah was the next person up, taking over from Jake. She wasn't thrilled at the thought of spending time alone with him, but at least it was only an hour until Frances took over Liv's shift. One hour, then she could get some sleep.

"You're here as well. You have eyes," Noah said without looking up from the book.

Annoyance boiled to life. This bloke was such a selfish, lazy bellend. She would have punched him in the dick—with her foot—if she could get away with it. And if it hadn't been for the sudden rustle of leaves and branches somewhere along the riverbank.

"What the hell was that?" She fished the small torch from her pocket and peered around Jake.

"What was what?" He turned, squinting at the sharp white light that she shined along the bank. Up and down trunks, back and forth, casting thin, long shadows wherever it went. Nothing. She aimed the beam at the red and yellow leaves on the ground. She could have sworn she heard something. She was beginning to think she'd imagined it when she heard it again. A rustling sound. Like someone raking leaves. Or running through them.

"Kill the engine." She flicked her light to the side, illuminating nothing but empty space.

"It's not like they haven't already heard us," Noah sighed.

"Fucking kill the engine," she hissed.

"Fine." The engine cut to an abrupt stop, and dead silence settled over them. She dragged the beam of light from one side to the other when Jake suddenly grabbed her wrist, stopping the beam in place.

"There." He pointed towards a gnarled tree with reddish-brown bark. She narrowed her eyes, staring at the trunk. There was nothing. She could see nothing. "Look at the ground."

A long, spindly shadow crept from behind the trunk, its arms and legs casting spidery silhouettes on the leafy ground. But it was standing completely still. Infected? No, they made gurgling or high-pitched screeching noises. And they certainly didn't hide behind trees. They chased and fed on everything. Everyone.

"He could be after the boat." Noah got to his feet.

Jake nodded and reached for the bat as he moved to the edge of the boat. "Maybe they need help."

"Wait." They'd run into enough tough situations to be reckless. "Let me try something first." She switched off the light, the button giving a sharp click as the light died out. Then, before whoever was behind the trunk could get too close, she switched it back on.

Nothing. The shadow was still there, like a patient predator lying in wait for its prey. She tried it again, waiting a little longer, but the shadow remained. Maybe it was just branches tricking their already skittish minds?

She tried again, silently counting in her head. One, two, three, four, five, six... The sharp crunch of leaves breaking under someone's weight startled her and almost made her forget to switch the torch on.

It moved towards the next tree with such speed they barely had time to see its shredded clothes and the grey, ripped skin that curled off limbs and arms, revealing rotting flesh.

It stopped dead in its tracks, turned to regard them, then let out a feral shriek. At first, she thought its high-pitched shriek bouncing around in the dark was an echo. As dark shadows moved in the field behind it, she realised those weren't echoes.

Those were answers.

43
JAKE

THEY'RE SO QUIET. I see their movements behind the first infected. Fast and deviously soundless as they speed through the field. Zombies aren't supposed to be quiet or *hiding*. They're supposed to be slow and mindless. Shambling about, moaning for brains. These infected are fast. And—a small, terrified voice in my head whispers—*smart.*

A twitch rattles the one by the tree, and his head wobbles as if it's barely hanging on. Its torn skin curls in revolting ribbons around dark-red flesh, and uneven yellow lumps cluster the surface of the flesh.

I shudder and lift my eyes, then suck in my breath. Something sticks out from his eye sockets. No. Something is *growing* out of them.

Red tendrils curl up and over his lids, latching on to his rotting skin. They've pushed the eye almost entirely to the side, but what little I can see looks weirdly yellow.

Movement jerks my attention from the horrifying face. The other infected, at least a dozen, are right behind him. Their heads are thrown back as if scenting the air. Scenting us.

"Ah fuck!" Noah throws a hand up to cover his nose, and Liv covers her face with her arm, breathing into the bend of her elbow. I couldn't smell the man before, but now that the rest of the infected have joined him, their stench is overpowering. They smell of something dead that's been left out in the hot sun for days. With a touch of shit sprinkled in for extra pungency.

I gag into my elbow when the smell hits me, and it draws Karma to where I'm standing. She sniffs the air, then tenses and growls as she heaves herself up on her hind legs and rests her paws on the railing. Her hackles raised, she watches the infected, a growl rumbling deep in her throat.

"Easy now." I give her neck a reassuring pat. She relaxes under my touch but keeps a steady eye on the infected.

Karma is a French mastiff, nothing but brawny muscle, and I don't doubt that she could take out at least one or two of the infected. That would still leave at least ten, if not more, that could take her out just as easily. The thought makes me feel weirdly vulnerable.

I put my arm around her and give her a gentle squeeze. “You stay right next to me, you hear that?”

She lets out a loud sigh as if to agree, albeit begrudgingly, before dropping to the floor.

“Good girl.”

“What the hell do we do now?” Liv speaks into her elbow, voice muffled.

“You wake the others while Noah and I keep watch.” I grab the bat that leans against the door but pause when I see her face. It’s a face of utter what-the-fuck-did-you-just-say. A face I’ve seen on Megan on more than a few occasions. *Oh shit.*

Liv fixes me with a penetrating stare as she slowly reaches down for the bat, not once breaking eye contact. Then she grabs it with one swift, determined motion and moves over to the railing without a single word.

Noah gives me a sympathetic grimace.

I clear my throat. “Right. I’ll wake the others.”

“At least they can’t get to us,” Fareena says as our group observes the infected from the deck. The short distance between us is unnerving, and I try not to ponder whether they could reach our boat if they lean over the edge of the riverbank.

They don’t. They pace around instead. Restlessly. Growling and shrieking in frustration. But every time they get close to the edge of the canal, they jerk back as if stung by fire.

“Do you guys see that?” I ask and point at the infected that just lurched away from the edge.

“I saw them do the same thing when we left London.” Angela hooks a small garden tool with three bent, pointy metal fingers, in her belt. “Could it be self-preservation?” she asks with a hint of fascination.

Self-preservation. Infected who cared about staying alive. Exactly what we need.

Liv shakes her head. “But when the soldiers shot at them, they just kept going. If they cared about not dying, why keep going?”

“Um, hello? I think we have more pressing matters at hand.” Fareena motions towards the riverbank. “What do we do about them?”

“Well, like you said, they can’t get us right now,” Roy says. “Maybe they’ll tire waiting for us after a while?”

"I don't know, mate," I say with a sigh. "But that one and the rest were lurking in the fields. And the one hiding behind the tree was very patient. I don't think they'll just go away."

"We have a motor, you know," Noah says impatiently.

Liv lets out a snort. "Have you heard our engine? If that guy didn't already alert every infected in town, good old *Gloria* will do the job for him."

"Okay, well, I have good news for you," Fareena says. "There's a lock just ahead of us."

A lock. That takes at least ten minutes to fill, twenty if we're unlucky, and barely twenty centimetres between the boat and the paved sides of the lock. If these infected follow, they'll be on the boat before the water is high enough for us to escape.

"How is that good news?" I try to keep the frown off my face.

"Well, because it means we don't have to argue about what to do. Also, I figured for morale's sake, it was better than 'guys, we're fucked.'"

"She's not wrong, you know," Frances says. "But what exactly are we going to do?"

Roy puts his hands on his hips, the way he always does when he means business. "We have to get off the boat. On the other side of the canal."

I liked to call myself a prepper, with bug out bags and all. But when push came to shove, instead of quickly grabbing my bag to leave, my first thought is how impractical it is to leave the boat. We'd be left without a vehicle, and we've stored all the new food in the cupboards. Not in our BOBs like a proper prepper would. I curse. Prepper? Liv was right. Fucking Hipster is more like it.

"Okay, so say we leave. What's to say they won't just follow?" I shove a thumb in the infected's direction. "Those lurkers don't seem to be the stupid kind of infected."

"How about a magic trick?"

A magic trick? We all turn to stare at Frances as if she's completely lost her marbles.

"What, like a card trick?"

Frances tuts and scowls at me. "Do I look like feckin magician? I mean, make them look elsewhere so they miss spotting the trick. Now you see me, now you don't."

"Oh… alright." Fareena nods her head and grins and I'm glad I'm not the only one who thought Frances was going bonkers. "So, what is the trick?"

"Well," Frances draws out the word, staring at Liv. It takes Liv a few seconds to realise we're all looking at her.

"What?" Something flashes across her face. Apprehension, then anger? "No." She shakes her head. "No!"

Angela's eyes dart between the two of them. "What?"

"I am *not* throwing away another whiskey," Liv hisses. "Someone else make a Molotov."

Angela's mouth falls open, Fareena and Roy's face mirroring hers. Frances just grins and Noah looks almost impressed, observing Liv with a new light in his eyes.

"A Molotov," I echo. First a hot-wiring lock picker who convinces me to steal a boat and now a Molotov-wielding pirate. My mum is going to be utterly appalled at the new company I keep.

"Anyone can do it." Liv dismisses me as if I just asked how to boil eggs.

"You're the only one with a bottle of alcohol, though," Frances says.

Liv's eyes dart between our faces and if it wasn't for the wild, almost primal look on her face, it would be a little funny. Is it because she can't bear the thought of throwing away good whiskey? Or is it because she can't bear the thought of not having it? For some reason, I think it's the latter rather than the former. And I shouldn't indulge her if that's the case, but we need that bottle because setting fire to the infected will create one hell of a distraction.

"There's whiskey at my dad's place."

"If you're lying to me..." Liv narrows her eyes, then jabs a finger in my direction. She doesn't need to finish her threat. When she's in a good mood and not brooding in a corner, she's nice. But when she gets mad or suspicious, she's got a red glare that promises death and destruction. I almost raise my hands into the air.

"I'm not lying."

"Alright, good." Roy claps his hands together, urging us into action. "Black Widow over here is going to sort the distraction. Now we only need a bit of a plan so we don't run off like headless chickens and get ourselves into a worse situation."

I'm not sure how a situation could be worse than the one we currently find ourselves in, but I get what he's saying. If we don't have a plan, the likelihood of us becoming separated and lurker food is somewhere near really-fuck-ing-high-probability on the scale.

"Okay, but wait." Noah takes a step forward. "If we can set them on fire, why leave the boat?"

That's a good question. I turn towards Roy. He is sort of the leader of our little group, after all.

"There's nothing to say all of them will catch fire. The ground is wet and might make it more difficult for the liquid to spread. And what if she misses?" Roy says calmly.

Liv gives a derisive snort, pushes past them, and lights the soaked kitchen towel that's stuffed into the bottleneck of her whiskey. Before anyone can protest, she hurls the bottle at the group of lurkers.

It's as if time slows to a stop. I watch the bottle sail through the air, arcing above the first infected, illuminating the dark like a massive firefly. It lands with a sharp crash, followed by a soft whooshing sound as the alcohol that's flowed across the muddy pathway catches fire.

Flames lick the infected's legs, latching on to them greedily, and their enraged howls launch me and the others into action.

"What the shit happened to the plan?" I try not to sound exasperated as I catch a bag that was chucked towards me by Roy.

"Not really a planner." Liv retorts. "And I don't miss."

"No shit." I haul my bag onto my shoulders and grab my bat. The lurkers shriek as they stumble around like drunk people on New Year's Eve. Arms flail and wave, spreading the fire. It catches quickly as if they're already drenched in oil. I glance at Liv.

She may well be the most impulsive person I've ever met, but I can't argue with her throwing skills. This should probably worry me.

"They're awfully flammable, aren't they?" I say as Roy sidesteps, making space for Angela and Noah to scurry back inside to pack our things. If the infected keep on burning like this, we won't have to get off the boat.

More infected catch fire, but my relief at the sight is curtailed by a strange voice in the dark. "Get off the boat!"

Who the fuck? I spin, trying to decipher where the voice is coming from.

"Get off the boat! They're going to blow!" a man's voice, urgent and insistent, shouts again. "They're too close. You need to get away!"

I look back at the lurkers a good few metres away. It's not enough. Not if they explode.

"Now!" another voice fills in, this one just as urgent.

I snap my eyes to the other side. We're not close enough to the riverbank.

"Mate, get off the fucking boat!" Whoever this guy is, he doesn't sound threatening.

"We have to jump," I say, grabbing Liv by the arm and dragging her away from the railing.

"Leave everything!" Roy's voice thunders. "We have to jump!"

Everyone rushes onto the deck empty-handed, then stop and turn their heads in the direction Roy points.

Noah hits the water first, Fareena, Frances, and Angela following closely after.

"Move away from them! Their spores spread further than you think!" the mystery man barks.

"Time to haul ass, Jake!" Roy throws himself over the railing.

The heat from the burning lurkers radiates through the short distance between us, warming my back. There's a popping sound behind me, like popcorn cooking on a stove. We have to get off the boat now. Before the small popping turns to one giant boom.

I grab Karma under her arms and legs, then launch her overboard. A hundred thirty pounds of dog tumbles through the air, then she goes under. I hold my breath. My heart slams frantically, and my hands shake. The thought of her not resurfacing settles in my mind. I climb onto the railing, seconds away from diving in, when she breaks the surface again.

She snorts, breathing through her nose, her jowls flaring against the surface. She sounds like a seal as she swims towards the others.

"Liv!" Fareena shouts, and I turn around. Liv hasn't moved. She just stands there, staring at the burning infected as if frozen by fear on the spot.

"Fuck!" I drop to the deck and grab her arm. She turns her head to look at my hand, but she doesn't move.

"Let me go." Her voice is eerily calm. It's almost as if she doesn't want to move. I blink in surprise. She *doesn't.*

Voices shout, urging me to get off the boat. I tug Liv's arm, but it's as if she's cemented to the floor. She has no intention of leaving. What the fuck do I do? Clearly, I can't force her, and if I stay, I'll be caught in the blast. I swallow. I must leave her behind. I can't wait, not if I want to survive.

I let go and take a step back. Her entire body relaxes, and she closes her eyes before turning towards the infected again.

I seize that moment and launch myself at her. I push off my feet and hope she doesn't have enough time to hear me coming. Throwing my arms around her, I use the momentum to lift her up, giving her no room to fight me.

She tries to struggle, tries to wriggle out of my grip, but I'm all adrenaline and fear. I want to live. I want to get away from the boat. I don't care if I break her ribs; I'm not leaving her.

I use all my strength to drag her to the opening in the railing, where I push off the edge. She goes limp in my arms as we crash through the surface into ice-cold water.

The water is so cold it numbs my skin and limbs as we sink like stones. My backpack weighs us down until we hit the muddy bottom of the canal with Liv's limp body pressing into mine, forcing air from my lungs. Sludge and soil billow up like mushroom clouds, muddying the waters. I blink, desperate to see something through the murkiness. To get my bearings.

Liv's hair floats above my face, but through the thin wisps I can see orange and yellow ripple and curl on the surface.

A dull bang rumbles from somewhere above, and the bright light from the fire expands out and across the river.

My feet slide across algae and mud, unable to find purchase as I try to lift us from the river bottom.

Liv hangs limp in my arms, and her head lolls. Her eyes are closed. Tiny bubbles emerge from between her lips. I need to get her above the surface before she runs out of air and starts swallowing water.

I roll us over, one arm still wrapped around her waist, the other pressing my fingers into the mud as I push our upper bodies away. It only takes a few seconds, but it feels like a fucking eternity until the riverbed is underneath my feet I sink down just enough to give myself power, and then I push with everything I've got left.

Gravity grabs hold, tries to pull us back, but I kick hard towards the surface, my lungs burning for air. I think we're about to break surface when I see something strange: a thick layer of something that reminds me of pollen, though it's thicker, denser. *Shit!* I try to find an opening, but there's nothing.

Panic claws into me, and I spin in frenzied movements as I try to spot somewhere we can surface. My lungs are almost empty, screaming for air, and I fight my own body as it tries to force oxygen into my lungs. It won't matter that I'm submerged in water, the instinct to breathe is too strong.

The bright beam of a torch penetrates my murky surroundings. One last push. Just a few seconds longer. I would close my eyes to help me focus on anything but that final primal inhalation, but I'm scared I'll lose my direction. I kick and beat against the water, but it's so heavy. Too heavy. The light is too far away. I give another helpless kick, but it's futile. The water is too strong, and my body is too tired. I reach with my free hand as if I could grab the light and drag myself towards it. When I find I can't, I take my first gulp of water.

I was thirsty anyway, I think, when something grabs my hand and pulls me the rest of the way.

We break the surface. I gasp and cough as strong arms pull us onto the cold riverbank. Someone holds me firmly under my arms, pulling me along, while someone else tugs hard at my jacket to help whoever holds me. It's a jerky, uneven tugging, and I open my eyes to see Karma with part of my coat in her mouth.

My arms are tangled up with Liv's, and it's not until Roy tells me to let go that I finally roll over onto my hands and knees. I vomit. Filthy canal water shoots out of my mouth and nose like I'm being exorcised. My chest heaves with gags when there's nothing left, and someone rubs my back between my shoulders.

"You're okay, kiddo. You're okay," Roy murmurs and hands me an open bottle of water. I shake my head, but Roy wiggles it in front of me. "You need to drink, kid. Just one sip."

Too tired to put up a real fight, and my arm pulsing with white-hot pain, I let him tip some water into my mouth, then wipe my lips and sit back on my knees while my breathing evens out. "Liv." I turn my head so fast that it almost makes me dizzy.

"She's fine," Roy says calmly, and I let out a sigh of relief.

She sits on her knees. Like me. Hands on her thighs, her head hanging forward as she heaves, but whether it's because she's trying to breathe or trying not to cry, I can't tell.

"What happened back there?" Roy looks at me with concern.

I don't know what to say. I know she wasn't too scared to move. At least I don't think so, but what if—in all the commotion—my brain misread things? Do I tell him what I think happened, or do I talk to Liv first?

It's as if she can hear my thoughts, or maybe she could see me watching her, but she lifts her head to look at me. Her eyes are damp and red. If I hadn't seen her on the boat, I would have thought it was from throwing up. But something behind the dampness, a hollowness I've never seen before, makes me shiver. She looks away and hugs herself.

I won our struggle on the boat. I saved her. So why do I feel like shit?

44

JAKE

THE NIGHT IS FREEZING cold, and it takes all my strength and willpower to get me on my feet. Roy still helps me keep my balance as we survey the boat. It's coated in the same stuff that covers parts of the canal's surface. It looks like pollen with the way it swirls in a wavelike pattern.

"What is that?" I say, my voice coarse and strained.

"Spores," a man says as he and his friend walk towards us. It's dark and the chilly night makes my eyes water, making it even harder to see.

Karma immediately goes into a protective stance, tail standing straight, lips curled as a low rumbling vibrates in her throat. Roy straightens beside me, drawing to his full height of six feet and then some.

The others quickly gather next to us, Angela and Frances holding on to Liv.

The man who spoke stops and raises his hands, the shorter one behind mimicking him. "We want no trouble. Is he going to attack?"

I look down at Karma. She's just dragged me out of the water barely alive. It would put any dog in a protective mood. I snap my fingers once and she sits down obediently.

"She won't attack, but I can't speak for this guy here." I nod at Roy, who doesn't move a muscle as he looms behind me.

"Okay, I'm Sam." The man lowers his hands, then motions to his friend. "This is Evan, my little brother. We only wanted to see if you were alright."

Evan, who looks to be in his late teens, nods. "We're not trying to knick your boat. We have our own." He points farther up the canal.

"Alright." Roy dips his head in a slow nod. "We're all okay. I suspect we have you two to thank for that."

Now that I know they're brothers and they're close enough, I can see the likeness between them. But whereas Evan is still working on a very sad-looking attempt at a moustache, Sam's face is rugged and unshaven. But they have the same round faces and large, slightly round noses.

"What are these spores?" Angela asks.

"These bastards are full of them. We ran into a bunch over in Culham. Patrick, my mate, whacked one of them over the head with an iron rod." Sam runs a hand through his hair. "Cracked like an eggshell."

"But then stuff comes out, yeah. Just fucking exploded, like one of them mushrooms that puffs out smoke." Evan holds a fist near his temple, then mimics the sound of an explosion as he moves it to the side and splays his fingers wide. "Like that, init."

"Pat inhaled it." Sam sighs. "He turned the next day."

"But why are you having infected up here?" Frances asks. "Surely it can't have spread from either Manchester or London already?"

Sam gives a dry chuckle. "Already? I first saw it a couple of weeks back. At the shipping firm where I work. Boxes coming in from London dusted with red pollen. Thought it was strange. Pollen at the end of summer."

At the end of the summer? That would mean this has been around much longer than what the PM indicated. We all exchange looks. "But the Prime Minister and the news said residue from the attack on London caused the infection," I say.

"And you bought that?" Amusement dances in his eyes.

"Don't be ridiculous. Those things overran London. Only an idiot would believe that." It's the first I've heard from Liv since we got dragged up on the beach. Charming as ever.

Sam's amusement melts into a frown. "Right. Well, we've been told the same thing. London, Manchester, Leeds, and Oxford. All overrun by the withered."

Oxford and Leeds as well? Fareena's family is in Leeds, and her eyes flicker at the mention of the city. The infection is spreading so much faster than we thought. I pause as a shiver racks my body. The cold is making it hard to think, and the more I try to resist the shivering, the more I shake. My teeth chatter. Roy has his arm around me, providing me with a little of his body heat, but it's not enough to help against the biting cold. For either of us. I can feel him tremble although he masks it a lot better than I do.

"Withered?" Angela says.

"That's what it looks like, humans withering to nothing but skin and bones. Seemed a fitting name for them," Sam explains.

"So, these... things?" Roy asks. "These withered, as you call them. Can't be killed by fire?"

"Or a blow to the head!" Evan raises his eyebrows. "Like, that's not at all what they taught us about zombies. Headshots, mate, init, but now it's all fucked up. Can't kill zombies with headshots."

"Oi." Sam glares at him.

"Or fire," Evan reminds us, but falls silent as he catches Sam's annoyed expression.

"Don't call them that."

"But that's what they are," Evan insists.

"No. It's stupid. It sounds stupid." Sam gives us an apologetic nod. I don't bother to admit I've been thinking in the same lines as Evan. "Listen, we're heading down to London, but we can stay here until tomorrow. Get your stuff dried."

I want to do the polite thing and say they don't have to help us out, but I'm too damn cold to be polite. And I want to get out of these wet clothes. I hate wet clothes. Besides, they shouldn't be trying to go *in* to London when most people are no doubt trying to get out. "You sure it'll be safe?"

He gives a shrug. "Feels like a lot of things aren't safe nowadays. But if we stay in the middle of the canal, we should be alright. Never seen a withered that swims."

I look at Roy. He's quiet, his face arranged in an unreadable expression. "I think we'd all appreciate getting dry," he finally says, and a unanimous breath of relief passes through our group.

"I don't doubt it," Sam says. "I'm cold and I'm dry, so you must be freezing your tits off."

"Yeah, I could use some of those magic hands of yours," Noah says to me, drawing curious looks from the others, and I laugh. That is the first joke he's cracked, and it's got perfect timing.

"Sure, mate, but can we get inside first?"

45

LIV

BY THE TIME THEY'D made their way over to Sam and Evan's boat, Liv had been so cold she couldn't keep from shivering. Wet clothes had clung to her, their dampness crawling in under her skin to penetrate muscles and bones.

Sam's boat was so warm Liv couldn't tell whether she was hot or cold when she'd first stepped into it. Wet clothes lined every piece of furniture and available space they could find in hopes that most of their things would dry overnight.

They all wore spare clothes that Sam and Evan lent them until it was time to go. However, two young blokes on a narrowboat left little room for clothes, it appeared. Especially not when they'd been travelling for a few days and had already accumulated an impressive load of dirty laundry. She looked around the narrow space at the bizarre and slightly outlandish mix of clothes.

Fareena wore a baggy t-shirt that read 'YOLO' in big red letters and a pair of PJ trousers with some sort of robots on them. Angela and Frances, who were sitting, playing a game of cards, wore hoodies and joggers, and Karma's fur was all puffy and fluffy like the hair on a pen troll.

And then there were the boys. Noah wore a nice suit shirt matched with a pair of red-and-green-chequered long johns. Roy, leaning against the wall, was dressed in a football jersey and a pair of silk boxers that looked like a pair of bicycle shorts on him. It took Angela at least five minutes to stop laughing.

Then there was Jake. He sported a pair of grey briefs with printed skulls and a knitted Christmas sweater. She wasn't sure she'd ever contemplate loaning someone else her underwear, let alone borrow someone else's, but then again, beggars can't be choosers.

She eyed Jake surreptitiously. She'd seen the way he'd looked at her after they'd been dragged from the water. Confusion, doubt, worry, and maybe even annoyance had clouded his dark eyes. He wanted to know what had happened back on the boat. He would eventually ask, and she would have no answer. At least not one she'd want to share.

No one else had asked what had happened. They'd been too busy discussing the fact that the infected—or withered as Sam and Evan called them—were now in Oxford as well as Leeds and Birmingham. She bit her thumbnail. That didn't bode well.

It had been bad enough that it hit London with their eleven million residents and God knew how many tourists on top of that. Trying to control the spread would be gruelling even with contingency plans in place. She sat up straight. "It was the contingency plan!"

The others regarded her with startled expressions, Angela pressing a hand on her chest in surprise.

"Liv?" Frances set down her cards.

Liv slid forward on her seat, arms held out to her sides in thought. "The bombs." She blinked, trying to make sense of her own thoughts. It couldn't be. It was too cruel. Which, of course, was the very reason it could be true. "The bombs were the contingency plan."

"What?" Fareena's face tightened with confusion.

"The bombs. The military shooting civilians. It was all part of the plan."

"That's not a contingency plan," Noah protested. "That's simply killing people."

"And what would you do if you had one of the most popular cities in the world infected by these things?" She let the thought sink in. "One for the many?"

"Sacrificing London for the rest of England? If so, they already failed." Frances looked sceptical.

"Unless of course..." Angela tapped her lip in thought, then let out a soft, "Ah."

"What?" Noah demanded.

"Unless the contingency plan failed, and London isn't the one. What if mainland UK is the one for the many?"

"Yeah, yeah." Roy nodded. "When we were on our way to the airport, we'd been told there had been severe delays. They could have been grounding flights even before the attack."

"To stop the infection getting out," Liv continued his thought.

"We know the infection got out of London, so what's saying it didn't escape England?" Jake spoke for the first time, his piercing eyes scrutinising her from the other side of the small seating area. Well, that was the million-dollar question, wasn't it?

"I don't know," she admitted.

Roy shook his head. "We all knew something wasn't right. All the more reason to get to Jake's dad. I have a feeling he'll have some answers for us."

"I hope so." Jake sat on the floor, leaning against the wall, his knees pulled towards his chest, his arms resting on top of them. Karma lay curled next to him, her nose pressed against the side of his thigh. He looked a little pale, and Liv felt a pang of guilt in her chest.

"Until then, I say we all focus on arriving in one piece. Let's start by getting some sleep," Roy said, and was answered with tired nods from the others. "Good, that's settled then. Ange and Frances in one bed; Fareena and Liv in the second."

She sighed. It was the gentleman's vein in him speaking. "You share with Angela. I don't mind sleeping on the floor." If sleeping was what one would call it. She'd probably be too busy fretting about Jake trying to talk to her. That and trying to come up with a good excuse.

"I think you two had quite a strenuous night tonight. I'll take the floor and use this one as my pillow." Angela patted her husband's stomach, earning herself an eye roll from Roy.

"You take the sofa," Noah said, drawing surprised looks from just about everyone in the room. "I'll take the floor if you don't mind sharing your husband for one night."

"Now hold up," Roy protested, "I'm not some bargaining chip to be passed around."

Angela smiled with a sort of pitying look and patted him again. "Of course not, sugar."

"Alright, alright." Roy waved his hand in front of him. "Everybody off to bed. We got a lot of things to figure out tomorrow."

For now, they would stay anchored in the middle of the canal. Sam and Evan offered to stay on watch to let the rest of them sleep.

Jake and Roy had tried to argue, but Sam and Evan had been adamant, saying that they needed to discuss their plan anyway. The boys had finally agreed, the decision of where to go was best left for tomorrow.

Everyone moved to get ready for the night, Frances and Fareena shuffling towards the bed as if they were already asleep. Wait. Liv blinked. Who was she sharing the bed with? Pushing off the floor, she made her way into the bow of the boat, only to find Fareena and Frances already in bed. The same bed. *Shit.* She gazed at the empty bed. Sam had called it a double, but that was not the word she'd use to describe it. *Fuck. Fuck-shitting-ball-wank.* Maybe she could swap with Noah. He sure liked to sleep in a bed.

She turned around, only to see the others settled in their places. "Hey, Noah," she whispered, but either he didn't hear or chose to ignore her. *Great.* Pursing her lips, she ran her fingers through her hair. If she slept close to the wall, then maybe Jake wouldn't think to talk to her.

She lifted the comforter just in time for someone to shove her hard to the side before ungracefully climbing into the bed.

"Oi!" She hissed as Karma crawled flat on her belly towards the wall. Then, as if it was the most natural thing in the world, she placed her head on the pillow and closed her eyes. "What the fuck...?"

"Oh, hey." His voice startled her into a jump.

"Fuck, you scared me."

"Sorry." He paused, observing her with his intense dark eyes. "I would say that I could take the floor but... I'm tired and aching so if you don't want to share, there's a floor you can have."

For some reason, his slightly belligerent attitude made her relax. At least he was too tired to have a chat, which suited her fine.

"Want to sleep next to your child?" She motioned towards Karma who lay snoring loudly.

He pointed at the thick sweater. "Honestly, I prefer not to tonight."

She smiled at that, then climbed into the bed. "Fine. I'll take one for the team."

He followed closely, the bed dipping ever so softly as he lay down beside her. They lay silent for a while, and she listened to his breathing grow slower as Karma twitched next to her, no doubt chasing rabbits in her dreams. Or withered. Who knew?

"Liv?" Jake's voice was soft and quiet. When she didn't reply, he continued. "You don't have to tell me what happened back at the boat." What was that supposed to mean? Was it a threat? He shifted and she watched him through the corner of her eye as he rolled from his back onto his stomach, folding his arms around the pillow. "But if you need to talk, I can be a pretty good listener."

She stared into the dark. That was it? No lecture about how what she did was wrong, that she was a coward, a piece of shit who couldn't take responsibility for her actions?

Jake wasn't stupid, far from it. He knew what had happened.

"Good night, Liv," he mumbled, "don't let the withered bite."

She smiled at the rather inappropriate joke and listened to his breathing grow heavy as he drifted off to sleep, leaving her alone with her thoughts. She blinked at the ceiling in a half-hearted attempt to stay awake. Rolling onto her side, she watched the sleeping man next to her. A stranger with whom she'd crossed paths by happenstance. Despite that, despite being strangers, he showed her—a broken and tired soul, too scared to live, too cowardly to die—a kindness she'd not found in many other places.

She stroked a lock of hair from his face, then gently pressed her lips against his temple. "Good night, Jake."

46

JAKE

SOMETHING WET CLINGS TO me as I stir in my sheets, and I groan. I must have been sweating in the thick knitted sweater. *That's disgusting*, I think until I hear the splashing of water against the side of my bed.

"What?" I sit up straight.

Water rushes in from everywhere, submerging half the boat. *Shit*! Air bubbles up and breaks the surface as the canal slowly but surely sucks the boat towards its sludge-covered bottom. I look for the others, but Frances and Fareena's end of the boat is completely submerged.

"Wake up! We're sinking!" Sam had warned us that our weight could shift the balance of the boat. If we weren't careful, the boat could tip over. We have to get out of here. I turn to Megan who somehow hasn't woken despite the water splish-splashing all around her.

"Wake up." I shake her hard and she sits up.

"Jake, I'm sleeping." I lift my gaze to her face, avoiding looking at anything else. Right now is *not* the time to think about what she looks like in the wet, see-through top that clings to her body.

"We're sinking." I grab her by the hand and try to pull her with me, but she remains seated.

"Why don't we stay here? Just you and me?" Her voice is soft as silk as she pulls me towards her, burgundy lips soft and inviting.

"The fuck, Meg?" We're sinking, and she wants to make out? She pulls me towards her lips and wraps her hands in my hair as we hit the water. I give in. I always do with her.

Rotten hands grab at us, clawing at my legs and arms as we sink to the bottom. A pair of fingers finds its way into my mouth along with river water. Murky, shit- and spore-filled water washes down my throat like expensive whiskey, and I scream.

I jerk awake, breathing hard, and sit up in the dark. The boat is still and quiet, save for Karma's snoring and Liv's breathing that whispers through the night.

The jumper sticks to my sweaty body, and I can't tell if I'm hot or cold as I struggle to get it off. I can't breathe, it's suffocating me.

My arms get tangled when I try to pull it over my head. The thick wool hangs like a veil, everything around me fading into dark shadows and silhouettes. I tug with frustration. I need to see. If I can't see, I can't know what's going on. I want to scream in unreasonable rage at my failed attempts when a pair of cool, soft hands touch my back.

"Let me help you," Liv murmurs, her voice draped with sleep. Her cool hands feel like heaven against my burning back, and my body gives an involuntary tremble.

"Thank you," I croak out as she slips the jumper off my head.

"Jake?" She places her hand on my forehead. It's feels so nice I press into her soft palm as if it might help cool the rest of me down. It takes a few seconds to realise what the hell I'm doing, and I quickly move away.

"Sorry." I squint at her through the dark, my head throbbing. Not that I can see much.

"Jake, you've got a fever." Her voice is softer than usual. I like it. "Do we have any ibuprofen?"

"There are some in my toiletry bag." I point at the small bag on a narrow table at the opposite wall. Lifting my arm feels like trying to lift forty pounds of heavy weights.

Liv pushes me down as she climbs over, hands pressing on the bed on either side of my head. I try to ignore how the insides of her thighs are pressing against my waist. I fail. Miserably so. Maybe because she's wearing nothing but a pair of boxer shorts and a too-big t-shirt with a generous V-neck that hangs low. I may be sick, but I still have eyes.

"Mate." She frowns down at me. "Are you perving right now?"

"I assure you that as a true gentleman, I would never dishonour a lady such as yourself."

She pushes off the bed with a snort. "Gentleman," I hear her mutter as she makes her way over to the table, and I chuckle.

The sound of the zipper on my bag seems to echo loudly through the sleeping boat. I lift my head to make sure the sound didn't wake up Frances and Fareena.

They're both sound asleep, not moving despite Liv rummaging through my bag. It hits me as I let my head fall to the pillow that my packer is in that bag. Sod it, I'm too tired to care.

Liv's rummaging stops as if she's found what she's looking for, but then continues until it stops again. She makes some more noise, then returns with the ibuprofen and a bottle of water.

"Take this." She makes me sit up, and I do, though I want to protest. Everything hurts. She leans down, her face close to mine, and whispers, "It'll help."

I exhale and hold out my hand. "I know, I know." I wash the pills down, thankful for the fresh taste of water. The taste of the mucky river is still in my mouth, so I take another sip from the bottle.

"Need anything else?" Liv pushes me against my pillow, and I shake my head. She climbs into bed, once again closing the distance between us. "You sure? Because if I have to climb over you one more time, your eyes might pop out of your skull."

Chuckling, I close my eyes. "Yes, ma'am."

"And stop thinking about it."

"I'm not." I grin and force the picture out of my head. I better get some sleep if tomorrow isn't going to absolutely suck. Taking a deep, slow breath, I will myself to fall asleep. My eyelids grow heavier and heavier. Liv murmurs something I can't decipher. I try to ask what she said, but give in to the warm, fuzzy feeling that spreads through my head. It's the serenity that settles just as you're about to fall asleep, and I let myself be carried away by it when I hear her whisper.

"Thank you."

47

LIV

MOST OF THEIR CLOTHES and things dried overnight, and judging by the others rising early and not complaining, they must have gotten some well-deserved sleep. Or perhaps they were all eager to get away from this place.

Liv pulled her jacket closed and took a drag from her cigarette where she sat on the bow of the boat. Sam's boat was different from theirs. Unlike *Gloria*, this one had its main outside seating on the bow.

She took another drag, her eyes resting on a leaf floating lazily down the canal. A thick layer of fog cloaked the entire canal and the surrounding meadows, the orange leaves a stark contrast to the white fog and grey skies.

The memory of orange and yellow flames engulfing the withered flashed through her mind. And then something else. The calm as she turned to face the inevitable explosion.

It had been so simple. An easy way out of the chaos and pain that was her life. One minute she was arguing to keep her whiskey, only to welcome the end with open arms moments later.

"Welcome to my life," she muttered across the rim of her coffee mug.

"Thank you." Frances sat next to her on the small deck seating.

Liv turned with a half smile playing on her lips. "You might want to wait on thanking me until you've been in it for a bit." She fell silent. What on earth had made her say that? *You're losing your grip, Liv.*

Thankfully, Frances either didn't notice or simply ignored it. "How's he holding up?"

Liv looked through the window at Jake, who lay still, sleeping in the bed. He'd woken her a few times during the night muttering through his fever. Each time she'd placed her palm against his forehead, and he'd sighed with satisfaction. He kept tossing and turning and didn't quite settle until the early hours of the morning. They were both going to be knackered.

"His fever keeps jumping all over the place, but he's fine. He'll have a hard time travelling, but at least it won't kill him." *No, that's what they have you for.*

She bit back the snarky reply to herself. After last night, she had racked up enough crazy points.

Frances nodded thoughtfully, then set her mug down. "And how are you holding up?" The way she said it was warm and careful, and Liv thought she could see a worried expression on Frances's face. For her? "Are you alright?"

Liv swallowed, uncertain what to say. "I'm not sick."

"I know that, dear." Reaching out, Frances put her hand on Liv's. Her breath quickened, her heart thumping as Frances observed her, brows pulled together in concern. Liv tried desperately to think of something else, force her exhausted mind to block out the emotions stirring to life.

She averted her gaze before those worried green eyes could cause her to unravel. She had no alcohol and hadn't gotten around to her morning dose of benzos. She wasn't ready for something like this.

"Liv?"

"Please don't ask me that." It was all she could muster. Any other answer would be a lie.

"Alright, Chicken."

"Oh God, no. Don't call me that." She laughed breathlessly. "Not now. I'll like it too much."

Laughing, Frances gave her hand a gentle squeeze. "That's the whole point. But if it makes you feel any better, I don't think many of us feel okay at the moment."

It did make her feel better. "I can't even understand what's happening. What these infected are. Where did they come from?"

"Well, I for one don't buy the terrorism angle."

Liv shook her head and glanced over at Frances again. "How the fuck do we even beat this thing?"

"We keep running."

"How long?" Hopelessness dug its claws into her. The virus was spreading faster than any of them had expected. How could you outrun something that didn't stop? That couldn't be stopped?

Placing her hands on Liv's arms, Frances's eyes burned with defiance. "We don't stop running or fighting. Unless we run out of luck, we keep going."

A week ago, Liv would've laughed at such a dramatic statement. But there was nothing funny about it now. Now it was how they survived.

"Hey," Angela stepped through the door, "everybody good?"

"Yeah," Frances said, giving Liv a quick hug. "All good."

"Well, it seems we're about to get ready to leave," Angela said.

"Any idea of which way we're running next?" Liv asked as she got up from her seat.

"Noah mentioned the Fens."

The Fens? They weren't exactly close to the Fens, the old, drained marshes turned farmlands. "Did he say what he meant by that?"

"Something about their roads being safer?"

"Safer?" She laughed. "I'm not sure that's what I'd call it."

The Fens was an area composed of marshlands and fields, with back roads running higgledy-piggledy through them. Though calling them roads was pushing it. She remembered driving from David's parents' in Norfolk to Cambridge a few years back. God, she'd been happy to be away from them. There was one particular road her GPS had directed her to. A shortcut, it said, saving her at least ten minutes of driving time.

She'd stared at the road, no, a trodden-down *footpath* running through the middle of a field. It was barely wide enough for one car, and she could see the tracks dip up and down through the muddy field. It was that or track back towards David and his insufferable family.

She shook her head. It had been a bumpy ride, but it got her where she wanted to be. That's probably what Noah was referring to when he'd mentioned the Fens.

"Should I be worried?" Angela tilted her head slightly.

"No. I think Noah might be right. We aren't near the Fens, but now that we're out of London, there are plenty of back roads we can use."

"Ah. Back roads," Angela said in a voice of someone who's had their fair share of them.

"It beats going through Oxford." She paused. "Can I just point out that there's one obvious flaw with this plan?"

Angela pursed her lips. "Yes, well, it seems our young hoodlum wants to find a suitable car to hot-wire."

"Of course she does." Liv shook her head. "Did you guys talk to Sam and his brother about London?"

"Yes," Angela grimaced, "but they're hell-bent on going. Got their mother and sisters there."

Frustration pulled her mouth into a scowl. "They shouldn't be going down there."

"I know." Angela gave her arm a gentle rub, motioning for Liv to go and get ready. "But people will do anything to get back to the ones they love."

Liv thought she could see something in Angela's eyes. A haunted, hollow sort of look. She looked away, scared that if she didn't, Angela would see her own expression mirrored in Liv's.

"I should go wake Jake." She excused herself and ducked inside to where Jake was sleeping.

Sitting down on the bed, she kept her eyes on Jake as Angela and Frances followed her inside. Angela stopped next to her momentarily, and Liv closed her eyes. She didn't want to talk to anyone. She needed room to breathe. Room to shift her mind into one set piece again. The way it had been before she talked to David. But instead of trying to talk to her, Angela gave her shoulder a gentle squeeze, then kept walking.

When she was sure Angela or Frances weren't looking, she followed them with her gaze until they disappeared into the kitchen.

"Did you come here to tell me something or are you just going to sit there?"

"Decided it was time to wake up now, huh? Slacker." She pressed her hand against his forehead.

He clicked his tongue in disapproval. "I'm fine."

Her lips twitched, but she bit down on the smile. He had a fever again, the first sign being the glossy eyes, the second his hot skin. She grabbed the pills and water bottle from the side of the bed. "Sure, you are. Now take these so we can get going."

He inspected the oval pills in her hand. "I could think of a lot more fun stuff to be bribed with," he muttered sullenly, and she raised her eyebrows.

"One peek and your brain has fallen into your testicles."

"What?" His eyes widened. "No, wait, I didn't mean it like that."

He was too easy. "Come on, let's get you dressed."

"I'm a grown-ass man. I can get myself dressed," he said and swung his legs across the edge of the bed to prove his point. "See." He stood up cockily and then, as expected, swayed forwards, almost crashing into the wall if it hadn't been for Liv catching him.

"Idiot," she murmured, her palm pressing against his chest. Her light-brown skin looked pale against the black solid ink that covered most of his chest. Except an intricate floral pattern that shifted from grey to skin colour across his collarbones.

He wasn't much shorter than her, but now that he was leaning against the wall with one hand, his face dangerously close to hers, she could see every little detail of the tattoo that covered his neck. Tiny dots etched into his skin in neat rows created a network of tiny triangles and boxes in a mixture of hard and soft lines.

"Well, this is embarrassing. Here I was going to impress you with my impeccable male strength," he joked.

She dropped her gaze to his well-defined pecs. There were certainly some things about him that were impeccable. "Colour me impressed." Her voice came out a little huskier than she'd meant, and he turned his head to her, surprise dancing in his eyes. And something else.

His eyes flickered as he considered her, and she wondered what he saw. The ghost of the person she'd once been or someone else? She gazed at his lips, generous and parted. She dragged her eyes up to meet his, their faces barely a breath away.

"Right, if you two are done wasting time, I brought you breakfast." Noah stood in the hallway with a tray in his hands, looking bored. Though the mischievous sparkle in his eyes didn't escape Liv when she took a step back.

"Thanks," Jake said, watching the floor now that Noah was there. "Just need to make myself presentable."

"Right, well, better get a move on; we haven't got time to waste." Noah gave Jake a hard slap on the back before leaving the two of them in the awkward silence that had settled.

She watched Noah retreat into the kitchen, then sighed. He wasn't wrong. The infection had spread all the way to Wallingford. They couldn't linger if they wanted to get to Huntingdon before the infection did. In fact—she glanced at Jake, who poked at the oatmeal with his spoon—they didn't have time for any distractions at all. And certainly not emotions. Regardless of their nature. Emotions got in the way of everything. Caring set one up for absolute failure.

She shook her head. How the fuck had she forgotten that? This would end now.

"I'll go fetch your clothes. And then you'll get dressed. On your own."

"What happened to helping me?" He shoved a spoonful of oatmeal into his mouth, his eyes glittering.

"I have better things to do."

"Okay, but so you know, this is a one-time performance. Sure you want to miss out?" He flexed his muscles and before she could stop it, laughter bubbled from her lips.

"You're an idiot." She stepped past him into the short hallway leading to the kitchen.

"I'm starting to think that's more of a compliment than an insult." She could hear him call after her, and she wasn't sure which startled her the most: that he was right or that he had figured it out.

48

JAKE

AFTER PACKING WHAT LITTLE things we were able to bring from the boat, Sam and Evan dropped us off closer to town. We tried to convince them one last time to stay away from London, but they've got their minds set. I don't blame them. If it were Mum and Tim, I'd do the same.

Impatience mixed with a tinge of worry stirs in my stomach. I should be home by now; Dad was counting on me. We may not see eye to eye on a lot of things, but when it comes to Mum and Tim, we were always on the same page.

I was seventeen when Tim was born. I still remember when Mum told me I was getting a sibling. It was at the end of June, and Mum had called me down to the kitchen for dinner. The moment I walked in, I *knew* something was up.

Mum had set our oak table with my favourite mackerel complete with a selection of my favourite banchan. Sticky rice, oyster mushroom, spinach, and kimchi. My mum smiled the same way she did before my grandparents came to visit. "I thought we could have something nicer tonight." She motioned towards my chair.

I watched her with increasing alarm and eased into my chair, looking at the meal as if it were the last supper. My mum had never cooked me a meal because *I* wanted it. I grew up by the rule of eat what's on the table or go hungry. I don't go hungry. Ever.

"Go on." She pushed one of the banchan towards me, putting some spinach on my plate.

"Mum." I picked up the chopsticks from the table. "What's wrong? Did something happen to Dad?"

Her shoulders slumped forward. "Not exactly."

"Not exactly? Mum, what does that even mean?" I put my chopsticks down.

She dropped her hands into her lap, and I could hear her flatten the napkin on it. "I'm not sure how to say this, but you are going to have a little brother."

My first instinct was to throw my hands over my ears and scream because I was seventeen and I *knew* how babies were made. But then I looked at my mum whose eyes were damp and glistening as she tried to keep the smile off her face in case the conversation went tits up.

I grabbed the oyster mushrooms. "Does this mean I'll get mackerel and banchan every day until he's born?"

She slapped my hand. "You're not angry?"

"Mum..." I grinned back at her. "I'm happy. I'm very happy, Mum. I always wanted a butler. It better come out ready to serve."

She laughed, leaning over and cupping my cheek. "*Saranghae*."

"I love you too."

Tim was born three months later, four months earlier than planned. So small he fit in the palm of my hand. And he's been sticking to me like glue ever since.

Once when I visited his school, he introduced me as his *hyeong* who was single and had a good job. I was both impressed the teacher knew enough Korean to understand I was his big brother, and equally embarrassed. When I awkwardly apologised to the teacher, Tim had tried to negotiate a good contract for her to marry me.

I smile at the memories. I have to make sure they're safe. I scan the area in front of us. We're on an open grass field with a camping ground next to it, the fog lingering as we make our way towards the town centre.

"Are you going to stick to the plan this time or are you going to almost get more of us killed?" Fareena glares at Liv as we cross a green that's supposed to lead to a car park where thick trees loom, which I'm hoping will help cover our slightly criminal activities.

I'm not sure why, but Fareena's been testy and irritable this morning. Especially around Liv, although I could be imagining that. She's probably missing and worrying about her family.

"Hey." I catch up to Fareena, who trudges across the well-trimmed lawn. For someone so short, she's fast, and the simple effort of keeping up with her makes me dizzy. "What's going on?"

"Nothing."

"Are you sure because you've been a little... tense."

She digs her thumbs underneath the bag straps, adjusting the bag. "I don't want things to go pear-shaped again, is all. Last time someone almost died."

Did Fareena blame Liv for last night? I glance at Liv, who catches me looking at her. She returns my gaze with one of her own, brows creased in an otherwise undistinguishable expression.

"You worried about your bestie?" I try to lighten the mood. "Because, you know, I'm fine."

"You're sick," she points out and suddenly I understand why she's worried.

A cold chill washes over me. I swallowed the water—water filled with spores—and I'm sick, displaying two out of three symptoms mentioned in the news. My eye gives an involuntary twitch, and I press my fingers against it to make it stop. It throbs with an intense ache.

The memory of the lurker from last night, the one with the blood-red tendrils growing out of its eyes, flashes through my mind. I shudder.

"Are you alright?"

"Yeah, fine." I drop my hand to my side. "I'll be better though if we can get this over with." I try to smile and quiet the thoughts of tendrils springing from my eyes.

"Okay, let's find our ride out of here, then. I need a Mazda, Ford Mondeo, Ford Escort, or a Volvo. Whatever you do, do not get me some new snazzy car because I don't have the right tools to break into them." *Tools?* Fareena pulls a screwdriver from her bag. "This is all I have."

I look at the thin screwdriver in her hand. "I thought you said you were a singer."

"No, I said I had my first gig. I never said what my actual job is."

"You a car mechanic? Because that's the only profession I can think of right now that isn't car thief."

"Shut up." Her face is less tense, but she chuckles, stopping by the mossy trunk of a tree at the edge of the car park. The others skulk in the shadows next to us.

"Psst." Roy points towards the far end of the car park.

An old yellow Volvo is parked at the far side, and three cars down stands an old red Nissan.

"Here we go," she mutters and ducks out from behind the tree.

"Okay, but *are* you a car thief? Should I set my watch to sixty seconds?" I follow her onto the asphalt.

"Do I look like a rookie to you?" She snorts and stops at the Nissan, then with a smooth movement she slides the screwdriver underneath the black handle and gives it one determined push downwards before pulling the screwdriver out.

"That's it?" I ask, and she grins back at me, then nods towards the handle. I pull, and the door swings open with no alarms going off, much to my relief. "Okay, I'm impressed."

"Wait till I get this started, then I'll rock your world." She squeezes past me and slides into the driver's seat.

"Maybe you already do."

Fareena laughs. "You say the nicest things to me." Using the thin screwdriver again, she fiddles around with something with her tongue sticking out of the corner of her mouth, her eyes narrowed in concentration.

We watch like she's some sort of late-night entertainment, almost forgetting to keep watch for anyone passing the car park. I pull my phone from my pocket. Five thirty in the morning is early, but even so it's unusually quiet. And with the streetlamps out, it's quiet and dark.

The engine sputters to life, and Karma's excited bark startles me into a jump.

"Shh," I warn her quietly.

"Let me get the rest of the doors, then you're good to get in."

We decided since I'm the one who knows where we're going, I'll be in the first car with Frances and Liv, who we all know drives like a bat out of hell.

Fareena barely has time to get out of the car before Karma bulldozes her way through the driver's side and into the back seat. I've never figured out why, but she loves going in cars, and now she sits in the back seat with an expression that says she's ready to roll.

As we get into the car, Fareena darts over to the next to work her magic.

"This thing is ancient," Liv says as she grabs the steering wheel. "Look for a map in the glove box."

I can't remember who said it, but the beauty of old cars is that they almost always have street maps in them. I peer into the glove box. No map. Well, shit. "No map."

"Look in the back."

I turn to look, but Frances shakes her head. "It's empty as well."

"Sure you don't have a handy little map from your creeper lair?" Liv asks.

"Creeper lair?" Frances leans forwards between the two seats with curiosity.

"It was a cupboard." I glare at Liv. "And no, I don't have a map."

"What about those mobile maps?" Frances asks.

The GPS has been spotty at best, which is why I didn't suggest it, but maybe it'll work.

"We can try it." I get my phone out again.

"Why do I keep you around?" Liv scratches the back of her head, but the left corner of her mouth twitches upwards, reminding me of her earlier that morning when she'd shocked me by letting loose a bright laugh.

"Because of my charming personality." I type in our current location, or the one I think it is, and then my parents' address.

"Right. Of course," she says dryly as I hold up my phone. The GPS isn't working, but at least it can calculate a few different routes. Following them will be a matter of its own. I press my finger against the grey line that snakes across the map.

Two hours if we only use back roads. One hour fifteen minutes if we bypass Oxford using back roads and then return to the main roads.

Car lights flash from our right and we see Noah behind the steering wheel in the Volvo. He lifts his hand in an are-you-ready-to-go gesture.

"Jesus take the wheel." Frances fastens her seat belt.

"What's wrong with me?" Liv gives her a sideways glance.

Frances's only reply is a silent stare. At that, Liv laughs, then says to me, "Buckle up." She rolls out from the parking spot in a smooth movement. This wasn't so bad.

"I have been in a car with you before," I point out.

"No really, love." Frances turns and points at my seat belt. "You're going to want to be strapped in for this."

49

JAKE

THE FIRST THING WE notice is the lack of streetlamps. Then the lack of traffic lights. Or, rather, the lack of working traffic lights. Every single one we pass is dark as we speed down the main road. The streets are empty, and I haven't seen any people out and about. Even for Abingdon's small size, it's a little odd.

I lean forward on the worn-out seat to get a better view of our surroundings. All lights, the train station, and a twenty-four-hour petrol station are dark as well. The only thing that cuts through the black night is our headlights. With the lack of other light sources, its bright and sharp beam makes my eyes hurt.

"Didn't they say they were only rerouting power sources in London?" I ask and cover my eyes with my hand.

"They said they redirected from London, though they didn't specify that it was only coming from London," Frances says from the seat behind me. "But even so, I can't see them needing power from out here."

"Check the radio," Liv says and turns onto a narrow road that lies squeezed between two big fields.

I turn the radio on, and it crackles with static despite being a popular station that should be airing music. I turn the dial unsuccessfully, finding more stations where static has replaced music.

"What the shit." I draw a quizzical look from Liv. "There's nothing."

"You sure you're on FM?" Frances asks, and I click my tongue.

"I'm not a complete idiot, you know."

"Well..." Liv drawls.

I open my mouth with an awesome comeback, but a sharp pain shoots straight through my head. I pinch my eyes shut and try to push the thought of eye tendrils aside. I am *not* infected. I open my eyes. But what if I am, and I end up hurting Mum or Tim? Or any of the others.

"Liv," I whisper, and she takes her eyes off the road for the briefest of moments. "I think I might be infected."

This time she looks at me for several seconds, then indicates with her light to let Noah know we're pulling off the road. "Why?"

"I have all the symptoms."

Once we're stopped, she turns to me in her seat, and Frances leans forward, both of them looking me over. "What symptoms?" Liv asks.

"My body hurts. A lot. And my eyes."

Frances feels my forehead with the back of her hand. "I don't think you are, love. I think you're just sick from that swim you had."

"Do we have a thermometer?" Liv asks, and I point at the bag on the floor below Karma.

"In my toiletry bag."

Frances leans over to grab it, but Liv waves her hands. "It's fine, I think I saw it last night." And I quietly thank her. The last thing I want right now is for everyone to have a peek at my private junk.

Someone knocks on my window. I turn to see Fareena and open the door. "What's happening?" she asks.

"Jake thinks he might have caught the infection," Frances says in a voice that clearly states I'm wrong. Fareena's eyes dart from me, then over to Liv, then back to me and finally to Frances.

"You were right," I say and try to give a casual shrug. "I'm sick. I swallowed water that had spores in it, and now I'm sick."

"That's not what I meant! And in any case, you're not infected." A whisper of panic touches her voice. "Is he?" she asks Liv.

Liv doesn't reply, simply shoves the thermometer into my mouth. Then we all wait, staring at the thermometer as if it's about to explode. Ten seconds never felt so long, and it's starting to feel like my eyes are going to get stuck staring at the stick in my mouth.

Liv pulls it out, looks at it, and flicks it over for the rest of us to see. Thirty-nine point five.

"No wonder you feel like shite," Frances says as Liv hands her the thermometer to hold.

"Unfortunately, you can't have any more paracetamol yet." Liv breathes on her hands and rubs them together for a few seconds. She places them on my neck, her thumbs resting against my jawline. She turns my head gently back and forth. "Does that hurt?"

I shake my head and try to ignore the way her hands feel on my neck. Something must have given me away because she wears an expression caught somewhere between a smile and a scowl. Her hands slide down, fingers adding careful pressure on the soft part under my jaw. The way her lips part when she's thinking, combined with the soft strokes of her fingers against my jaw, makes me think of the night before. And just like that, I'm in dire need of a cold shower. At least it might help with the fever.

She lets go and drops her hands into her lap. "You've got a high fever and swollen glands. Your neck doesn't hurt, so by all accounts you've caught a bad case of the cold. Worst case the flu."

"But the symptoms," I say.

"You've not shown any signs of aggression and no nosebleeds. I say that unless we see unmistakable signs, you're not infected."

I release a sigh of relief. "Okay. So I'm just very sick."

"Told you so." Fareena squeezes my shoulder. "Typical case of man cold."

I laugh, and it hurts my head when—unexpectedly—the radio gives a loud crackle, followed by a long beep.

"On Friday night, we were told that the Residue virus, which was released upon London in a vicious attack, could be contained within the city. We implemented the Cordon Sanitaire immediately to control and eradicate the virus. It is with regret that I must inform you the infection has breached the Cordon Sanitaire in London, and the lockdowns in Manchester, Leeds, Oxford, and Birmingham. As of nine o'clock this day, I, the Prime Minister, declare the United Kingdom in a state of emergency and under martial law."

There's a pause where I find myself staring at the radio in shock. State of emergency.

"We ask that civilians follow our instructions and cooperate during this difficult time. Protection shelters have been established as of last night and will continue to be set up in various cities through the UK.

"Those who have food and supplies are advised to stay home for their own and others' safety. If you or your family have no supplies, seek help at the protection shelters.

"All borders have been closed. We urge civilians not to attempt crossing mainland UK borders. The Coast Guard patrols our coasts and airports, and the military are present at our land borders. Measures will be taken against anyone who violates these rules." She pauses again. "We face challenging times ahead of us, but it is not Great Britain's first time overcoming adversity. Like before, we must work together. If we do, we will prevail."

The radio crackles again, and then silence settles once more.

50
LIV

THEY SAT IN SILENCE, all of them trying to comprehend what they'd just heard.

Frances was the first one to speak. "I need to call Kerry."

Liv remembered Frances mentioning having family in Dublin. That was where she was heading. Liv's stomach grew heavy at the idea of Frances leaving, and it struck her that Frances's presence had become somewhat comforting. The realisation surprised her and made her uneasy at the same time.

They all had lives before all of this went down. Of course the others would have people they wanted to contact. To make sure they were safe and alive.

Liv had no mobile, and even if she did, there was no one to call. She tapped her thigh with her fingers, waiting patiently as the others tried to ring their families. Noah was the only other person who wasn't trying to ring someone.

He stood in the background looking somewhere to his side, and she wondered why someone like Noah didn't have anyone.

Frances lowered the phone from her ear with a puzzled look. "It won't connect. At all."

"Neither does mine." Jake shook his head. "Probably a case of everyone trying to get a hold of everyone."

"What do we do now?" Noah's brows furrowed.

"They mentioned protection shelters," Angela said, though her voice was hesitant.

The protective shelters that were being set up to keep the people inside safe. From the infection on the outside. It sounded good, but the thing about people being "safely" locked up in one place was that it worked two ways. It kept things out, just as well as it kept them in. Regardless of what was inside with them.

Liv had spent two years in prison, long enough to learn that it only took one thing to go wrong before everything went tits up.

"I don't think the shelters are a good idea," she said, hoping no one would want an explanation as to why she thought so.

Roy nodded. "I agree. I think we're better off staying away from crowds of civilians. At least for now, while we don't know what this thing is."

"So, we go to my parents' place, hunker down, and wait for my dad?" Jake asked.

Liv had nowhere else to go, and now it appeared it was the same for the others. But there was an unspoken hope that Jake's dad would have the resources to help the rest of them get back to their families. Maybe they were right. Either way being out on the roads seemed like a bad idea, especially now.

"Then we go now," Angela said, pointing at her wristwatch. "I don't think the roads will be empty for long after that announcement."

They all agreed and—when Angela pointed out that the PM didn't mention the spores—they decided to go through Aylesbury, a small town with a hardware store and some food shops, according to Jake's mobile. They could replace some of the food they'd lost on the boat. More importantly, they could get protective masks.

With that plan in mind, they rolled out from the side of the road with Jake fast asleep and Frances lost in her own thoughts.

Liv drummed her thumb against the steering wheel, her eyes set on the road. If she concentrated on driving, she wouldn't think about the growing knot in her stomach at the uncertainty of the whole situation. It was an all too familiar feeling. One she hadn't thought she'd ever feel again.

On her first day of prison, the warden had led Liv into the cell block late at night, then locked her in a cell with another inmate who spoke no English. She had no idea what to expect. The only thing she knew for certain was that life would never be the same. From that moment on, every day would be a battle.

She checked the rearview mirror, always watching her back. She'd left prison knowing that as long as she stayed in line and played her cards right, she would never have to return. Never have to feel that same feeling of complete and utter loss of control.

The first tendrils of ice-cold panic moved through her, and she gripped the steering wheel hard, her knuckles whitening. England and the rest of mainland UK were in a state of emergency. Under martial law. Was anyone certain of what that meant? Was the military patrolling the country or just the borders?

It reminded her of prison right before the top dog was released, when everyone locked up wondered who would take her place. When they waited to see who would battle it out and worried how it would affect the rest of them.

Liv chewed her lip. During a situation like this in prison, she'd be working on stocking up on things like fags, prison-issued shower gel, and hand-wash powder. Inmates like her were especially targeted, and those were valuable things that had saved her skin on more than a few occasions.

There had been multiple changes in command during her stay at Her Majesty's Pleasure and each time she would make herself wake up every other hour. When they came for her, she would be prepared. It was how things worked in prison. If she was prepared, she could deal with it. Only this wasn't prison. This was the real world.

In prison, they all knew they were worth shit. They were criminals. Not to be trusted. Out here, the so-called good people could justify any action in the name of doing what's right. It made people unreliable and dangerous. If they wanted to stay alive, they would have to prepare. Not just against the infected, but against the living.

51

JAKE

ANGELA WAS RIGHT WHEN she said the empty roads wouldn't last for long. We try to navigate our way, avoiding main roads, but soon even the back roads fill with people leaving their homes. We pass through small towns that should be quiet and calm, but instead people run in and out of their houses, packing their cars.

Shops have been looted, and I screw my face up in dismay at what people choose to loot. Clothes and electronics.

"This is probably what they've been trying to avoid," Liv says as we roll through Aylesbury. A man carrying a TV scampers down the street.

"He's not doing a very good job though." I tut and shake my head at his poor choice of loot.

"No," Liv agrees, "he should be getting fags and soap."

I lift an eyebrow at her. "Is this where we learn about your Prison Daddy expertise?" I think I see her tense for a millisecond, but she recovers quickly.

"You got that list ready for the others?" she asks and tilts her head towards a shop with a yellow and blue sign. I tried to convince them to let me help, but I gave up after five minutes of arguing with both Liv and Frances.

I wave the small paper in the air. "I have the list."

Liv pulls to a stop, and I open the door when Noah and Fareena appear. Noah looks tired with a few days' worth of stubble and noticeable bags under his eyes.

"You alright?" I ask when they reach our car.

"Yeah," Noah says, but his eyes flicker and he brushes a hand through his wavy hair. Fareena gives me an uncharacteristically sombre nod.

"Right, that should be it." I hand them the note with all the things we came up with in the car. "This is pretty shit, isn't it?" I say once they're out of earshot. When even Noah isn't trying his utmost to be a jerk, things must be bad. We all knew London was terrible, but I don't think any of us could have foreseen this development, even in our wildest conspiracy-driven scenarios.

"It's all a bit of shock." Frances exhales slowly. There's a slight quiver to it.

Liv observes Frances from the rearview mirror, a barely noticeable wrinkle creasing between her brows before her expression softens. "What are you thinking?"

"I thought I would have more time to get back to Kerry." Regret weighs Frances's shoulders down and she blinks away the dampness in her eyes.

"There's still time," Liv says even though we all know Frances won't be able to reach her family now. I wish I could promise them that my dad will help them get home, but I haven't heard from him since London. Right now, I'm just hoping he'll make it home. Maybe then we'll get actual answers—not lies to keep us calm.

We wait for almost ten minutes, then Fareena and Noah emerge, speed walking from the shop with two big bags.

"Wow," I say and peer into the bag Noah hands me.

"You know, we should probably get going," Noah says in a voice that is too nice. It's only now I notice him rocking on his heels. Fareena keeps trying to tuck hair behind her ear, one hand shoved in her pocket.

Liv tilts her head. She looks at Noah and Fareena, then at the shop, then back at the fidgeting duo. "Why did you steal these things?"

"We didn't—" Noah starts, but Fareena's grunt interrupts him.

"We waited and tried to pay, but there was *no one* there."

I was never the kid to go shoplifting with my mates. I was the one smoking pot in the alleyway while waiting for the others who shoplifted makeup in Next or whatnot. "At least tell me no one saw you nick it."

Fareena's lips twitch. "Apparently tools shops aren't the place to be."

"Right, well, if Bonnie and Clyde get back to their car, we so can get going." Frances's voice drips with amusement.

As we pull out from the front of the shop, a loud buzz vibrates the dashboard. My phone.

"Mum?"

"Hyeong!" Tim's voice cries.

"Timmy?" I ask in surprise.

"Hyeong," he cries again, "I'm scared."

I instantly swap to Korean. "Little brother, what's wrong? Where's Mother?"

"She's in the kitchen, and she's really angry."

Mum angry? Mum rarely got angry, and when she did, she didn't show it. "Why is she angry?"

He sniffles. "She says she has a headache. That her eyes hurt. And she's been shouting at the mirror and throwing things."

No. No! My head screams at me. It can't be. Not my mum! I told her to stay inside. I feel my heart pace pick up. How could the infection already be in Huntingdon? The noise of my chaotic thoughts grows into a deafening crescendo, and I find it hard to breathe.

"Hyeong?"

I snap back to reality. I have to keep my shit together for Tim. "Timmy," I say in the calmest voice I can muster. "I need you to do something for me." There's a long moment of silence and for a heartbeat I worry we lost our connection. "Timmy?"

"Okay," he says after a while, his voice small.

"I need you to tell Mum I'm outside and when she's outside you lock the door and you don't open for anyone."

"Why?" he exclaims in unbridled shock. "I don't want to. I'm going to be in trouble."

"Listen to me. I *promise* you won't be in trouble, but I really need you to do this for me. Please. Just till I get there, and then we can talk to Mum."

There's a brief silence as he ponders this, then a sigh. "Okay."

"Don't open the door. Not until you see me. And you're going to have to be super quick about it, you understand?"

"Yes," he says, breathing into the phone.

"When are you allowed to open the door again?"

"When you're here."

"That's right. Now go do it. Keep me on the phone with you." Worry roils through my entire body as I hear him move through the house.

"Umma?" *Mum*? His voice shakes when he calls her.

For a terrifying moment, all I hear is the rustling of someone running, and then my mum's angry voice as she shouts at Tim. She sounds different, though. Her voice is cold, melting into sinister. Like the old lady at the shop. Then the sound of the door slamming and locks clicking reaches my ear.

"Tim?" There's no answer. "Timmy!"

"Yes," he breathes after a while, and I drop my head into my hand.

"Alright, now lock yourself in your room in case Mum gets in."

"Why is she so angry?" His voice quivers. "Did I do something wrong?"

"No, little brother," I try to reassure him, but Timmy was always a sensitive kid, and I'm not sure it's helping. I try another approach. "Mum's not feeling well. I'm going to get her help when we get there. I promise."

"I don't want Mum to be sick," he cries, and I regret my not so great way of dealing with it.

I swap back to English. "She's not angry at you, buddy, and when I get there, we'll help her, okay? I've got a friend here who's a doctor." Liv gives me a sidelong look. "She can take a look at her."

"She can make Mum better?" He seems to perk up at this.

"Maybe. But I need you to stay in your room. Promise me."

"Promise."

"No, Hyun-Promise me," I demand. It's the sacred brother promise that may never, ever be broken. I let Timmy make up the rules on that one.

"I Hyun-Promise," he whispers solemnly.

Satisfied, I look at my watch. "I'll be there in an hour. Keep an eye out from your bedroom window."

"I'll use my binoculars." The sheets on his bed rustle as he moves to sit by the window.

"Sounds good, buddy."

"Okay, bye." He sounds almost a little excited, and it makes me smile.

"Whoa, whoa, buddy." I stop him before he hangs up. "Did you forget something?"

"I love you."

"Love you, too." He hangs up, and I look down at my phone, still trying to comprehend what happened. Mum infected? My stomach twists with dread. I know we must grow up at some point, but thinking about my mum dying isn't something I've done before. Mums aren't supposed to die. Not until they're old and grey and you've had a lifetime to prepare for it.

"Shit." I tug at my hair in anxiety, stress and worry churning my stomach.

"What's wrong?" Frances asks carefully, but I don't know how to answer. Somehow thinking I'd been infected was easier than thinking of Mum being infected. "Jake?"

"My mum," I finally say. "My brother had to lock her out of the house." I don't know what else to say. The crestfallen looks on their faces tell me they understand.

"He'll be fine," Liv says as she speeds up.

Frances gives my shoulder a squeeze.

I wish it reassured me, but now my brother's life is at stake and I'm still an hour away. A lot can happen in an hour. And maybe time wouldn't be a problem if some of the infected weren't lurkers. If they weren't somewhat smart. The lurker at the boat waited us out, tried to trick us. If Mum really wants to get into the house, eventually she will.

My heart races. I have to get to Tim before Mum does.

52

JAKE

"THE BRITISH ARMY IS working to establish help zones in various cities throughout the UK," a woman with a nasal voice informs us over the radio.

"In Greater London, the Army has organised more than a hundred and twenty camps to aid people. The government has confirmed that they have planned protection packages for specific drop-off points at a nonspecific date later this week. If you cannot get to one of those drop points, the government and PHE advise the use of masks at all times when leaving your house."

It's the same news that's been repeated for what seems to be every minute this past hour. I've stopped listening. Instead, I keep my eyes on the road. I'm not the Christian type, or any type of religious, but I silently pray or bargain with any god I can think of that we'll make it to Tim in time.

We've passed fields where camps are being built, only to pass a group of infected just a few miles down the road. They give chase for as long as they can or until we get too far away.

The highways are packed tight with cars that stand painfully still. Their drivers honk in frustration as if it will magically get the line moving. I wonder if they've considered the noise they're making. Or do they not know the infected are drawn to the sound of people? To the sound of prey.

Houses, streets, and cars all blur into seamless multicoloured streaks. It's not until we reach St. Neots that I start to pay attention to my surroundings. I know these parts like the back of my hand. This is where Cait lived before we both left for university in London. I've driven this route so many times I know every speed bump, every shortcut.

We follow the winding roads until we see a white sign that reads Welcome to Godmanchester in black letters. I want to cry in relief. Even though the traffic is backed up all the way to our location, I know that if need be, I can jump out of the car and run home.

Some houses have broken windows and doors, obviously vandalized. Others have boarded windows, and some residents are still fortifying their homes, preparing to stay low until the infection is under control. The street next to the post office is littered with plastic bags, clothes, and food items dropped by people in their haste to loot the post office corner shop. A red Closed sign hangs ajar on the door, and I feel sorry for the owner at the sight of the shattered shop windows.

A Black guy in a military-green bomber jacket steps through one of the windows and surveys his surroundings. He looks slightly familiar, and when he turns my way, I recognise him.

Justin Davis. We went to college together and every time I visit, we try to fit in a pint so he can tell me about his awful life as a carefree single guy.

I roll down my window. "Justin!"

He can't see me, and he strokes his chin in thought as he scans the street.

"Oi! Over here, mate!" I stick my arm out the window.

"Jake!" His face lights up, and he quickly crosses the road. "Man, you look like shit."

I slap my hand into his. "Gee, thanks, always knew how to compliment a guy."

"And women." I roll my eyes. Still an arse. Then he spots Liv, and his lips twitch goofily at the corners. "Nice catch, mate. And she's got a sister."

"Oh, he's a charmer." Frances peeks out between the seats.

"Stop it." I give him *the look*, and he lifts his hands in an I'm-on-my-best-behaviour gesture. He's not. Justin is the tough bad boy the girls *love*. He's got that deep, sexy voice and an easy-going vibe about him. "What happened here?"

His expression turns serious as he scans the street in front of us. "Sick, init? People have gone batshit crazy. I didn't believe it when my sister first told me. Thought she was off her rocker. But then I saw my neighbour chew on her own husband's face."

His expression turns my stomach into knots. I've never seen him this serious. "How did they get here before us?"

"You coming from London?" It sounds more like a surprised statement than a question.

I nod. "Have to get to... get home."

"Megsters?" I don't know what to say, so I shake my head. "Ah shit, I'm sorry, bruv."

"Do you know why it's so backed up?" I change the subject.

"Military setting up shop in the fields behind Goddie park." He nods towards the tree line on our left, then sniggers. "Bellends were trying to set up in the park."

I exhale in amusement. Goddie park is a sizeable park on a small island that rests in the Ouse, and in good British tradition it floods entirely every year. "When did they twig?"

"This morning when it was flooded."

"Ouch."

"Yeah, moving everything over to the field now, most people are heading over there."

"What about you?" I cast a quick glance at the line of cars that haven't moved at all.

"Nah, going to my sister's after dropping some stuff off at Mr. Hannigan's next door. Poor sod, lost his wife and one of his kids." He hoists his bag up onto his shoulder. "I really should get going."

"Alright, mate. Be safe, yeah." I hold out my hand. He grabs it and gives it a small squeeze.

"Yeah, mate, you too." He flashes us all one last disgustingly charming smile and takes off zigzagging between the cars.

"Hey, Justin!" He turns to look at me. "You know where to find me if you need anything."

He gives a small wave, and I watch him until he disappears between two white houses as the line finally starts moving.

I take a deep breath and almost miss the white bridge that connects Goddie park with the rest of Godmanchester.

Godmanchester Chinese bridge. Where Megan once kissed me, and we promised each other forever. We were only kids back then. Earlier this year, I came here after finding out about her and Cait. We'd been stupid to believe in forever.

Exhaling, I pull my gaze away from the bridge with its white timber and oriental design. I should keep my head in the now, but it's hard not going down memory lane when this is where all the memories were made. Where I grew up.

"Withered!" Frances points at a green field less than twenty feet away.

Infected move across it. Some fast, others slower, but with the same raw determination as the infected we barely escaped in London.

In the cars ahead, people point frantically in the direction of the infected. I silently pray they will curb their instinct to leave their car behind and run. The last thing we need is an abandoned car blocking our escape route.

Two of the cars speed up, but a red car right in front of us panics. The middle-aged driver tries to turn into the opposite lane, only to get hit by an oncoming car in the other lane.

Liv curses and turns the wheel a millisecond before hitting the red car. *Holy shit.* She really drives like a car thief. Looking in the rearview mirror, I see Noah hot on our heels as we speed after the other cars.

When we near the Old Bridge, the one that connects Godmanchester with Huntingdon, crowds of people pour from the other side. Some run, some flee on bikes. Some cars try to alert them by honking, but they keep running.

My stomach tightens. "If those people are running from the infected..."

"The honking will draw them this way." Liv's jaw clenches. We crawl across the Old Bridge until we see the Ring Road, the road that loops around the town centre.

It's packed with cars, some emptied and abandoned, others with their owners honking angrily at the unoccupied cars and too busy to see the infected that rush up the street.

"We need to leave!" I kick my door open. Our car will block the ones behind, but the traffic is too jammed. We're not going any farther now, anyway.

Liv and Frances grab our bags and abandon the car, waving for the others to follow. They pile out of the car and rush over.

A high-pitched wail pierces the air, and we turn. Behind us, a lady carrying a small white dog gets knocked to the ground by a group of infected. More infected swarm around the woman with the dog, the smell of fresh blood stirring them into a frenzy.

One of the infected looks a little bigger, a little less crazed. Blood covers his face, a strip of flesh or gut hanging from his mouth. He throws his head backwards, and an ear-piercing shriek rips from his mouth, the same sound as the lurker on the canal. It's a calling sound.

"Let's go!" I spin, cricket bat in hand, and sprint up the road and onto the high street. I take the shortcut to our right through an arch. It leads us away from the mayhem on the main road and down a quieter alley.

Something clatters to the ground, and I hear Roy curse. But I don't stop. I need to get to Tim.

The others shout at me to wait, but I'm already halfway down the street, moving so fast I almost topple over as I swerve around the corner.

I pass brick houses and fenced-off front gardens until I see our house. White walls stark against the yellow brick houses and dull street cobble. At the top, I can spot Timmy's window and a shadow behind it.

Speeding up, I draw closer to the house in time to see Tim wave excitedly, then he disappears from view, no doubt rushing down the stairs to greet me.

"Wait!" I try to shout, but I'm too far away and he's already gone.

I'm almost by our gate when I see his tiny face peer out the living room window. He looks this way and that, and I hold my hands up in the air, motioning for him to stay put.

That's when I see it. The shadow behind him. Twitching and jerking. Moving towards him.

"Tim, get out! Tim!" I shout at the top of my lungs, wheeling my arm around in the air towards myself. "Tim!"

I watch in horror as his eyes widen. He spins around and screams, and I leap across the short gate just as the door flies open and Tim stumbles out.

"Jake!" Fear rattles his voice, and he slows slightly to run down the stairs. I throw my arms out, reaching for him.

Mum launches herself, mouth wide open, arms stretched out like a panther leaping onto its prey.

He tumbles to the ground with a frightened cry. Mum lands on top, yanking him around by the neck like he's a rag doll.

"Mum!" I grab the back of her shirt, but the creature, the infected, whatever this thing is now—is not my mum.

She releases him and spins to stare at me, red vines growing out of her eyes, yellow spores mixed with fresh, dark blood coating her teeth and what remains of her eyes. I freeze. My bat clatters to the ground.

That used to be my mother. Whatever it may be now, that was the woman who raised me. Scolded me when I was naughty, laughed with me, held me when I was sad. The woman who loved me. I can't kill her. All I can do is watch her advance, the others still too far behind to help me.

She grabs at me with fingers that are brown and dirty from blood and flesh.

"Mum, please," I whisper. "Please." My pleas fall on deaf ears, and she hurls herself at me.

Something blurs past, knocking her off course, and she lets out an angry howl as Karma drags her away.

The others round the corner, sprinting down the street towards me. I dash to where Tim lies on his back.

Blood pools from his neck. I drop to my knees, using my hand to cover as much of his wound as I can. It's warm. Sickly warm. It seeps through the slits of my fingers. Panic roils through my body, but I clamp down on it.

"It's okay. It's okay, Tim. You're going to be fine." I pull him into my arms. Seconds later, Liv drops to her knees, pressing a piece of fabric against the wound on his neck. It soaks with dark-red blood almost immediately.

His round, rosy cheeks are stained with tears, his small hand clutching the front of my shirt.

"Hyeong," he cries, his small mouth quivering, chest rising and falling in quick shallow breaths. Somewhere behind me I hear Karma's snarl, and an odd thwack followed by a crunching pop, then everything around us falls silent.

"It's okay. Don't be scared." I steady my voice and cup his small face with my hand, then gently wipe his tears away with my thumb. It looks so unnaturally big against his tiny cheek. "Hey, do you remember that time we went fishing? With Mum and Dad. Over at Elvesden."

He nods, his breath growing ragged, and my throat tightens into a knot. He's so small. He's always been small, even for his age. He used to follow me around whenever I was home. I could barely even go to the loo on my own. I'm not ready for him to stop following me around, to stop asking me what I'm doing. I'm not ready to let him go.

"Buddy, can you do me a favour?" I ask.

He blinks sluggishly.

"Why don't you close your eyes, so you can really see it—the lake."

He nods again, a shiver running through his small body, and he clutches frantically at my shirt. A shaky cry slips across his lips.

"It's alright, bud. Just close your eyes." I stroke his face and smile with every ounce of strength I have. I can't let him see how I'm breaking at the thought of losing the little brother who once fit in the palm of my hand.

He finally closes his eyes, his breathing heavy and strained.

"That's my boy," I whisper and put my forehead against his. "Can you see the lake? With the funny trees and the little boat. And the fishing rods we used to catch that big fish." He nods again, lips moving as if he's trying to speak. I close my eyes to keep my tears from falling, but I can't stop them. They roll from my eyes, down the bridge of my nose and onto Tim's face, mingling with his.

I take a deep, shaky breath. "Do you see Mum and Dad?" Another nod. "Mum's wearing that green dress with the big silly animals on them. And Dad is in his..." For the life of me, I can't remember what Dad wore that day. "He's in his favourite jeans."

His hand tugs at my shirt. "Are you there?" he asks, his whisper almost inaudible.

I try to speak, but all that comes out is a sob, and it hurts my entire being to swallow down on it. "Yeah, buddy," I whisper, "of course I am."

His chest rises again, and then it falls with one last soft whisper. The hand that clutches my shirt falls to his stomach.

I hold it against my chest as if somehow my heartbeats will bring him back, then I press my face against his and weep.

53

LIV

THE KITCHEN WAS BIG, with white walls and pale-yellow cupboards, bright and pleasant. An almost cruel contrast to their sombre mood.

Fresh herbs in tins, dried chillies in glass jars, cookbooks and vegetables cluttered the work tops. Two large windows and a door opened to a large garden, giving the room a warm, sun-kissed atmosphere.

Liv sat with her arms wrapped around herself. That way, she didn't have to look at them, wasn't reminded of the blood that had stained them earlier.

Jake sat at the far end, his eyes and nose a swollen red. She hugged herself tighter at the sight. It felt like they were all intruding by being in the kitchen when Jake's mother lay dead in the front garden.

Frances walked to the table and stopped by Jake. When she put an arm around his shoulders, he sagged into the embrace.

"It's alright, Chicken." Frances kissed the side of his bowed head.

Roy leaned across the table and placed his big hands on top of Jake's, giving them a squeeze. "We're going to find a way to put them to rest."

Jake didn't reply. His shoulders shook, fingers twitching beneath Roy's hand. Liv looked at her lap, unable to watch. Jake's pain was too real, too familiar.

Someone touched her arm and she flinched away.

"Liv?" Fareena watched her with concern. Liv clenched her jaws. Her head and throat throbbed from trying to control her emotions.

"I'm fine." This wasn't about her. She wasn't the one who'd just watched her family die.

"Okay," Fareena said.

"I'm sorry." Jake inhaled sharply and held out his hand in apology. "I'll pull myself together."

"Jake, honey," Angela started, but Jake waved his hands, cutting her off.

"I can't just sit here and feel like this." It was barely a whisper, making him sound small and vulnerable. "We need to start... preparing, I guess."

Roy nodded. "Things are looking even worse. For now, our best option is to stay put here."

Everyone nodded in agreement. What else was there to do? Where else could they go?

"We need to start thinking about water and food supplies," Jake said, his voice less fragile.

Frances motioned to the kitchen tap. "Well, there's still running water and gas. But for how long?"

"Not long. If people stop going to work, power and water reservoirs will be unmanned. We should start thinking about filling up on water while we can."

"What about food?" Angela pondered out loud.

"Mum should have enough for a few weeks. She'd always stock up."

Roy leaned back, and his chair creaked in protest. "I know a thing or two about foraging. It should help keep us going."

For the first time since they'd arrived, Liv smiled. Of course, the restaurant owner knew how to cook with moss and twigs.

"A thing or two." Angela rolled her eyes. "He's obsessed with it. Paid nearly three thousand dollars to get a Wild Food Culinary diploma."

"It'll keep you fed in the coming days, woman." Roy shot her a mock dirty look.

"Megan used to bang on about learning to forage." A smile pulled at Jake's lips. Though it didn't reach his eyes the way it usually did.

"I'm sorry, you guys, I'm being a city brat. What are we talking about?" Fareena's nose scrunched up.

"Food you can find in nature. Fungi, berries, certain weeds. No, young lady, not that kind of weed." Roy grinned when Fareena's eyes lit up.

"I could probably make a contraption for catching water," Noah said.

Liv let out a huff. "A contraption?" What was he, a mad scientist?

His cheeks flushed. "I used to tinker in my spare time."

"With what?" Fareena looked as if she was about to laugh, which, Liv reminded herself, would be highly inappropriate at the moment.

"Does it really matter?" Noah scowled at Fareena, who lifted her hands in a half-hearted apology.

"There are tools and planks in the shed outside. We have to board up the windows. I have to—" Getting up from his seat, Jake swayed.

Frances grabbed him by the shoulders. "You need to rest, love."

"The rest of us can handle this," Angela reassured him.

Roy slapped his hands together, startling them all, and rose to his feet. "Right, that's settled then. Frances makes sure Jake gets some rest. I'll get some food going. Noah, contraption. Ange, windows. Liv, Fareena take a pick where you want to help."

"Do you want help with your *contraption*?" Fareena said to Noah.

"Sure." He shrugged, but Liv could hear the change in his voice. To say it was excited would be like describing a toilet roll as adventurous. But something had started to creep into his behaviour over the last couple of days. Something not as unlikable as before.

Liv moved to where Frances and Jake stood. "Here." She pressed one of the blister packages into Frances's hands. It was unlikely Jake would be able to sleep. His mind would replay the last moments of his mother's and Tim's lives. Every little detail. Trying to remember everything. As if his mind was trying to solve a puzzle. It was how the brain worked.

"This is probably not the best time for you to stop self-medicating, love." Frances gave her a knowing look. She'd known? For how long?

"I'll be fine; he needs it more than me."

"Why don't you have a little rest as well?"

Liv shook her head. "I have something I have to do."

The others could start with the windows and water. She would help, but first she needed to see to Tim and his mother. When Jake came back down, he'd want to see his little brother and mother. Someone should make sure it wasn't harder than it had to be. And it had to be her. After everything, she owed him that much.

54

JAKE

EVERYTHING AFTER OUR ARRIVAL at the house is a blur. I don't know how long I stayed with Tim or how I found the strength to get up. Maybe someone helped me. I can't remember. But I remember Roy carrying Tim into the house, and I remember Liv.

The stricken expression on her face. How she held her arm in front of her mouth, her hand shaking uncontrollably. Round and impossibly heavy tears rolled down her cheeks, burning them red, and when I met her eyes, it felt like I was swallowed by a sea of grief almost as endless as my own.

We left my mum in the garden after covering her with a sheet and black plastic bags. We don't know exactly how the infection spreads, but with the spores we can't take any chances. We have our masks, but we don't know what touching the spores does. Until we have proper protective gear, we can't move her. Not without risking infection.

It makes me feel like the worst son in the world. The thought of her out there like discarded rubbish. I *know* it's too dangerous to do anything else, but it feels like shit.

I sit on the floor in Dad's office where Tim lies on a blanket, a pillow propped under his head. Someone has cleaned his face and neck and put him in new clothes. A pair of jeans and a blue turtleneck to cover up the bite on his neck. I don't know who did it, but I'm eternally thankful. He looks so peaceful, as if he's sleeping. But then I realise he's not, and I wipe tears from my eyes.

He and Mum were the sole reason for my trip here. Now I'm here, but they're both gone. Yet their presence is everywhere in the house. All my senses tell me they should be here. Every time I've walked into the kitchen, I've expected to find Mum watching one of her favourite Korean TV shows while preparing dinner. And every time it takes my brain a few seconds before it remembers. Before my world crumbles all over again.

I lean forward and kiss Tim gently on his forehead, then leave and walk outside. It's late, and everyone else is asleep. They spent the first day boarding up the windows, making the house look abandoned, while I was knocked out in bed, drifting in and out of feverish nightmares.

The soft, wet grass squelches, and I pass something that looks like a mutation between a mini radio tower and a parasol turned upside down. A thick pipe sits in a large barrel and a blue tarp at the top catches the rain.

Noah had mentioned a contraption. I assume this is it. Black netting sticks out from under the lid that covers the barrel and Noah even installed a small spigot. This water system is a lot more sophisticated than the barrel and lid I had in mind.

I don't know which surprises me the most, that Noah built this complex structure or that Dad had a spigot in the shed. I suppose mum wanted it for her gardening.

Mum. My eyes fall on the plastic bag in the corner beside the shed. How can my mum be under those bags? Mum, who was first in her family to graduate from university. Who flew to New York to study for the New York State bar, where she met my dad. She was always so brave and headstrong.

It seems impossible she's under those bags. I swallow and move towards the body. My heart hammers in my chest. I shake my head when I picture her just before she died. I don't want to see her like that. I don't want to know what she looks like now. I want to remember her the way she was.

I stop and look down at the black bags, at the unmistakable body shape underneath the plastic. She's completely still, lifeless. Now that I'm close, I see a hand has slipped from under her black shroud. Pale fingers slightly curled, nail beds tinged with blue. It seems so unreal. So impossible it's her hand.

"Mum?" I whisper as if she can still hear me. Mum was my safe harbour. She made me feel less wrong and broken, made me feel loved even when I didn't think myself worth it. I was so sure I'd come here, and she'd tell me everything would be okay. But I'll never hear those words from her again, and I don't know what to do. I'll never feel her warm embrace. Never hear her or Tim's laughter again.

I fall to my knees. "Mum," I cry touching her cold, cold hand with mine. "What do I do? I don't know what to do." I can't fathom life without her or Tim. I suck in a hard breath, squeeze my eyes shut, and press my fist against my mouth. Tears roll down my nose and between my fingers, but I will myself to swallow the grief that threatens to tear me apart. When I open my eyes again, my chest quivers as I inhale deeply.

Losing my shit won't help. It won't bring them back. I tell myself this before I stand on unsteady feet, grabbing the old shed for support.

The shed contains our old things like bikes, a wheelbarrow, and shovels. I grab a shovel and walk to a spot under one of Mum's cherry trees. This is a good spot for a homemade fridge, and with the electricity gone most of the time, we need one to keep food fresh. And I need the distraction, need to do anything to keep this unbearable pain at bay.

The rounded tip of the blade slices through soil softened from days of rain. Earth falls onto the ground as I lift it. Mum would have gone mental if she saw me now. The thought makes me smile until heaviness settles in my chest.

55

JAKE

I CAME HERE TO keep my family safe. But they're gone. Everyone is gone. Megan and Dad too. It's absurd to me that the world keeps spinning when mine has been shattered. What the hell is the point? Even if the world was set right tomorrow, a world without my family seems unbearable.

I look at the wooden fence that separates us from surrounding houses. Green ivy grows along the panels, and two neighbouring trees dip into our garden on the far end. Mum used to love sitting underneath their blossoming crowns during spring, tea in one hand, her trusty pruner in her lap.

The panels are tall, but I could climb them easily, slip across and into the night before anyone noticed. The others are safe. For now. There's nothing more I can do for them.

I trudge through the wet grass and reach for the top of the fence, heaving myself onto it.

"Dangerous times to be sneaking out for a midnight stroll, don't you think?" She stands in the garden in one of the oversized, knitted cardigans she liked to wear. Pale against the night, like a ghost.

"Mum?" My heart lurches in my chest and I stumble towards her.

"No, sweetheart," Angela says, and it feels like I lost my mum all over again. For a second, I really thought it was her, that the corpse in the front garden was someone else. Angela must see it on my expression because she cups my face with her hands, her brown eyes sad. "I'm so sorry, Jake."

I nod to imply that it's fine, that I'm fine. I don't want to cry in front of her, but my emotions aren't listening to me.

"Where are you going?" She wipes my tears with her thumbs.

I raise my shoulders and let them drop because I genuinely don't know. I don't even know how to breathe through these emotions. "There's nothing left here."

"I know it feels like that. You've lost your mother and little brother. But is that"—she nods towards the fence panel—"what your mother would have wanted for you?"

"Does it matter?"

"Oh, sugar, of course it does. I'm dying to see my daughter again, but above all else, I want her to be alive, well, and *safe*. Even if I can't be there with her." She curls a finger under my chin and lifts it so my eyes meet hers. Her eyes are damp but whether it's because of me or the thought of her daughter, I can't tell. "I can tell you with a hundred percent certainty that she would not have wanted you to stop living. To go out here and become infected. To become nothing but a husk of your former self. It would be a parent's worst nightmare."

I drop my head. "I don't know what to do."

She pulls me into her arms, holding me tight. "It's okay not to know; the only thing you need to do now is remember to keep breathing."

I try to breathe through my stuffed nose. "Easier said than done."

Something between a sigh and a soft laugh slips across her lips. "I think I can help with that." She snakes her arm around my waist and leads me towards the house.

Grateful for her presence, for anyone to hold on to, I put my arm on her shoulder and pull her close. She's not my mother, but right now she's the next best thing.

56

LIV

"MUM, CAN I HAVE a phone?"

"A phone?" She stroked his pale cheek. "Why do you need a phone, darling?"

His small fingers plucked at a seam on the hospital sheets. She picked up his hand and kissed the tiny knuckles. "It's okay, you can tell me."

"If I have a phone, you and Dad can call me when I go away." His face fell. "If you miss me."

"No, darling," she said so fiercely she almost startled him. "You're not going anywhere. That's why we're here. So that you'll get better."

He looked at her then, his brown eyes round and sad.

"You're not going *anywhere*." She pressed her face against his cheek, and as her hair spilled across her shoulders and onto the bed, dark against his sickly pale skin, he picked up a strand and twisted it between his fingers.

"Okay, it doesn't matter."

"No?"

"No," he replied with a serious expression. "I'll always be able to hear you, anyway."

She leaned over to kiss him then but found the bed empty, as if he'd vanished into thin air.

"Ellis?" Liv woke herself up whispering his name. She rolled over to her side, looking at the pillow beside her.

Empty. She sat up in the dark room and rubbed sleep from her eyes, her mind still dazed and slightly confused. The dream had felt so real. She swore she could still feel his skin under her fingertips. That she could still hear the beautiful sound of him breathing. She dropped her face into her hands. It was a dream; it was always just a dream.

She'd had them for a long time after Ellis passed away. They were all different, but he was always in them giving her cryptic messages. Some days, she almost believed it had really been him. Talking to her through her dreams.

Then, in true Liv fashion, she'd gotten angry. Angry at the empty room that still held all his clothes and toys. Angry at David for being stuck in meetings when Ellis passed. And finally, angry at herself. What kind of paediatrician couldn't even save her own child?

Liv sighed in frustration. She hadn't dreamt of him in ages and that's the way she liked it. But then Jake's little brother had died. Had bled out on the wet ground, frightened and small, clinging to his brother. She should have kept herself together. But the entire world had spun and warped until they became a single focused pinprick. Jake and his brother. The blood on her hands. Tim, Toby, Ellis, Teresa. She couldn't tell the difference where she sat on her knees, unstoppable tears clouding her view.

There was nothing she could have done. So why did it feel like something inside her had broken?

Distant noises reached her ears, and she opened her eyes again, forcing the images of the children from her mind. It sounded like people walking down the street. Or was it the withered? They'd boarded the house, making it difficult for outsiders to get in, but that didn't mean they wouldn't try. Eventually, looters might come their way.

Throwing her covers to the side, she put her feet on the floor, stifling a gasp at the cold wood against her bare soles. Jake's house wasn't covered in carpets like most homes in England, and without heat, it made the house *freezing*.

She exhaled slowly, her warm breath turning the air white. They had released her from Chadwick Hall in spring earlier this year, and David and Lisa had so kindly offered to let her stay with them. She had declined, with two fingers thrown into the air, as she let them know she'd be picking up her mail in a week's time.

Probation meant she needed an address of residence. In her world, that didn't mean she actually had to live there. It may have been cold outside, but she'd rather sleep in her car than be anywhere near David. Lisa, she didn't mind. Gullible, sweet, and boring. *And really fucking judgy.*

April had been cold, but nowhere near as cold as this. She sucked air through her teeth, hugging herself and stroking the prickled skin on her arms. Careful not to wake Fareena, who shared her room, Liv tiptoed across the floor until she reached the door. The handle creaked, thwarting her efforts to be quiet as she stepped into the moonlit hallway.

A tall dark figure stood in the shadows, still and quiet, staring at her. Fear seized her heart, and she fumbled for something to defend herself with until the figure stepped into the moonlight.

"Liv?"

"Jesus, you could've killed us both, Jake!" She slammed her hand against her chest.

Jake had spent the past four days in bed, riddled with the fever. To say that she did not expect him to be lurking outside her door was an understatement. If he didn't still look a little poorly, she'd have punched him.

"Shh," he hushed her, a finger pressed to his lips as he jerked his head towards the window. "Over there."

Mildly annoyed at being shushed, she crept closer to the window. Situated on the second floor, it overlooked the street in front of the house.

With none of the lamps working, the street lay dark save for the soft moonlight. It provided enough light to illuminate dark shadows creeping down the street.

She leaned closer to the glass. Infected? The way they moved was too controlled, too human. Dressed in all dark clothes, moving in and out of houses like burglars or looters, looking for any valuables left behind.

A few days ago, items like jewellery, laptops, and tablets would've been considered valuable. Now, valuables amounted to edibles or supplies that could help keep you alive. Food, fluids, clothes, and anything that looked like a decent weapon. At least for those trying to survive outside the military camps.

Most owners had abandoned their houses to seek shelter at the military camp Justin had pointed out earlier. That left many homes empty and easy to loot.

The sound of glass breaking could be heard through the still night, and she leaned against the window to get a better view.

A growl came from the other side of Jake but he made a hushing noise and the growl died out again. As friendly as Karma looked, Liv had seen the massive dog a few days before, ripping at the infected attacking her owner. In that moment she looked terrifying, muscles straining, lips pulled back in a ferocious snarl, eyes dark and focused on one thing only: protecting Jake. If she hadn't, he would've probably been dead or infected by now.

It was an unpleasant thought and she turned her attention back to the four figures, cloaked by the dark, advancing down the street. They turned in at the brick house two houses down. Two held machete-like weapons in their hands, but the taller of the four held something aimed in front of himself.

Liv froze. A shotgun or a rifle. The darkness and awkward angle made it difficult to tell.

"Are your neighbours still home?"

Jake shook his head. "I didn't see them when we arrived. They're an old couple; they probably went to the camp."

"If they don't leave after clearing that house, we should wake everyone. Look at that one." She pointed at the shotgun looter. One of the smaller looters moved past him towards the door and knelt by the lock. He remained for a minute or so, and she snorted. "Fareena would have gotten it in less than half that time."

"Noob."

Another moment passed before the lock-picking looter signalled for the others. She watched Lock Picker duck down as Shotgun raised their weapon a little further.

It moved so fast she barely had time to see it, shooting out from the house as if it had been waiting for someone to finally release it.

Lock Picker scrambled backwards, arms and legs flailing in panic. Shotgun lifted their gun as if they were going to shoot the infected man when muffled shouts and chaotic scuffling drifted from farther down the street.

One of the looters aimed a torch in the direction of the sound, the beam lighting up the night. A group of infected shambled towards the group of looters. Their bodies were riddled with bites and various wounds, their clothes looking like they'd been crawling in mud. She could imagine the stink of vomit, piss, and days' old rubbish coming from them. The thought of being close enough to smell them made her shiver with terror.

These monsters, these once-people, were unstoppable. Bullets didn't stop them. Fire might stop them, but it would also infect more. Turn people into mindless husks.

She watched the looters sprint up the street, the infected following behind. Was it wrong to feel relief that the fleeing looters drew the attention of the infected?

"I'll never get used to seeing them," she whispered when she was sure the infected and their prey were out of earshot.

"It's fucking terrifying." Jake's breath fogged up the glass.

Terrifying. Now that was an understatement if ever she heard one. The cold seemed to rattle her bones and she hugged herself.

Jake turned towards her, his brows scrunched. "How are you not freezing to death?"

She looked down at herself. A new pair of boxer shorts and a top with thin fabric that didn't keep anything warm. She thinned her lips. "It's not like *I* have my childhood room here stuffed with my old clothes."

He let out a soft and humourless laugh. "Fair point. How about I let you pick some of my warmer clothes?"

"Considering I've been taking care of your sick arse, it's only fair."

He rolled his eyes, then beckoned her to follow him across the landing. "Ladies first." He pushed the door open to his room.

His room was big with white walls that were decorated with video game posters. A navy-blue rug that read Keep Calm and Don't Blink lay on the floor.

She stepped into the room and smiled at the sight of the bookshelf taking up half a wall. Books, DVDs, and video games were stacked higgledy-piggledy on the shelves. It looked as if it were going to explode. Jake had definitely been a geek growing up.

"Bit of a bookworm?"

"You know what they say, 'there's no friend as loyal as a book.'" Bitterness had snuck into his voice.

"I think you might be onto something."

A wry smile pulled at his lips. "There are clothes in there and the dresser drawers. Knock yourself out."

Shirts and t-shirts hung in neat, colour-coordinated rows ranging from white to black. She looked over at Jake, who stood by his bedside, then back into the wardrobe. "You're shitting me, right?" She pointed her finger at the clothes.

"It makes it easier for me to find the right top." He scratched the nape of his neck with a lopsided smile.

"I'll be honest. I'm not sure if I'm scared or impressed." She regarded the well-organised rows of clothes and spotted a blue flannel shirt. One couldn't possibly go wrong with flannel during British winter. Especially when it was going to be spent with no working heaters. Pulling it off the hanger, she slipped it over her head.

"There's an extra pair of joggers in the drawers. And thick socks."

Jake was wearing another pair of joggers. They hung low on his hips, revealing a well-toned and inked abdomen. Unlike the ones he'd worn on the boat, these weren't tatty and worn out, but shamelessly tight in exactly the right places. As eye candy went, they worked perfectly as wrappers.

She dragged her eyes up towards his face. "This should do it. You'll have it back once we've found more clothes." She owed him enough as it was. The less of a debt she accumulated, the better.

"Yeah, sure, no stress." He took a step to the side, allowing her to pass, but when she pressed her hand against the door handle, he spoke again. "Thank you."

She turned around, releasing the metal handle. "For what?"

"Angela told me what you did for Tim and Mum after they"—his voice turned thick—"after they passed."

"Of course, I..." Her voice trailed off when he dipped his head, ever so slightly looking at her.

"Are you alright?" Inquisitive eyes searched hers. Was she alright? Parts of her wanted to laugh. She could scarcely remember the last time she felt anything that resembled alright.

"You're asking me?"

"You looked a little—"

"I'm fine." She interrupted him, hoping that he'd leave it alone. Just like last time. When he said nothing else, she turned to leave.

"Hey, Liv?" His voice stopped her mid-turn. "Do you want to grab a cup of tea? With me."

She couldn't help but laugh. Of all the things he could say. "Are you asking me out?"

His eyes crinkled at the corners. "Promise I'll have you back by dawn?"

"Fine, but only if you hand me your joggers." She held out her hands and watched a big grin work its way onto his face. "The ones in your drawers."

"Sure, sure," he said innocently, though the way he looked at her was anything but.

The living room was the first room they'd stepped into. Bright with pale-yellow walls and large windows that had once let in light. Now, layers of newspaper covered them to help with insulation. It didn't do much, but in the apocalypse, one couldn't be choosy.

The best part, however, was the carpeted floors. It was the only room in the house with carpet, and Liv couldn't be more thankful as she sat waiting for her tea.

Tea wasn't exactly her thing. She'd much rather have a drink of whiskey, but with this bone-penetrating cold, she'd take anything warm she could get.

To her side, a flat screen stood next to a large fireplace. A fireplace that could keep them warm if the smell of burning wood wouldn't alert everyone nearby of their presence. Jake had said that determining where the smell came from was difficult, but until the worst of the looting had passed, they used it sparingly.

Jake had brought her a pair of woollen blankets and made sure she was wrapped up before leaving to make tea. She'd known since that first day in his creeper lair that he was a bit of a sappy romantic. What she hadn't known was how much she'd appreciate someone wrapping warm blankets around her.

Pulling them close, she let her eyes wander to the wall. Framed photos hung behind the telly. Ones of the entire family, ones of Jake's mum and brother. Then there was one of a young girl and a much younger boy. They both smiled into the camera, looking as if they'd just stopped tittering about something. The small boy looked particularly mischievous. Liv shook her head. Exactly like Jake.

"Sorry, Mum only has green tea left." Jake set their mugs on the polished wooden table, then lowered himself onto the couch. He sat rigidly, back straight, mug in his lap, and stared somewhere into the distance.

"I'm sorry, is this a business meeting or are we hanging out?" She rested her mug on the top of her knees, drawing a soft chortle from him.

"Alright." He pushed himself further into the sofa and pulled his legs up from the floor.

She stuck her toes underneath his thighs, drawing a curious look from him. "You're a living, breathing heater, remember?"

His Adam's apple bobbed in amusement. "Right, I keep forgetting."

She took a sip from the hot tea, revelling in the warm feeling in her chest. "That's a cute picture." She motioned with her head towards the photo.

He let out a groan. "I wish Mum wouldn't have it out, but she loves that photo. Loved," he corrected himself.

"I think that's part of parenting, though. Having pictures of your kids they'd rather be shredded," she mused. "Did it bother you a lot?"

"Sometimes," he admitted. A short silence followed, and he dropped his head against the sofa cushion. "It's so weird being here. Without them."

She lowered her mug but said nothing.

"I can still feel them. They're gone, but they're everywhere." He swallowed thickly and closed his eyes, his chest rising.

"It sucks. And it's going to suck for an insanely long time."

"Do you have a better time frame than 'insanely long'?" He cracked one eye open, the whisper of a smile on his lips. The kind of smile everyone had smiled at some point in their life. The smile of someone with enough hurt inside of themselves that they could barely make sense of it.

She shuffled closer to him. "No. But you have to get out of that bed every morning and keep putting one foot in front of the other."

"God, I'm tired of moving onwards and forwards." His weariness was so palpable she could nearly touch it.

"It's only tiring if you try to do it alone."

He looked at her then. "Speaking from experience?"

He might as well have doused her with a bucket of ice-cold water with the way her body shuddered. Jake was a nice bloke. He'd saved her an annoying number of times. Maybe she owed him. Not the entire truth, but some of it. "I lost someone when I was growing up."

He didn't speak, didn't ask her to continue, but waited patiently.

"Growing up was a little different for me, I imagine." She looked around the tidy living room. One could tell by the photos on display, the stylish but well-placed ornaments, and the books left out in various places, that this house was lived in.

She'd grown up in a small council flat with windows so dirty the sun was hardly able to break through. Where Jake had family photos on his walls, hers had been covered in stains from water damage and smoke.

"Where did you grow up?"

"Hoxton. And yes, all you've heard about it is probably true. My dad, Swedish born and bred wife beater, alcoholic, and petty criminal."

"Well, you know what they say, Swedes are cold-hearted wankers."

She laughed. If only he knew. "That's putting it mildly. But it wasn't all bad. For a little while we lived with a really nice couple." She trailed off. Marie and Henry, a couple in their late thirties who lived in a terrace house in Battersea.

She could still remember the taste of the roasted potatoes Marie and Harry would make for their Sunday roast. Back then it had been like living at a castle, and Liv had felt every bit the princess. She had her own room and clean clothes. Like a real princess.

"For a while?"

"My dad decided he wanted his kids back. So back we went, just like that." She picked at the blanket. "Things weren't so bad to begin with, and I thought maybe he'd changed. I should have known better."

"You were only a kid."

"My dad got upset about something. Started smacking my little brother Toby around. I threw a plate at him, thinking maybe he'd lay off him. He lost his mind. Hit Toby so hard he fell over and knocked his head on the kitchen counter." The crawling panic always started at that part of that particular memory, like a buzzing noise that grew into loud explosions in her ear. PTSD, the doctors called it. Her mind's way of protecting her from triggering memories.

"You don't have to tell me."

She ignored the intense, *imaginary* sounds. "People don't always die when they break their neck. But if you do, did you know you don't die instantly? It took Toby seven minutes to..." She swallowed the lump in her throat.

"I'm really sorry you had to go through that." Usually, the redundant sorry phrases annoyed her. Instead of being comforting, it made her feel like she had to explain to the other person that 'oh no, it's fine,' when—in reality—it wasn't fucking fine.

But Jake had just lost his own brother, the way he said it was different. Like someone who knew what it felt like. Like someone who actually gave a shit.

She caught herself reaching out to touch him and quickly withdrew her hand. He grabbed her wrist, his palm soft and warm against her skin. She could pull her wrist free if she wanted to, but perhaps most surprising to herself, she reached out and brushed her fingertips against his scruffy cheek.

"Careful, Liv." The way he said her name, smooth with a tint of whiskey vapour to it, sent a pleasant flutter through her.

"Or what?"

"Or I'll think you actually enjoy having me around."

57

JAKE

LIV'S LONG HAIR SPILLS across her shoulders and falls in her face, hiding it from view. She does that a lot. Rolls her shoulders forward and tucks her chin in towards her chest like she's trying to hide.

"Keep dreaming, Hipster." Her voice is a low hum, and I can imagine the raised eyebrow and crooked smile hidden somewhere behind the curtain of dark-brown hair.

Her hand is still on my cheek. Warm and comforting. I'd forgotten what it feels like. Everyday intimacy. The small touches here and there. The ones you use instead of words. To say: I love you, I see you, I'm here for you.

I know this isn't what she means, but it feels good. Every time she touches me. And it makes me wonder why I stayed with Megan for so long. A misguided sense of security and complacency?

"So," Liv says and drops her hand to the mug in her lap. "Tell me about your mum and Tim. What were they like?"

What were they like? I smile at the thought of them alive and well. The way they used to be. Mum almost always knew what I was thinking, and she was the first person I wanted to talk to if I had a rough day. Tim liked to play traffic police, forcing me to drive the cars "realistically" or I'd get a fine. There are so many good memories, I don't know where to start.

"Mum was the best."

"That's not very descriptive."

I laugh. "Fine. Mum was always there for me and always supported me. Didn't matter what I did. Unless, of course, it was something naughty. Man, if you disobeyed her, you would know it."

"How so?"

"My mum *never* yelled or scolded. She'd sit down, hands clasped on the table in front of her, and look at me, almost teary-eyed. And then she'd explain why my actions made her sad. And guess how she'd finish."

"Grounding you?"

I shake my head. "I wish. She'd tell me that it didn't matter who thought what. The one person I would really disappoint was myself."

"Ouch!"

"Right?" I sit up a little straighter. "I can take someone shouting at me, but my mum being sad... and the fact that me screwing things up would make me feel disappointed in myself. I can't even."

She laughs. "Master manipulator."

"I'll say." I exhale in defeat and sink back against the cushion.

"She sounds pretty great."

"She was." A sudden wave of sadness tugs at my chest, and I clear my throat. "She reminds me of my mum."

Her expression is different when she views me this time. Not so guarded. I think she's trying to distract me, but the fact that she's sharing things about herself in order to do so makes my chest tingle. "Yeah?"

"When Dad wasn't around, she'd bring out paper and crayons and we'd spend the day drawing. And we'd have pancakes for lunch. Even though she hated pancakes. 'Pancakes isn't proper food,' she'd say."

"Where is she now?"

"She passed away giving birth to Toby."

Both Liv's mother and her brother died when she was still only a kid. I've been so caught up with my own problems I didn't realise. For some of us this cruel world of death and destruction didn't just begin. For some, it tore their world apart long before the infected.

The thought makes me want to wrap her in my arms and keep her safe. She'd probably kill me if she knew, so I opt for waving my pack of cigarettes in front of her. Talking is nice, cathartic even, but there comes a point when the only right thing to do is to have a fag. "I think we both need one of these."

"We bloody deserve it." She stands and drags me off the sofa. Then, in true Liv fashion, she shoves me in front of herself with the excuse that I make a better meat shield than her.

"I'll have you know I'm very sinewy, not a very enjoyable meal," I protest as we step outside.

The cold is biting despite the thick blanket I wear, and I can't control the shudder that ripples through me.

I light my cigarette and inhale, closing my eyes briefly at the sensation of smoke filling my lungs. It shouldn't feel this good, but I guess that's addiction for you.

I'm not sure when I first started loving smoking. My gran smoked, always shutting herself in the bathroom, standing by an open window. I'd sneak up on her and open the door because I loved the smell, and she'd shoo me away with a thin, wrinkled hand. After that, the smell of smoking always reminded me of my gran. It was familiar and safe. The step to smoking wasn't all that far. I have no idea how I'll quit.

"Fuck, it's cold." Liv rubs her hands together, trying to warm them up.

"Here, take this." I hold the fag towards Liv, whose hand shakes when she reaches for it.

"So cold it's almost not worth wasting your fags on this."

"Turn around." I make a circular motion with my hand.

"Why?"

"Because I'm going to warm you up."

Her eyebrow rises. It's not quite suspicion, but not complete trust either.

"It's strictly professional."

She turns around, but not before I catch the glint in her eyes. I wrap my arms and blanket around her and pull her close. She doesn't stiffen up like I thought she would, but leans into me. She's not much shorter than me and her body is warm against mine.

I press my cheek against the side of her head. For heat. Strictly professional.

"I'd forgotten how warm you are." She holds the fag to my lips and I take another drag.

"It's my superpower."

"Good, then you can keep me warm when we go to sleep."

"Oh, can I now?" Last time we shared a bed, things got rather interesting.

"As two professionals." I can hear the jest in her voice.

"Okay, but what kind of professionals are we? I'm open to suggestions here."

She ribs me with her elbow, and I laugh. Maybe I shouldn't laugh so soon after my family passed away, but for an instant life almost feels normal. It's not much, but it's enough. For now.

58

LIV

THE PLAN HAD BEEN: sleep in Jake's bed because, boy, that man was hot. In every sense of the word. Then, before everyone else got up, sneak to her own bed.

Her plan had been successful but for one thing on that list. Because, contrary to popular belief, some people were crazy and got up before five in the morning. And if she had to choose between being sandwiched between Jake and Karma, perfectly warm and comfortable, or the walk of shame, it wasn't going to be a tough choice. So much for getting her home before dawn.

She looked down at her underdressed self. It appeared sleeping in joggers and a flannel shirt where Jake was concerned was not an option. Halfway through the night, she'd had to shed some of her layers. It very nearly ruined the authentic feeling of camping outside in winter.

Not that Jake would complain. He was, of course, the perfect gentleman, but he was also someone who seemed to appreciate her physical appearance. His eyes lingered, and he was too fine a specimen for her to object.

"Are you watching me sleep?" His voice was drowsy as he turned around.

"Nope. You're the only creep in this room."

"It was *not* a creeper lair." Jake squinted at the morning sun that peeked in through the window. Rays skittered across his messy hair, leaving a trail of blue reflections in their wake. Morning puffiness had his already full lips looking even plumper and more inviting. And devilishly soft.

"I'm sorry, I have to ask. What happens to your lips when you sleep?"

"My lips?"

"I mean, they're so big. Are you letting Karma chew on them or something?"

He let out a coarse laughter. "Leave my lips alone."

"And here I was going to show you my gratitude for warming me up last night."

Jake's eyes widened. "Well, I mean, I'd be willing to make an exception. This one time. I'm professional like that, you see."

"Like last night then?"

"Exactly."

A soft knock on the bedroom door silenced them both, and she hoped to sweet baby Jesus that it wouldn't swing open.

"Jake honey?" Frances's soft voice asked from the other side of the door.

Jake bit his lip in an oh-shit grimace. "Yes?"

"Do you feel well enough to come down for breakfast?"

"Um, yeah, yeah." Jake usually interacted with other people with ease. Liv had to admit there was something highly entertaining about watching him squirm.

"I'm glad to hear that, Chicken."

"I love it when she calls us that," Liv whispered, drawing a smile from him.

"I'll see you in a bit then." The floorboards creaked as Frances withdrew from the door. "Oh, and Liv, can you make sure Jake showers before he joins us?"

Liv felt her jaw drop, and she had to stifle a mortified gasp with the pillow.

"I'm not sure which is the best: Frances knowing or your face right now." Jake's eyes crinkled in amusement.

"Oh God." She was thirty-two years old. It had been a long time since getting caught in bed with someone else was a big deal. And yet she felt like she was going to be in trouble.

"I don't even know how she knows."

"Well, you do smell." She threw off the covers that landed on top of Karma. The big dog merely raised her ears, then went back to sleep.

"Holy shite, that's cold."

"And to think you're about to have a cold shower," she teased and headed for the door. He followed her gloomily until she turned around.

He wore a pair of tight, black briefs. Because why wouldn't he? She impressed herself by not letting her gaze linger too long. Despite the defined muscles that ran the length of his hips before diving in under the brief's lining. The word "pump" was printed on the lining, which proved more than a little unhelpful in curbing her wildly inappropriate thoughts. *Jesus, constrain your thirst!*

Taking her own advice, she raised her head. He watched through half-lidded eyes as she leaned forward and brushed her lips against his cheek.

When she moved away, he wore the same expression he had that first morning on the boat. Like he was trying to figure her out. A smile pulled at her lips. *Good luck with that.*

59

JAKE

FAREENA LOOKS LIKE A Cheshire cat when I walk into the kitchen after my ice-cold shower. We really need to do something about that. Frances, on the other hand, wears a neutral expression. It's only when she places my cup of tea on the table and sits down, hands clasped together, that I know things are about to get awkward.

I open my mouth to speak, but the way she looks at me and Liv—with her lips set and chin lowered as if observing us over the rim of her reading glasses—silences me rather effectively. I look over at Fareena for moral support, but she grins like she won the bloody lottery.

Roy sets a plate in front of me. "Scrambled eggs," he announces, as if I couldn't tell.

"Talking about eggs," Frances says pointedly, and I put my fork down. I see where this is going. "When two people find each other attractive, they sometimes decide to indulge in—"

"Woah, okay!" I shake my head and wave my arms to stop her talking.

"Really," Liv cuts in, and I'm thankful for the support. "All we did was sleep together."

I turn and scowl at her with the heat of a thousand fiery suns. "That sounds like something it *wasn't*."

"You mean like, closing your eyes and breathing heavily," Noah offers.

"Yes!" I gesture towards him like I'm demonstrating the locations of emergency exits on a plane. Fareena and Angela titter, and I groan. "No. Shut up, you two. I mean, like, resting."

Roy chuckles where he leans against the fridge, and Frances's eyes are full of mirth. "So, I don't have to talk to you about how babies are made?"

I shake my head. "God, no. Please. Don't." I know how babies are made, and there is no way in a million years I could make one with Liv.

"As much as I would appreciate nine months without my period, that's not going to happen." Liv gives me a conspiratorial look. "I was cold, and Jake simply offered to keep me warm."

"I can buy that. I shared a bed with him once. He's like a furnace." Fareena gives Liv a knowing nod.

"Well, then I have to say, the attic is pretty cold. I could use some Jake tonight," Noah says dryly. He bites into his cheek to keep his lips from twitching.

Liv picks at her scrambled eggs. "Make sure he's not wearing a shirt."

"I'm still here, you know." I look around the table. "I can hear everything you say."

"Maybe we should make a schedule?" Angela offers. Helpful as ever.

"Okay, but as best mates' privilege, I should be the one to have him tonight." Fareena puts forward her argument like a barrister in court.

I laugh. "You bunch of utter knobs."

It gives me a break from the heaviness that has settled in my chest. And I'll take it. Anything to keep my head above the water right now.

Roy sits and puts a meaty arm around my neck. "Don't let these fools think they have a chance. You're warming *me* tonight. They said England had warm winters." He looks at me gravely. "They *lied*."

"Well, I suppose for the delicate American, I should."

He leans away, looking indignant. "Delicate? Oh, I see how it is. Well, you wouldn't want this delicate man to keep you fed, I suppose."

"That reminds me. Scrambled eggs?"

"Well, seems someone dug us a fridge. Turns out it's pretty darn good." He ruffles my hair and gets back up.

The fridge is but a hole in the ground. An unused metal drawer from dad's old file cabinet pushed into it. With the cold weather and a piece of polystyrene I found to insulate it with, it works perfectly as a fridge.

It's stupid how chuffed I feel. "Right, well, if you're all done mocking me, Liv and I saw people looting the neighbouring houses. They were armed to their teeth. One of them carried a rifle."

"And so it begins." Angela looks to Roy, who nods thoughtfully.

I fancied myself a beginner prepper, but there are a lot of things I haven't learned yet. Luckily for us, Angela and Roy were experienced when it came to looting during the hurricane and flooding season. They'd been the ones to suggest making the house unattractive to looters with barred doors and windows. It only leaves us with the back door and attic window as an escape route. But having seen the looters last night, it might be preferable to worrying about them kicking down our door.

"Have we decided what to do yet?" Fareena asks. "Now that Jake feels better?"

Everyone looks over at me. "I think I'm good." Whatever that means.

"Good enough to travel?" Angela asks.

"I think I could go." I pause. With the spores and the infected swarming Huntingdon and the streets around it, trying to go to the Danby base would be suicidal. "Should we, though?" I ask. "It's at least a two-day walk."

Roy heaves a sigh, shaking his head. He and Angela want to get back to their daughter, but he knows we barely escaped the bridge with our lives. A two-day walk is too big of a risk.

Angela clasps Roy's hand in hers. "I had hoped for better news, but we spotted infected all over town."

"Even the big roads. And they're filled with cars," Fareena says.

"And their hungry drivers," Noah adds darkly. He seems different, but I can't put my finger on how.

"Well, if we stay, we have to go back to keeping watch at night," I say to the sound of several low groans.

"We do," Roy agrees and levels a grave expression our way. "There's another matter we should probably address as well."

I cock my head.

"Keeping watch ain't enough. The looters had a rifle of some sort. We have a few sticks to defend ourselves with." He motions at the two cricket bats that lean against the door.

We lost pretty much everything else on the boat. Except for Angela's tiny garden tool.

"We need weapons, and we need to know how to use 'em." Roy crosses his arms.

Now the others start inspecting the kitchen as if my mother kept a secret stash of illegal firearms in the oven or something. Unfortunately, the closest thing to a weapon in this place are Mum's kitchen knives. And the tenderizer.

"Ah..." Noah opens his mouth to speak when Fareena's eyes light up.

"Tinkerman can fix it!"

He deflates ever so slightly. "You had to go and steal my thunder, didn't you?"

She fires off a sugary sweet smile. "But you *tinker*."

He looks back to us, face serious as if he's about to take an oath. "I have experience with creating similar things."

"Similar things?" I'm curious what this tinkering business of his is. A hobby or latent murdering sociopath tendencies?

He tries to look casual. I say try because more often than not, Noah looks effortlessly arrogant. Not now though. His fingertips tap the table, and his gaze lingers somewhere on his empty plate. "I may have enjoyed the craft of creating costumes."

The craft of creating costumes? "Wait, is that your poncey way of saying you're a cosplayer?"

His face reddens. "It's an art form."

"I know. I used to love cosplay! Please tell me you can make me a Death Knight costume." I hold my hands up, fingers crossed for luck.

"I already have the sword," he says with pride, and I think I see him sitting a little straighter.

"That is bad arse, mate."

"I'm sorry," Fareena drawls, "can we go back to speaking English so the rest of us can understand?"

"Dress up." Liv pushes her scrambled eggs to the side and picks at the mushrooms on her plate.

"It's *art*," Noah scowls.

"More like Halloween every day of the week."

"Now, hold up." Angela puts her hand on Roy's shoulder, silencing us. "What exactly can you make?"

Noah shrugs. "Depending on what I can find, pretty much anything."

Angela tilts her head, eyebrows rising in approval. "Now, this is what I like to hear. You telling me all we need to do is find you some material and you make whatever?"

"Pretty much?"

"I like this boy." Angela winks at Noah, and either I'm still fever hallucinating or a pink blush creeps up his cheeks. "Well then, we find material and Noah works his magic while the rest of us keep working on the house and scavenging."

When Angela begins to delegate different tasks, it's easy to see she's a copper: assertive, determined, and charismatic. When she speaks, people listen.

We spent another hour planning our next steps: finding food, reinforcing the house, and working out a watch schedule. Roy cheekily suggested Angela be in charge of scheduling responsibility, stating that as a police officer she was the one with most experience creating watch rotas.

Fareena, Noah, and I have been tasked with going to the garden centre to get everything we need for a homemade water filtration system.

The thing about rainwater is that although it looks fairly clean, the roof and tarp it has been collected from might not be the most hygienic surfaces.

Though the moss from the roof helps filter the water, there's still bird shit that could contaminate it. And though I'm all up for new experiences, pissing from my arse and vomiting at the same time isn't one of them.

On top of that, I'm helping Angela with the training she insists we do. Strength and cardio combined with self-defence.

Even though the others—mostly Liv—protested vehemently at first, there's no denying that being chased by mindless, unstoppable infected demands a certain endurance. One most of us don't have.

It's not only running. It's dodging things, other people, and infected. Climbing fences, bins, and brick walls. And it's fighting tooth and nail to stay alive.

And that's something I know how to do. I'm not a trained fighter, but when you grow up tiny and scrawny compared to the boys, you quickly learn how to fight dirty. And in a fight right now, it doesn't matter how you win, it only matters that you're the last one standing.

60

JAKE

RAIN HAMMERS DOWN AS we scurry along the thin alleyway. Me first, Noah and Fareena right behind. We run hunched forward, and my poncho drags across the ground, spraying water in its wake. I duck behind the cover of a large rubbish bin.

We've loaded up our bike's trailer with sand and gravel for the water filtering system, but then I remembered the outdoor shop nearby. It would really help if we could nab some sleeping bags now that it's getting colder. Because as much as I don't mind sharing a bed with others, I am *not* going to be some portable heater passed around.

I shiver in my wet clothes. I hate the rain. I hate the sticky feeling of wet clothes as they cling to my skin.

Noah and Fareena drop to a crouch next to me and we sit quietly in case someone or *something* hears us.

One good thing about the rain is the way it masks our footsteps. We remain still for a few minutes, listening to the rain smatter the asphalt. Partly because I've watched enough horror movies to know not to peek out too soon. And partly because the longer we wait, the more it freaks me out.

What if I look around the corner and one of the infected is right there? I really do not fancy running face-first into a group of withered. Or even worse, lurkers or those shrieking snitches, the ones who call to the other infected, alerting them to prey.

"We look absolutely ridiculous." Noah adjusts his scuba mask as we press ourselves against the wall.

The goggles combined with face masks work as protection from the spores. We think. We don't know how the spores work exactly, but it seems like a reasonable assumption to cover mouth, nose, and eyes. Better safe than sorry.

The masks press against our nostrils, making us sound wonderfully nasal whenever we speak. Which sent us into a fit of inappropriate giggles. It's difficult taking someone seriously when their entire face is squished into a pair of goggles, leaving them with a pouty fish mouth.

Until you have to step outside and hope that you don't see any infected. And if you do, that the masks will help.

"I don't know, it works wonders for your cheekbones." I wink at him.

Fareena lets out a soundless breath and ribs me. It is definitely not the right time for jokes, but I don't know how else to handle the fear that lies like a hard knot in my stomach.

I lean onto my palms and peer out, the wet ground hard and cold against my hands. I bite down on a shiver. Nothing. Not a soul. I stand and step out from behind the bin. "Come on, let's check out that store."

We run on light feet down the rest of the alley until we reach the opening between the two buildings. I can't hear anything but rain. I ease myself along the coarse brick wall, then crane my neck around the corner.

The store front is as empty as the rest of the area. I glance around the car park to make sure nothing is lurking behind one of the vehicles left behind.

"Anything?" Noah asks from behind me. I shake my head.

"Okay, but before we go in, can I ask *how* are we going to get in? Breaking one of the store windows?" Fareena asks quietly.

"Too loud." I'm mostly referring to the withered. Although we saw looters a few nights ago, we haven't seen them since. But why risk drawing unwanted attention from either looters or the withered?

"Then how?"

"Can't you..." I wiggle my fist from side to side in the air.

Fareena scowls at me. "Yeah, cars and crappy house doors. I'm not Houdini, you know."

"Well, that's rather disappointing." Noah frowns. He's rewarded by a glare from Fareena.

"Okay, we'll wing it." I push myself off the wall and jog towards the glass doors to press my face against the display windows. No point in trying to break in if it's chock-full of infected.

The store lies dark and untouched. You couldn't tell the world was going insane outside by looking inside. Which—right now—is a good thing. I walk the rest of the way to the doors. Electricity is gone again. Some days it works, others it doesn't. This time we haven't had any for a day or two. Whether the government is cutting back or the grid has gone down is anyone's guess. I hope it's the former. Because if the grid's down, we're in a lot more trouble than we could have ever imagined. It'll mean we're no longer getting electricity from France, and the only reason for that would be if France's grid is down as well.

"Maybe we could pry them open with something?" Noah motions towards the doors. If we can find something to use, it could work. Now I regret not bringing a crowbar.

"Fareena, did you bring your screwdriver?"

"Do birds fly?"

"Can you get one of those boots open?"

"Why do you even ask me such silly things?" She sighs melodramatically. I grin and push her towards the closest car.

Within seconds, she's in and popping the boot with a satisfied grin. Then she passes me with a raised hand, and I give it a well-deserved high five.

"Nothing here." Noah pops his head from the boot.

"Try the blue one." I point at the next car.

"Err... please."

"*Please*." I give her my sincerest please-do-me-this-favour face.

It never stops to amaze me how quickly she gets these cars open. They're old shitty cars, which is probably why they were left behind, but regardless, it's impressive.

The obligatory blanket and spare wheel are in the back of this one and—Fareena high-fives me again—a crowbar.

"Let's go." I wave the crowbar in the air.

"You know"—Fareena flashes her teeth at me—"you're getting better at this criminal lifestyle thing."

"Yeah, well, you have a bad influence on me." I shove the crowbar into the thin slit between doors. I've seen it done on TV before and I know it takes a lot of strength to pry doors open, which is probably why we stare, dumbfounded, as the doors give way and slide apart with no trouble at all.

"All that work and someone already had them unlocked?" Fareena's nose wrinkles.

Someone had this place unlocked? Or did the locks stop working when the electricity went out? Whatever the reason, we better be alert.

I raise the crowbar with both hands and step into the store like a burglar not wanting to get caught. I half expect someone to be in here, but there's nothing. It's completely empty and looks untouched.

We pull off our masks and squint into the darkness. This is like a kid's dream. An empty store to peruse and pick whatever they want. I shut the glass doors behind us. The last thing we want is for infected to come pouring in.

"How has no one looted this place?" Fareena lifts a jacket from its rack.

Noah clicks his tongue. "What would you pick: food or clothes?"

She narrows her eyes at Noah. "Do you have to be so arrogant whenever you exist?"

His eyes widen, but then his expression goes back to its normal disinterested self. "I was only saying, in a life and death situation, surely you'd think more about food than clothes."

"Well, yes, but you don't have to be so *you* about it."

I let them bicker while I sweep my gaze across neatly arranged shelves and clothes racks that litter the store.

Mum used to bring us here to let us pick things for the fishing trip. The sudden memory and the realisation she's gone hit me like a gut punch. The thought of never seeing her again, that she and Tim no longer exist, leaves me reeling.

I inhale and hold my breath, slowly counting to ten, then I let it out. I have to focus on what I'm doing. On why we're here.

I exhale, ignoring the ache in my chest, and focus on scanning the store for any lurking dangers.

It's eerily still, and something gnaws at the back of my mind. Why leave this place unlocked and untouched?

Dread latches on like cold fingers to the back of my head. We shouldn't be here.

"Hey, let's get what we need and get out of here. This place is creeping me out."

"Why? Because it's dark?" Noah smirks.

"Well, yeah, but something feels off."

Noah clucks. "Take Fareena with you. I'll go look over there."

"Uh…" Fareena's voice drips with annoyance. "How about you hold Jake's hand? And *I'll* go look over *there*." She motioned at a section filled with boots and rain gear.

I narrow my eyes at the two of them. I do not need someone to hold my hand. "We'll get bags and tents. Meet you back here in five?" I turn to Noah. "And I'm *not* holding anyone's hand."

"Well, this day keeps on disappointing me. You won't warm my bed and now you won't hold my hand." Noah drops his hand to the side, eyes glittering with amusement, then he turns and walks off. Did he make a joke?

Fareena looks as perplexed as me. I guess miracles do happen. I shrug, then trail after him.

We weave through the racks, and I imagine swapping some of the dry clothes for my wet ones. But I'd rather not get caught off guard and have to make a run for it naked. The hangers creak as we push ourselves past tightly packed outdoor gear until we reach the tents.

"Which one?" Noah bends down to survey the neatly stacked tents.

"There's seven of us."

"Eight." Noah turns one of the tent packages in his hands.

"Eight?" I'm not that good at math, but I'm not *that* bad.

"Yeah. That dog of yours is the size of a large, very hairy man."

I snigger. He's not wrong. "Right, eight then. Three tents?"

Piling another two tents into his arms, he scowls. "These are heavier than they look."

"Well, that's why you have me here, isn't it? Big, strong, and handsome." I pluck two of the tents from his arms and fire off a smile.

Noah blows air through the corner of his mouth, a lock of blond hair falling in his face. "Only one of those statements is accurate."

I narrow my eyes. Ever since this morning, Noah has been unusually nice to me, and it makes me suspicious. Noah isn't nice to anyone but himself.

"Why are you being nice?"

He gives me a blank look. "Keep your friends close..."

"You have friends?"

"Oh, har har, aren't you funny?"

"Why, thank you, you're too kind." I bare my teeth in a smile and let my eyes trail the section for anything useful.

"It wasn't a compliment."

"No?"

Noah huffs as I spot a blue sign that reads, Outdoor. That could mean anything and if we're lucky, we could find something useful there. Probably not the sort of goods Roy is so desperately longing for, but something. If nothing else, at least we might find bits and pieces Noah could work with.

I zigzag through wooden showcases littered with the typical sports gear until we reach the Outdoor aisle.

Climbing gear like rope and harnesses line the shelves in neat rows. I grab two packs of rope, threading my arm through the hoops. I cast a glance around us. It's still a crazy feeling to walk around an empty shop, grabbing whatever you need. Guilt strikes, and I have the absurd thought that we should leave a few quid by the till. Or an IOU.

"Oh, yes." Noah picks up speed and jogs down the aisle. I scurry after him, not wanting to be left behind. He stops by a wall mounted with ice axes.

I 'ooh' and put the tents on the floor and grab an axe. I've played enough video games to know these things come in handy for more than climbing. It's lighter than I thought, but the jagged teeth and sharp-looking blade look comforting to me. Never thought I'd say something like that.

I spin it in my hand when the sliding of doors catches my attention. Fareena? Feet shuffle across the store floor, and low voices drift towards us.

Noah's brows draw together. The feet stop, the voices falling silent. Whoever entered the store knows we're here.

What do we do? Noah mouths at me. I shake my head. I don't know.

"Whoever is in here, we know you're here." The voice has a hard edge to it. "You got about thirty seconds to show yourselves, or me and my boys will find you."

The speaker and his group are somewhere between us and the entrance. There's no way we can pass them undetected. And there's Fareena. She's still somewhere in the shop.

"Do we show ourselves?" Noah whispers.

I nod and hook the ice axe into my belt. The question isn't what to do. The real question is, friend or foe?

61

JAKE

"WELL, HELLO LADS." A gruff-looking grey-haired man with hardened lines around his mouth and eyes greets us as we step from the aisle. My gaze falls to the rifle mouth pointed at me.

"Sir, we're only trying to find some supplies." I raise my hands. I haven't been around guns enough to respect them, only fear them.

"These aren't from the safe zone." A tall, lanky guy points a baseball bat in our direction. Nails puncture the top of it and something chunky, vaguely familiar, clings to a few of the rusty nails. Skin?

The older man's eyes drop to the mask around my neck. "You're not infected?"

"No, sir."

The lines around his eyes tighten. "Where are you coming from?"

"Huntingdon, near the Market Square. We're not from Goddie Park." I avoid telling him we came from London. We're not infected, but they have no reason to trust us.

He inspects us a few seconds longer, then lowers his rifle. Either he trusts us, or he realises that no matter if we're honest or not, he's the one with a rifle.

Tall and Gangly's gaze flickers towards him. "Keith, we don't know they're telling the truth."

"It's fine, James." Keith gives us another stern look. "Isn't it, lads?"

"Yes, sir." I almost salute him as if he's a ranking officer. James lowers his bat, but I can tell by the way his brows furrow he doesn't trust us.

"We've had some trouble with looters." Keith rubs a curled finger at the side of his bushy eyebrow. It's only then I see the bracelet. Mismatched Perler beads in neon colours wrap around his wrist. I'm no fashionista, but I'm pretty sure that's not a bracelet from the latest men's autumn collection.

"Looters from outside the safe zone," James fills in.

I frown. "You're not allowed to leave?"

Keith gives us a strange look. Like I've told a bad joke. "You haven't heard?"

"Heard? We've been staying hunkered down." This isn't the right time to tell strangers I've been sick. Not with infected running rampant on the streets.

"The military's safe zone fell after only a week. Some of the people who got in... well, they weren't showing any symptoms, but some of them were infected."

"Shit..." Noah breathes next to me.

"Yeah, don't go near Goddie. That place is swarming with them things now," James says.

A week. I'm still shocked by the rate of the infection and the speed at which society keeps collapsing. The government had barely gotten camps up and running, and already safe zones are falling.

If the Huntingdon safe zone got run over in a week, I don't want to think about what could happen in bigger cities. But maybe they have more military and other resources than a town like Huntingdon. Or maybe, a small part of my brain niggles at me, maybe this virus had been around for longer than we know. How else could it spread so fast?

I'd worried we'd made the wrong decision about avoiding the safe zone. I thought maybe I'd read too many books or seen too many movies. Now I'm glad we stayed at my house. I can't imagine a safe zone turning into the chaos we saw in London and on our way here. How many families with children were in that safe zone?

"We lost a lot of good people." Keith's eyes are downcast and now that I dare look closer, I see the weariness in his eyes. In the way his shoulders rise and fall with a deep sigh.

James is younger, with spiky hair and hollowed eyes. He glances at Keith, then back at us. "A group of us escaped to Tescos. But them raiders chased us out. Took everything." The corner of his lip twitches, and the grip around his bat tightens.

I can only imagine the anger of having someone take all our supplies. Leaving us with nothing to fend for ourselves. I bite down on a groan. We lost most of our supplies escaping the boat. I'm not sure which is worse.

"We would have shared if they'd only asked us. Times like these..."

"We need to help each other." I finish Keith's sentence after a moment of silence. "Don't worry. We're not raiders. I'm Jake. I grew up here near Barney's Plaice."

"Best damn chippy in town." Keith's face lights up. I can't disagree.

"This is my friend Noah." I motion towards Noah and try not to smile at the surprised look on his face. "Our friend Fareena is around somewhere."

"Well, I'm Keith; this here is James. We're the ones on patrol duty today. I'm sorry for the harsh greeting, but we can't be too careful."

"No, I get it. We saw looters around the house the other week. Most of us are just trying to stay safe."

"Listen," James says and lowers the bat that rests on his shoulder, "we have women and children. If you do, you better get something to protect them with. Those fuckers don't go down easy." His jaw works, and I'm not sure if he's referring to the infected or the looters.

A moment ago, James reminded me of the creepy guy in the movies who wigs people out, especially girls. Now he looks like the overprotective big brother all girls should have.

"We found some of your ice axes." Noah gives them an apologetic smile as he unhooks one from his belt.

Keith chuckles, and James gives an approving nod. "Those are good," he says, "but there's something even better we stashed at the back. Come on."

The small part of me, the one that sometimes believe in conspiracy theories, hesitates. They seem friendly enough, but we don't know enough about them or their intentions.

I wish Angela were here. It's like the woman has a sixth sense for sniffing out dodgy people. Guess it comes with her profession. I glance at Noah, but he shrugs and follows James.

Keith observes me quietly. Something tells me he doesn't miss much. "I think I'd worry if you weren't on your guard."

I let out a breath. "That obvious, huh?"

"Let's just say you're lucky we're not playing poker."

Noah's laughter reaches my ears. "No. Poker never was my strong suit."

"Fareena can verify that when she turns up," Noah calls across his shoulder when James hushes all of us. He flicks his hand up and down, signalling for us to quiet down.

Keith moves to the front. Quiet and fast.

I stop next to James. My eyes dart from side to side, the spotlight of my torch trailing my gaze.

A thick layer of fine dust swirls in the beam. Red and yellow tinted dust? No... Spores.

I grab James' shoulder. He's not wearing a facemask and the air in front of us is laden with the spores. Both James and Keith turn to look at me.

"Spores." I pull my mask up and goggles down and point at the spores with my torch.

Keith pulls his scarf up, and I grimace. I'm not so sure simply covering your mouth without some sort of air filter will do any good.

A wet gagging sound rolls through the darkness, and a cold sensation creeps up the back of my neck.

Infected. Because where there are spores, there are infected.

My hand drops to the axe, and I unhook it with shaking fingers. The unmistakable warbles of the infected resonate through the store.

"Help…" The word, despite being a muffled whisper, punches through the eerie noises.

The beam of James' torch jerks in the direction of the voice. My breath catches in my throat.

The infected is massive. Despite hunching over, it towers over us by a few heads at least. Large patches of yellow lichen and strange discs that grow in clusters cover its bloated body. Red moss and roots web through and between them.

We should run. Flee. But I stare, my mind racing, the instinct to run fighting with the notion to stay quiet and undetected.

"Help." It comes out stronger this time.

We all look at each other. I've never heard one of the withered talk before.

Its hands, swollen with torn-off fingers, clutch at its head, the massive body twitching back and forth.

It heaves and gags. Something hits the floor with a wet squelch and the sickly stench of death rises from the floor, permeating the air.

James backs into me and the beam of his torch flashes across the back wall. That's when I see her, and my entire body goes cold.

Fareena pressed up against the wall behind the withered.

62

JAKE

FAREENA PRESSES HERSELF FLUSH against the wall, her eyes wide behind her goggles, and I realise it wasn't the infected talking. It was Fareena. The wall is covered in thick wet-looking roots. The biggest roots are pale pink, like worms, and they move ever so slightly.

I point, drawing the others' attention to her, then motion at the infected. We need to take it out before it notices us. Unease tightens my stomach. Something isn't right about this one.

The heaving stops as if it can hear my thoughts, and it turns its head towards us.

My pulse stutters.

Thick pinkish roots and red tumour-like bulbs have pried its skull open. Big mushroomy lumps bubble from large cracks, forcing their way out. Smaller roots sprout from eye sockets and nostrils, latching on to whatever part of the head they can reach. No wonder it can't hear or see us.

It tosses its head back and forth, clouds of spores puffing from the cracks and crevices that carve through the bulging body.

Keith lifts his rifle, but Fareena's curls bob around her face as she shakes her head, her eyes wide. She points to her side, careful not to draw the thing's attention.

Wait. I wave my hands at Keith. His brows lower. I motion to where Fareena points. James follows my finger with his torch.

Three withered loom near the wall only a few steps away from Fareena. Eerily still and slightly hunched. They're smaller than the big one right in front of us. Roots and tumours grow in thick clusters all over their heads, pushing milky eyeballs from their sockets. Yellow stems with tiny capsules grow like moss on rocks.

I shudder. These people, these *things*, all seem oblivious to our presence. Does that mean we could take them out? One by one, without the others noticing. We could try, but the infected don't die like us. You shoot them once, they keep going. You cut them down, they get back up.

We need a plan before we rush in and get ourselves killed. Or worse... infected.

The hulk-like withered gurgles out a coarse, grating sound and the smaller ones shuffle in their spot.

I force myself to stay in place despite the fear that twists my stomach. We need to get Fareena and get the fuck out of here.

I glance at her. She's small and light on her feet. Maybe she could skirt around the infected. If it didn't hear us approach, it most likely won't hear her either.

Come here, I mouth to Fareena and wave at myself, urging her to leave her spot and slip over to us.

Her brows furrow, and she shakes her head.

"They can't hear or see us," I whisper as loudly as I dare. Because why poke a sleeping... infected in the eye? If it had any.

Fareena's eyes narrow dubiously. Yeah, I wouldn't simply take someone's word for it either.

I point at the infected, then cover my eyes, then my ears.

Her eyes light up with understanding.

"Slow," I mouth, and she nods. Her chest rises as she inhales deeply, then she takes a hesitant step to the side, her eyes on the withered. It doesn't react. She takes another step, and Keith moves towards her. Quietly, he pushes a clothing carousel to the side, making space for Fareena to pass through. The wheels roll soundlessly across the floor.

The infected's head snaps that way. Its mouth opens and closes, head swivelling.

Startled by the sudden movement, James backs into me, knocking my axe from my hand. It clatters loudly to the floor.

A vibrating, creaking sound rips from the infected's cracked lips. The three other infected spin around, arms out to the sides like rugby players ready to attack. They snap and hiss, sludge and slime dripping from their open mouths.

Grabbing James by the shoulder, I back away and drag him with me. Noah moves next to us, axe gripped hard in his hand. He doesn't notice the barrel of trekking poles behind him.

"Noah!" I hiss too late as the barrel topples over, trekking poles cascading onto the floor.

The infected burst into motion and head straight for us.

We scramble backwards, panic seizing my heart. They're so fast. We won't be able to outrun them. I yank at a large box filled with footballs. It spins and falls over, the balls spilling to the floor.

The big, brutish infected stops dead in its tracks, jerking around as the balls bounce across the floor.

Using the commotion as a distraction, Fareena and Keith break into a run.

The other infected stop as well. They spin towards the balls that spring in all directions. *Thump, thump, thump.* Their heads whip back and forth.

James keeps running, but I stop and watch the infected chase after the balls.

Thump, thump.

The usually harmless sound feels like it reverberates through the entire store. Reverberates. The footballs roll to a stop.

"Jake, come on!" Noah stops and whirls towards me.

Four heads whip away from the balls. The brute howls, knocking carousels and boxes to the side as it thunders towards Fareena and Keith.

"Jake..." Noah urges me. "We have to go."

I take a step backwards, expecting the infected to chase us down. Instead, they bolt past me and Noah towards where James runs as fast as he can.

A shriek draws my attention. The infected has cornered Fareena and Keith.

"Hey!" I shout at the top of my lungs. It ignores me or it can't hear me. I'm not so sure anymore.

"Jesus, Jake!" Noah snaps, grabbing my shoulder hard.

"Oi!" I clap my hands over my head, trying to draw its attention away from Fareena and Keith.

"Are you trying to get us fucking killed?"

It shouldn't surprise me that Noah wants to leave everyone behind. But I'm not leaving Fareena. Or Keith.

"Over here!" I wave my arms in the air, but once again it just stands there, head twitching. I scowl. It's not hearing me again.

"We need to get the fuck out of here, Jake. Now." Noah breathes heavily, fear making his breath shudder. He wants to leave. He wants to survive. And yet, he hasn't left.

"We can't leave her."

"Fine," he mutters, "but can you try not to be a moron about it?"

"I make no promises."

The brute swipes a meaty arm at Fareena, who ducks and rolls out of reach. Keith jerks backwards, barely getting himself out of the way in time.

"Hey, fucker!" I stomp my foot hard, just as Noah chucks a sleeping bag at it. The infected whirls around.

"And you call me a moron?" I turn to stare at Noah.

"Well, you wanted its attention."

That I did. The brute froths at the mouth, brown bubbles foaming at the corner of its lips. It snaps and twitches, searching for its prey. For us.

Behind it, Fareena steps to the side on light feet. Feet? I look down at my own. The brute didn't pay me any attention until I stomped my foot. Same with Keith and the carousel. And the balls bouncing off the floor. Could it be...?

"Hey, knob face," I mutter, then before I can think any better of it, I lift my foot and stomp down hard.

It reacts instantly, charging towards us as if I've lit a giant bull's eye above our heads.

"Oh, shit..." I steel myself against the instinct to run. If vibration is how these infected sense us, every hard slap of my soles against the floor would alert them of my whereabouts.

"Jake..."

I kick the carousel next to me. It rolls away, wheels and hangars wobbling as it goes crashing into another one.

The brute veers after it. That's it! They follow the vibrations through the ground. Not the sound.

"Use these!" Yanking a wheeled display box, I send it rolling in the same direction.

Fareena and Keith grab at anything they can find and shove that way. They break into a sprint, Noah and I shoving store equipment in all directions to mask their heavy footsteps.

A scream filters through the chaos around us. Not Fareena or Keith. James. Terror builds in his voice as we kick and push everything we can reach.

"Help them, I'll get James." I turn around, but before I can take another step, Noah fists his hand in the hood of my jacket.

"No."

"Noah, what the fuck." I try to pull free from him.

"I said *no*. You can't save him. If you go in, we'll either have to rescue your arse or explain to Angela why you're not with us."

"Let. Go."

His grip tightens. "You can't save everyone. And I don't want to risk my life because you're being naïve and stupid. James is *gone*."

The screams have been replaced by a pitiful gurgling moan. My pulse thrums loudly in my ears.

"Now, if they're done with James, they're coming for us. So you better get your shit together so we can get the hell out of here."

I push him off me, and he finally releases his grip. He's won and he knows it.

"Guys," Fareena breathes as she and Keith arrive.

"Where's James?" Keith looks at us.

I shake my head, unable to meet his eyes.

"Fuck." He throws his head forward as he spits out the word. For a second, I think he's going to punch one of us. But he lets out a heavy breath instead. "Let's go."

We circle out and away from the brute and the other infected. We don't see them, but the wet sounds and gurgles give me a haunting idea of what keeps them busy. Either our footsteps are light enough not to draw their attention or we are too far away for them to sense us. Whichever it is, none of us dare so much as breathe until I slip my fingers through the glass doors and pry them open.

We pull off our masks and goggles and let out a unanimous sigh of relief as we slide down behind a car.

"What the actual fuck was that?" Fareena asks, staring at us.

"I've never seen anything like it." Keith shakes his head. "We scouted that store the other week."

"And they weren't there?" I ask.

"We shut some infected into the delivery corridor last week, but that was barred and nailed shut. There's no way they could have gotten out."

Maybe not regular infected. But the big brute we saw, it could probably melt through one of those doors. I don't say it out loud, but glancing at Fareena and Noah, I know they're thinking the same thing.

"I'm sorry about James." I look back at Keith. "If we hadn't..."

Keith gives a hard shake. "No. We would've run into them anyway. With or without you guys."

I know that's true, but it doesn't make me feel any better.

"He was my responsibility. Not yours," Keith says after a moment of silence. "I should get back and tell his sister."

I nod. We should get back as well before it gets too dark. "Listen, if you or your group need anything. Mark the bin outside Boots and we'll meet up on Peeping Sam's roof at noon."

He chuckles at my nickname for the small pub situated on High Street. "Alright, kids. Be safe out there, and watch out for the raiders; they aren't the kind type."

We watch him duck out from behind the car and run across the street. He disappears between two houses, rifle gripped tightly in his hands. Though I bet he won't be using it anytime soon. It draws too much attention out in the open. Not to mention bullets being a scarce commodity. You'd want to hold on to what few bullets you had.

I wish we could do more to help, but we need to get back with our loot. The others are waiting for us. Depending on us.

For now, he knows how to send a message our way. That'll have to do.

“Come on,” I say, standing. “We should get back before we run into any more surprises.”

63

LIV

"DID YOU FIND ALL of this in the forest?" Jake had looked around the kitchen, eyes large with wonder.

Jars of pickled cattail, wild mushrooms, hawthorn jam, and sourdough starters cluttered the countertops. Several bundles of plants hung on the wall above the jars; yarrow, thyme, basil, and burdock roots were a few of the things Liv had tied up in neat bundles.

In other words, Roy had kept them all busy foraging the forest nearby and helping him clean and prep all the food.

When he'd handed her the flour and water, he'd joked that it was no more work than taking care of a low-maintenance pet.

She wouldn't trust herself with something others would have to eat, let alone a small pet that needed feeding. Unfortunately for everyone, Roy hadn't listened.

She glared at the jar with the white-looking gloop in it. He better not be putting all his money on that horse because if he did, they would all starve or suffer food poisoning.

She'd been mixing dough starters until the three mismatched amigos returned. They'd stumbled through the door, soaking wet, words pouring out of them as they recounted their adventure. It was like listening to a group of overexcited children talk. Until Frances told them in her most motherly voice to 'shut their traps for one second.'

They'd had a run-in with some sort of mutated infected in a store. The way they had described the big one made Liv's skin crawl. The lurker at the boat still had her on edge and now they were telling her there were other types of infected out there. Other *mutated* infected.

"What kind of withered did you say it was?" She pulled her hair into a messy bun, biting down on the hairband.

"We don't know." Fareena slid into the armchair beside her, a purple towel turban-wrapped around her head, one stubborn curl sticking out from the confinements of the towel. For someone who'd been chased around half of Huntingdon, Fareena looked like she'd been merely out for a stroll. *Bitch.*

"They're attracted by the footsteps of running though," Noah filled in. "The vibrations."

Great. Not only did they have fast infected to run from. Now they also had fast infected attracted by running.

"There has to be an explanation to the different infected we keep seeing." Liv tapped the armrest. Her brows squeezed together as curiosity pulled at her thoughts. She tried to beat it back down, but the doctor in her had always been too stubborn. Too hungry for knowledge. Even as a student she was more comfortable diving into research than connecting with other people. Relationships were flawed, the root to pain. Science was not.

She locked her eyes on the carpet, tuning out everything else. What did they know so far?

The infection spread by bites, bodily fluids, and spores. It caused severe headaches, flu-like symptoms, and eventually hyper-aggressiveness. That was when the infected patients attacked others. Those were like Claire. The mindless, seemingly unstoppable runners.

Somewhere along the infection, a mutation must trigger, taking it to the next stage like the lurker at the canal. It appeared they kept enough cognitive awareness to stalk and wait out prey. That one had called the attention of their fellow infected once prey had been sighted. The withered near the bridge when they first arrived in Huntingdon looked nothing like the lurker. And yet it too had called nearby infected. Could the call be a separate behaviour assigned to some infected, regardless of mutation?

"This brute, was it like that when they locked it in?"

"Keith said they had been regular withered." Jake ruffled his hair with the towel. He wore a t-shirt that fit his broad chest snuggly, and she tried *really* hard not to imagine him naked.

Though the memory of him from the night before did not help her in the slightest. He'd been warm, his muscular arms wrapped tightly around her, and she'd felt comfortable. Safe. With his bearded cheek pressed against hers, his warm chuckle brushing her ear. Which inevitably made her think of other situations where he could be *just* as close. With fewer clothes on.

"Liv?"

"Hmm?" She snapped her eyes up towards Jake and away from his... other parts.

"You kind of zoned out there, girl." Fareena's eyes sparkled.

She blinked. "Sorry, I, uh, was thinking."

"Yeah." Fareena snickered. "We could tell."

She harrumphed. "About the infection."

"Of course."

Ignoring Fareena, she looked at the others. "How long did this bloke say the withered had been locked up inside the delivery passage?"

"A few days? He said they locked them in there last week."

"They had gone from regular runners to this in a few days?"

Jake nodded and she felt dread bubble in her gut. "That's so fast."

"What is?" Jake pushed away from the doorframe he was leaning against.

"The evolution of the virus. A few days from a regular runner to that... it means the virus is moving incredibly fast. And we know hardly anything about it."

"Because the government isn't telling us everything," Noah said.

"Then we should find out for ourselves," she said, silencing the others' murmurs.

Jake was the first to break the silence. "How would we do that?"

"We capture one and study it."

64
LIV

"I'M SORRY." FAREENA BLINKED. "I thought you said we *capture* one."

"I did."

The room exploded with loud voices as Jake, Fareena, and Noah expressed a surprisingly unanimous, *are you out of your mind*?

The living room wasn't big, and though they'd covered the windows, the volume of their voices could still carry to the street. She winced, hoping neither withered nor raiders could hear.

"That's a terrible idea," Noah objected. It wasn't *that* bad.

"What's a terrible idea?" Frances asked as she stepped into the kitchen, Angela in tow. "If it's another concoction of Liv's, I'm not sure I dare know."

"Ahem." Liv glared at Frances. "I've been known to come up with quite a few *explosive* ideas, I'll have you know."

"Oh yes, my dear. That's exactly why I'm so worried." Frances turned to the others. "If you ever see Liv with a bottle of whiskey and a sock, run."

"I think we've all had enough of Liv's whiskey tossing, thanks," Noah said.

"So ungrateful," Liv muttered as the rest of them chuckled.

Frances put her arm around Liv's shoulders, pulling her close. "You know, I have a feeling you and Kerry would get along like a house on fire."

It was said lightly, though Frances's arm tensed in reaction to her own words, as if they'd slipped out. Before Liv could ask, Angela cut in. "Care to share what this terrible idea is?"

"Liv thinks we should go get ourselves an infected." Noah motioned towards her, annoyance crinkling his handsome features.

Angela tilted her head, amusement lighting up her eyes. Like she was about to hear a really good story.

"We don't know how the infection works. And the government isn't telling us. What they've told us, that's merely the tip of the iceberg. We *need* to study them."

Angela looked at the others. "And you think this is a bad idea?"

Of course they were all going to think it was a bad idea.

Noah scratched the nape of his neck. "It sounds dangerous."

"Do you agree?" Angela turned to Liv.

"Well, yes, but if we learn more about these withered, about this virus, it'll be worth the risk."

"I don't know." Fareena screwed her face up. "Doesn't it feel a little... unethical?"

"They're dead."

Jake flinched and Fareena grimaced. "Yeah... but they were probably *someone's* family."

Family. Now that was a concept Liv hadn't cared about much. Not since Ellis passed away. The others, however, still had their families. When they looked at the infected, they still saw the faces of the people they loved. Feared they could become like them.

"I think she's right," Jake finally spoke. "But I also think Noah and Fareena are right as well."

Jeez. Way to take a side, Jake.

"I think you're all right. Your government isn't telling us what we need to know. They're still lying to us." Angela shook her head. "We can't rely on anybody but ourselves right now. And that means we've got to find out what we can on our own."

Feeling victorious, Liv cocked her head with a grin.

"*But* that doesn't mean we go grab infected by the neck and start experimenting on them."

"Aww." She mock pouted, earning herself an eye roll and a playful slap on the arm from Angela.

"What exactly is it you want to do?" Jake asked.

"I want to study the mutation. How fast it happens and how far it goes."

"So, we wouldn't necessarily need to keep one in the backyard." Jake's expression of pure relief almost made her laugh. That man had the worst poker face.

"If we could find one and make sure it can't get out, that would be good enough."

"Well, we saw some of the shambling type not far from here," Fareena said. "Near that fire station?"

"Oh, yeah..." Jake turned towards the windows. "They actually have a fenced parking lot there."

"If we could get one or two inside," she said, "we could study them."

"How close is this fire station?" Angela asked.

"It's only around the corner, maybe a three-minute walk. One, tops, on our bikes."

"Close enough for us to get there safely now that we've cleared out the surrounding houses. But far enough for them to not be a threat?"

Jake nodded. "I think so."

Angela's brows lifted. "You think so or you know so?"

Jake's eyes flitted from her to Angela, deciding which one of the women he wanted to back. "I'm not sure I want a brute in the making that close to our house..."

Well, shit. That made sense.

"There's another place we could use though," he said slowly, like he was still piecing together his thoughts. "There's a church not far away. All you do is cross a few allotments to get there. They have this really sturdy metal fence. It'll be trickier to get to, but safer to keep infected at."

The room went silent as the others mulled over Jake's words.

"It doesn't absolutely suck," Noah said. "Though I opt for not letting Fareena go off on her own. We all know how that ends." Much to Liv's surprise, Noah drew laughter from the others. Fareena gasped in fake outrage and reached to shove him.

"Too soon!"

"Alright, alright." Angela laughed before turning serious, one hand on her hip, the other pointing at them. "We do this, we have to stay safe and be smart."

The others nodded.

"Good, now before my husband kills us, we better get our behinds into the kitchen."

They piled into the kitchen in time for Roy to set a big iron pot on the table.

"That forest you showed us, Jake, was a gold mine." Steam puffed up and a rich smell of herbs and wine filled the kitchen as he lifted the lid.

"What is that?" Fareena elbowed her way past Jake and peered into the pot. If Liv hadn't already sat down, she would have done the same. Where food and Roy were involved, everybody wanted the first taste.

"Scarlet Cup and meat stew cooked in our marvellous fire pit. Now get gone." He shooed Fareena towards her seat.

The fire pit was a simple hole dug into the ground in the garden and filled with large stones they looted from nearby gardens.

Eager to taste his latest concoction, the rest of them gathered around the table.

"It smells absolutely glorious, doesn't it?"

Liv smiled. What a Frances thing to say. Glorious. Chicken. Fecking shite. "It does."

It didn't just smell amazing, it tasted unlike anything she'd ever had. Earthy with a rich flavour of beef. Although she'd spent the past two years in prison. Perhaps her expectations weren't all that high.

The others sat quietly, too busy enjoying the food to talk. Fareena let out tiny noises of pleasure with each bite. Jake nodded to himself, and Noah licked the leftover sauce from his plate. That man must inhale his food because she'd barely taken three bites of hers.

She couldn't think of a time when their table had ever been so quiet. Then again, it had been quite a day.

"And now, to finish a great meal." Roy tossed five bags of instant coffee onto the table. The others wrinkled their noses at the brown bags. MRE coffee made prison coffee seem like something from the Ritz.

She stirred her mug, then sniffed it and let out a disgusted grunt. It smelled like a swimming pool.

"When are you going to learn not to smell the MRE stuff?" Jake's eyes danced.

"Never, apparently." She grimaced at the burnt taste in her mouth. It tasted like an American coffee. Bland and burned.

Her father hadn't been good for much, but if it was one thing the Swedes knew how to do, besides damn good princess cake, it was how to make good coffee.

"I keep thinking it'll taste better the more I drink." Fareena set the mug on the table. "But it never does."

"The definition of insanity." Noah swallowed his coffee, then stuck out his tongue with a grimace.

Fareena huffed lengthily. "I'm going insane alright. I'm PMSing, and my knockers feel like fucking water balloons about to burst every time I walk."

Noah choked on his coffee, and even Roy looked a little unsettled. Unsurprisingly, Jake wasn't bothered at all.

"You know the worst of it, though?" Fareena's eyes narrowed.

"No snacks." Jake's top lip curled upward.

"No snacks! Roy, mate, what's this all about? We need food *and* snacks."

Chuckling heartily, Roy crossed his arms over his chest and leaned back in his chair. "Don't you think our precarious situation tops snack cravings?"

"Roy..." Fareena locked eyes with him and leaned on her elbows. "What scares you the most? The withered or Angela in the mornings without coffee."

"Now that's plain unfair! Ain't nobody in their right mind trying to haul Ange out bed without no coffee." He protested to the laughter around him.

"Well, that's what PMS without snacks is to me."

"She's got a good point, mate." Jake gave Roy the just-nod-and-agree look. *Good man.*

Liv let her eyes linger on him. He was a good man. The kind to stay away from. If she had any self-preservation at all.

"See, Jakes understands me."

"I know exactly how you feel," Jake said with a grimace.

"Do you though?" Noah smirked. "Or are you collecting points?"

Her eyes snapped back to Jake, who usually had a clever retort to most things. Instead, he remained quiet, his brows furled, fingers tapping the table. She wanted to reach for him then. To tell him he didn't need to explain himself to Noah. Or anyone else.

There were moments in life when brief silences were required, and no one thought anything of it. Then there were situations where the silence became so palpable it forced something to change. But if Jake didn't want that one change, he shouldn't have to.

65
JAKE

I'VE ALWAYS FOUND COMING out to be awkward. I spent the entirety of my teens and twenties coming out. To family, co-workers, and new friends.

When you're younger, it's scary, then something to be proud of. As you grow older, it becomes tedious and sometimes even annoying. Because I *have to* come out. It's like a rite upheld by society dictating that if I'm a certain gender, I should follow certain rules. And if I don't, I have to explain why.

Granted, I could have chosen to not correct people when they assumed I had a boyfriend. Sometimes, if it didn't feel safe, I chose not to. But being a lesbian of colour was part of who I was. I was proud of that version of myself. Soo-Yun, or Yun, as most people called me, was someone to be proud of.

She was a proud, open lesbian, unafraid of who she was. But she was also shy and awkward and uncomfortable around new people. Uncomfortable in her own skin.

The feeling had always been there, but I could never put my finger on it. I grew up a tomboy, so I simply put my feelings of discomfort to insecurity. I figured I didn't like my body and appearance because I didn't fit the general idea of what girls should be like or look like. But as much as I kept telling myself that, I always felt *wrong.*

It wasn't until we'd watched *Tipping The Velvet* for the first time, and Megan started calling me 'Uncle' that something changed. I liked the term uncle much more than butch. And, thinking about it, I definitely preferred the noun uncle over aunt.

I was eighteen when I first realised I was transgendered, nineteen when I finally accepted it. Reading trans guy blogs and watching YouTube definitely helped me come to terms with my new identity. But then there was the question of coming out. *Again.* It hadn't really gone the way I thought it would.

I look at the small group I've been travelling and living with for the past weeks. They were strangers back then. Strangers I knew nothing about. But over these past weeks, they have come to mean more to me than I thought they would. I like them.

My gaze slides to Noah. For all our differences, I even like him. Or at least I like him more now than I used to. I'll settle for that.

It's one thing to say you don't care what people think about you. If they like you or not. But with people you care about, it's different.

It means more. I care more about what they think. I can pretend all I like that it wouldn't bother me, that I don't care. But it would. The rejection, the feeling of not being enough. Not being worthy. But I like these people, so it's a chance I'll take.

"I actually do really know because I'm a trans guy."

Six sets of eyes watch me. Roy raises his eyebrows in surprise, but that's all the reaction I get. And it scares me a little bit. Is it good or bad?

Noah blinks, brows pulled together in thought. Frances and Angela, however, seem suspiciously unfazed.

Fareena's amber eyes are round as she watches at me, then her eyes dart to Liv, who shrugs. "You *knew*?"

"I helped him get his testosterone prescription."

It hadn't occurred to me she'd know what my prescription was. I thought the packer gave me away. Apparently, I'd been wrong. She'd known since Wallingford. "Yeah," I say, "I've been on T for... eight years? Yeah, I started when I was nineteen."

Fareena gawks, her eyes widening more. "Wait, you're twenty-seven? You're younger than *me*? Is he the baby of the group?" She looks at the others. "Is he the baby of the group? Noah?"

"Twenty-nine." He rubs his chest.

Liv opens her mouth to speak but is interrupted by Fareena who clicks her tongue. "Girl, I don't even need to ask. You're thirty-two."

"How did you know?" Liv frowns.

"I went through your wallet. What? I grew up with petty criminal brothers, don't judge me. I see that look."

I think everyone sees the look on Liv's face. Especially when she heard my age. Liv has known about me being trans since Wallingford, but it hasn't changed the way she acts towards me. How she is with me. How she looks at me. But now that Fareena has figured out my age, she looks at me like I've grown a second head. And it has nothing to do with my gender.

Her eyes only narrow when she's judging someone or thinking hard about something. For a fraction of a heartbeat, I think she's displeased about my age, but then something tugs at the corner of her mouth. My stomach flips when she smiles with a shake of her head.

"You know, that makes you a cradle snatcher." Fareena flashes her teeth at Liv, who drops her head into her hands with a groan.

"I think I must agree. Jake being a wee baby is definitely the most shocking thing I've been told this evening." Frances winks at me.

Try as I might, I can't keep myself from joining when the others break into laughter. I'm both amused and immensely relieved that their reactions are better than I could have hoped for.

"I'm sorry I didn't tell you sooner but—"

"Son, ain't nobody else's business what's in your pants or who you used to be. It don't change who you are. If somebody thinks it does, you tell them to go straight to hell. In fact, send them my way, and *I* will." Roy hooks a thumb at his chest.

My entire chest grows warm with a buzzing feeling. Maybe it's because we've been through so much in such a short time that I see Roy as something of a father figure. Maybe I'm so starved of love from my own father. Whatever the reason, the man I hardly knew until a few weeks back is the closest thing I have to a father.

"I'm proud to know a fine young man like you, Jake."

My throat tightens with emotion, and when Roy puts an arm around me to pull me into a side hug, I blink as the emotions get the better of me.

"Right, well, since you slackers don't have watch tonight, I'm leaving you to clean this mess up." I excuse myself quickly, and before anyone can point out we don't start watch until everyone goes to sleep, I hurry up the stairs.

After excusing myself, I retreated to the roof with the excuse of taking the next watch. Angela's and Frances's dubious expressions said they didn't believe me, although they had the good grace to not call me out. They're like the mums everyone wants. Calm, knowing when to give their kids space and when to give them the rollocking of a lifetime. The thought amuses me and makes me sad at the same time.

What hit me the hardest was Roy's supportive hug. When I came out to my dad, there was no hugging. No words of encouragement. Only an ice-cold disapproving silence.

That was the last time I spoke to my dad. Until a few weeks ago. Mum had tried to talk sense into him. I was his child, after all. But it stings. Every time I think about it. That he considered his only daughter dead, and the new person I was a complete stranger. It stings that my mother didn't try harder. Didn't put her foot down or stand up for me. Had my back.

Guilt washes over me. I shouldn't think of her like that. Not when she's not around to defend herself. Not when she's dead.

I take a deep breath and gaze at the roofs stretched out before me. I watch the houses that were once full of people. People I grew up with, people I've known for a lifetime. They're all gone now. I wonder if they left, if they made it to the safe zone only to be killed or turned by the infected.

A roof with orange tiles covered in patches of moss a few houses away from me catches my attention. Megan's old house. There's a sting of bitterness in my chest. Megan had not taken my coming out well, going into a spiral of self-doubt and panic. If I were a man, what did that make her? She'd lived her entire life as an open lesbian. And now she was going to turn up with a boyfriend. It was too much, and she needed time to wrap her mind around it. Turned out she never managed to do that. The same as Dad, she saw me as someone new, someone she couldn't recognise anymore. A stranger she couldn't love.

She had stayed, though. So did I. Transitioning, I had to discover myself again. Parts that had always been there but never been allowed to surface. It was all new and scary, but Megan, our life, was familiar. Comfortable. Maybe I was scared of anything else. I'd been with Megan for so long. Would I even know who I was without her?

I pull out my phone and unlock the screen. Chat conversations from Mum, Tim, Megan, and various friends light up my screen. I shouldn't waste the little battery I have left on this. But tonight is different.

I pause, hovering my thumb above Megan's picture. Do I really want to see her? Or will it open a can of worms? *Just leave it.*

As always an expert at taking my own advice, I press the round picture, and it pops across my screen. She's wearing her black-rimmed glasses, chin tilted upwards as she glances down at the camera. It's that look of hers. The one where she's utterly unimpressed by you and yet all you want to do is impress her enough to get her attention.

I let out a long sigh. Being loved by her made me feel special. Like I mattered. As if I were someone. I found a home with her, somewhere I belonged.

Then she left me. Like I was nothing. My chest twinges. I rub at it. And now she's gone again. She left me. Again. And I'm left with a million complicated feelings I never even knew I had: anger, hurt, sadness, and loneliness. I'm so tired of it.

"Ugh." I shake my head in frustration. I can't keep doing this to myself. I have to let her go. Once and for all.

The tiles behind me creak as someone steps on them, and I shove the phone into my pocket.

"Hey, stranger." I look back to see Fareena coming towards me.

"Hey."

"Mind if I join you?"

"Not at all." I pat the roof.

"So." She sits down. "I'd be lying if I said I wasn't surprised."

"That kind of makes me happy." I grin at the ground. If people I come out to are surprised, it means their first thought wasn't, 'that's a chick with a beard,' which was probably one of my worst fears. Looking like a butch lesbian playing drag king. It's what kept me from transitioning until I did. I know it's not right, that's not how gender works. It's not either-or, but I guess fear isn't logical. It simply keeps us in check. It definitely kept me from being true to myself for too long. "You don't think it's... weird?"

"Weird?" She scrunches her nose in the way I've come to think of as a perfectly Fareena manner.

"You're not put off, I mean." I don't want Fareena to be put off. I don't want any of them to be. It didn't seem like they were, but sometimes people mask their true feelings very well.

"Of course, I'm not put off!" She sounds a little offended. "I'm a little sad you didn't tell me." She hugs her knees. "When you told Liv."

I take a deep breath to collect my thoughts. How do I explain this?

I choose my words carefully when I decide to speak. "Coming out isn't just going 'Oh. By the way, I'm a trans dude.' It's inevitably about asking people to respect me for who I am. And with people who matter, to support me." I twist the twig I found on the roof in my hand. "Megan couldn't look at me the same way. Said she couldn't recognise who she saw. And then she fell in love with my best friend. Caitlin. My dad won't talk to me anymore..."

Fareena's eyes go dark. "I don't want to say this about the people you obviously love. But Jake, they *suck*."

I let out a soft chuckle. "Don't get me wrong, I'm proud to be a self-made man. I've pulled myself out of some really dark places. I fought to become me, who I am today, and I'm happy. I've had shitty luck with the whole coming out process."

"I know it's not the same. I mean, how could it be? But you have us now." She snakes her arm around my waist and leans her head against my shoulder.

She's right. Of course she is. She's lost her family as well. All of us have lost the lives we had before this, everything that was familiar to us. And we've been thrust into this crazy, dangerous world that wants us dead. But somehow we're surviving.

"How are you holding up?"

"Half the time I don't know what's a nightmare or reality. Andy, my family..." Her voice trails off, and she wipes at her eyes. "I mean, even my stupid brother Affie."

The way she says it, singling him out, makes me wonder why. "Why 'even Affie'?"

She shakes her head. "Affie always got into trouble. Drugs, fights, car theft... It's like he could never give my parents a break. And then, of course, the stupid twins go and take after him. I hated him sometimes. And now I really miss all of them."

"We could try to go there," I lie. We couldn't. Not without risking our lives. But if we could, there was nothing keeping me here. I would go with her.

She lets out mirthless laughter, tinged with sadness and a bit of bitterness. "We can barely cross the street."

"Yeah..."

She sighs. "I'm scared out of my mind, Jake."

One wouldn't be able to tell. Fareena is always such a ray of sunshine. It's hard to think she could be struggling. But I suppose that's what silly jokes and cheerful smiles are all about: hiding the turmoil inside.

"Me too, but for whatever it's worth, I'm really glad I got to know you."

Her cheeks are rosy from the nipping cold, and her eyes glisten as she views the vast sky above us. In this light, she's beautiful. Putting my arm around her shoulders, I pull her close and kiss the top of her head. "I couldn't do this without you."

"Liar," she whispers, but I can hear the smile in her voice. It's the second time I've made her smile through her sadness, and it makes my chest warm.

"You're stuck with me now. No matter what happens."

"Forever?"

"Forever."

We stayed on the roof until our arses got so cold they felt numb. Then we climbed into the attic. With a kiss on my cheek and a hug, Fareena slips into her and Liv's room, and I head downstairs to let Roy know he's up for watch.

"The prodigal son returns." Roy rises from the sofa and grabs his jacket.

"It's freezing out there." An ice-cold shudder runs through me.

"Sounds like I'll have a fun night then." Roy zips his jacket close. "Right, well, you two sleep tight."

"I would say you too, but you know..." I pull a face at him. He chuckles before disappearing up the stairs, and I turn to Liv.

She sits on the sofa wearing two layers of sweaters, my favourite joggers, and no doubt my long johns as well. Karma lies next to her, and I know she's a bundle of warmth.

"K, let's go get some sleep." I pat my thigh to get Karma's attention. I've been sitting outside for the past three hours. I think I deserve sleep and a little extra heat. It appears my dog doesn't feel the same. She doesn't even move. In fact, I think I see her scoot even closer to Liv, who grins back at me.

"What kind of treachery is this?"

"Well, she's my," Liv pauses, a twinkle flashing in her eyes before she continues, "beastie."

I stare at her. I'm not sure what surprises me the most. That Liv, girl of stony glares and five layers of protective walls, made a joke or how terrible it was.

She breaks into a fit of sparkling laughter. Maybe at my confused expression or maybe at her own joke.

"You should see your face," she wheezes out between laughter.

"Because it's that handsome?" I fire off a grin in her direction.

She doesn't stop laughing, but it slows until it dies out with a low chuckle, then she stands up and steps towards me.

"I would answer that." She looks up at me and bites her lip as if contemplating something.

I watch her, fully aware of and completely ignoring how close she is, barely a breath away. I try to think of a clever comeback, but then I see her cute smile, and I suffer a brain fart of epic proportions.

"Keep this up and I'm going to think you really like me."

"Well, we can't have that."

"Absolutely not." And with that, she sidesteps me and climbs the stairs, leaving me standing.

I let my gaze follow as she disappears. Suddenly, I don't feel so cold anymore. *What is this girl doing to me?*

Liv is not the type you get attached to. She's the type you stay well away from. She's got baggage, a lot of it. As do I. Then there's the whole end-of-the-world thing. This isn't the time for something as trivial as flirting. Surviving, that's what we must focus on.

The memory of her straddling me on the boat has been haunting me with all kinds of inappropriate thoughts ever since. I shake my head, hoping to shake off the warmth that grows in the pit of my stomach when I think about her. Perhaps one of those awful cold showers could help.

A disgruntled sigh sounds, and Karma starts to drag herself off the sofa with a grumpy expression etched on her wrinkly face.

"Stole your sleeping partner, huh?"

She huffs in response, her hind legs stretched out on the sofa. It always took her a good two minutes getting off the couch.

"Yeah, well, I know how you feel," I mutter as I climb the stairs. "But you're stuck with me tonight."

I stop abruptly at the top of the stairs. Karma walks headfirst into me and snorts impatiently.

Noah stands outside my room wearing his pyjamas. "Not the bunk buddy you were hoping for?"

"Uh..." My brow furrows. "Not exactly."

"Well, I spoke to Liv earlier, and she agreed to share. Meaning, *I'm* sleeping with you tonight."

"Are you serious?" I'm not sure whether I should be amused or insulted.

"Dead. Serious," he deadpans. Not a single twitch or barest hint of a smile.

I sigh and throw my hands up in surrender, then open my bedroom door. "What exactly did you bribe her with?"

"My ration of the Caramel energy bar."

I stop and stare at him. "The disgusting one?"

"Yeah." He chuckles.

It's a caramel bar that tastes even worse than it smells. Like days-old dried milk mixed with some sort of chemical that's supposedly caramel flavour. I tried a bite once and gagged.

"Well, now I feel cheap."

"It could have been worse; it could have been a mint," Noah points out as we crawl under my covers, Karma curling up by our feet.

We lie quiet for a long time, the entire thing somewhere between awkward and really fucking weird.

"Do you know who you remind me of?" Noah finally speaks.

"If you say Jackie Chan, I swear I'll shove you into the next group of runners we see."

Noah laughs softly and for the first time, it sounds genuine. "No. My brother."

That's not the answer I was expecting. "I didn't know you had a brother."

"Yeah, well, he's sort of an arsehole."

"Right, so it basically runs in the family?"

"I guess you could say that."'

"Wait, did you call me an arsehole?"

He chuckles. "No, you're not like him like that. I mean in the way he's good at everything he does."

I don't even bother to keep my face neutral, but I turn my head and narrow my eyes. "I'm not sure how any of that relates to me."

"Fred walks into a room and all eyes are on him. Everybody instantly likes him. You're like him. People instantly like you. You're very confident, you don't even have to try."

"Wait? Did you miss the entire trans guy thing? The last thing I feel is confident all the time."

He groans next to me. "Are you going to make me spell it out for you?"

"Did I tell you I'm slightly dyslexic?" It's true.

"I get insecure, okay? And then I act like a tough guy so that you won't know that I'm not."

I contemplate this. Being insecure is something I can relate to. If I had a penny for every situation that made me feel insecure, I'd be a billionaire by now. But there's more to Noah than being insecure and acting like an arse. He's not telling me everything.

"I don't believe you."

He squints at me. "What do you mean you don't believe me?"

"Honestly? I think you're scared people won't like you, so you act like a jerk. That way you give them a reason not to like you."

He looks as if I've slapped him. Forehead wrinkled as he glares. I'm certain he's gone back to the sulky, pouting Noah, but then he speaks again.

"My brother was always a competitive knobhead. He'd gloat about being born a minute before me. He'd rub my face in it when he beat me in sports. He was the golden boy, couldn't do anything wrong. My parents *loved* him. Worshipped him almost. Everything he did was amazing."

"Sibling rivalry." Read about it, seen it on TV, never really experienced it myself.

"It was more than that. I never fit in with my family of overachievers. I like video games and crafting, but in my family that meant I should be the best craftsman or top e-sports player. 'Only successful people are liked, Noah,'" he mimics what I think is his father's voice.

I remain quiet, waiting for him to continue. My dad was a bit of an overachiever, but I can't remember a time when he forced me to be the best at anything. Or implied I had to be the best for him to love me.

"I didn't like my family. And they made it pretty clear they didn't like me."

I know, deep down, my father loves me. Even if he's angry or disappointed, he loves me, and my mother loved me. I don't know what it's like to have parents that don't seem to love you or even like you. I can only try to imagine what that feels like.

"Fuck, that sucks, mate."

He puts his hands behind his head and stares up at the ceiling. "Grow up being told enough times that no one will ever like you for who you really are, eventually you believe it. Guess being an arse is easier than being not liked."

Tough, poncey Prince Charming suddenly feels small, like one of the lost boys, and curse my bleeding heart, but it makes me feel all sorry and protective of him. And it also makes me feel a little shitty that I haven't given him the benefit of the doubt. That I haven't taken his baggage into account. Or the fact that we all have it. That we're all shaped by the experiences we have. I knew nothing about him and still I judged him as if I did. What does that make me?

"But I digress. I wanted to say that I know a thing or two about being brothers and being family. You did everything you could for your family."

I still find it difficult to think about Tim and Mum. But it hits me when I least expect it, and it still hurts too much to talk about. My chest and throat go cold and tight. And yet, Noah's words feel comforting. "Thanks."

We fall silent again, and I look out the window at the trees that form dark shapes and shadows on the neighbouring houses.

"Noah?" I ask when he hasn't spoken for a while.

"Yeah?"

"You were right."

"I was right?"

"Back at the store." I hate it when I'm wrong. I hate it extra much when someone calls me out on it before I realise I'm wrong. But Noah did. Not because he was being selfish, but because he genuinely cares about us. "We couldn't have saved James. I only would've gotten us into more danger."

He remains quiet for a short moment. "It's like you have some sort of hero complex."

I nod.

"And it's really annoying because it makes you the good guy."

I laugh. "Not if I get us all killed. I think you're the good one here. I'm the reckless arsehole, risking everyone's lives to save one. If it wasn't for you, I might have gotten us all killed." Now that I've said the words out loud, it makes my stomach lurch unpleasantly.

"Oh..." He sounds surprised. "I guess you're right."

It's both sad and funny. Mostly sad that Noah isn't used to being told he's a good guy. "You know, someone recently told me the same thing I'm going to tell you: they suck. Your family. And I'm sorry that I've been a bit of an arse to you."

He heaves a heavy sigh. "I probably deserved it."

"Yeah, well..."

Noah snorts. "I can't imagine any of you being all too happy to have me tag along."

"Hell no, I hoped you'd be lurker fodder that first day, mate."

Noah's expression goes from full of contemplation to outright indignant. "What the fuck!" He punches my arm, and I laugh.

"At least you're not on top of my list anymore."

"Seriously, bruv." Noah glares at me.

"I'm fucking with you. Now stop chatting my ears off and go to sleep."

He blows air through his teeth. "Liv did say you were a grump when you get tired."

"I think the two of you might be spending too much time together."

"No need to be jealous." There's jest in his voice and I can tell he's got his Prince Charming smirk in place.

"Good night, Noah."

"Night, Jakey, don't let the lurkers bite."

Now I *know* he's been hanging out with Liv far too much. "Shut up."

66

LIV

PLANNING A TRIP TO a church less than fifteen minutes away shouldn't take long. But in a world overrun by monsters, science had to take the back seat.

Things like building a water filtering system and making a smoker from two large terracotta pots were, as it seemed, more important for their survival.

Liv would argue understanding the infected was as important, but Jake had a point about hungry people. Hungry people did stupid things.

No one had said it out loud yet, but they all knew the hope that everything would go back to normal, that the virus would pass—was gone.

The safe zone had been run over in a week. The *safe* zone. Or as the government liked to call them, protection shelters.

The irony. Even with armed forces, they didn't stand a chance. They couldn't protect anyone. Not here, not in London.

The government was still broadcasting daily "news" to keep the population informed. It was the same message every time.

Great Britain was still in a state of emergency, and scientists were working around the clock trying to find a vaccine or a cure for those taken ill.

Liv gave a derisive snort. Fancy speeches to keep them content. Keep them from asking too many questions. But people weren't stupid. At least not the ones still out there fighting to stay alive. While the government no doubt sat somewhere safe, broadcasting their so-called news, people were scrambling to survive, whether it be fighting the withered or scavenging for food.

Their small group had food for now. The regular staples like rice, pasta, noodles, a variety of dried beans, canned vegetables, an insane amount of kimchi, and Gochujang paste. Which she could have sworn she saw Jake dip his finger into as if it were chocolate cream and not spicy hot chilli paste.

Despite the generous number of things in the pantry, food was still scarce, and there were seven of them.

Even if they rationed it to one small meal per day, they wouldn't make it through winter without scavenging and hunting. Jake was right, the more they stockpiled now, the easier winter would be. The easier surviving would be.

Going out meant taking risks. The less they needed to do that, the better. And that's where all the scouring of the nearby area for food and building a smoker came in.

The meat in the fridge wouldn't last forever. Without electricity, any meat they could hunt would go bad. Lucky for them, Roy knew how to smoke and dry meat. And Jake knew how to build a smoker.

She gazed at the water-filled bathtub that stood next to the deck. A small fire burned underneath, heating the water.

Turned out a smoker wasn't the only thing Jake knew how to make.

After burying his family, he'd spent two days finishing it, digging nonstop until he was so out of breath he wheezed.

They'd all left him alone to grieve in his own way. Personally, she would drown her sorrows in alcohol and Valium. Or Xanax. Or whatever other benzos she could get her hands on.

Beggars can't be choosers and all that. A shudder ran through her. *Junkies can't be choosers, you mean.*

"Shut up," she silenced the nagging voice. Karma whined, giving her a hurt look. "No, not you, darling." She scratched the big dog behind her ear.

Karma had taken to following her around when she wasn't sleeping on the sofa. For a big muscular dog, Karma did an awful lot of sleeping. And a lot less guarding. Liv glanced over her shoulder through the window.

Jake sat in the living room with Fareena, Angela, and Roy, his hands gesticulating the way they always did when he talked. It was as if the man talked with his entire being. Angela laughed at something, her entire face lighting up.

It was odd to think that somehow Liv was part of this group. Even stranger that they seemed to appreciate having her around.

At another window, Frances stood by the sink, washing dishes with Noah. Frances caught sight of her and lifted her chin, the corner of her mouth kicking up in a smile.

Liv chuckled softly, an odd light feeling spreading through her chest. She walked towards the tub. Perhaps the strangest thing was that she enjoyed being part of it.

She stepped behind the wooden screen, built to give the bath a bit of privacy. Karma followed and plonked herself down as if to keep a watchful eye on her.

Liv dipped her hand into the water. Into the *warm* water. Who would have thought she'd be so excited to sink into a hot bath filled with river water?

It wasn't the cleanest water, but it was clean enough to swim and bathe in. After weeks of cold showers, a hot bath was a welcomed luxury. And it could help with the icy shivers that spasmed through her, leaving her hands shaking.

Some days, she had to clench her fists to keep them from shaking wildly. Most days, it helped with both the shaking and the constant nausea.

She could blame her shaking hands on the cold. The throwing up, however, if someone found out, that would be more difficult to explain.

At least this morning had started well. No throwing up, and it was already past breakfast.

Hopefully, the warmth would stop the crawling under her skin. Like ants skittering through her limbs, making her want to crawl out of herself.

One of the bushes rustled.

She jerked her hand from the water, her eyes darting around the garden. Nothing. But she could have sworn she'd heard something.

Karma let out a loud snore. Liv frowned. Karma never missed a single sound. Whenever a group of stragglers shuffled by, Karma's hackles rose, a low growl rumbling in her throat. But not this time.

She huffed out a breath, shaking her head. Not taking her meds had her jumpier than usual. With the withered roaming around the slowly crumbling world, who could blame her?

Another rustle sounded, and she saw something move out of the corner of her eye. She whipped her head towards the end of the garden, at the door that led to the street.

She blinked. There had definitely been something there. A shadow, but now there was nothing.

She stared at the spot until she was certain it was her own paranoia playing tricks on her.

"Stop freaking yourself out, you silly bitch."

"Liv?" Frances stepped out from the kitchen. "You alright, love?"

Liv nodded, hoping Frances couldn't hear her heart hammering with adrenaline. "Mm-hmm." The last thing she wanted was for the others to think she was crazy. *Crazier.*

Frances eyed her, then shrugged. "Okay, well, don't let that water get cold."

"Never." Liv fired off a smile and watched Frances retreat inside. Turning back towards the tub, a voice called out through the damp midday air. High-pitched and searching.

"Mum!"

She froze.

"Mummy!" the voice came again.

She shook her head. *No. It's not you.*

"Mum, help me," the voice cried, small and frightened and as clear as Frances's voice had been. It came from the other side of the fence door, and against her better judgement, Liv walked towards it.

"Mummy, open the door."

Her hand trembled as she reached for the latch to unlock the gate. The latch slid from its place. The gate swung open.

She sucked in a shuddering breath.

He stood in the alley between the two houses, his small frame cowering in the cold. He was the same height as when she last saw him. Had the same dark locks as his father.

"Ellis?" She took a step, expecting him to vanish. Impossible. He couldn't possibly be there. He died. He'd *died* in her arms, and it hadn't been beautiful. He'd cried and been scared, clawing at her chest, trying to free himself from the tubes and wires connected to his body. She'd held him until he stopped fighting. Until he stopped breathing.

But Ellis didn't vanish, only stood there watching her as if nothing had changed. As if he hadn't been gone for four years.

She rubbed her eyes, but Ellis was still there when she opened them again. "You can't be here," she whispered.

"You're so silly, Mum." A giggle reached her ears, familiar and bright like a song.

Pushing the gate to the side, she walked, reaching out for him, but before she reached him, Ellis darted down the alleyway, laughing loudly.

"Wait!" she called. "Ellis!" Before she could think better of it, she chased after him. Down the alley, out to the street, around the corner.

He rushed towards the yellow brick house, dark hair bouncing as he slowed enough for her to almost catch up. Then he slipped through the front door.

She quickened her pace, trying to catch him, her arms reaching for the marine-blue door. A red cross hatch crawled across the door. It should warn her off. But it didn't, and she pushed the handle down. If Ellis were in there, she had to get to him.

"Liv, no!" someone called. She ignored them, stumbling into the empty, quiet house.

"Ellis?"

Shadows clung to walls covered in floral wallpaper, and a smell of stale air and dust filled the house. No one had been in there for a while. Laughter trickled down the stairwell.

She looked up at top of the stairs, well aware that children's laughter in an abandoned house should scare the living shite out of her. But it was Ellis, her son. She knew that laughter like the back of her hand. She could pick it out in a crowd full of people.

A cold white-painted railing brushed against her palm as she walked up the stairs. The carpet, with its hideous pattern, softened her footsteps when the stairs creaked beneath her feet.

"Mummy, come look." His voice brimmed with excitement.

"Ellis!" She ran the last few steps, coming to a halt at the top.

A baby-pink door slammed shut at the other end of the walkway. Hesitation tried to pull her attention away, but she brushed it off. Ellis was in there. She'd seen him with her own eyes. As clearly as she could see the pink door.

Curling her fingers around the handle, she sucked in a breath and held it.

The door creaked open in time with her slow exhale. She blinked through the thin crack of the door.

Nothing. The room was empty. Except for an empty baby cot and toys haphazardly strewn across the floor, and... a shadow in the corner of the room.

Part of her tingled with warning, the other whispering that her son could still be in the room, when the shadow blurred towards her with a wet snarl.

An infected in a flowered dress, half her face covered by the red roots sprouting from her orifices, rushed towards her. Her arms were stretched out, reaching for Liv.

"Move!" Jake pushed her to the side. Where'd he come from?

Curses poured from his mouth as he jerked at the handle, trying to slam the door shut, but a rotten hand with a few missing fingers held his wrist in a tight grip.

Teeth covered in ghoulishly grey and brown slime snapped at his face. "Fareena!"

Liv's eyes flickered from his fingers curled around the door handle to the space behind the infected woman. Ellis stood still behind the drooling, shrieking woman. *No!* Jake was going to shut Ellis in that room.

"Back away, love." Frances grabbed her by the shoulders, startling Liv, just as Fareena pushed past with a cricket bat raised above her head. It made a sickening crunch as she shoved it through the gap straight into the snarling woman's face.

A shriek of indignation ripped from the infected's mouth, and she staggered backwards.

Jake slammed the door shut.

"No!" If Jake closed the door, he would lock Ellis inside with that woman, that *thing.* She couldn't lose him again. Adrenaline surged through her like a switch being flipped, and she lunged at him, trying to push him away.

Fareena sidestepped with a yelp, spinning on the balls of her feet. "What the hell?"

"Stop it!" Jake grabbed her wrists, keeping himself between her and the door. "Liv! Stop!"

She yanked free of his grip, slamming her palms into his chest. It drew a grunt from him, but instead of moving, he wrapped his arms around her, pulling her close.

"You need to stop it."

She struggled briefly, but his hold on her was too strong.

"Get off me!"

His arms loosened, though he didn't fully let her go. "Liv—"

"I said get off of me!" She wedged her arms between them and pushed him hard in the chest, sending him stumbling backwards.

"I'm trying to help you!"

"You're not helping anyone, Jake." Her temper flared, and he was the one who had lit the fuse. Lit the spark she had tried to defuse for so long. Who the hell was he to keep her from her son? Whenever she was given an opportunity to see Ellis again, Jake just had to *help*.

Rage bubbled up. All the anger and resentment she'd locked away. It was all coming out. Every single bit of it.

"You try to be so fucking perfect, but all you do is stir shit you have no business stirring! And you drag everyone along with you."

"Liv!" Fareena's eyes blazed with anger, but Liv couldn't care less. She had been so close to getting to Ellis. To being with him again. And for a second time, Jake had ruined it.

"Who have you actually helped? Jules? That woman at the house? Me? Or your—"

Dark eyes, almost black, flashed at her. The muscles in his jaws worked. "I guess no one."

She blinked, the edge in his voice sobering her up. One far too familiar to her. Self-loathing. What the hell was she doing?

"Jake..." she whispered, coming out of her daze. But he pushed past her and walked away.

"What the fuck is wrong with you?" Fareena shouldered past her, following Jake. Even Frances looked at her with disappointment in her eyes.

Well, fuck these people! Liv balled her hands into fists. They didn't know her. They had no idea how difficult things were for her. She twitched, the ants crawling all over her again. She needed her benzo, but she was trying to stop. She did that for them, and this was how they thanked her?

"Let's go, love." Frances gave her elbow a gentle nudge.

Liv refused to look at the older woman. Frances would give her the same look Marie had given her. The one that said, *I'm disappointed in you, but I'm here for you*. And although she had acted like she didn't care back then, even as a kid, she knew what it meant.

It meant they cared. They cared enough to be disappointed by her. Perhaps that's why she had done it so many times in her life. To see who really cared.

"I don't know why I did that..."

Frances touched a hand to her cheek. "We both know why, but this isn't the place to be talking about it. We need to get home, and you need to take your meds."

67
LIV

TO SAY THAT THE rest of the day had been awkward was like saying that the sky was blue or winter was cold.

Jake had avoided her completely, steering clear whenever they were in the same room. Maybe she had avoided him, too. Because facing him meant facing things about herself she wasn't ready to face. Shame, anger, and hatred. Ugly things. Things that boiled under the surface.

This was the exact reason she stayed away from other people in the first place. It was easier to lie to herself when she didn't have to see the truth in other people's eyes.

Parts of her felt justified in her reaction. As if she had simply triggered an inevitable event. People were going to leave eventually. Why prolong the wait? This way, at least, it was her choice. She made them leave.

And yet, Jake barely looking at her during dinner felt wrong. Dinner had been unusually quiet. And it wasn't only because of Roy's insanely tasty wild mushroom ragu.

Frances and Noah had tried asking Roy about the food, momentarily breaking the heavy silence. It had been a pleasant moment, listening to Roy talk passionately about what he could do with the wild food in the area around them.

The things he could cook or pickle that had never crossed her mind were embarrassingly many. Mushrooms, cranberries, and fruits. Though granted, she would poison herself if she'd tried anything like it on her own. According to Roy, there was an entire science behind what to can and how to can it. If done wrong, one could apparently top oneself off.

"Well." Frances sat down, pushing a glass of water Liv's way. "I dare say that's the most awkward family dinner I've ever had to attend. And I had to bring a girlfriend home to a Catholic family in the eighties. So that says quite a lot about tonight."

Liv paused, looking at Frances with narrowed eyes. "Girlfriend?"

"Focusing on the wrong thing, dear." Frances quirked an eyebrow.

"Right, I—" Liv cleared her throat and picked at her cuticles. Frances already knew what had happened earlier, and judging by what she'd said before they returned to the house, she knew why. "How did you know?"

"If I hadn't been working with addicts for the past forty years, I don't think I would've known."

"Of course," Liv scoffed. Of all the people who could find her during the apocalypse, it had to be a substance abuse nurse. "I thought I hid it better."

"I see everything, Liv. The shaking hands, the muscle aches, and spasms... and the look of someone who's on a high. I can see it from miles away. Even when you hide it well." Frances paused. "How much are you on? By the frequency you took them at and your withdrawal symptoms, I'd guess around four or five milligrams?"

Shame washed over her, the familiar feeling making her want to disappear. Her normal response would be to kick off and flee. Didn't matter what she said or who she hurt, as long as she didn't have to stay and bear that shame.

More often than not, she ended up in a bar. Or in her car with a bottle of vodka or whiskey, depending on what she could get. And a handful of the small white pills. The ones that made her feel so good. So calm. If only she could take one now, to calm her nerves a bit. To still the crawling in her skin. Take the edge off the shame and guilt.

"More?" Frances nudged her.

She shook her head. "Three or four. Mostly four."

"For how long?"

For longer than she cared to admit. During med school before Ellis and then after. Exactly like her good-for-nothing father, addiction ran in her blood. The first thing she'd done leaving prison was get drunk and high. The relief of not having to spend every night forgetting or bearing the guilt, the memories, was too great to resist. If only for a night. Just. One. Night. And then one more and another one after that. Soon, one night became every night. "Six months this time."

"And you decided to simply quit."

She nodded again, knowing full well what the nurse was going to say next.

"That was extremely reckless and dangerous. Benzoates differ from other drugs. You need to wean off them or you could suffer severe side effects." Frances put her hand on her wrist and squeezed it, locking eyes with her. "You could seizure or *die*."

Liv dropped her gaze to the fingers curled around her wrist, a palpable silence settling in the dimly lit kitchen.

She knew what she would see if she looked up. That same expression everyone had when silence was answer enough. One of confusion and pity. And she hated it. Hated the resentment that welled up inside her. How could they possibly understand? What she had done. What she had lost. No one could. Even death was not punishment enough. She was not worthy of death. She didn't deserve to escape this hell, this suffering.

Death would be a mercy too kind for someone like you. I hope you live a very long life with what you've done.

She could still hear him in her mind. Could still hear the slight tremble in his voice that somehow, despite its quietness, seemed to shake the world.

Angela, done with the washing up, sat down with a soft sigh. "I don't know what happened to you, hon." She leaned over the table, pulling Liv's hands into her own. "And I know saying 'it's okay' is about as helpful as..."

"A bull's tit," Frances filled in.

Laughter bubbled from Angela's lips, the sparkling sound contagious. Liv laughed, the familiar feeling of guilt creeping into the back of her head. She shouldn't be allowed to laugh. To enjoy life, when she was responsible for...

"It's not exactly the phrasing I would use, but it'll do." Angela shook her head, still smiling. She gave Liv's hands a gentle squeeze. "But it will be okay."

Liv shook her head. "I don't know that it will be."

"Oh, it will be. You may not feel like it right now, in this moment. But every day you're still here, you're choosing to survive, to fight. Every damn hour, you're a fighter."

Liv bit the inside of her cheek. Angela's words were too much. They were too kind, and she didn't deserve kindness.

"You don't know... I have no right."

"Your mistake, whatever it was, does not mean you've lost your right to exist. To *live*." Angela locked her gaze with Liv's.

She blinked, her vision growing blurry. Stupid tears. "I'm not sure I believe that."

"You know, I understand feeling like you don't belong. Like you have no right to exist. I'm a Black woman in the police force." Angela smiled but her eyes shone with a rare sadness. "I don't ever get to step into a room and feel like I belong. As if I have the right to be there. I have to fight for that space. For my right to exist in the same room as my white colleagues. As a woman of colour, I'm sure you know this feeling too.

"You hear me when I say that I understand trying to protect yourself. Keeping everyone at an arm's length. But it gets *lonely*. Doesn't it?"

Liv swallowed against the dryness in her throat. She'd always been alone. By choice. It was safer.

Even with David and his family, she'd chosen to stay distanced. But after Ellis, she felt... lonely. The crushing ache to see him again only to realise over and over that he was gone. It was the kind of loneliness and pain that chipped away a little piece of her soul every time.

Then this group of people happened in some side street in London, and before she'd realised what was happening, she'd become part of it. And she liked it. Liked being a part of something, liked them.

Frances with her calm demeanour, Angela with her stern motherly look, and Jake with his pensive dark eyes.

The man could be all fun and games, yet when he thought no one was looking, he grew quiet and contemplative. When he got caught, he'd fire off a disarming smile, one that would trick those who didn't pay attention. But his eyes always spoke more than his words.

He was a puzzle, a mystery. Something about him pulled her in. Like an invisible force causing her to gravitate towards him. His presence and patience calmed and soothed. It made her want to stay. Made her want to belong to this haphazardly thrown together group of people. And she hated it. What a cliché she was.

He—all of them—made her feel like she was a part of a large, very strange family. And still she'd done what she always did, treated him like he was the enemy. She was good at that. At pushing others away. At breaking things.

"I think... I'm too broken."

"Sugar." Angela's smile was back. Warm and genuine this time. "We're all broken. Just to different degrees."

Liv wiped her tears. "I'd like to be a little less broken."

"And that is why you self-medicate," Frances said. As if self-medicate wasn't simply a nicer way of calling someone a junkie.

She nodded, trying to ignore the shame that wrapped itself around her like a second layer of skin.

"I gather you know about the side effects of your medicine."

Another nod.

"And you know what happens if you go cold turkey."

"What *can* happen," she corrected Frances before she could stop herself.

The older woman let out a dry laugh and leaned backwards. "You kids all think you're the exception to the rule. 'We're doctors, we know what we're doing.' Well, as someone with over forty years of experience as a mental health nurse, benzoates alter the chemicals in your brain. If you don't wean off it slowly. It. Could. Kill. You."

Perhaps that wasn't such a bad—

"Or as evident by earlier, one of us."

She dropped her gaze to the table.

"You may not care about your own life, but I *know* you care about the rest of us. You don't want to be the reason someone gets hurt or worse."

Liv shook her head.

"Then let me do what I do best. Let me help you get clean."

She nodded. "Okay."

"This will only work if you really want this." Frances tilted her head forward, searching her face.

"I do." The thought of being the reason someone else died, someone she cared for... it was too much. She nodded again. She needed to do it. "I *want* to be clean. But what if I can't do it?"

Angela squeezed her arm. "No one else but *you* has kept you alive this long. You're stronger than you think. Imagine what you could do with a little support."

"I've tried before, so many times." She looked at Angela and Frances. "I don't think I cannot drink for the rest of my life. I've tried."

Frances smiled, calm and reassuring. "You don't have to not drink for the rest of your life; you just have to not drink today. One day at a time."

68

JAKE

IT'S NIGHT, THE COLD and mist creeping in, when I hear the door creak open. Karma stirs, her tail beating the deck and, by the force of it, I can guess who's standing behind us.

"Hello, puppy," the soft voice murmurs, and Karma grunts in approval. *Traitor.*

"You realise she's a grown-arse dog, right?" It comes out harder than planned.

"You're angry." She doesn't dance around the topic. Though it's not like we spent most of the day avoiding each other. *Hashtag sarcasm,* I mutter inwardly.

"Would it be that weird if I was?"

Her gaze flickers. "Honestly? A little bit."

My annoyance flares to life. Fuck her. Fuck everyone who always thinks they can treat people however they want with no consequences. I open my mouth to tell her where to stick it, but she lifts her hand into the air.

"It's just... you're always so levelheaded."

"Oh, I'm sorry I don't go around shoving people and hitting them below the belt."

"No... but I heard something about a punch."

I glare at her attempt to lighten the mood. It draws a sigh from her, and she averts her eyes. She looks small, tired, and sad.

"Ugh," I scoff at myself. I'm so weak. "*He* pushed me first."

"So you *punched* him?"

I nod.

"Did you want to punch me?"

"What? No."

Her lips thin into a straight line. "Why not? I pushed you. Are you sexist, Jake?"

"No! I—"

"Relax, I'm teasing."

"Yeah, of course..." I narrow my eyes. "I *knew* that."

She smiles, almost shyly. "Thanks for not punching me."

The odd sincerity in her voice sobers me. I forgot how she grew up. My chest twinges when I think about it. "I would never hurt you..."

"I deserved it."

"No." I shake my head hard. "No one deserves to get punched."

"Not even that awful American president?"

I let out an exasperated noise. "Yeah, okay, but not someone who isn't a political figure or famously bigoted."

"Not even Noah?" She tilts her head as if I'm about to tell her a secret.

"Now why do you need to call me out like this when I was trying to make a good point?"

She laughs and it pulls a smile onto my lips. She sees it, and her big, hazel eyes turn contemplative, focused somewhere behind me.

"Hmm."

"What?"

Her gaze returns to my face. "Why did you bring everyone here? You don't know us. You don't know me."

I pause. Why did I bring this lot? I didn't have to. Now that I know them better, the thought of leaving them behind seems absurd. But I didn't know them at all back then. And I don't actually like people all that much, so what made me tell them to come with me when I could've left them at Westminster? Safety in numbers? Or altruistic selflessness?

I wish I could say that was the reason. I shake my head. No, it wasn't pure altruism. It was guilt. All the people on the train. I left those behind to drown. Or worse...

I still hear the screaming and chaos from that carriage sometimes. Now I know it wasn't people fighting or trying to break their way out, and it makes my stomach turn.

I grimace, trying to quiet the memories. If I told Liv why, if I told her what I saw, what I *did*, what would she see when she looked at me? A murderer responsible for hundreds of deaths. But what's the point in trying to hide it from her? If I don't tell her, one of the others might. If they haven't already. Maybe that's why she asked.

"Before we ran into you, we were stuck in the tube."

"Yes, Fareena gave me the rundown of it. You got everyone out."

"Not everyone..." I pick the seam on my jeans, bouncing my leg up and down. "You were right about what you said."

"No." She pushes her hand against my thigh. "What I did was fucking shitty. I'm not... well. And I know that doesn't excuse what I did." She shakes her head hard. "What I said was hurtful and cruel."

I remain silent, unsure of what to say.

"I'm sorry I said those things... you're pretty awesome."

I scoff. "I assure you there's an alarming amount of people who'd disagree with you."

"Well shit, Jake. When have I ever cared about what other people think?"

I laugh. "Fair point."

"They're all wrong about you." She touches her palm against my cheek, her brows knitting in concern as she searches my eyes. The way she looks at me—the way she touches me—is something I've longed for.

Megan would look at me and see someone else. Someone I used to be. Someone who wasn't me. I—Jake—was always invisible to her. But Liv looks at me; she *touches* me like she wants to. And sometimes when she looks at me, I wonder if she wants more.

Her thumb brushes my cheek, and it feels so good. But the way she lashes out... it hurts just as much.

"Why?" I ask, as if she can read my mind and knows what I've been thinking. Why does it feel like as much as she wants to touch me, she wants to hurt me? Whatever her reason, I've already done the shitty relationship thing. I don't want to do that again regardless of how much I like someone.

She takes a deep breath. Her gaze dances around, and I put my hand on hers. "I'm not angry. I only want to understand so I can help."

"I'm scared," she says after a long moment of silence. We're all scared. There must be more to it. I wait for her, giving her time to compose her thoughts.

"I'm scared I'll hurt you."

I could pretend and make her feel better by saying she didn't. But I'm tired of acting as if everything is fine when it's not. Civilisation is crumbling to the ground all around us. We've lost families and friends, everything that's familiar to us. Nothing is fine anymore.

"You do hurt me. When you lash out instead of talking to me. Or anyone. I get it. Telling people how you really feel is scary, but so is the world right now. It's fucking terrifying out there. So... why not let us in? I mean, what could you really lose?"

69

LIV

What could you really lose? It both annoyed and impressed her how bluntly he simply threw the question out there. Had he never heard of betrayal and backstabbing? The worst enemy was the person who knew everyone's secrets. That didn't apply only to her experience with Doctor Lindeberg or prison. Or did it?

She studied him a moment longer. Neither he nor the others had given her any reason to distrust them. Perhaps that was the problem. She was always waiting for that moment when they realised what a fuckup she was and left her behind. Waiting for when their true colours would show and prove she'd been right all along, that people suck.

But none of that had happened. Not even after today. Instead, they had embraced her and encouraged her to not give up on herself.

How was she supposed to do that when it felt like she'd given up a hundred times before? Not only on herself, but on others as well. On life. But this group of people she'd met, they were different. They were a broken group, but they were considerate, and they did their best to get along. Maybe she wasn't ready to fight for herself yet. But Jake and the rest of them were worth not giving up on.

"I'm not good at accepting help," she said slowly, "but you... you want to help everyone."

He grimaced. "I know. It's a fault of mine. I think—or maybe I wish—I could help, but not everyone needs it or even wants it."

"It's not a bad thing. It's brave, reaching out for people, throwing them a lifeline, but we're not all brave enough to take it."

He remained silent, his eyes pensive and dark as he took her in.

"Help usually comes with some sort of condition, or maybe that's the only experience I've had."

"I don't want anything back." He almost sounded a little hurt. "I want you to be well. I want people to be okay."

She smiled. What a Jake thing to say. Perhaps the exact right thing to say at that very moment.

If she wanted to get clean for good, she couldn't stay the same, couldn't keep up the same patterns as before. As scary as it was, she was going to have to let them in. She needed their help, no matter how much she tried to deny it. She'd already tried to do it on her own so many times.

She chewed the inside of her cheek. She would have to try, even if it meant letting them down, and they left her behind.

"I do want your help... but I'm scared."

"That it won't work?"

She shook her head. "I didn't plan on liking any of you lot," she said, testing the ground and when he didn't react, she continued, "but the awful truth is, I do."

"Why is that awful?" His brows creased.

"Because I don't know how to deal with that. Now..." She fell silent, picking at her fraying cuticles.

He put his hand on hers to stop her picking. His palm was warm and welcoming, the motion so natural that parts of her wanted to melt into him. His thumb brushed across her skin, pulling her from her silence. "Now?"

"I could lose you. All of you. Anything could take you lot away from me, and I don't know if I can lose someone else."

He exhaled heavily, his breath fogging up the night air. "I can't tell you what the future holds, but I can promise you I will do what I can to make you feel safe."

She let out a breath. Jake was anything but safe. He was the type that could get others to jump the ledge into the unknown. Hell, if she weren't careful, she'd race towards it and throw herself off for the rush of being near him.

With David, she'd been in control. There was no ledge, no crazy desire to stray from the safe side of the fence. Jake was unknown to her. Unknown and unsafe. And she had already calculated all the ways letting him in could go wrong.

"I'm not scared of the world around us."

"Then what are you scared of?"

She looked away from him, her instincts telling her to keep quiet. To not let him in. But Frances and Angela were right; her instincts were off. They had done nothing but get her into trouble this far.

"Myself."

"Yourself?"

The night suddenly felt colder, the space around them smaller. The instinct to run fought with her need to belong. To feel right again. To do more than barely survive day by day. Like one of those creatures, those mindless infected roaming the world outside.

"Why?" he asked again. She hated that he knew when to wait her out and when to nudge her to answer.

"I hurt the people around me." She held her breath, the truth big and scary to say out loud.

"How?"

"People around me die. If they don't, I push them away."

Understanding flitted through his eyes. "Toby? I know it doesn't help to hear, but it wasn't your fault."

She shook her head. Not Toby. Not Ellis. She knew she couldn't help them. Parts of her knew, other parts liked the torment of thinking she could have somehow prevented it. A fitting punishment for the crime. But there was one she could have saved. There was one that was all her fault. Teresa Miller.

The walls were white, sterile, and clean. Exactly what one might expect from a hospital room. The buzzing noise of voices and rubber soles squeaking across the floor quieted as she closed the door behind her.

The little girl looked back at her from the window where she stood in her mother's lap, trying to peer outside.

The woman, Alicia Miller, gave Liv an apologetic smile. "Tess is determined to count all the red cars."

"Is that so?" Liv smiled and sat down on the bed, putting her pad beside her. Sitting down would help keep her tethered to the room. Stop her from turning around to leave. No matter how crowded or suffocating the room felt around her, she had to stay. This little girl needed her.

Teresa Miller, five years old, in desperate need of a heart transplant. It was Liv's job to do that. To gift her and her family with that.

"There are thousands of them." Teresa grinned, and by thousands, she of course meant two.

"That's a lot of cars." Liv crossed her leg over the other and stuck her hands into her white coat pockets. It would keep them from shaking.

Teresa nodded, black curls bouncing around her head as she did.

"Do you know why you're here today?"

"We've talked to Tess about it." The dad, Brian Miller, put his hand on his daughter's head. Teresa nodded.

"Do you have any questions you want to ask me?"

"Can I try your stethoscope?"

A smile pulled at Liv's lips. Kids. Tell them about the end of the world and they would still focus on all the things their imagination could conjure up.

"Do I get to listen to your heart first?"

Tess pursed her lips but allowed herself to be placed next to Liv. "Doctors always want to listen to my heart."

"Do you know why?" Liv adjusted the earpieces. She always hated the feeling of them in her ears.

"Because mine's broken."

"No, darling." She pressed the metal diaphragm against Teresa's chest. "The sound of your heartbeat is like music. It just needs a little help to keep its rhythm."

Thud, thud-thud-thud, thud. The same irregular pattern as the first time she met Teresa. But in two weeks' time, God willing, her new heart would have a much healthier sound.

"Can you take a deep breath for me?"

Teresa's chest rose and fell with the breath.

"Good, that's great." Liv pulled the earpieces from her ears. "Well, everything sounds good. If things progress like this, and I don't see any indication that it shouldn't, she'll be approved for her upcoming surgery."

"Oh, thank God." Brian's shoulders dropped in relief, the blood returning to the knuckles on his fist that squeezed Alicia's hand.

Alicia covered her mouth, nodding, her eyes turned towards the sky as if she were quietly thanking a higher power.

Liv had seen that look on many parents' faces. The one when they knew their child was going to be alright. She'd always felt a sense of euphoria seeing it, knowing she was part of that. Now she felt numb.

She turned to Teresa. "Do you know what that means?"

The little girl's brown eyes went round as she saw the stethoscope held out towards her. "I get to listen to *your* heart?"

Liv chuckled. "Yes. Yes, it does."

When Teresa Miller was too busy listening to Liv's heart to pay them any attention, Liv had told her parents the hospital would do anything they could to help Teresa. That she was getting the best care at one of the top hospitals in the UK. Teresa was in good hands.

The surgery wasn't scheduled for another two weeks. She had two weeks to get her act together. She thought she had enough time.

She'd been wrong.

70

JAKE

"Liv?" I PULL HER focus back to me. She'd said a girl's name, then she'd got lost in her own thoughts.

"I lost my son."

Son? I blink in surprise but quickly recover. "I'm sorry... I can't imagine what that's like."

"It's like having the room collapse on top of you. Every. Single. Day." Her lip quivers, and she bites down on it, dark-pink flesh turning white underneath her teeth.

"What happened?" I don't know if I should ask or say anything at all. But not asking or saying anything would be pretending she hadn't told me she lost her son.

Her expressions are usually difficult to read, but now her brows scrunch and though her mouth is set, the corners quiver despite her best effort to not cry. "Ewing's Sarcoma." Dampness fills her eyes and she blinks against it, wetting her dark lashes. "A rare type of cancer. We tried everything, but it was too aggressive." She wipes at her eyes and pulls her knees towards her chest.

My mother's auntie died from cancer, and though it's not at all the same, I know it changes your life forever. "I fucking hate cancer. And I hate that you lost your son to it."

Tears roll off her quivering lips, and she exhales. I do the same when I try to steady my breathing. Did the same when I lost Mum and Tim. I understand the pain of breaking inside, not having the words to express it.

Despite that, I don't know the right words to say. I don't think there are any. I do the next best thing and slide my hand under hers and link our fingers together.

"Nothing makes sense when you lose your child. I can't even make sense of myself anymore. So I try to forget."

I give her hand a gentle squeeze and I hope it's enough for her to know that I understand. Or that I'm trying to and that I'm here for her.

She shakes her head and looks up at the sky. "I've done awful things, shitty, unspeakable things. And I wished it would end. All of it."

All of it. Her words echo in my mind, and I remember that night on the boat. The look on her face. I didn't understand it then, but now it makes sense.

"Is that what happened on the boat?" I ask carefully.

"Sometimes, more often than not, I wished it was me. It should have been me." Her voice breaks, and she gives a hard shake of her head. She closes her eyes and curls towards her knees as if to disappear into herself and shut the world out.

Liv is all protective walls and distance. Maybe not as much anymore, but there's still that level of self-control. Always in place to make sure she can't be hurt. But what's the point? What's the point of being around people if you aren't going to let them in? If you can't even be honest with them about the things you feel or don't feel, then there is no point. It's not worth it. It never was.

We're all vulnerable. We all want to belong, want to feel safe, fit in somewhere. That doesn't make us weak. Not when we have each other.

I pull her into my arms. Without hesitating or offering her a cup of tea first, and she hides her face in my jacket.

"I'm sorry." What else is there to say? "What do you need from me?"

She's quiet for a long moment. "I could really use a friend."

I smile. "Well, you're in luck. Because I hear Noah is a superb friend."

Her shoulders shake with something between a laughter and a sob, and I squeeze her tighter. "I don't want to brag but... I've been told I'm a pretty good friend."

"Why are you so nice to me?" she whispers into my chest. "I've done terrible things after I lost Ellis. I'm not safe."

"I see you're trying, even if you think it's not enough. That's all that matters."

She shakes her head. "How can you be so sure?"

"I'm a pretty excellent judge of character."

She snorts and I smile. I'm a terrible judge of character and we both know it.

"Well," I murmur, "I like you. I like that you came into my life, all of you. I want you here. I think everyone else does as well."

"Why?" It's barely a whisper as she leans further into me.

I press my lips against her hair. "I don't know. I just do," I confess. I can't explain it, but in a world where so much can't be explained, maybe this can remain a mystery.

Emergency Broadcast

This is an Emergency Broadcast from the government. Please stand by for further information. This is not a test.

The virus is spreading rapidly in the larger cities.

Roads and airports will be closed for military use.

Phones will be restricted for emergency use and information only.

These are the following symptoms of the virus: hyper-aggressiveness, bleeding from the eyes, headaches, fever, and confusion.

If a member of your family has been infected, do not approach them or try to care for them.

Please make your way to a protection shelter in one of the following locations: Brighton, Kirkwall, Cardiff, Snowdonia National Park, or Scarborough.

71

LIV

THE WORLD HAD GONE silent. TV and radio stations no longer broadcasted, landlines and mobile networks were down. Not even the internet had been able to outrun its inevitable death.

They hadn't heard a single piece of news in the past four weeks. Last they'd heard, scientists were confirming what Liv had already suspected. The virus, R3-D, wasn't a virus at all. It was a parasitic fungus that attacked the brain and spread through exposure to the spores and the bodily fluids of the infected.

None of them was sure what R3-D stood for, but the others called it the Red Death. She supposed it was appropriate with the red spores the fungi around them emitted.

The parasite caused severe aggression in the host, or in the substrate as scientists called it, driving it to attack others around them, thus spreading the infection further.

The reports hadn't mentioned the mutated version of the infected. Did they not know or were they not telling them? If it weren't for Liv's field studies, their group would be as clueless as most others likely were.

They never got around to capturing an infected. A flower store in a side alley took care of that for them. Three infected were already trapped inside, but none had yet turned into a brute. The crusties, as she had named them, were like the ones from the camping store Jake had described. They didn't seem to actively look for prey, only wandered around or stood staring into space. The more days that went by, the more spores filled the small shop and the more the infected mutated.

Everything about the infected was still a puzzle she had to solve, but too much information was missing. And though the government was working on a cure, they weren't sharing their findings.

She only knew scientists were hard at work on a vaccine and a cure, the government estimating a two-to-three-month period of the current state before the country would slowly return to normal. Until then, everyone was to go to the nearest protection shelter.

Liv grimaced and picked at her caramel bar. There was no way they'd have a safe vaccine or cure within a year, let alone a month. Even if it would make the perfect Christmas gift. Maybe if it had been a virus they'd seen before, but a fungal parasite completely unknown to them? It was but a lie to induce a false sense of control and security. But there was no security left in the world.

The parasitic fungus had already found a way to get past the human defences and survive. If their body heat and immune system couldn't keep these fungi out, it would be extremely difficult to destroy. Humans and fungi were too similarly built. What harmed the parasite would harm the host as well.

Even if they came up with a vaccine within a reasonable amount of time, things would never go back to normal. How could they? Whatever normal had been was shattered by the substrates attacking and killing people in the streets.

Either way, after that last message, everything had gone silent. There were no more radio or TV announcements. Nothing but the same emergency alert telling the public to make their way to the safe zones. The message had been updated a few times to remove safe zones that were no longer safe.

She sighed. It seemed more safe zones had fallen than were still standing.

They'd done the right thing by staying away. The neighbourhood was eerily quiet as well. The only other survivor they'd seen was Keith. Other than him, neither the looters from the first night nor the people who ran whatever remained of the safe zone had come to their area. And there'd been no sightings of those military planes dropping off rations. The world was quiet. Quiet and dead.

She popped a chunk of protein bar into her mouth. It was the last of the MRE bars, and though the others frowned at it, something about the chemical preserved flavour felt familiar. Comforting even.

Her uncle, a stout man with thick dark-brown hair and a kind face, would sometimes visit from Asansol when she was growing up. Whenever he did, he would sneak her caramel sweets from the airport, despite her mother berating him for it. Anything but homemade sandesh corrupted the minds of the young, her mother would tease him. Nonetheless, Liv had been allowed to eat them. And although the stale caramel was not nearly as nice as the sweet, cardamon treats her mother made, it was one of the few things she remembered about her mother. That and the sweet smell of her shampoo.

Liv let out a soft, barely audible laugh. It wasn't often she thought about her mother, but in the past week it seemed she'd popped into Liv's mind more often. The good moments Liv rarely liked to think about. The ones that caused the sort of sadness that left you with a lot of regrets but no peace. Lately though, Liv thought more about her mother, feeling... at peace? Perhaps Frances's incessant talking sessions were helping.

Liv chewed the bar, mulling over the past six weeks. With Frances's help, they'd weaned her down to one and a half tablets per day. Half her dose. And no alcohol. Not a single drop.

She still itched for the bottles of liquor stashed in the garden shed and found herself outside it on multiple occasions.

One night when everyone was asleep, she tiptoed through the thin paths snaking through the garden beds and the crops Jake planted for an early spring harvest.

She was only going to peek inside the shed. It couldn't hurt to look. It wasn't like she'd actually drink anything, she'd reasoned with herself. Or maybe—on second thought—she could have a small sip. She could handle that. Only to take the edge off.

After a quick sweep, she'd found the bottles at the back of the shed. It had been night and dark, but she could still make out the weird notes stuck to the bottles. She crept closer, like a thief taking cover in the night.

A handful of yellow and pink square notes with black lettering in different handwriting covered the entire body of each bottle. She pulled off the first note.

A mathematical equation. She frowned, adding and subtracting numbers in her head until she found the answer. Putting the note in her pocket, she turned the bottle around, eyeing the other notes. A riddle, a miniature treasure map, arrows followed by an instruction: ask Roy what you can do with fiddleheads.

The next day she'd gone back to the shed, pulled the note off and asked Roy about fiddleheads only to be subjected to a two—if not three—hour long, very passionate lecture about fiddleheads and dandelion hearts. By the time Roy was done, and she'd planted another batch of herbs, she was both so tired and fascinated that she'd completely forgotten about the liquor in the shed. And why she wanted it in the first place.

Liv shook her head. Those lovely fuckers had made her personalized alcohol patches to help fight the urge to have a drink. And over the past month, she'd learned everything from wild foraging and cooking to the best way of getting Jake on his back.

Liv grimaced at the thought. Her body ached. Every muscle and sinew. As if a freight train had hit her. Twice. And yet it beat the shooting pain through her limbs that weaning off the benzoates caused.

She took solace in the fact that the reason for the pain was because she'd finally knocked Jake on his arse earlier that morning.

Granted, it had taken her over a month to finally outwit him in hand-to-hand combat. The man was a slippery fucker. He was fast and strong, with insane reflexes. It was as if he could tell what she'd do before even she knew it.

Jake fought differently. He didn't go in swinging blindly, relying on his strength. Instead, he charged like a guy at a bar fight. Or rather like the winning guy in a bar fight. Fast, light on his feet, with low blows to take his opponent down.

She couldn't count the times she'd had her legs swiped from underneath her since they began their training together. It was a small consolation that the others had been tricked as many times as she had.

She rubbed her shoulder. It was going to bruise. If she were lucky, Fareena would take pity on her and give her neck a well-deserved massage during the evening's entertainment.

With the electricity completely gone, they'd taken to spending the nights reading books aloud. Jake had picked the book he'd showed her in his prepper lair. He was a good narrator, reading with passion and emotion and, she had to admit, he had her sitting at the edge of her seat sometimes.

During their commercial breaks, Fareena would sing all the jingles she could remember, and if they were lucky, she'd take requests while whoever was narrating the chosen book sipped their tea.

One night Fareena had picked a song herself. As she sang, they all sat transfixed by the song and the way her voice was low and rich before it rose into a pitch so delicate it was barely a gentle whisper. The Arabic words rolled off her tongue, exotic and foreign though the raw emotion in her voice needed no translation. When Fareena's voice faded into silence, Liv found she wasn't the only one whose eyes were damp. Fareena wiped at her eyes and smiled when Frances clapped her hands together before giving her a hug. The rest of them followed suit. For all the moments of grief and sadness, there were a handful more filled with laughter and camaraderie.

Liv pulled another crumb from her bar. As life went, however messed up the world was, it was a surprisingly good one.

"Still picking on that thing?" Jake sat down on the flat roof. He'd been peering above the stone ledge, keeping an eye out for their visitors and any signs of trouble—whether that be the living or the substrates. Or withered, whatever one chose to call them. It seemed everyone had different names for the infected.

Keith had left them a note on a green bin asking them to meet by noon in a week's time. He'd dated the note and luckily for him, even without charging their phones on the car batteries, Roy kept track of the days.

"You'll be sorry you missed out when the world runs out of caramel."

Resting his head against the chimney wall, Jake closed his eyes and grinned up at the warming winter sun. At least Keith had picked a good day to be hanging around on rooftops for hours.

"Of all the things I'll miss," he pursed his lips, "*caramel* isn't one of them."

He didn't even bother to say 'if the world ends.' They both knew it already had.

"Let me guess, you'll miss all the anchovies on your pizza."

Laughter spilled from his lips, and he rested his arms on top of his knees. "Amongst other things. But you know what?"

"What?"

"I won't miss having to pay bills."

She tilted her head. "Now this is a much better game."

"Or going to work."

She laughed. If only he knew how awful work could be. "I'll toast to that."

He cracked an eye open, glancing at her.

"With... water." She rolled her eyes.

"You could at least treat yourself to some squash."

"And I suppose you're sitting on a heap of extra squash?"

The corner of his lips twitched. "I bet Roy could whip something up."

Of that, she had no doubt. "I swear he could turn sand into gold."

"Or even better, grass into salad."

A crude reminder that in this new world, food was worth its weight in gold.

Leaves crunched on the street below them. They'd swept up big piles and strewn them around the house. A simple but handy trap. Although lurkers retained enough cognitive awareness to hide and wait, they weren't smart. No intelligent substrates that could open doors or windows, not yet. She mentally knocked on wood.

Jake craned his neck around the chimney.

Is that them? she mouthed when he turned towards her.

He nodded. "Two of them. You think we're good?"

"I don't think I'm the best judge..."

He gave her a sharp look.

"Okay, fine. We can totally take them if we need to."

Silent laughter slipped from his lips.

"Alright," she conceded, "you could. I will try to remember all the wrestling moves I've seen."

"Sounds good to me." He stood up and whistled to the people below, then waved his hand. They must have acknowledged him because he motioned towards the side of the house. "We'll meet you round the back." He hoisted his backpack onto his shoulders and walked towards the ledge. "Let's go."

She pushed herself up, following as he swung his legs across the ledge. The drop to the tall white stone wall wasn't far. From there, they scuttled along the wall until they reached the roof of the back door. They slipped onto it, then dropped the last bit down to the big paving stones.

She landed with a hard thud and grimaced. Her body was still too sore for these sorts of acrobatics. Or maybe she was too old.

"Looks like you've been keeping well." A man with greying hair and pale skin gave Jake a friendly slap on the back. That must be Keith.

"Glad I can say the same about you."

"Yeah, well, that might not be the case much longer. Unless you can help us."

Cutting straight to business. She liked this man.

"We're running low on medical supplies like antibiotics. We also have people who need meds for diabetes and epilepsy."

"And we need anxiolytics," a tall Black woman with a shaved head and perceptive eyes said. With her forest-green fatigues and a maroon bomber jacket, she looked like something the infected should fear, not the other way around.

Anxiolytics? Liv's brows drew together. Those were used to ease anxiety and relax the body. More commonly, they were used for surgery. "Why do you need anxiolytics?"

The woman glanced at Keith. Keith, in his turn, looked at Liv.

"That's used for surgery," she prompted him when he didn't answer. "Do your people need medical attention?"

If he realised she was medically inclined, he didn't say as much, but she thought she could see a gleam in his eyes.

"A precaution. Eve here used to work for the military. She's been coordinating what needs to be done in our home base."

Ah. So Keith was merely a figurehead, a puppet king. Eve was the real leader.

"Why do you need our help?" Jake asked. It was a valid question. Keith and Eve looked more than capable—not to mention qualified—to scavenge for meds themselves.

Hell, even Liv and Frances had done so on their own. And although Frances was not to be shamed for her age, neither she nor Liv looked like they were plucked straight from a military squad.

That last item on their list, however, wasn't a drug commonly stored in pharmacies. Hospitals, on the other hand, would have it in large quantities. *Huh.* She nodded as the penny dropped.

"They want to go to a hospital."

Jake's mouth fell open. "Hinchingbrooke? That's a death trap. We can't risk that." He slashed his hand through the air.

Liv wasn't what one might call well versed in nerd culture, but even she knew that hospitals in a zombie apocalypse were a poor bet.

"Under normal circumstances, I'd agree with that assessment," Eve said in a posh, stern voice one would expect from military people.

Normal circumstances. Liv let out a noisy breath. Under normal circumstances, none of them would even be there. Let alone avoid hospitals because of the walking fucking *dead.*

Eve fixed her with a hard stare, her jaw rigid, before turning back to Jake, clearly deeming Liv unworthy of her attention. "I was part of the military setting up the safe zone. Before we got overrun, we had planned a mission to the hospital to stock up for supplies. I was the Major in charge. I know the layout and where they keep the medicines."

Liv tried to keep the scowl from her face. What was it about people thinking hospitals left all kinds of drugs lying around?

"That's great, but you realise without an actual—"

Eve pulled a chain from the neck of her jacket, the key chain clinking as she shook it demonstratively.

"Key..." Liv finished her sentence, if only to be obstinate.

"That still doesn't explain why you need us," Jake said.

"Most of our group are families and children. We have some that could go, but I'd rather leave them to keep the others safe. You and your friends seemed... able." Keith dragged a hand through his hair. "Without these meds, my people won't last long. I'd rather not subject them to the raiders."

Jake lifted a hand, scratching the side of his beard. "What do you think?" he asked her.

Eve made it sound easy. Too easy. But if Keith's group depended on those medicines, could they really say no? What kind of people were they if they refused to help people whose lives depended on it?

She bit the inside of her lip. Even if they didn't want to risk it for a bunch of strangers, they needed to stock up on medicines as well.

Noah had gotten caught in rusty barbwire, cutting a deep gash along his shoulder. It was red and swollen with infection. Nothing a little antibiotic and careful looking after couldn't handle, but it meant using a sizeable chunk of their medicine stash.

On top of that, she needed more benzos for her treatment, and Jake needed to stock up on his hormones and syringes.

With Eve's knowledge of the place and keys, it was an opportunity they could hardly refuse. Dangerous or not, it was a risk they'd have to take.

She gave him a nod.

"Okay," he said, "but I need to run it by our group."

"That's fair," Keith agreed, "how much time do you need?"

Jake remained silent for a moment, his gaze wandering as he contemplated his answer. "A week. We need time to prepare."

Keith's eyes wrinkled in a smile. "A cautious guy, I can appreciate that."

Jake ignored him, instead looking over at Eve. "You said you were military."

She nodded once. A curt nod, barely a dip of her chin. Everything from her posture to the air around her was so proper.

"So you know what was happening." It wasn't a question, and judging by the lack of protest, Eve knew as much. "You must know Catterick then."

Eve's brow twitched, but she quickly rearranged her face. Finally, something that seemed to surprise the stoic soldier. "I do. What of it?"

"My father, he was on his way to Catterick. Do you know if..." Jake didn't finish the question.

"The last thing I heard Catterick had been destroyed. I'm sorry."

Jake looked away from her, the muscles in his jaw working. "And the rest of Europe?"

"You've heard the transmissions."

"I've only heard what they want us to hear. We have no electricity." Jake returned his eyes to Eve's, challenging and determined. "I think you know why just as well as I do. And I don't think you'd be risking a hospital raid if you didn't know something. You'd be holed up, waiting for rescue."

Liv tried—and failed—not to smile. Jake was sweet and kind, but he was also intelligent which at times made him enticingly dominant. *Down, girl.*

Eve opened her mouth and inhaled before speaking. "The last transmission I heard, it looked bad."

"How bad?" Jake asked.

"It's all over Europe, Asia, and North America. We weren't quick enough to stop it."

Asia and North America. It wasn't a surprise that they'd been lied to, and yet Liv felt a pang of anger in her chest. They'd believed that the virus was contained in the UK—or at least they'd hoped it was. That way their suffering meant the rest of the world would be safe. And for Angela and Roy, it meant their daughter would be safe. But not anymore.

"Thank you," Jake said. "Give a us week to prepare. Then we'll meet you on the car park of the hospital."

"Alright, you stay safe until then." Keith patted Jake's back.

"You too." With that, Jake put his hand on Liv's shoulder and motioned for her to leave.

They made their way around the corner of the house and took a sharp left into another back alley. From there they'd enter the abandoned pub and wait until Keith and Eve had left before making their way home. Allies were great, but until they knew exactly how good of an ally they were, it was smart to be cautious.

They sat on the leather barstools in front of a mint-green bar. The bottles at the back had been smashed along with most of the glasses, and black signs with white handwriting hung askew on the wall.

"Oh, shit, I'm sorry."

She looked to Jake, who observed her. "Why?"

"This probably wasn't the best place to take you." He looked sheepishly at the bar, his broad shoulders slouching forwards. She imagined him sitting in the same place a month before, probably laughing with his friends, wearing that nice tight grey Henley.

"So, distract me then."

"Uh... how?"

"Did you used to come here?"

"Not really." He shrugged and looked around the room furnished with a mix of tables and chairs and the odd leather armchair before he grinned back at her. "Too clean for me. I need something way more dingy to enjoy myself."

She laughed. "I did see a Cromwells bar the other week."

"Yes, that. Dirty, bad food, and cheap drinks."

She shoved him. "Liar. Did you come here with Megan?"

"Sometimes. Before I transitioned and we still enjoyed each other's company."

She remembered that day in Jake's creeper lair. When he said they'd stopped recognising each other. "Did she really not accept it?"

He shook his head. "I thought maybe if I gave her time she'd come around. But then she fell in love with someone else." He let out a scoff.

"Fareena told me. That was a bitch move." Jake dropped his chin towards his chest with a chuckle. She grabbed the underside of his seat, pulling her stool and herself closer. "Fuck her. And not in a good way."

This time, Jake's lips parted in a wide smile when he lifted his eyes to hers. "Trust me, that's not going to happen."

"Good, because you deserve someone who adores you for you. Not who you were, who you could be, but for who you are right now."

"Thank you." He sounded surprised.

Her knees brushed the insides of his thighs and suddenly she became painfully aware of the position of her hands. Between his legs, fingers curled around the edge of his seat. Jake, however, didn't seem to notice—or maybe he hid it better. Her cheeks warmed, and as her gaze slid past the discreet bulge and up to the top button of his jeans, she felt a hot flash wash over her body.

She was either hitting menopause two decades too early, or she hadn't had enough alone time to get Jake out of her system.

"Yes, well"—she released the chair—"you're welcome. I read it in a fortune cookie."

He laughed. "Well, thank you for sharing it with me."

"Anytime." She punched his arm and hopped off the stool. "We should probably get back home."

"Yeah." His smile faded, and he sighed. "We have to tell the others."

"Yeah." Her own smile disappeared. The quarantine had failed, the government, the military had failed. The Red Death would spread to the rest of the world.

72

LIV

THEIR MOOD HAD BEEN as sullen as the weather for the past two days. The others had taken the news Liv and Jake brought back as well as one might expect. Angela had cried, and Roy had wrapped his arms around her while he shed tears of his own.

They'd all taken their time to grieve, as much as one could when infected roamed the streets. Two days, and then Roy had done what he did best: found the silver lining and told Angela that they'd better survive this thing so they could get back to Ash. Because she, just like them, would not die. They'd raised her strong and smart.

It seemed it was the pep talk Angela needed. Now she walked a few steps behind Roy as they scoured the nature around them for anything edible.

Wet leaves squelched under Liv's shoes as they picked their way through the dense forest of birch, fir, and large oak trees. A bird squawked behind them, the sound echoing through the woods, their footsteps soft against moss and leaves. Light drizzle landed with barely audible pops on leaves and pine needles. It was deceptively relaxing.

Her red wellies sunk into the rain-dampened mulch and soil, but at least they kept her feet dry. Unlike a mud-covered Karma who walked beside her, nose fervently sniffing the mossy ground.

Every now and then Karma would break her concentration and frown up at Liv, then at the others, her wrinkled face stubborn yet contemplative. When she couldn't sense any danger, she returned to her sniffing as though ignoring them all. Liv doubted that was really the case.

Jake had insisted they bring Karma along. He and the others were going to investigate the Essential Supermarket. When she'd pointed out most supermarkets would be picked clean, he'd explained this wasn't the typical grocery store for a place like Huntingdon. This particular one took a more oriental approach: Indian, African, and Asian food with some Polish sausages thrown in for good measure.

When Jake finished his argument with the fact that Roy could teach Karma how to scent the mushrooms, they'd all agreed to bring her.

Liv remembered Karma outside Jake's house. The way the massive dog had leapt without hesitation to protect her owner from the infected. Good at scenting or not, Liv knew that mushroom hunting was not the real reason Jake wanted Karma to go with them. Besides, Karma already had an unrivalled knack for sensing and alerting them of infected.

It should annoy her that Jake thought they needed more protection than he and the others. It did irk her, but not as much as it should. It was nice that someone cared about their safety.

She groaned under her breath. *You're acting like a damn schoolgirl.* She kicked at the leaves on the ground. November was drawing to an end—as evidenced by the endless raining—and temperatures would drop lower, making foraging more difficult.

Jake and Roy had built cold boxes to sow kale and cabbage for late winter and early spring harvest. Other boxes had been prepared with next year's vegetables, but those wouldn't be ready for harvest until late spring. They needed food long before then.

She peered into her bag filled with bullace fruit and chestnuts. It didn't seem like much, but when your nutrition consisted of snack-sized meals, anything to fill it out was better than nothing. Even if it was just a spoon of bullace jam or chestnut pie.

A twig broke, and she whipped her head to the side. Roy lifted and dropped his shoulders guiltily.

"That man," Angela said in a low voice once they were sure no infected had heard them. "He's going to be the death of me."

"Good way or bad way?" Liv stepped over a log and was rewarded by a dry chortle.

"In the best kind of way, but I ain't letting him know that."

Liv smiled. The two were so different and yet perfect for each other. Angela was intellectual and logical. Someone who'd twist and turn the problem until she had a solution, or at least an understanding of the problem. Liv had been like that once. She understood the need to comprehend things, to find logic within the chaos.

Everything had a reasonable explanation. Everything could be fixed or solved. With enough knowledge, there was very little one couldn't accomplish. Perhaps that's why she'd chosen to train as a surgeon. It demanded knowledge, skill, and precision. It demanded excellence, nothing less.

Roy moved beside them with careful steps, his brows furled at the ground. He was the dreamer, no doubt. That wasn't to say he wasn't an intellectual, but he had that dreamer quality that'd allowed him to start his own restaurant. When Angela launched into a new discussion theorising about the infection,

Roy got to his feet to work on new meals for them. While Angela steam wheeled into a theory, Roy seemed to slow her down just enough to stay on track.

Liv could have deduced this without observing them for hours. But observing other people from her corner was what she liked best. It was like getting to know people without them ever seeing her. She'd imagined what they were like, what their life was like, but it always turned out different.

Roy let out a triumphant hiss and knelt on the wet leaves in front of a thick trunk. White, round caps grew in clusters from the cracks of the dark-brown tree bark. He reached for the knife in his bag and carefully sliced their stems, dropping them into his paper bag.

Liv bit into her grimace. The clusters of fungi reminded her a little too much of the infected.

"Never been so nervous about eating fungi before," Frances said in a low voice, voicing Liv's thought.

"Roy's a professional though; he wouldn't feed us zombie mushrooms." Liv watched Angela walk up next to him. "Right?"

"Not intentionally."

Liv turned to Frances only to see the older woman's eyes crinkle with amusement. "Not. Funny."

"Your expression was quite entertaining."

"To think the best entertainment available to you is my face... it is truly the downfall of society."

It drew a low chuckle from Frances. "How is today?"

A few weeks back her regular response would've been, it's a mind your own business kind of day. But not anymore. She was a changed person, a better person.

She let out an audible scoff. If only it was that easy. Weaning off her medicines and quitting drinking might help her body, but it did nothing for her mind. Did nothing to quiet the incessant voices in her head, the ones that whispered reminders of everything she wanted to forget. Of what she'd done. Of what she truly was.

She inhaled slowly. "It's better than yesterday."

"Better than yesterday is good." Frances gave her arm a light squeeze. "Remember, one day at a time."

Liv sighed and watched the forest around them. "I feel like I'm failing. What if I never get better?"

"Oh, Chicken." Frances pulled her into a hug. "You are doing so well. Everyone has bad days every now and then, but what are you going to do when it happens?"

Inhaling slowly, Liv leaned into the warm hug. She wasn't a hug person; she didn't like hugs. Or maybe she resented the way they made her feel needy and vulnerable.

"Well?" Frances prompted her again.

"Ask for help."

"And you know everyone is here for you."

She could try to deny it, but even Noah had put small notes on the bottles in the shed and forced her to create makeshift armour from scrap metal and old tyres. "I don't need everyone when I have you."

Frances chuckled and squeezed her harder. "Well, you certainly know how to brighten an old lady's day."

"You're only fifty-what? Five?" Liv scowled.

"Seven, but who's counting?"

Liv blew air through her closed lips. "We're in the apocalypse. You can pick any age you want. Reinvent yourself."

"Oh, well, then maybe I'll be twenty-five from now on. And Scottish," Frances said in barely passable Scottish.

"Um... Twenty-five totally believable, but maybe pass on the Scottish."

"To be twenty-five again," Frances said, resuming their walk. Karma had stopped, observing them with her sad amber eyes, but now she let her nose guide her back and forth and across the ground. That dog was really interested in whatever it was she smelled.

"Do anything differently?" Liv said.

"What wouldn't I do differently?" Amusement filtered into Frances's voice though the sigh that followed was heavy. "I think I would've liked to be braver."

Liv frowned. "You are brave."

"Because I have to. If I want to get back to Kerry. Maybe if I'd been braver sooner, perhaps I wouldn't be in this situation." Frances smiled sadly, her eyes suddenly downturned and faraway. "But I suppose there really is no use boiling your cabbage twice, eh?"

Kerry. The one person Frances kept trying to get back to. Who was she? Sister? Or maybe a daughter she hadn't mentioned. "Were you able to get a hold of her?"

Frances shook her head. "No. I never did. I just hope she's..."

Frances didn't have to finish the sentence. Everyone was hoping their loved ones were okay. There were times when Angela didn't think anyone could see her. When she'd rub the golden cross that hung from the chain around her neck, her eyes locked on the horizon, her lips moving in silent prayer. A mother praying for her child, inaudible words spoken softly, as if the wind might carry the words across the Atlantic.

"I'm sorry," she said, guilt rising in her chest. At least she knew what had happened to Ellis. She even knew David was most likely still alive. And she didn't even like the man much. But the people she was with—her friends—were all living with that uncertainty, torn between hope and despair. "Who was she?"

Frances sighed, lost in a memory for a moment. "Someone I let down. Someone I should have been brave for."

"She sounds like she was special to you."

"She was. I loved her very much." Frances let out a soft scoff. "Love, I suppose."

She put her hand on Frances's arm. "I'm sure she knows you're trying to get to her."

"Oh, I don't know. I left her a long time ago. There's only so long you can leave someone waiting for you. Eventually, they move on."

They both fell into silence, Liv uncertain of what to say. Should she ask what had happened between the two or leave it alone? The decision was made for her when a deep growl rumbled from her right. The big dog stood facing an opening in the trees, head lowered, shoulders stiff and hackles raised.

They stopped and listened for sounds of the infected. But there was nothing.

"What's wrong, girlie?" Roy moved towards them on quiet feet.

Karma whined in response, not moving from her spot. Last time Liv had seen Karma act similarly, it had been on the boat just before they discovered their first lurker.

Liv swept her gaze across the trees and mulchy ground. Thick branches of fir and oak covered most of the view, a faint midday sun breaking through the foliage and mist. Nothing seemed out of place. There were no strange noises, no shrill shrieking or trilling sounds. Just the regular chirping of birds and trickling of water from the nearby stream. At least where they stood. Liv followed the direction in which Karma stared.

That section of the forest looked darker, as if less sunlight filtered through the canopy of fir and trees. She frowned, focusing on the trunks farther in. They looked deformed and strange, odd lumps protruding in various places. She stepped closer, and Karma's whine turned into an agitated growl.

"Liv," Frances hissed, but Liv ignored her and pulled the Noah-made metal shiv and machete from her belt. The others carried pipes and axes, but the shiv and machete were light and small. Easy to handle, though deadly sharp. "At least put your mask on."

She slid the gas mask over her face. The others followed suit. Only stupid people went unmasked when there might be infected or spores nearby. She walked closer to the trees and made a mental huff. Only stupid people walked towards the possible threat. This could no doubt turn out to be a terrible idea, but so far, her chances to study the infected had been almost non-existent. Studying infected locked up in a store was like studying wolves in captivity, only to make an awfully inaccurate assessment.

Karma's muscled body brushed against her as they drew closer to the trees. Thick roots pushed through the moss and grass. Knotted and gnarled, they twisted up and around the tree trunks like thick snakes. Along the length of the roots, bright red and purple, thin stalks waved in the cold breeze, almost weightless. Spores floated in the few sunrays that punched through the canopy of fir. Familiar red tendrils webbed out from the centre of the trees. Liv squinted through the visor. The roots and tendrils weren't growing from the ground, but from something at the bottom of the trunks.

She stepped closer to what looked like a stump split in half. Tendrils and roots grew from within, curling their way past disks of fungi and... She halted at the sight of dirty red Converse sticking out from under the mass of growth.

Her heart rate picked up as she observed it further. Long, white branches poked through the mass of moss and roots, curled like fingers. Liv swallowed the nausea that rose in her throat. Not branches. She stepped backwards, away from the trees. The white branches were a rib cage torn open, the rest of the body unrecognisable underneath the fungi's growth.

"What is it?" Roy asked.

"I'm not sure, but you see those?" She pointed at the shoes with her machete.

"Jesus." He aimed his torch at the pile. "Are those roots growing from the ground?"

Liv shook her head. "They're growing into the ground."

73

JAKE

I SHOULD'VE KNOWN FINDING the Essential Supermarket plundered but not completely empty was too good to be true. Someone had either been and left or—judging by the three substrates we disposed of—been and got stuck.

We returned with four twenty-kilo bags of rice. All the fresh food and vegetables were bad, the rotten stench of oozing plantains and black, mouldy meat permeating the air in the small store. But there were plenty of cans and dry food to last us until summer.

We brought back three carts filled to the brim with rice, canned black beans and ham, jars of pickled okra, ginger, and enoki. And whereas Noah stuffed his bag full of chocolate protein bars, I stuffed mine with noodles and Panda biscuits. I think Fareena cried at the sight of an entire section of hair products for African hair.

The thought of being well fed for our trip to the hospital tomorrow had given me confidence that we could do it. That we could survive until all of this was over, until the government and the military could get the world back on its feet.

I watch Fareena drag her thumb across the teeth of a comb as we sit in the living room. She looks as ashen as I feel. I swallow thickly, my fist pressed against my lips as if it might force down the nausea welling inside.

Noah presses his forehead against his palm, his wavy hair sticking through his fingers while he stares slack-jawed.

Liv just finished telling us about the corpse they found in the forest, nestled between the thick tree trunks. Instead of decomposing, fungi took root and sprang from inside the husk, latching on to the trees and growth around it, its roots burying into the ground.

I've watched enough *Star Trek* to know what a mycelium network is. If the fungi have spread to the environment, if it's growing in the forest and not just on humans, it's going to be everywhere. Fungi already are everywhere. It grows in large networks deep in the soil beneath our feet. One measly branch in the network can have trillions of end branchings and each of those another trillion of branchings.

If the virus—the parasite—works the same, it too will be everywhere. I think back to Eve's words: It's all over Europe, Asia, and North America. We weren't quick enough to stop it. If we want to get rid of this parasite killing us, we'll have to scorch the earth.

74
JAKE

THE WORLD WILL NEVER go back to what it once was. We already knew that, but I guess hope really is the last thing to abandon humanity. Yesterday was a harsh reality check. Everything we've left behind, everything we've lost, it's never coming back.

The fungi will keep growing and spread through the mycelium. The substrates aren't going anywhere. If we want to survive, we have to learn and adapt. We have to fight. If we don't, this is how humanity ends. The thought is a heavy one, a scary one, but I clench my jaw as I push my feet down on the pedal.

We're on our way to Hinchingbrooke. Now that most of the town is deserted, save the infected and the other survivors, the big Ring Road is empty of traffic. Abandoned cars, and cars with their dead drivers, dot the streets. We zigzag between them as carefully and quickly as we can.

The wind brushes through the leaves as we roll closer to the bridge where we left the cars we borrowed. They're still there, doors ajar and windows broken. It seems like a lifetime since we faced the wave of substrates pouring down these streets.

They're gone now. The street—just like much of the town—is empty and abandoned. At least for now. But the infected are still around on the streets, in back gardens, and in the stores around town. We've seen them banging on the windows as we've rushed past, mouths opening and closing at our shadows. We stay well away, the memory of St. Thomas Hospital still fresh in our minds.

This is the third, and hopefully last, time we have to do this journey. Angela, not one to blindly trust the word of a man she's never met, has scoped out the route and hospital with me and Roy. We have two different escape routes and marked at least four different entry points. I think it's the police officer in her that likes to feel she has the situation under control.

Hinchingbrooke Hospital is the biggest and only hospital in Huntingdon and consists of multiple two-storey buildings that house over hundreds of patients. It's big, and it's likely filled with infected.

Keith gave us a week to decide and then meet by the car park next to the hospital. I watch the others ride in front of me: Angela, Roy, Frances, and Liv.

The latter two were the obvious choices, as they were a nurse and some sort of doctor type person. Liv still hasn't told us what she used to do before all of this. Considering her knowledge of gun wounds and other medical emergencies, I'm pretty sure she's a doctor.

Fareena stayed home with Karma to watch the house and Noah. *Someone's got to make sure these two don't burn down the house,* she'd joked. Noah had cracked a half smile. Or grimaced. Sometimes it's hard to tell with him.

We travel at night even though it makes it more difficult to spot lurkers, and—as Liv calls them—crusties and snitches, the ones calling the other infected. She has created her own classification system to differentiate all the infected we've seen.

Travelling in the dark is a two-way street. We can't see them, and if we don't use our torches, they don't spot us either. Neither do the raiders. And we like it that way. In a world where safety is a somewhat loose concept, this seems to be the closest thing to it.

We continue along the Ring Road, passing empty or dark houses, nothing but the creaking of our tyres disrupting the otherwise quiet night. Huntingdon is eerily quiet, none of the regular traffic lights lighting up the dark.

I've driven down this street so many times or sat in the car with Mum as she gave me a lift to the train station. My chest pains as we pull up to George Street and turn left.

Don't forget the series finale to Beullaek *next weekend. Don't make me wait to watch it.* Mum and her Korean dramas. Some more important than others, this one in particular. We'd watched every single episode together. When Dad wasn't home. And every time she dropped me off, she'd remind me that she didn't like having to wait for me to get my sorry arse back home until she could watch it.

I swallow against the dryness in my throat. I'd made her wait for the series finale. We were going to watch it that weekend, but I decided it was more important to get an extra shift in. If I hadn't, I would've been there. I could've protected them. Maybe they would still be alive.

I push the thoughts from my mind when we reach a couple of trees by Hinchingbrooke's car park. I gently press the brakes on my bike, rolling to a slow stop alongside Angela.

"Now listen." She looks us dead in the eye. "I know I've already said this, but we don't know what to expect in there. We have to stay safe and *be smart.*"

I nod, the others doing the same, not daring to speak so close to the hospital.

"Remember, we are helping them, but if it gets too hot in there, we leave. Everyone clear on that?"

We nod again.

"Good. Then we do this." She waits, perhaps to see if anyone protests, but when no one does, she straddles her bike.

We follow, and unease tightens my stomach. I always hated the dark. Being at a hospital, and an abandoned one at that, is probably one of my worst nightmares come true. But I have no choice. Yet, as the two stories tower over me, I feel myself shrink. I don't want to be here.

The car park and tall glassed entrance look empty, but we've seen infected circle the hospital. Some wearing gowns, others in military gear or regular clothes.

Movement to our side pulls my attention from the substrates that shamble outside the hospital. A white circle dashes across the hospital facade. I follow the beam with my eyes towards a set of large oaks. A dark figure stands next to it—Keith.

I let out a breath of relief, pushing my inner wimp down as we roll to him and Eve.

She stands slightly behind him, looking as stone-faced and ominous as she did the other day.

"I almost didn't think you'd be here." Keith sounds as relieved as I feel.

"Boss said we should help." I nod in Angela's direction, who smacks her lips and rolls her eyes. She doesn't consider herself our leader, but I don't think any of us *don't* see her as that. A brief flash of curiosity touches Eve's face.

"I am no one's boss," Angela states, "but I will tell you right now, if I don't like what I hear, I will take my group and leave."

I bite down on a grin and see Liv scratch her top lip, hiding a smile.

"Fair enough," Keith agrees and motions towards Eve. She steps forwards, her face set, two pistols resting on her hips.

"We're going around the east side and up the fire escape ladder to the roof. There's an emergency exit there that leads into a staircase. Now listen carefully. *Do not* go to the west wing," Eve instructs us.

"What's in the west wing?" Angela voices the question no doubt burning in everyone's minds.

Far too many seconds whisper by in the dark night. Distant moans and groans remind us about the stakes.

"Ground zero," she finally says.

"I'm sorry," Liv breathes out a chuckle, "I thought you said Ground zero."

"I did. But"—Eve holds a hand in the air, palm down—"we've barred them inside. There's no way they can get through. Unless someone intentionally opens a door."

"How exactly have you"—Angela makes air quotes with her fingers—"*barred* them inside?"

Keith gives Eve a sidelong look. He knows if the answer is that they "closed a couple of doors," Angela will march us out of here in no time.

"Hinchingbrooke was the first place to get hit here. My platoon was flown in to help contain the situation. We... cleared out most of the infection in the basement section, but parts of it were unreachable."

Whenever someone with military or government connection uses terms like "contain" and "cleared out," they always mean wiped it out. As in, shot it to pieces. But if they couldn't even reach some parts of the basement when they first arrived, it must have been bad. "How bad was it?" I ask.

"Half my platoon didn't make it." Her expression remains the same, indifferent, but the muscles in her jaw work. She straightens a little. "We resorted to welding all the doors shut on the lower level. It gave us enough time to block all entry points to the west wing with anything heavy we could find. I doubt even a group of strong humans could push through it now."

"Eve has monitored the place. No infected have come out. They're contained inside," Keith offers when Angela's frown deepens. "There might be stragglers, but with the seven of us, we have enough to grab supplies and keep watch."

"Stragglers?" Liv asks.

"The slow ones."

"Oh." She glances at the slow shambling infected in front of the hospital. Her forehead wrinkles in thought, and I make a mental note to ask about it later.

"I know the exact route." Eve lifts her chin, bringing our attention back to the plan. "If we go in quick and quiet, it should be an easy in and out."

"What about these?" Angela motions with her hand towards the lot littered with infected.

"Warm up," Keith tries to joke, though his smile falters when Angela crosses her arms.

"Ma'am, we need those medicines, and I suspect since you're here, so do you. If we work together, we can dispose of them."

Angela leans backwards and looks at us with a raised eyebrow. It's that look she wears when she both agrees and disagrees with something.

We still have enough for Noah's infection, but he'll need more soon. We could go later, but the problem would remain the same. The infected aren't leaving anytime soon. It's better to do this now with the help of others than wait for more infected to turn up. Or, even worse, for them to turn into brutes.

"We got this." Roy tightens the straps on his rucksack and zips his leather jacket closed. Frances nods, slipping Noah's homemade spiked iron bar into her hand. *Okay,* I agree with a dip of my head. Their determination makes me think we can do this.

I pull my cricket bat from where it's hooked on top of my handlebars. Long rusty nails pierce the top. I strapped my fire axe to the back of my bag. Hopefully, I won't have to use it.

"You have any of those to spare?" Angela points at one of the pistols strapped to Eve's hips. Eve hesitates, but Angela holds her gaze, her top lip curled.

"You know how to use one of these?" She pulls a black gun from behind her back and holds it up.

Roy laughs, a low amused laughter. "Not only are we American, but *she* is a police officer." He dons his leather gloves and hooks a hammer to his belt. "And a damn good one."

"Huh." For the first time since we met, I see a smile pull at Eve's lips as she hands over the gun. "You should be familiar with this one then."

Angela takes it and turns it in her hand as she inspects it. Then, with a smile, she drops her hand to the side. "Feels like home."

"So, are we good to go?" Is Keith fidgeting? He seems a lot less relaxed than the other times we've met him. And one of those times was facing down a bulger.

Angela motions for him and Eve to lead and we fall in line behind them, walking on quiet feet along the tree line that hides us from view. We won't be able to avoid the infected forever, but better to take on fewer of them than all of them.

We put on our masks. It's easier to kill them when you don't have to worry about inhaling their spores.

We're only halfway along the tree line before the first infected stumbles into our path. Eve steps forward, lets it grab her, then jabs her knife through its eye. It drops to the grass with a thud.

The sounds draw more infected, and we raise our arms, readying ourselves. A large man hisses and snarls, eight more infected turning around to follow him. They move slower than the ones we've seen so far. Cracks and crevices split some of their heads. Yellow and pink fungi protrude from the cracks. Tendrils sprout from their eye sockets—if they still have eye sockets.

A substrate in jeans and what used to be a white shirt staggers towards us, its face completely overgrown by what looks like green moss lichen, with the ever-present red tendrils crawling through it. Blood and dark-brown slime drips from its mouth. I touch my mask to make sure it's in place, then I look at Angela. She nods, and we sprint towards the group of infected.

I swing my bat, the nails slicing through the cheek of Jeans Man, then I twist it. The skull cracks open, brittle from whatever grows inside, and he drops to the ground.

Liv moves like a dancer, darting from one infected to the other in smooth, quick movements. They spin in frustration, but she ducks, rises, and wedges her blade up and through the back of their necks.

Head shots or head kills aren't necessary. But they're quicker.

Frances clubs a woman in military gear, the sharp, rusty spikes tearing through her neck. The skin ribbons and curls, dark blood pulsing from the open wound as the woman drops to the ground.

The sounds of more infected reach us, but our route to the ladder is clear, and we dash for it.

Liv pulls up, shadows hiding most of her face. A slice of moonlight cuts through the treetops, illuminating one of her brows lowered in thought.

"You good?" I ask as we duck and cross the grassy area next to the parking lot.

She nods quietly, seeming subdued. When faced with life-threatening situations, Liv usually responds with snark or outright defiance. But this mood is unlike her. Maybe she's scared we'll fail, despite taking down a dozen infected just now.

I touch her arm as Eve starts the climb up the fire escape ladder. Liv turns to me, gaze darting back and forth.

"We'll be fine," I say.

She smiles, but her eyes are haunted.

"Hey, I didn't tell you earlier, but Noah's holding on to another caramel bar for you. As an incentive to come back."

This time, her smile is brighter, and she shakes her head. "There is no way Noah still has a caramel bar. He's been sleeping with you for the past two nights."

Frances climbs the ladder, and Liv grabs the sides of it to pull herself up.

"Um... *next* to me," I correct her with a hiss and when she's climbed the ladder far enough, I pull myself onto it and follow.

When someone says they have a foolproof plan, I always think it's something that will go tits up. I'm surprised that we've made it to the hospital roof, through one of the emergency exits, and into the abandoned east wing of the hospital. The air is stale and smells of mould and old wet socks.

Eve has taken point walking in front with Keith, both holding their guns at eye level. I don't know that shooting anything should be someone's first response when seeing an infected, not since sounds seem to attract them. Sounds and the smell of blood.

Our group walks a few footsteps behind them. The once lit-up corridors have been thrown into complete darkness, our torches fireflies dancing up and down the walls. Angela looks every bit the police officer, her gun raised, torch resting on top of it as she sweeps the beam from side to side.

I grip my bat harder and scan the corridor. The narrow hallway is littered with unused gurneys, capsized waiting room chairs, dead potted plants, and a janitor trolley.

Dark stains and smears cover the floor and wall farther down. Large windows on our right reveal a laboratory. It's empty save for the lab equipment, papers, and books that lie discarded across the desks and floor. Looks like whoever was working left in a hurry.

Ahead, the corridor splits in two. Eve stops and motions with her hand for us to stop.

A gurgling warble followed by hissing coughs punches through the dead silence. I push down the fear that causes my neck hair to stand.

Eve moves on light feet, drawing closer to where the corridor branches. She disappears around the corner, and I check on the others.

It's a habit we've taken up lately, always knowing where everyone is. Like the buddy system in school. Only we don't hold hands.

Angela wears one of Mum's old hiking jackets. Green and black, it helps her melt into the darkness. She's peering inside the lab, mumbling in a low voice to Roy, probably planning our escape route should we need one.

Liv stands to the side, a machete in one hand, a torch in the other. It casts a soft light on her face. Her usually messy hair has been pulled into a ponytail, and wisps of hair spring from it. She blows the few annoying hairs from her face and rubs her forehead with the back of her hand.

She wears a brown leather jacket zipped tight, one of Mum's chequered shirts sticking out from underneath it. Her dark blue jeans hug her curves nicely.

I look away the instant the thought enters my mind. If there's one thing testosterone does, it's kick one's libido into gear at the most inappropriate times.

Frances bumps me gently with her shoulder just as Eve returns, saving me from an embarrassing moment.

Eve dips her chin in a nod, then points with her rifle to the corridor on the other side. Keith jerks his head in a *let's go* motion.

I exchange looks with the others. The moaning and groaning haven't stopped. It sounds close, but Eve doesn't look like she's got a bunch of infected at her back. "I guess we're good, since she isn't hightailing it out of here."

Liv snickers and we follow, though I glance into the left corridor, where I make out the vague shape of a wall made from cabinets. I can't see it well, but since light attracts some varieties of infected—though which ones we're unsure—I'm definitely not shining my torch there to find out.

Moans and scratchy noises drift from behind the cabinets. So long as we don't make too much noise, reek of blood, or shine our torches at them, they should remain where they are.

Eve leads us into a corridor filled with medicine cabinets and furniture stacked along the walls. Only a very narrow path leads to a blockade farther down, where lockers have been pushed into the corridor, blocking anyone or anything trying to get through. A small gap at the top of the lockers allows for passage.

We creep through the gauntlet of furniture, careful not to knock anything with our bags.

Eve stops at the lockers and grabs a chair. She moves so slowly that she almost looks frozen in time, but she places the chair in front of the lockers and opens the door. Unhooking her bag, she steps onto the chair and pushes the bag through the small opening. She grabs the top of the locker with both hands and uses the shelf inside for a step, heaving herself on top. Once up, she slides into the gap.

I'm wondering how she's going to get out on the other side without falling flat on her face when she spins on her stomach until she faces us, bag in hand. Her face is set, her eyes glued behind us, most likely at the other corridor and the infected lurking behind the wall. Her jaw clenches, then she pushes herself backwards before she disappears from view and lands with a soft thud on the other side.

I let out my breath. I hadn't realised I'd been holding it with the same intensity as someone watching a football game.

Climbing over lockers isn't difficult, but a single slipup could be the difference between life and death.

Keith is next, squeezing through the gap slowly. It's not too tight, but I glance Roy's way. He's a hulking mass of muscle, and his pillowy man bosom is going to have to *really* squeeze through.

Minutes tick by in agonising suspense as each of us makes our way through the top of the barricade. When Roy finally lands behind me, fifteen minutes have passed.

This part of the corridor is pitch-black like the other one. I run my beam across sterile white walls. Frames with colourful art punctuate the boring walls.

Chairs, tables, and medicine carts lie on their sides, with all sorts of medical supplies scattered around them.

At the top of the wall farther down, red and brown tendrils catch my attention. I 'psst' in warning, then illuminate them and raise my mask.

Tendrils mean spores, and spores mean dead or long-term infected like the brute and its smaller minions. The fresh ones, the runners and lurkers, don't emit spores into the air around them. Only if you crack their heads open, like one of those puff balls.

We sneak down the corridor. Yellow and red spores float in the stale air all around us. It grows thicker, like a mist, the farther we get.

When we looted the fire station a few weeks back, I thought the gas masks we took might be overkill. Now I'm glad we have them, along with the boxes of clean filters.

Windows open to a room next to us, though the thickening fog of spores makes it difficult to see. Something moves inside on the other side of the glass.

We drop to our knees on instinct. We might not be able to see them, but they might sense us. There's still so much we don't know about the virus or the infected. Studying them for a few weeks has taught us some, but not nearly enough.

Something shuffles in the room—or some*things*. A sign extends from the wall by the door. Mess Hall, it reads. Shit. A fucking lunchroom? How many people were in there when shit hit the fan? I push myself up and peek across the ledge of the window. How many are still in there?

I bet none of them thought they'd be on the menu when they went for their lunch.

I squint into the room, faintly lit by our torches, and I can just make out dark shapes moving inside. I can't see how many or what kind of infected. I pray none of them is a brute.

"How many?" Roy whispers.

"Not sure." I check the door. At least it's locked, if we're lucky.

Eve leans from the wall and looks at me.

I hold up five fingers but lift my shoulders and tilt my head in the universal "not quite sure" gesture.

She looks thoughtful. After a few seconds, she gives a determined nod and points at a door a little farther down on the opposite side.

Okay, I mouth, and she ducks towards the other door. The others are quick to follow, moving quietly.

Glancing one last time at the lunchroom, I catch up with the others. I'll be happy once we're out of here.

Windows allow us a view inside the stockroom, but the spore-filled darkness makes it difficult to see. There's something inside. Or maybe my mind's playing tricks on me, seeing infected everywhere.

It doesn't matter. We have to get inside. We need that medicine, if not for Noah, then for future use. And we need Liv's medicine as well. She's running low, and although we could make her cut down faster, the price for it isn't one I'm willing to pay.

If there are infected in that room, we can take them out quietly, drawing no attention to us. We just have to be smart about it.

I rummage through my bag. Perhaps one of those LED road flares might finally come in handy. The others teased me when we returned home from scavenging for supplies last week, and I had only grabbed a handful of LED lights from the paint shop and a box of sugar.

I hand the round flare to Frances, who passes it along until it reaches Eve. She looks at it with a frown, then at me, one brow raised.

Maybe it *was* a stupid idea after all.

But she twists the flare, covering the bright-red light with her palm. Carefully, she pulls the door handle and slides the flare into the room.

Something slithers across the floor, or crawls. It's difficult to tell. Shuffling noises move towards the red glow that flickers in the dark.

I glance back at the lunchroom we passed. The light isn't strong enough to attract the lunchers' attention. Neither are the raspy, scratching groans from inside the storage room.

There are only four of them. Even in a room, four can be a lot to handle, but there's enough of us to make quick and safe work of it.

I almost laugh. Safe is a relative term nowadays, but I'm not sure anyone would call this safe, even under the best of circumstances.

Eve opens the door, the infected inside too busy with the flare to notice as we fan out into the room. They cluster around the red glow, which lights the space and casts their large shadows on walls and floor. Eve creeps towards the flare, the rest of us moving to the side, quickly circling the infected.

Liv and I duck in behind a shelf, and the others crouch low behind a desk. We skirt around the side when Eve pounces, reaching for a woman with a missing jaw. The woman swings her arms, her rotten tongue flapping. Eve sinks her knife into her temple.

The other infected spin towards her.

Pushing off the floor, I lunge for the third. Its back is turned towards us, its sight on Eve. I use the momentum of my lunge to swing my bat. It connects with a crunch, spikes sinking through bones and tissue. The force of my swing sends me spinning. The spikes rip through the skull, slowing my spin, and spores explode into the air. It tumbles to the floor, the insides of its skull leaking onto its dirty, ripped lab coat.

I shake lumps of hair and flesh off my bat. They drop to the floor with a sickening plop.

Liv knocks over a man in a janitor's uniform. He spins, landing on his hands and knees, limbs twitching like spider's legs.

I stumble backwards; I fucking hate spiders. But Liv plunges her machete into his head, her fists tight on the grip.

The man thrashes underneath her, but she saws back and forth with the machete. Then, with one final push, the blade cleaves the side of the head open.

Spore-covered mushroom-like things spill out on the floor. I frown. What is that?

Liv must wonder the same, for she picks at them with her blade. Stabbing one, it deflates, black goop seeping onto the floor.

"What the hell is that?" Roy asks in a muffled voice from inside his mask.

"Not important. We have to get the supplies and leave." Eve wipes her knife on the side of her leg. I grimace. Wiping substrate gloop on your clothes can't be sanitary.

Liv pokes the pile at her feet, regarding it with narrowed eyes. Like someone picking at their food. Whatever it is she's looking for, I'll have to ask about it later. For now, Roy, Angela, and I have to make sure the room stays safe while the others get the supplies.

The red light gives the room a spooky glow as I weave between the rows of shelves. Angela checks the other side of the room and Roy guards the door. Our earlier brawl with the infected went unnoticed by the lunchers. One less thing to worry about.

I pass a door on the short side of the room and peer through the window. It leads into another hallway. I tuck the knowledge away in case we need it later and return to looking around the room.

Keith stands in one of the rows, opening boxes and peering inside them, but he looks up as I get closer. "Seen anything interesting?" he asks in his gruff voice.

"Just a door over there." I point with my beam. He grunts back a confirmation and returns to rifling through the boxes.

Shadows dance across the walls, the red light giving the spores a bizarrely beautiful glow. Stacked boxes fill the shelves. The quiet sounds of boxes being moved and opened drifts towards me as I shine my light back and forth.

I turn a corner into the middle aisle, where rows of shelves branch out in both directions. A thud and a rustle come from the row on my left. I spin my beam, lighting up the narrow aisle. An unopened box sits on the floor. I stare, my brain trying to make sense of the noise.

The others are still at the far end of the room. Roy is by the door. Maybe it was Angela?

"What are you looking at?" a familiar voice asks from behind me. Definitely not Angela. There's no way she knocked the box over and had the time to circle around me. Besides, now seems an especially cruel time to play a prank.

"I'm not sure, but I think—" Spores stir above us, as if a gust of wind sweeps through the room. I drag Angela to the ground, barely in time to avoid the rotten hand swiping at us. "Lurker!" I warn the others and jab upward with my bat.

The lurker shrieks, jerking backwards. It avoids my attack, retreats, and disappears into the dark.

"Where did it go?" Angela pushes off the floor.

"I don't know."

The sound of bare feet slaps across the floor. We spin, trying to locate it. The shelves give a shake, boxes falling as the lurker scrambles to the top.

"Over there!" I point my torch towards the lurker. Its shriek is followed by loud creaking sounds as it lurches off the shelves.

I watch in horror as one side of the shelf tilts into the air. It's too heavy to grab—I'd go down with it. It topples, crashing into the shelf behind it. That shelf goes down, then the next, and the subsequent shelves fall like dominoes, smashing into each other with ear-shattering clangs of metal.

"Everybody move!" Angela orders at the top of her lungs. The lunchers will have heard the ruckus. No point in trying to be discreet anymore.

A painful shout echoes through the room. Roy! We sprint towards the door.

"Goddamn, you motherf—" Roy cries out in pain, grasping at his leg. Angela drops to his side. His thigh is wedged between two shelves, bright-red blood pulsing from a large rip in his jeans. When I peer closer, I see skin curled inwards around a deep gash. It's so deep I can see things I don't want to see. *Shit. Shit, shit, shit.*

"What the fuck do we do?" My heart beats like a jackhammer pounding in my ears. The shelves are too heavy. The blood is a siren call to every infected nearby.

Liv and Frances arrive and drop to their knees. Liv barely glances at the wound before she's back on her feet again. "I need more gauze."

My gut twists as her figure disappears into the darkness.

"What happened?" Keith demands as he and Eve run up to us, hefting a big bag onto his shoulders.

I open my mouth to answer, but the sound of breaking glass snaps our attention to the lunchroom.

Infected pour through the broken windows. They climb and pull at each other, their shrieks and moans growing thunderous.

"You need to help me with this." I snap out of my panic and point at the shelf. "We need to lift until we can pull him out."

"Leave him." Keith gives me a hard look.

I stare. I must've heard wrong. "What? We're not leaving him."

"Then I'm sorry. You're on your own." And with that, he moves to leave.

"Keith!" Eve's usually stiff and calm voice rises.

"We go. Now," Keith says over his shoulder as he walks towards the other door.

"You can't do that." Eve stands frozen in place. "We're not leaving them."

He abruptly stops, anger burning in his eyes. "You know what's at stake. It's them or us. I'm leaving now."

"You son of a bitch," Angela spits out.

"But—"

"Now!" he barks.

Eve's gaze darts between us and Keith's retreating figure. The urge to stay, fighting with whatever is at stake back at their camp. Anger and helplessness flash across her face. "I'll try to leave you a trail," she whispers, her voice muffled by the mask. She presses an orange gun into my hand, then she spins on her heel and sprints after Keith.

They left. They just *left.* I stare at the flare gun in my hand.

Roy moans. The noises from the hall louden, the smell of his blood drawing every infected in the corridor our way.

"Hold that door." Liv sinks to her knees and drops small packages and bandages to the floor.

I slam my back against the door and slide down until I'm sitting, then push my feet against the fallen shelf. Angela drops next to me as the first wave of infected hit.

Liv rips open the packages of thick gauze. "This is going to hurt." Roy gives one hard nod, his jaw set. With a fistful of gauze, she presses down with both hands on his leg. He jerks, his chest rising and falling in quick succession.

"Slow breaths. In through your nose, out your mouth," she instructs him as another wave of infected slam against the door. Our knees bend, but we push back hard. Something squelches and cracks as the door slams shut. A severed hand plops to the floor.

"We can't hold this door much longer," I grit as we push back against another wave of infected. Hands slap and bang the thick glass windows. Sweat beads my upper lip, and my head slams against the door every time we push it shut.

"Almost there." Liv works fast, her hands moving methodically. The wad of gauze that covers Roy's wound is more white than red. It must be working, though Roy looks as if he's about to pass out, his eyes unfocused and his skin clammy.

The infected claw at the wooden door and it gives a horrifying crack.

"Help Angela with the door." Liv motions to Frances, who joins us. "Jake, help me with this shelf."

I wait for the pressure on the door to lessen. It takes too many heartbeats, but when it finally does, I scramble away. Frances sinks into my spot and kicks her feet against the shelves.

Running to Liv, I scan the room for something to use as a lever. Something heavy I can slide between the two shelves. Heavy, sturdy, and thin.

My gaze drops to Roy's iron pipe. I grab it and position myself next to the lockers.

"Let me help you." Liv moves to stand, but I shake my head.

"No, be ready to pull him out." I jam the pipe where the two shelves meet and push down hard. It barely moves. Fire races through my arms. Frustration pounds through me, and I push harder, scared the pipe will snap and cause Roy more pain.

My arms shake as I lean over, sinking my entire weight onto the pipe. I need to take a breath, but if I do, I'll lose my grip. *Come on!* I scream in my head, willing the shelf to move.

Inch by agonising inch, the shelf moves. My arms and legs tremble. Even my arse cheeks twitch from tensing my entire body. I can't hold it much longer.

Roy cries out, but I'm too focused on keeping pressure on the pipe.

"I've got him!" Liv shouts, and I collapse against the shelf.

Roy grunts, eyes rolling back into his head. Liv slaps his face, waking him up. "I need to wrap his leg."

"Hurry!" Angela's voice shakes the way it does when she's angry, upset, or scared.

I'm not doing any good standing here, so I run over and shove my bat at the infected who claw and bite through the slit between the door and broken hinges. Brown liquid sprays all over my legs and the side of Angela's face, coating us with the smell of rotten fish.

Her worried eyes are so round I can see the whites through her mask, and her head bounces painfully with every thump of the door. Frances's face is set, her eyes closed as she pushes.

An infected with discs growing out of its split head rams through the thin gap. Big puffs of spores waft into the air.

I back up a few steps. The windows are breaking, glass shattering across the floor beside Frances, and someone lets out a scream. The windows are breaking, more infected trying to get through the doorway.

I sprint and smash my shoulder into the door. Angela and Frances scream with the effort of pushing. The head of one of the infected implodes from our pressure with a crunching pop.

"I'm done! Let's go!"

Spinning on my heel, I wheel over to Liv, and we hoist Roy up between us. He groans in pain, sweat rolling down the side of his face. I steer us in the same direction Keith and Eve had left.

Angela and Frances push off the floor, dashing after us. Infected pour like water through the broken windows and the door.

We push the door open and step into the empty corridor. It's pitch-black, save for a green glow stick that penetrates the dark farther down to our left. Eve left us crumbs. We take off towards it. A door is slightly ajar. I kick it open and we burst into a stairwell.

We make our way down the stairs at a snail's pace. Carrying Roy isn't doing us any favours. I pant, my breath coming hard and short. A series of loud bangs come from behind our backs. Angela fires her gun. Then the metal door to the stairs slams shut.

Sweat beats my upper lip, dripping from my brow. My chest pounds with terror. I'm scared we won't make it. We're going too slow.

Roy grunts, but his arm around me tightens as he starts hopping along with his good leg. Either the drugs are finally kicking in or adrenaline is boosting him.

"I'm okay, I'm okay."

He's not, but now is not the time to remind him. At the bottom of the stairs, Liv kicks open a grey metal door.

Stumbling out into a corridor, more warbling and gagging reaches our ears from farther down the corridor. And it's coming towards us. Fast.

Throwing my arm out in front of me, I aim the flare gun and pull the trigger. The flare tears from its mouth, the sharp light blinding us.

An infected runs chest first into the flare and stumbles backwards. The spores in the air fizzle and pop from the heat as the infected bursts into flames. I expected the other infected to either be too dumb and run into the flames or be distracted by them. But they don't. They halt and veer off to the side. *What the fuck?*

Liv pulls us in the other direction. A door on the opposite wall stands ajar, its electric lock smashed. That has to be Keith and Eve. I hope. There are no more glow sticks, no crumbs to show us the way.

We hesitate for a heartbeat.

"No time to dillydally." Frances ushers us towards the door, the rumble of hundreds of feet thundering towards us. The door at the top of the stairs must have given way.

"Go, go, go," Angela breathes hard, stumbling down the stairs.

We stagger through the door, and my heart plummets. The windows into the corridor are all broken.

Though it's dark, my eyes have adjusted to the moonlight that filters in through large windows, allowing me a good look of the room. Tables lie overturned. A shelf blocks a door into the corridor that runs along the far side of the room, but infected crawl through the broken windows. They groan hungrily at our noises and the smell of Roy's blood. There's not enough time to break one of the windows and climb out with Roy. Cold sweat runs down my back. I can see the car park where we left our bikes. It's so close. But so far away.

"There!" Liv drags us towards a door held open with a fire extinguisher. A small glow stick sits on the floor beside it.

"Hurry." Angela pushes at our back. "Get in there now!"

Liv and I dive through the door Roy held firmly between us. Angela follows closely behind.

This room has no windows to the corridor, only one to the room we came from and another to the outside.

Cool night air breezes through a broken window. I let out a breath of relief. Liv grins back at me. Guess that's our way out.

"Well, I'll be damned," Roy's voice trembles.

"We have to—"

The door slams shut behind us.

"Frances?" Angela says. Her beam sweeps the room. Frances was right behind us, but now she isn't. I look at the closed door, then at the window into the other room. Frances watches us from the other side of the window. Her brows pull together and her quivering lips part with shallow breaths. She looks paler than usual in the faint moonlight.

"What are you doing?" I pull at the handle, but the door won't budge.

Frances smiles sadly and holds up the handle from the door's other side.

"Open the door!" Liv demands.

Frances shakes her head.

"Open this door," Angela says in her stern police tone, but the quiver in her voice betrays her. Frances's throat bobs as she steps away from the door.

Angela's hand falls to the gun on her hip, as if she plans to shoot through the thick netted window. "What are you doing? Open this door!"

Tears roll down Frances's cheeks. She shakes her head, her lip quivering. *I'm sorry*, she mouths through the window.

"Frances!" Liv slaps a palm against the glass.

Angela pushes one of the room's chairs in my direction. It's heavy, but I hoist it up with my free hand to throw against the thick glass.

"No!" Frances sobs, placing her palm on the window. "Jake, no." Her voice is muffled, barely audible through the glass. Then she lifts her jacket.

The side of her blue shirt is torn and stained with dark blood. Her fingers shake as she runs them over the bleeding wound. Over the teeth marks in her pale skin.

No! I drop the chair to the floor. Not Frances. Not one of us. One of our family.

Liv presses her hand to her mouth. Angela shakes her head with a desperate, "No, no, no."

"Please," Liv cries. "I can't do this without you."

Frances smiles and steps forwards. She presses her hands against the glass and nods. *You can.* She glances to the side when something at the other end of the room catches her attention. Looking back at us, she presses her lips together, then she takes a deep breath and lifts her chin.

Go.

Liv shakes her head fervently.

Go!

The first infected reaches her and she spins, swinging her iron bar. It's a battle she can't win. But knowing her, she'll take down as many as she can before she loses. A scream rips from her mouth as she hacks through the infected.

Her voice rings in my ears as a man in dark-blue scrubs runs face-first into her spiked bat. The spikes bury themselves in his face. She gives him a hard kick and twists the bat. His face cracks open, and spores wisp into the air around them.

She swings, taking down more. One, two, three infected. But more robe-clad figures pour through the side doors that have swung open under their weight. It won't be long before she's overrun.

"We have to go," I say, but Liv shakes her head.

"Hon," Angela says, "she wouldn't want us to see..." She can't finish the sentence. None of us can.

"No," Liv says, determination in her voice. "I won't let her think she's alone when she—"

I nod. Liv's right. We will stay with her. So that she knows she's not alone. She may want to spare us what comes next, but she would *never* abandon us.

We won't abandon her.

Angela puts her arm around Liv, who holds on to Roy on her other side. Roy's hand squeezes mine, and I squeeze it back hard.

Frances raises the bat, clubbing a young, slack-jawed girl in tatty and torn PJs. When the group of infected finally reaches her, they swarm around her to bite, claw, and rip. She screams, her voice shrill and deafening. I don't want to hear it, but I can't shut it out.

She staggers, agonised cries ripping from her lips. A rotted hand digs into her thick hair, twisting and pulling mercilessly.

She spins around, the whites of her eyes bright in the dark. Maybe it's wishful thinking, maybe my mind is trying to protect me, but I think I see her smile. Then her eyes close and the infected drag her to the floor, burying her underneath them.

75

LIV

"NO..." HER VOICE SOUNDED foreign to her own ears as Angela and Jake pulled her into motion. Frances's screams had stopped, the twisted snarls and growls from the infected the only sound that remained. She didn't know which was worse: hearing Frances's screams or knowing that she was gone. Dead.

A brief image of Frances walking slack-jawed, flesh ripped open and chewed, flooded her mind. A wave of fear and nausea washed over her.

Angela wiped tears from her cheeks, then squared her shoulders before climbing onto the table by the window. She turned around, reaching for Liv. "We have to go now."

Go and leave Frances? She glanced behind herself as if her brain had only imagined it. How could it be possible? Frances had been there only seconds ago. But Frances was gone. Only the infected stood at the glass, pounding and pressing their faces against it.

"Okay," she whispered. She grabbed Angela's hand and climbed up onto the table.

"Okay," Angela echoed. Her jaw was set, though her lip quivered.

They helped Roy climb up onto the table. Jake followed shortly after, pulling his axe from his bag. Liv guessed he'd lost his bat. "I'll go first, to make sure it's clear," he said, his voice low. "Can you take him?"

"Yeah." They were safe for now. The window was too high for the infected outside to reach, and the door behind them was locked. She watched him grab a chair, dropping it to the grass below. He gave a stiff nod, then dropped after it.

She shouldn't let him go alone, but with Roy depending on both of them to help him walk, it was better not to risk having to fend off infected.

Outside, dead bodies lay on the ground, once-people in colourful clothes now dirtied and shredded. To their left lay a pile of smaller bodies. Children. She quickly looked away.

The sight of dead bodies was gruesome. But the sight of children so small was too horrific to linger on. She turned her focus to a few stragglers who shambled around on the grass a stone's throw away from Jake. She wanted to help him, but she couldn't leave Roy and Angela.

A gust rattled the tall grass beneath their window, the heads of the lumbering infected snapping towards the sky as they sniffed the air. No doubt scenting the fresh blood from her hands and Roy's leg, carried by the night wind across the lot.

She swallowed, her throat dry when she saw Jake sprint across the grass. There was a big, red stain on his backpack. Blood, enough of it to attract any nearby infected.

She should warn him about it, but the sound of her voice would only make the infected notice her. With Roy injured, the risk was too big.

Look at you being all sensible and shit. She scoffed quietly as a crouched Jake pushed off the ground with his feet, lodging his axe into the skull of a suit-clad straggler.

Jake moved like a shadow, quickly and quietly. She watched him dispose of two more infected, then he sprinted into the darkness ahead. The pitch-black night made it difficult for her to see.

"I hope he hurries," Angela muttered next to her. "That glass won't hold much longer."

The quiet nights made everything easier to hear. Crisp leaves crunched on frosty grass, owls hooted, the wind rushing through tree crowns, pulling roughly at them, and the insistent battering at the door.

She threw a quick glance over her shoulder, praying the glass would still be intact. Infected pressed themselves against it, their dead faces leaving smudges of dark blood and brown goop.

A woman with red bursts of fungi growing from her ears dragged her face back and forth across the glass. Her lips and jaw were chewed off, and she chewed at the air with horridly exposed rotten teeth. Another infected slammed its dirtied hands against the window. The hands were missing parts of fingers, ripped off by dull teeth. When the glass didn't break, it slammed its head against it. The crack reverberated through the quiet night. The infected pulled its head backwards. A thick sludge coated the hair.

Liv squinted at the window. Was it fresh blood? Bright-red liquid covered the crack in the window. Infected didn't have fresh blood. It was a dark, coagulated, thick mucus.

Wet hair parted, revealing the infected's pale neck, the flesh torn off and chewed into right above the all too familiar blue shirt. *No!*

She looked away before the next slam echoed. The window moaned from the impact.

No, no, no! She couldn't see Frances like that. Frances wouldn't have wanted any of them to see her that way. Pulling the backpack from her shoulders, Liv dug into it in a frenzy.

"We have to go, we have to go," she whispered like a mantra to keep herself from turning back.

"Liv?" Angela asked.

"Get ready. We're going to have to run for it." Her fingers brushed against the cool neck of one of the whiskey bottles from the shed. She pulled it from the bag, her hands shaking.

"What are you doing?" Angela frowned, turning to look behind them.

"Don't." Liv wrung the cap off the bottle, using her shiv to rip a shred of fabric from the curtain next to them. "Don't look. Just get ready to help Roy down."

Angela nodded as she pulled herself closer to the edge of the window, hesitating only momentarily before she slipped off.

Working quickly, Liv pushed as much fabric as she could into the bottle without spilling any on herself. When she was done, she set the bottle aside and nudged Roy's shoulder. "We need to lower you gently. I won't have time to stop another bleed."

"Alright." Roy fired off a tired smile. She squeezed his shoulder. That was Roy, always trying to keep everyone's spirits up. Even when he was on the brink of bleeding to death.

"Can you do it yourself, or do you need me to help?"

"I could use a little help."

"Okay." She looped her arms under his armpits, planting her feet against the sturdy windowsill. "*Don't* land on your left leg."

He let out a breathy laugh. "Hell, if I could, I'd princess hop into Angela's arms."

She chuckled quietly. "Now that might be something I'd like to see. When we're not being chased by infected."

"Copy that," Roy said, then shimmied towards the edge. Slowly, he pushed himself off, and she strained against the table to keep her hold. What the hell did this man eat? Bricks? Fear that she might drop him shot through her mind. Sweat ran down her back, and her legs started to shake. Then, finally, the pull on her arms lessened as his foot found purchase on the chair below.

"I'm good," Roy whispered, and she released her hold.

"You guys ready to haul some arse?" Jake said in a low voice as he rolled up with his bike.

"You ready?" Angela asked Roy.

"No time to dillydally." Roy grabbed Angela's hands for support as he stepped down from the chair.

"Hop into the trailer." Jake didn't have to tell Roy twice. Hobbling over, he got into the trailer.

"Go ahead, I'll be right behind you." Liv motioned in the direction of the town centre. Jake narrowed his eyes, not entirely believing her. She didn't blame him. "I promise."

"What are you going to do?" he asked.

"I can't leave her like this. Like... one of them. I just can't."

He exchanged glances with Angela. Liv worried they might try to stop her, but after a moment he gave a nod. "Okay. Let's go."

She watched them scurry across the grass, silhouetted by the moon, until they were out of sight. What a strange feeling. Usually she did the running away. Turning back towards the room, she watched the crack expand.

"Stop it," she whispered, knowing they wouldn't. Knowing Frances wouldn't.

Dead, milky eyes met hers, their usual warmth gone. Clutching the bottle closer, her thumb tapping the lighter, Liv waited until the first shard dislodged from the crack. She watched, mesmerised, as it fell to the floor. Then the rest of the glass broke in cascading shards.

With one last look at the woman she'd come to know—her mentor and friend—Liv lit the wick of her Molotov and threw it.

She watched the bottle sail through the air, landing somewhere among the infected. Orange burst to life, fire latching onto anything in its wake.

Flames licked Frances's clothes and hair, but the fire wouldn't stop them. Not instantly. Liv pushed herself away from the burning crowd of infected. Their shrieking would attract more, and she had to reach her bike before they arrived.

She turned and leapt through the window, landing with a hard thud on the grass. Ready for a mad dash towards her bike, she pushed off the ground.

Someone moved in the dark. She froze. The shapes drew nearer until she could see Angela and Jake biking like bats out of hell. Angela used one hand to steer—the other towed Liv's bike.

Emotions stuck in her throat. She wiped at her eyes and ran towards them.

"You came back." She panted, grabbing her bike mid-sprint and swinging her leg across the bar.

"Knew we couldn't stop you." Angela smiled as they turned around. "Figured we'd get your ride ready."

A boom reverberated from the hospital. Bright yellow and orange flickered to life in the pitch-black night. Flames danced, casting shadows at their backs, urging them to flee. To get out before more infected arrived.

We don't stop running or fighting. Unless we run out of luck, we keep going.

76

LIV

THE FIRST SNOW STARTED falling as they fled into the night. White flakes wafted lazily through the cold air, landing on Liv's bloodied hands. White and pure, like a cruel reminder of the world's insanity. When they reached the house, the ground was covered in snow. They rushed in, Angela and Jake dragging Roy between them. By the time they placed him on the floor in front of the fireplace, he was shivering and beads of sweat coated his forehead.

"Where's Frances?" Noah inspected the room. Jake only looked down at his feet and shook his head.

Fareena raised her eyebrows at Liv in an unspoken question. Then she saw Liv's puffy, red eyes and swollen nose. "No." Fareena buried her face in her hands, bending as if someone had punched her in the gut.

With barely a moment's hesitation Noah stepped forward and put his arm around her. If Liv had had the time to be surprised, she might have stood there gobsmacked. Instead, she motioned for Jake to get the first aid kit as she dropped to her knees by Roy.

She wrangled out of her jacket; the tight leather confined her movements. Working as fast as she could, she pulled a pair of black scissors from the first aid kit. They felt familiar and comforting as they sliced through the thick jeans.

Jake and Fareena helped her pull off the jeans, but she stopped before reaching for the bloodied bandage. What was she supposed to do? Roy had already lost too much blood. She wasn't sure he'd survive losing much more. Had she made a mistake back at the hospital, stressed by the situation?

Roy moaned, and she jerked her eyes to his face, pulling his eyelids down. The typically pink mucus membrane had a grey-blue cast, and sweat coated his forehead. He needed a hospital with proper care or he was going to die. He needed *real* doctors. Not some drugged-up medical has-been.

"I can't..." Her hands shook. Frances was always by her side, helping. She was the extra set of eyes that could catch Liv's mistakes. But Frances wasn't there anymore. Frances was gone, and there was no one to make sure Liv didn't hurt anyone else, that she didn't—

"Liv." Fareena put her hands on her shoulders, snapping Liv out of her spiralling. "How can I help?"

What would Frances usually do? "Uh... syringe, needles, and sutures. And I need gloves. From my backpack."

"Okay. I know what those things are. What else?" Fareena asked as calmly as if she were asking Liv how her day had been.

"Gauze, one of those brown bottles, and one green sheet." The more she focused on Roy's leg and Fareena's questions, the clearer her mind became.

Angela set a bowl of hot water in front of her, and Liv quickly dipped her hands in it, scrubbing them clean.

"Put the gloves on my hands."

"I feel like one of those nurses on TV," Fareena mused as she pulled the gloves onto Liv's hands.

Liv smiled and wiggled her fingers, then grabbed the scissors again. Fareena would make an excellent nurse. She had the right instincts. Holding her breath, Liv cut the bandage. It split and fell to the side, but no blood came pulsing from the wound.

Gently, she peeled away the layers of gauze until the laceration was exposed. Jake made a noise and turned away. She smiled. Jake, on the other hand, would make an *awful* nurse.

"If you could poor some water on that," she instructed Fareena.

Water mixed with the blood, turning it pink until Liv could see the full damage. Torn and jagged skin revealed bright-pink flesh and then the dark red of the muscle. *Fuck.* Muscles were difficult to repair, even when proper medical care was available.

"Someone grab the surgical kit from my bag, please. And I need that white box with vials in it." Local anaesthesia wasn't optimal, but it would have to do. She gritted her teeth. She had grabbed all those things for an emergency. She hadn't thought she'd be using them so soon.

Fareena placed the plastic package next to her. Liv took a deep breath. It had been a long time since she last used a pair of those. "Alright, now the brown bottle. You're doing great, Far."

An almost shy smile pulled at Fareena's lips but was quickly replaced by an "Eww" as a sludgy, brown goop came out of the bottle. Jake, ever sensitive to smells and gore, retreated to the kitchen.

Terrible nurse. She spent the next hour cleaning and stitching the muscle and wound. While Angela stroked Roy's head, Fareena watched her with curious eyes. She finished dressing the wound as Jake returned with sleeping bags and pillows.

Roy was better off sleeping on the floor in front of the warm fire rather than in a cold bedroom. With the snow, they all were. Sleeping in the same room would generate more heat. After a night like this, everyone would need it.

She sat back. Roy slept peacefully. He would need a lot of rest and antibiotics, but he would survive.

"Thank you." Angela's voice was thick when she spoke. Her usually strong, determined face looked haggard, the round cheeks damp, and the corners of her lips twitched with emotion. She'd almost lost her husband, and she had lost her friend. They'd all lost a friend, and though they all deserved to mourn and say goodbye, this world wouldn't let them. It took what it wanted without prejudice. It always had, and it *always* would.

She was scrubbing her fingers in the freezing water. This constant fucking cold water that never made her feel clean. She wanted to scream in frustration. Or maybe anger. She kept massaging the spot between her thumb and finger. The blood wouldn't go away. Its metallic stench still filled her nostrils and all she wanted was for it to disappear.

"Hey," the deep soothing voice murmured behind her. "Maybe this will help." Jake poured hot water into the bowl. A shiver ran up her spine, and she wished she could sink into the bowl. Sink into the warmth and comfort of the water, shutting out the rest of the world and the pain.

He poured more water into the bowl until it reached above her wrist then he stepped closer, so close that her shoulder blades pressed against him. She let her head and shoulders drop with an exhale. She both hated and loved the way his presence comforted her.

Dipping his hands into the bowl, he touched his soft palms to her wrists. It tingled and warmed her at the same time. Gently, he ran his hands up and down, massaging her wrists and hands with soap. Bubbles formed and floated across the water's surface.

She shuddered, his touch leaving goosebumps in its wake. She leaned into his warmth and his arms tightened around her. He made her feel safe. At home. Just like Frances had.

He pulled their hands from the water, the blood was washed away, as if it had never been there. Much like the woman who had woken Liv up from her drunken sleep all those months ago. Liv blinked, her eyes growing damp at the memory of it. Something heavy grew in her chest, expanding in every direction until tears blurred her view. She let them fall onto her wrists. Jake patiently dabbed them dry, then he turned her around and pulled her close. She let him. Let him wrap his arms around her, let herself cry into his chest.

"I know," he whispered, his voice thick and low with his own emotions, and she realised he was clinging on to her as much as she to him. "Nothing's okay, but it will be. Someday, it will be. *We* will be."

Coming up for air, she nodded into his neck. Everything was wrong, and things weren't okay. But she couldn't remember the last time they had been, anyway. At least this time, she wasn't alone. Digging her fingers into his back, she looked through the kitchen window behind him.

Angela hugged Noah and Fareena as their shoulders shook with pain and sorrow. For Frances, their friend, their mother figure. For all the people they'd lost since that day in London. They'd lost everything they knew and loved. But they had this. *She* had this.

77

JAKE

I SIT IN THE back garden underneath the dark night sky. A vast canopy of stars sparkle back at us. It's a quiet night. All nights are quiet now that we have no electricity, and the majority of England's population and maybe even the world is either dead or hiding. But, still, it's quieter than normal.

The streets outside are vacant of the slow shuffles of infected looking for prey. I always thought the living dead would be driven by a primal instinct to feed. It never occurred to me that they were looking for hosts. Hosts that would help spread the infection.

Despite that, I take in the calmness of the night, the crisp December chill pinching my cheeks as my breath fogs up the air.

There was a time I would have ached for Megan to be here with me. But for the first time, I don't. I don't miss being alone next to her. I don't miss being invisible.

Karma stirs by my feet, and I scratch the fur between her shoulder blades. I'm not alone anymore. Better yet, I don't feel alone.

"Cashew for your thoughts." Liv sits down, the small nut pinched between her fingers. I let out a noisy breath. No one ever says a penny anymore because money is useless to us. Food is a much better bribe nowadays. Most people won't say no to any extra nutrition they can get their paws on. I'm no different.

"It's a nice night." I snatch the cashew from her fingers.

"Oh, for fuck's sake," she blurts out. "You do not get to eat my cashew for 'it's a nice night.'"

I laugh. Always the diplomatic one. "It's all so different now."

She sighs. "Yes."

I should tell her a joke, lighten the solemn mood that has settled, but I can't. How do you joke when it's the end of the world? It's a beautiful night, and I feel guilty for thinking so when so much has gone wrong with the world. When the dead—kept alive by a parasitic fungus—feed on the living. Use our bodies as soulless husks. And amongst those of us who survived, the strong prey on the weak. The world was always cruel, but now it's even more so.

"I wish things were different," I say.

"We all do, sugar," Angela says as she steps out from the kitchen, closely followed by Roy, who limps carefully across the deck. They must have finished in the kitchen, leaving Fareena and Noah to put the dishes away.

Roy hugs himself, his breath fogging the air. "Go to England, they said. They got warm winters, they said."

"Are you positive you're not thinking of some obscure town in America called England?" Liv raises her eyebrow.

"Happy New Year!" Fareena hoots from the door and we all turn as she raises her hands in the air. She wiggles two large wine bottles and then, when Noah doesn't, she shoulders him until he does the same with the bottle he holds.

"Is that..." Liv starts.

"Bitch, you wish," Fareena says and somehow makes it sound like a compliment. "I didn't put up with you being a cranky bellend for a month only to feed you alcohol again. No offense."

"None taken," Liv mutters as Angela sits down with a chuckle and pulls her into a side hug.

"What is it?" I frown.

"Homemade mulled... squash." Fareena fires off a proud smile. "Made by yours truly."

Someone clears their throat in a not so subtle *'and,'* drawing a dramatic sigh from her. "And Roy."

Noah doesn't say anything, but he glares sidelong, pointy daggers at her.

"And Noah." She hangs her head, the rest of us bursting into laughter. The thirsting one act who never gets the spotlight quite to herself.

"It's usually made from wine," Roy says and passes small paper mugs to the rest of us. "And we only had the MRE powder drinks. So, I had to be *creative*."

Fareena and Noah pour the warm mulled squash into our mugs, and I take a sip. I've never had mulled wine—squash—before but it's warm, sweet and, oddly, tastes a lot like Christmas with its mixture of cinnamon, orange, and anis.

Sitting down beside Angela, Roy holds his arm in front himself and checks the time on his wristwatch. It stopped working ages ago, at twenty-one minutes to twelve. "Looks like we got twenty minutes to go."

It's ridiculous. We all know his watch isn't working, but somehow it makes it feel like a normal New Year's Eve. Twenty minutes to go, then we start a new year. The six of us.

We've lost so many people along the way, and I don't think we'll ever heal. Not when the world constantly threatens to take us out. To take what we love. But maybe, when one of us falters, the others will help them up.

If Frances taught us anything, it'd be that life is not only about surviving, but about the people we choose to love. The ones we call our family. Not by blood, but by bond, trust, and friendship.

Everything we knew, everything we were, has changed. And it will keep on changing. This new world, whatever it holds, will never be the same.

I don't know what next year has in store for us, and perhaps that's alright. I take another sip of the warm drink in my hand and allow myself a look at the others. Angela, who always holds her mug between two hands. Fareena, who can sing any song prompted by any word. Roy, who isn't a man of many words, but always has the right ones when you need them. Noah, who is slowly coming out of his shell and can turn anything into a weapon. And then there's Liv. Whose hair is never more than a heartbeat away from a bird's nest and whose filter is nonexistent.

I smile at the sight of the ragtag group of strangers who have become family. People I couldn't make it without. They've pulled me out of danger, out of hopelessness. If it weren't for them, I'd be on my own. In a world like this, I wouldn't stand a chance.

No matter what happens, I won't face it alone. And as Fareena slips her arm into mine, leaning into me, and Noah gives Roy a gentle pat on his shoulder, I know, we're in this together.

Thank You For Reading!

Want to know more about the characters and the world of *How We Survive*? Visit my website! And if you want to stay up to date and **be the first to know** when the sequel ***How We Survive*** drops, sign up to my newsletter on my website: lmjuniper.com

Other places to connect with me:
TikTok: @lmjuniper
Facebook: @lmjuniper
Instagram: @author_lmjuniper

Afterword

THIS BOOK HAS BEEN a labour of love, as are most books ever written, and I'm so proud to see it out there in the world. It took me five years to write this book and it's been a wild ride.

I've made many friends and learned many things over the years working on this book and there are some in particular that I want to thank.

My fanfic followers: The OG crew, the nerds, the Bioware and Odyssey superfans, the ones who believed in me and loved my writing before anyone else. Thank you to all of you who have followed my fanfics, left reviews, sent messages, and made fanart of my stories.

Before fanfiction and your support I thought writing were only for "real writers", for those that publishers said were good enough. But you showed me that I am good enough. You helped me believe in myself.

Thank you.

Sarah Lyons Fleming: My favourite Space Cadet. I can never thank you enough for your patience, kindness, and wholesome quirkiness. I wouldn't be the writer I am today without your help. Thank you for always helping me, for letting me pick your brain and for leaving the funniest comments in my dreadful first drafts.

You were the one author I looked up to who told me that: "if you write, you're a writer." I took those words to heart and I ran with it.

Michele Miller & Jen Anderson: For always helping, encouraging, and having my back. And for helping this book become what it is by beta reading, giving me cover feedback and final formatting control. I couldn't have done this without you two!

Beta readers: Michele Miller, Jen Anderson, Nisha Addleman, and Jess. All your input and help has been invaluable.

Ashia Monet: Who helped make sure I write Black characters in a respectful way that doesn't perpetrate harmful stereotypes.

Kimberly Dawn: My editor, thank you for your invaluable help and corrections and for having the patience to teach me grammar and writing rules.

Kim Graylock: This virus and the world in this book wouldn't be as fleshed out without your help, and for that I'm eternally grateful.

Donyale M: For helping me with the final round of blurb edits. Adding that extra little oomph to it all. Thank you so much!

Jess: Last but not least, my beautiful and amazing wife. Where others doubted me and my choices, you never once stopped believing in me. You stood by me through thick and thin. You've always encouraged me to write and to chase the dream of publishing. Thank you for being awesome, I love you until the end of the world. ♥

Glossary

Crawlers: Infected that crawl with limbs much like a spider.

Crusties: Smaller infected, further along in their infection. Slower, but still somewhat fast.

Brute: Mutated infected. Massive in size, has no visual or auditory senses. Reacts to vibrations in the ground. Fungi discs, roots, and lichen cover its body, hardening its skin. The brute is incredibly difficult to kill due to its armoured exterior.

Lurker: Infected that stalks their prey by hiding. Lurkers are recently turned thus are faster and retain some of their cognitive functions.

LYM-1: Lysurus Mycosis 1 virus caused by a parasite. Symptoms range from: severe headaches, extreme aggression, loss of impulse control, fever, and nosebleeds.

O-Zone: The Outbreak zone where the London Cordon Sanitaire was set up.

Rotter: Another term for infected humans.

Snitch: An infected that alerts the horde to prey. An infected can (but doesn't have to) be both a lurker and a snitch, much like the one near the canal.

Substrates: Official term for infected humans.

Withered: Person infected by LYM-1 or in layman terms: the Red Death.

Zonites: People left inside the quarantine zone.

Printed in Great Britain
by Amazon

57790487R00202